LOVE CAN SAVE US ALL

Olivia Coppin

ISBN 9798832103570

Cover illustration by Fred Coppin

For Mum,
for filling our lives with more love than we could have imagined.

PART 1

THE LAKE.

Although she would never admit it aloud, Anna enjoyed the respite of her turn in the Welcome Cabin. Age was beginning to seep into her bones, a feeling shared by the cabin itself. Anna had built the cabin with the very hands that now swelled and moaned, just as the ageing oak did. She must be in her mid-sixties, late-sixties perhaps. She didn't know for certain, she'd stopped counting the number years ago. It was irrelevant. And yet, label or no label, the process didn't stop.

She settled into her shift, sinking deeper into a wooden chair that had been born from the same tree as the rest of the cabin. They'd found the ancient oak already felled, and that had been their signal. It must have withstood hundreds of storms, before gracefully bowing out when the time was right, and allowing Anna and her friends to breathe new life into where it had stood.

And new life into its old bones.

Its hefty trunk still lived as the cornerstones to the oldest buildings on site. Larger branches had been used for roof segments, most of which had now been reinforced, but were still there too, silently sheltering. The smaller branches and twigs had provided kindling for months. And, once the women had grown more competent with their tools, they carved the chair from its offcuts to look throne-like and comical. Anna felt a great affinity for that oak tree. The life partner she had never required had perhaps quietly been there all along.

She'd planned to use this rota-ed time away from camp to make her annual list of tasks to be done when the seasons changed. After this many years she did not really need to. She knew by heart what needed to be picked, planted, raked and sewn over the next few weeks as summer drew to a close. But being a list-maker was one practice that had persisted from her old life. She had tried for years to kick the habit, to not be constrained by the need to quantify and plan. Until one day,

she'd made peace with it.

She figured it was more serene to live as her authentic, organised self than to force spontaneity. It would be her only vice. But she did not begin the list right away. The tattered notepad and pencil sat on the arm of the wooden throne, and she closed her eyes. It would be a while until the postman was here anyway. She didn't know the exact time (another unnecessary marker) but the early choristers, the thrushes and wrens, were still singing as if no one was listening. Although out here, they sang like that all day. There was nothing to quell their confidence or quash their sweet song in this quiet corner of the earth. Anna would simply close her eyes and listen, sure to hear the postman's car crawling up the track when she was needed.

From the main road – as main as the local roads could be – there was a subtle turning onto a country lane, which was winding and narrow, but a mappable road nonetheless. This rumbled on for an undulating, pot-holey kilometre, until the concrete rolled into flinty rubble and was hugged even tighter by hawthorn bushes and dogwood shrubs. It was a further two kilometres down this wild track to their site. But this final stretch seemed too much to ask of postal workers and visitors. Anna didn't want their own desire for seclusion and tranquility to be a nuisance to others, so they'd built the Welcome Cabin just four hundred metres down the rubble track, on the boundary between privacy and cooperation.

It was little more than a shed, with the word 'Welcome' etched into the door. It had high windows on each side, out of which the tops of ash trees could be seen, and in from which poured the hazy morning sunshine. All the cabin contained was the chair, and a chest of items that they had once deemed useful for this halfway house. In turns, someone would wait here once a week for the postman, or when collecting scheduled visitors. And the visitors were always scheduled, for it was near-impossible to mistakenly stumble upon their home. A few times a year, tourists would accidentally trespass at the other end of their site, next to the lake's edge. It was not uncommon for an adventurous, or uninitiated, trekker to veer off the popular walking loop so far that they reached their campsite clearing. And whilst they welcomed anyone with open arms, most of the lost souls hurriedly disappeared back into the waterside woodland, in fear of these mysterious women and their tipis. The tipis which would be dismantled over the coming days as the warm weather retreated and stored away for another year.

Anna hadn't realised that she'd drifted away from the calls of the birds, until she was startled by a, *creeeeeeeeeeeeeeeek.*

In the cabin doorway stood two women.

One of them was thin as a rake, with see-through skin. The lines of her sinewy muscles were etched across her limbs like a medical drawing, where they poked out beneath polyester football shorts or lay limp at her sides. She wore no bra beneath her stained vest top, but there was barely a hint of breast. Whole sections of her skin were bruised, in shades of purple and yellow and green, spreading across the contours of her body like a heat map, which burned most brightly around her neck. Her age was unclear. Her adolescent body alluded to youth, but her dark eyes sunk with experience. Dried blood crusted around her nostrils and her top lip protruded at an angle.

The other was merely a child,
with afro curls splaying out of two buns.

Anna stood up from her throne. The two bodies stayed quite still, save for the heavy rise and fall of their chests.

I'm Layla, *she's Robyn.*
It was the child who spoke.
Then Robyn collapsed to the floor.

ROBYN. 1993.

Mr Jagait had three eggs that morning, for strength.

He tapped their shells with the butt of a teaspoon. The cracked casing peeled away with ease to show shiny white sponge, a sign he'd boiled them to perfection. Then, each egg in turn, he sliced the top off with the teaspoon rim and dunked toast soldiers into the sticky yolks. It was a practice his wife had taught him only a year ago, and he'd had two boiled eggs for breakfast every day since. But never three.

He toasted a fourth slice of bread for the third egg, since the third slice had somehow disappeared. Unconsciously eaten, whilst his mind thought only of the errand ahead. An errand which had also been the brainchild of Mrs Jagait-Jones.

Mr Jagait loved being a landlord. He loved hearing the stories of those who filled his flats, what paths they had weaved to find themselves in his care. He took pride in ringing up tenant references, hearing the worst and giving them a chance anyway. He even enjoyed the panicked weekend calls when a pipe had burst or a boiler was broken and he could sweep in to the rescue. As his collection of properties had grown, slowly and steadily, he'd chosen not to invest in more upmarket apartments and inflate his prices with the going gentrification rate, but instead he stuck to the modest flats in the darker corners of the city, where he could offer the most vulnerable a secure roof and turn a blind eye to the odd late payment.

Unfortunately, with Emily, in 99B Wilkins Road, it had been more than just the odd late payment. For two years she'd rented the cheapest studio flat he had, and barely made six payments. The pregnant teen had arrived to the viewing, bloodshot-eyed and bulbous-bellied with a gentle northern accent and one bag of belongings, and Mr Jagait had handed her the key there and then. He'd reached out constantly in the first few weeks. Ringing to check if she'd settled in ok, if the water was hot enough, if she was familiar with gas cookers, if the smoke alarms needed testing and never to check if she had the money she owed. Each time, he hoped she would sound a little brighter, or mention having people over, or at the least, confess to the struggles of her solitary pregnancy. But not once, within her monosyllabic answers, did she address the baby growing inside her, until finally she stopped picking up the phone all together.

After a month of radio silence, Mr Jagait had been attending to a swollen front door at 99A Wilkins Road, when he'd heard a baby's cry and a mother's coo. Relief and heartache had washed over him so strongly that his knees had buckled, and he'd lent against the distended door.

It had taken Mrs Jagait-Jones six months after Emily moved in to notice that no contracts were rolling for the flat on Wilkins Road.

Still can't fill 99B? Maybe we should re-repaint it,

she'd asked, with stacks of bookkeeping papers spread across the kitchen table.

Oh, there's someone in there,

Jagait had mumbled, head buried deep in the fridge.

What? Who?

Her hearing was impeccable.

Just a young mum.

He inspected a strawberry yoghurt.

Oh for heavens sake, Vish,

she tutted, well versed in his unrelenting generosity. Envelopes with varying amounts of cash had dropped onto their doormat at random intervals over Emily's tenancy, but even these had dried up completely. He'd got through to her once on the phone, where he'd apologised profusely for the inconvenience, but still no envelopes appeared.

We're not a charity,

his wife said softly, kissing him on the temple, before she left for work that morning, aware what was eating him up inside as he ate up his breakfast. He belched a sulphurous burp into the silence of his empty house.

Mr Jagait clutched onto the eviction notice buried deep in his pocket as he knocked on the door of 99B Wilkins Road. His clammy hands were spoiling the handwritten letter, that he'd rewritten four times, each one less severe than the last. The coward in him hoped that she wouldn't answer and he could slip it through the letterbox. But the caregiver in him wanted her to open the door and hush her apologies and begin a paternal friendship over a cup of tea.

When there was no answer, neither the coward nor caregiver felt satisfied.

He stood for a moment in the hallway. The muted space felt like a vacuum. It was designed for coming and going, rushing segues and passing visits, not to stand there with nowhere to go. Someone came up the stairs behind him.

Oh hi, Mr Jagait!

It was Lukas, one half of the Finnish couple renting 99A.

Lukas! How are you- wait, wait– mi- tä kuu-luu?

He clambered over the phrase he'd learnt especially for them.

Ahhh very nice! I am good thank you.

Just finished my night shift. And you?

Although Lukas's accent was strong, his words appeared dexterous compared to Jagait's awkward Finnish.

Yes, I'm very well thank you.

You here to fix something?

Lukas pointed towards Emily's front door.

Jagait felt the letter in his pocket. He wobbled his head side to side, as his smile simmered. Lukas nodded back, fully understanding the noncommittal answer.

I haven't seen her for a time,

Lukas's attempt to forge on in the conversation hung even heavier in the air.

The two men stood in the hallway, against its purpose, as dread began to prickle across their skin. Neither wanted to breathe life into their fears, which were unfounded, extreme, ridiculous, surely.

Well I–

Yes, yes, sorry, don't let me keep you, you must want to sleep.

Nice to see you Lukas. Farvel!

Farvel,

Lukas said back, without the heart to tell his landlord that they'd just parted in Danish.

Lukas looked back once more at Mr Jagait, with a small smile, before slipping inside his home. Jagait rapped against the door, his sweaty hands now trembled slightly. He bent down to the letterbox flap but could see only an inch of floorboards, that gave away nothing. Was he imagining the smell?
Emily? It's Mr Jagait.

Your landlord,
he added, trapped between not wanting to assume familiarity and not wanting to flaunt his regal-like title.
Emily? I just want to check you're doing ok, that's all.
He tried to speak directly through the letter flap, not wanting to be overheard by Lukas, who may think he was meddling.

Still no answer and no hint of movement came.
She's probably just not in,
he muttered to himself, standing up straight.

But he had not fooled himself into reassurance. He ran through his options in his head, (ring his wife, ring the police, post the eviction notice and stop overreacting) whilst the spare key to the flat sat heavier in his other pocket. In truth, his subconscious had forewarned of this scenario and quietly slipped the single key from the array of hooks in his own home.
Emily? Look, I'm going to come in, ok? I have reason to believe –I think you might –
Official wording he often heard recited by fictional police officers escaped him.
If you don't want me to open this door, just say so. You don't have to talk to me, just tell me to go away.
He scrunched his toes up, and wished more than anything that she would tell him to go away.
Ok well,

I'm coming in then.
Mr Jagait wiggled the spare key in the high-security lock that he'd had fitted especially.

Emily's lifeless body lay on the floor, in the slither of space between table and sofa. The young woman's features were puffed up. Her bloated limbs shone a reddish hue. She did not look peaceful, nor did she look in pain. She looked as if she were a waxwork: artificial and vacant.

But Mr Jagait did not recoil at the horrifying discovery, he remained quite still.

Because, next to the body of her mother, sat the toddler. Wide-eyed and unflustered. She had a plastic spoon in her mouth that had been so chewed and sucked on it looked as though it had melted. She squirmed a little, shifting her bottom around inside her saturated nappy.

Hello,

Jagait whispered, his voice only a touch less frozen than his body.

The child looked up at him, with a distinct lack of expression.

Hello, little one.

He began to thaw.

He started to edge towards her, and moving only an inch closer, he was hit with smells, of faeces and decay, strong enough to break the barrier of shock. But still he continued on, moving in slow motion as one might move towards a volatile predator, convinced that this infant might drop her air of nonchalance at any moment. The child sucked her cutlery, watching him creep closer. Mr Jagait stepped one leg carefully over the mother and reached down towards the toddler, and then he stopped.

It was at this point – straddled over the dead woman, with his clammy hands stuffed beneath the child's armpits – that he worried he might be interfering with a crime scene. Tampering with evidence. Putting his fingerprints all over suspicious matter. A bead of sweat trickled down his forehead, racing towards the child he overhung. The child who simply watched this strange man. The child who had gone perhaps days without her mother, without food, without care. Perhaps a lifetime. And with this thought, he picked her up, held her close to his body and phoned 999 from the landline.

For twelve minutes, Mr Jagait rocked the infant back and forth on his hip, the way he had once imagined he would do to his own children and grandchildren, who had never arrived. Then efficient paramedics swept through the studio flat, carrying away the mother and child, and leaving Jagait alone again, in the vacuous hallway.

Mr Jagait was left in the dark for weeks, only called upon when police or social services needed access to 99B. His phone calls concerning the child's welfare and the conclusion of Emily's death were bounced around departments,

I'll have a look into that for you,

I can't discuss that with you, I'm afraid,

Ooh, that doesn't sound good does it,

My manager is on holiday at the moment,

Look, Mr Chuckhate, the sooner our time isn't wasted with these phone calls, the sooner we can do our job.

At night, he lay so still and breathed through his mouth in the hope that his wife wouldn't realise he was crying, as he tormented himself over alternative pasts where he had reached out to his tenant earlier.

Then one afternoon, as he bled the radiators in another soon-to-be-let flat, his mobile phone rang.

Hello, is that Mr Jag, Mr jgjit?

Yes, hello, speaking.

Hi, my name's Philip, I'm calling from Southwark Social Services.

Oh yes, hello.

He sat down, with his back to the radiator.

It's regarding the passing of the unidentified adult woman, I believe she was your tenant, is that correct?

Unidentified? You mean Emily? Yes. Yes, she was my tenant.

The possessive pulled at his sense of failed duty.

Well, she remains unidentified until you hand over the paperwork to the police.

Philip hissed his esses and tutted his tees.

They haven't, they haven't asked me for anything.

Mr Jagait's heart began to thump. Not with rational rage at their incompetence, but at his own. He knew he had nothing to offer them.

What, what do they need?

Well, there was no sign of personal documentation in the residence, no passport or driver's license, nothing with her name on whatsoever actually, so they're going to need the copies of the tenancy agreement, etcetera, when she presumably gave you all that information.

There was gleeful spite in Philip's presumption.

But for now, if I could just get her full name it would help to speed up the process of finding a guardian for Robyn.

Robyn?

The child, yes. If you remember correctly there was also a child living in your rented residence, or were you not aware of that?

Yes, no –

Yes or no Mr jgjit, which one is it?

Philip laughed.

No, yes, I was, am aware. I didn't know her name was Robyn.

Yes, they found it on a birthday card down the side of a kitchen unit, he said with the air of gossip one might share in a staff room.

I think that belonged to –

Jagait's explanation that the previous tenant had been a German exchange student called Robyn Weber was cut short.

I don't need your thoughts, sir, I need your facts. The deceased tenant. Can I get her full name, and if you have a date of birth to hand that would be helpful.

Her name was Emily –

he hoped her surname would just roll off the tongue.

Emily,   erm, er,

His mind raced back to the day they'd met. Emily had rung him up, responding to the advert blu-tacked in a newsagent shop window. It was in its fourth week of being displayed, nearing the end of Jagait's paid advert run, with no takers. Then she had called him, with her quiet voice.

She was Northern,

he said aloud.

Right ok. So I'm going to inform all families in the north of England that if you have a young female relative, who may or may not be called Emily, she's sadly passed away and there is a highly vulnerable infant that needs looking after? That's what I'm going to do, am I?

Jagait began to pant. His chest heaved under the weight of his own negligence.

May I ask if there's a reason you're being so obstructive here, Mr jgjit? Because may I remind you that no self-preservation, no selfish concerns over landlord rights or immigration issues should take precedent over the welfare of a child.

No, no,

Mr Jagait wept, not noticing how his back burnt against the radiator,

no.

That was the first and last time anyone contacted Mr Jagait regarding the incident at 99B Wilkins Road, but he was reminded of the mother and child every time he demanded a new tenant present their documentation and sign on the dotted line.

ELIZABETH. 1980.

It had rained all day, when Elizabeth was born at tea time.

Grey clouds interlaced their fingers and trapped London beneath dark palms. Mary watched people scamper across the grass outside, using jean jackets for umbrellas. Their bronzed limbs were still exposed as they refused to succumb to this momentary lapse in July weather. Droplets appeared from nowhere, tapping against the gothic windows and Mary thought of the weddings that would have been ruined today. The unlucky couples with marriages doomed before they'd even begun. Quiet beads sloped down her cheeks, tears that would not have looked out of place upon the gloomy glass.

She kept her head turned away from the rest of the ward, and from the newborn she held loosely in her arms. In all bays but her own, fathers sat by the mother's sides, holding hands or babies or balloons. Though everyone spoke in hushed tones, the presence of love was heartbreakingly loud. She hoped she could lay there so quietly, so still, that she would be forgotten about altogether.

Mary was not the same human being as the pregnant woman who had told the nurses a few hours earlier that her husband was in the army. That he was serving as a soldier, a hero, in an undisclosed location and therefore could not be reached by telephone. That giving birth alone was not representative of the loving family unit that she, and soon enough her daughter, were a part of.

It was another tall tale in her string of fables,
like telling her colleagues at the Post Office that her ankles were swollen from the heat,
like telling her parents across a crackling international phone line that it was simply a stomach virus,
like telling herself that he would be here, that he'd bring flowers, or a gift, or nothing at all, but he would be here.

Even when she'd arrived at the hospital in the final throes of birth and found its vaulted ceilings and arched windows were nothing like the clinical setting she'd seen in the vision she fell asleep to each night, she still used this daydream to ease the pain.

It was only as her sweat dried cold and the baby's cries subsided that reality finally suffocated her imagination.

Mary Ojo had met Tristan Coles in the dark depths of a piano bar. It had been two weeks since her brother Charles had returned to Nigeria, and she was settling into her independence, basking in the mundanity of routine. Charles had blamed the cold weather, but Mary knew the truth. She'd watched him shining the shoes of the men he thought he would be, those who scoffed at his degree as if all relevance had washed away on their overseas journey. Whereas Mary, for whom expectation to be uneducated was consistent across continents, had landed a secure job and made friends and said things like 'cheeky' and 'brolly.' She was the breadwinner, wiring slices back to their anglophile parents, and spending a Friday night in Soho was just what she did now. And as that evening had unfolded with the businessman,
as he handled the bar tab,
as he held open the taxi door,
as he gently unbuttoned her dress in his hotel room,
as he tenderly claimed her virginity for his own,
Mary felt as if the curtain had finally lifted on the opening night of her life. She was the living, breathing protagonist.

And the performance ran for three months. Bright, sparkling months in which the London she'd been calling home for over a year seemed like a rough draft. Months in which the city looked neater, twinkling in little pockets, when viewed from bridges and balconies. And buildings looked more regal, as she strained her eyes upwards in the back of taxis, to catch a glimpse of the ornate carvings that decorated embassies and framed townhouses the size of hotels. It was the first time in her life when she looked no further into the future than what outfit she would wear that evening or whether she'd have room for dessert or to what depths Tristan would pleasure her. Even her most colourful fantasies were pale by comparison to this rich reality. She finally longed to be no one and nowhere else.

In fact, nothing outside of them existed at all. She didn't feel a pang for home, where half the neighbourhood would be dropping into her parent's house in the lead-up to Independence Day celebrations, dropping hints of their expectations for their annual party. She stopped worrying about how Charles was readjusting to Lagos life and the mistruths he was weaving about his departure.

And she didn't lend a single thought to the life thread around Tristan's golden ring finger. For a man of Tristan Coles's arrogance doesn't remove his wedding band to be with his mistress. It makes for light work when returning home at the drop of a hat, or a bombshell. He could slip back to northern suburbia, kiss the forehead of his twin boys and quietly assign Finance Niall to tend to any future business in the capital.

He only removed the ring months later, on a surprisingly damp July day to save it chaffing beneath his wet golf glove. It had rained all day, but he would not miss his tee time.

The nurses were courteous enough to leave Mary alone to wait for the taxi that would never arrive. On the bus, she held Elizabeth so close to disguise how newborn she was from strangers.

She placed the baby down in a dip on the sofa that still sagged to the shape of her brother's sleeping body. It had taken Mary nearly a year to grow accustomed to the quiet of the flat without him. And now, after nights listening to the squeak of nurses' shoes and the clatter of wheeled beds, the wound reopened as if it had never healed. She could still see them squeezing past each other in the narrow hallway, running between the three rooms, their feet barely touching the English soil they were so happy to be on.

The pulse of her heart was conflicted, for every relieved beat that Charles had not stayed long enough to witness her downfall, there was a thump that violently longed for his presence.

Mary stretched her arms out straight and thought her elbow creases might tear. For hours, she had held the baby. The baby who stayed so silent that Mary paused every so often to watch for breath, holding her own as she did so, then feeling a wave of nausea at her twisted disappointment when the tiny chest lifted. She sat for minutes, countless, mindless minutes, staying just out of reach of Elizabeth. When she noticed the blood staining the seat cushions beneath her own traumatised body, she did not have the energy to weep. Instead, Mary would begin to move with the mechanical stamina of a mother. An autopilot that did not have the privilege to falter. She'd danced briefly and boldly in the light of freedom and now she was to see out her days in the dark.

да я ем овощи мама,

one side of a conversation echoed out from the back of the convenience store.

Mary reluctantly waited for her turn in the cubby-hole that would connect her to the outskirts of Lagos. Her eyes glazed over the small selection of infant items. She pressed her back against the aisle shelves to let shoppers past, the true convenience store patrons who came in with purpose, who were fetching a pint of milk or a crucial ingredient. Those who browsed were either numbed by life or awaiting the international phone line, or both. Mary picked up nappies, months too large, and pureed food, that wouldn't be needed for weeks, and wandered to another aisle.

She'd fashioned a sling for Elizabeth, the type she'd seen infants carried in for years. But hers was not made from colourful cloth. It was a large scratchy scarf that she'd bought from a market stall as emergency cold-weather wear in her first London winter. The newsagent tallied up her array of items. Behind him were the bottles she'd once thought so aloof and untouchable, like the potent secrets of an apothecary. She remembered the first time she'd brought a bottle of red to a dinner party and felt as if she had sealed her adulthood in a single transaction. She remembered the sparkling wine that Charles had bought on their first night. He'd shaken it up and sprayed it across the flat, to celebrate with extravagance. They hadn't cared for the wastage, for they'd been so sure that frugality would soon be swallowed by abundance.

I should get a gift,

she half-whispered the lie, and pointed to the cheapest bottle of dark rum.

Telephone's free, the shopkeeper handed over her items and nodded to the back room. With the bag of randoms goods at her feet, she dialled the only number she knew by heart.

Well how am I supposed to know that, eh?

Though it was her mother that spoke, it was her father's breathing she could hear, as the pair crowded too close to the receiver. The image of them hunched together in a cloud of concern made Mary's organs feel too big for her body.

Because I told you,

she tried to keep her sulk loud and volume low,

They cannot fire you for being SICK.

Her dad spoke now, and Mary had to pull her ear away as the consonants exploded across the four thousand miles.

They haven't.

Elizabeth squirmed a little in the sling,

I'm just moving,

Mary readjusted the baby,

branches.

Where to? To Greenwich? or Hammersmith?

Mary could still see the London map she'd grown up with on their kitchen wall. She knew, because they had told her, that it was now decorated with the postcards she and Charles had sent back home. Quintessential pictures of red buses and black cabs in streets of the capital that they'd never been to. They had picked a new one off the swirling stand in their local newsagent once a month, and scrawled fantastical tales across the back.

I don't know yet.

Elizabeth puckered her lips and jutted her chin in search of milk.

Somewhere with,

Mary bounced from one foot to the other to delay the inevitable,

with more career progression.

She accidentally kicked her groceries, clonking the bottle.

You're being promoted, I knew it! I knew it, I knew it, I said, eh –

Well, you will have to go and collect it,

her mother interrupted him.

Such an expensive parcel and the next time you get sick –

I'm better now Mummy –

I said the NEXT time, the next time –

Okay! Okay. I will collect it.

She quashed the conversation with an empty promise and an easy pacifier.

Mary would not, could not, return to the Post Office branch where her colleagues had apparently gone along with her charade of oversized clothes and frequent sick days. She still flushed to think of her manager pulling her aside in the break room and uttering, *maybe it's time you take some leave now.* He'd continued to send payslips these past few weeks, despite no contractual entitlement to maternity pay. But she would write and request a transfer. She couldn't give up the job altogether. It gave her the best rates on naira and a way to send parcels home for the price of postage to Dublin. And it gave her an independence that she would reclaim shortly.

Elizabeth began to cry out.

Good. Your brother is – is that a baby?

I can't hear you, sorry, someone's baby –

Mary? We can't hear you?

I can't hear you. I have to go.

There's a baby making –

I'll call you soon.

She clonked the receiver down so hard that Elizabeth was jolted from her cries for a second.

Then she started again, louder.

Mary tried to make it home, but the incessant wails were deafening. The handles of her shopping bag were cutting the circulation to her fingertips and the knot of the scarf-sling rubbed at the nape of her neck. She walked as fast as she could, her nipples chaffing against her cotton bra. She kept her head down past strangers who winced at the screams coming from the cocoon. Her finger pads bulged. The scarf's scratch was spreading across her whole upper body. She couldn't hear anything beyond the crying and it made her feel disorientated, dizzy. All she could imagine was ripping off the sling and dropping the carrier bag and watching rum soak across the pavement in silence. She hurried her feet faster. Her palms clammed with impatience and rage and strain and all she wanted to do was let go of the carrier bag, let go of –

Autopilot diverted her into an alleyway. She squatted behind an industrial dustbin and removed a breast from her shirt. Soon there was only the sound of suckling, and water sloshing inside a network of pipes somewhere.

As Elizabeth fed, Mary drained. She slouched fully onto the alley floor, leaning against a brick building. When the baby was satisfied, Mary realised tiny threads of her scarf were caught on rough bricks behind her and this minor resistance required too much effort to overcome. She stayed on the ground. Feet pattered past, beyond the dustbin, and shards of conversations blew into the silent alley. This was where Mary belonged now, sat in life's lay-bys, feeling the rush of air of those who travelled past with somewhere to go.

She rummaged in her groceries for a snack and found herself surprised by each item, as if she were rifling through someone else's shopping or a disappointing goodie bag. Autopilot broke the seal on the dark rum and Mary took a sip. It coated her tongue, igniting buds until flames pressed against her palette and she had to gape her mouth open, panting hot breath. The fire glowed in her chest, sizzled in her belly and fizzed down her nose. She took another sip, then another, chasing feeling with anaesthetic.

Mary tried to suppress the wrenching emotion but it stabbed out of her. Short sharp bursts,

her shoulders punching

and her throated knotting

and her chest convulsing,

as if her heart were trying to leap out of her body altogether to find a better home and Baby Elizabeth was rocked to sleep by the rhythm of her mother's pain.

THE LAKE.

Anna rifled through the chest.

It's ok, it's ok, you'll be ok,

she said as she rummaged.

Layla, the child, had simply lain down next to Robyn, without the energy for concern. She'd tucked herself into her grown up, placing a gentle hand on Robyn's chest, which still faintly moved.

Anna found an air horn. It must have been thrown into the box fifteen years ago, back when the possibility of danger still rattled the edges of their existence.

Ok ok, let me get some help.

She stepped over the two bodies.

Just outside the cabin, she held the horn high and pressed down hard on the plastic,

but nothing happened.

She shook the rusted canister frantically, hearing a small rattle inside grow looser, then tried again, using both hands.

BRRRRRRRRRRRRRRRRRRP

Birds flew from the nearby trees in their droves,

BRRRRRRP

BRRRRRP

BRRRRRRRRRRRRP

a rude awakening, a mass exodus.

Cynthia was the first to arrive. The most recent addition to the community, having lived with them for just over a year. The ex-athlete had barely broken a sweat from her impromptu two kilometre sprint. It would be a while until the others came.

What's happened?

I don't know, they just turned up and they – we need the cart and the first aid kit and blankets.

Cynthia ran back down the track as quickly as she had come.

You'll be ok. You'll be ok my loves.

Anna crouched next to the two skeletal frames.

It took four of them to heave Robyn's body into the cart, which they'd lined with blankets ahead of the bumpy journey down to site. Though she looked slight and fit well within the confines of the wooden crate, she was dense with muscle, and the wheels stuck in defiance. They were more used to transporting mounds of sheep's wool or small barrels of fresh water from the river at the heaviest. Five women pushed and pulled the cart, navigating the rocky path, teetering between cautiousness and urgency.

Anna followed closely behind, carrying Layla on her hip. She watched her footing on the ground, just as she always did, despite knowing the track so well. She always travelled it with purpose, marching between the deciduous trees to fetch or deliver, eyes internally focused on where she was going. And yet her peripheries knew all two kilometres from memory, which had been divided into mental chunks somewhere along the way:

> the Welcome Cabin to the woodland entrance, where fringe fir trees still keep their distance from one another > the crossroads where the chalky path flattens into dense peaty soil > the slight decline after the tallest oak and the return of rubbly pathway > the section that's hugged a little tighter by evergreens > the sudden steep slope of the path, before it rolls out into the flat of the site courtyard

It was here where the cart-drivers picked up speed, and six other women stood waiting, springing to attention at the sound of the clattering.

They wheeled as close to the main building as possible, the largest of the five outhouses, then plucked Robyn up and carried her over the threshold, her limbs spread between carriers.

They burst into the open-plan space, which prior to the intrusion had sat still, wallowing in the comforting smell of baking bread. It had been purpose built to stay warm in winter and cool in summer, so it fulfilled its thermal duties and chilled the women as they barged in on this sunny morning. Cynthia carried Robyn by herself for the final steps, and lay her down on the sofa, which was a wooden base swaddled by woollen stuffing and cloaked in a quilted blanket. Without words, the women backed away and allowed Maria to see to the unconscious woman.

Maria would never claim she had co-founded the commune, since it didn't feel like something structured enough to be founded.

But she had been here since day one, by Anna's side. Maria left Portugal to train as a doctor, with every intention of returning home, until a tragedy had swallowed everyone she loved and there was nothing to return to. So she'd wandered listlessly through life, until she met Anna, and their desire to simply breathe a little deeper had snowballed into this self-sufficient life.

Maria checked Robyn's pulse, and leaned in close to feel her soft breath. She gently lifted her eyelids, and looked at the dark irises that did not look back at her. Maria ran her hand over the bony frame, delicate but firm over the vital spots: skull, neck, chest.

Ok, she's severely dehy-derrated,

In thirty-odd years, Maria's accent had never faded.

I need some water please.

She spoke calmly towards the crowd of women.

She ran a wet finger pad gently over Robyn's lips, chapped and disfigured.

I think she may have broken some ribs, so I don't want to keep moving her, but I think we should settle her in the bell tent, for warmth. We will just have to keep an eye on her for now. I don't know where else she is in pain.

Maria felt tears appear as she brushed the young woman's face. She was reminded of a small sparrow she'd nursed the past winter. She'd found it with a wing badly broken and a gash to its chest, and the brutality of injuries to something so fragile had winded her.

And the girl?

Maria looked up at Anna, who still clutched the child to her chest.

No obvious injuries. I think she's just exhausted, but probably the same.

Anna held out Layla for Maria to make her own assessment. She stood up and took the child, who obediently slid her arms around her neck, on top of Maria's thick black hair. Hair that used to be her pride and joy, that used to hang heavy on her hips, until she'd lopped it off one of the first weeks living in the commune, and it had never grown back further than her collarbone. She couldn't bear to pull Layla too far from her body to inspect her properly. Instead, she held her tight and said,

Let's move them to the water. Let them rest there.

ROBYN. 2004.

A bitter cold swept across the netball court, snapping at the bare legs of the Year Seven girls. The court was scattered with potholes and weeds toiled out of the concrete cracks. The faint painted lines, which were masked entirely by moss in some parts, were intended for tennis. But a metal hoop had been wheeled to either end, making it a netball court.

Miss Rowland frantically blew her whistle, attempting to organise the smatterings of eleven- and twelve-year olds, who were spread as far as the collection of rolling netballs. A few feebly attempted to throw a ball, some nudged them with their trainers, but mostly they shivered and huddled and whined.

Oh come on. It's not that bad, Matilda,

Miss Rowland said, whistle still gripped between her teeth, as she zipped up her second *gilet.*

Robyn stood by herself. She prised her hands open and closed, examining how the cold had stiffened them. Her pitch-black hair blew across her face and her matchstick limbs were covered in a fishnet pattern of purple and orange, but she didn't join in the complaints of her peers. She rarely joined in with her peers at all. The teacher's erratic whistle-blowing blurred deep into her background, as her mind drifted somewhere nondescript. Until she was drawn back to the court with a

SMACK.

Robyn became acutely aware of her nose. Where it stuck out from her face, how it throbbed. The cold air felt shocking in her nostrils, as if they were only breathing for the first time, and her eyes began to sting.

She blinked,

once,

twice,

then the bobbly imprint of a netball began to tingle across her forehead and cheeks.

The whole class was finally quiet and focused.

You'right there Robyn? Shake it off,

Miss Rowland called across the court.

Robyn looked at the face of each of her twenty-two classmates. She saw surprise diluting into stifled laughter, but her gaze tripped over one girl, Alice Levy.

Alice was the tallest in the class, with a wide face and long blonde hair. She wore mascara everyday and had both earlobes pierced in two places. When she got a detention for talking in class or rolling her skirt up or smoking in the loos, she would wail *ohmygoddddaaaaaa* and stomp away in her all-black trainers. And now, she held a palm to her mouth, in delighted shock.

Good girl,

Miss Rowland nodded, as Robyn walked towards the group, but Robyn did not slow down.She marched closer, balling her frozen fists, led by her thumping heart, and nose.

A few girls cowered as she approached, but not Alice Levy. Not Alice Levy who sat on the top deck of the bus and had a boyfriend in the year above. She would never cower away from the mute, ratty, weirdo.

Then, Robyn punched Alice Levy in her big, wide face.

Whatthefuck you psycho

ohmygoddddaaaaaa

As Robyn sat on a cushioned chair in the Admin Corridor, she inspected her hand again. This time it was not the cold that tried to clamp it shut, but her rapidly-swelling knuckles. She had never punched anyone before.

Robyn had never lived long enough in one home to develop that sibling-like bond that could withstand play-fighting (or real fighting). She'd often witnessed scuffles in the playground between older boys shouting, *COME ON THEN!* and caught glimpses on television when the movement was alluded to with a THUMP and a posthumous black-eye, but she didn't know that she had internalised the mechanics. She didn't know that the rage, which resided quietly in her gut, could take that form when provoked. It had been instinctual, and somewhat satisfying.

The door to an office swooshed open against the felt carpet, and Mrs Rowland exited, with the whistle still dangling around her neck. She gave Robyn a *what-are-we-going-to-do-with-you* half-smile, and headed off down the corridor, *swish-swishing* away in her polyester tracksuit bottoms.

Ms Watkins appeared in the doorway. At nearly six feet tall, she had long since adopted a small stoop to mask her height, which was exaggerated by her slenderness. But she still wore small heels, as a big EFF YOU to the faculty members who resorted to privately attacking her femininity when threatened by a woman in charge. She wore a pencil skirt and cashmere jumper and wire spectacles on her spindly nose.

Come on in, Robyn.

Robyn wasn't intimidated by offices. Before every new journey, and every new chapter, of her life she found herself on this side of an oversized fake pine desk. She was familiar with their sad-looking plants, their strategically placed family portraits, their nameplates: Ms Watkins - Headteacher. *Ms. Mzzzzzzzz.*

Now Robyn, we both know, what you just did to Alice was totally unacceptable.

Ms Watkins had a way of not talking down to the pupils. She might have gently scolded her colleagues or her husband or her cat in the very same level-headed way.

I can't imagine, to act so out of character, that it was unprovoked, but violence is never, ne-ver, the answer.

Robyn noticed the silver chain that attached one arm of Watkins's glasses to the other. She thought it seemed odd, as a headteacher, to be so brazen about her disorganisation, to tell the world that she would likely lose her glasses unless they were physically strung around her.

I'm sure you can sort things out with Alice with an apology,

Ms Watkins looked down as she carried on,

but, we do have a zero-tolerance policy when it comes to violence.

Robyn looked at the teenaged son in the family photo, angled just so she could see it. He wore glasses like his mother and had a neck as long as hers, stretching out from a black t-shirt. His smile was a bundle of crooked teeth, but wide nonetheless. Robyn wondered what his name was. If he called Watkins Mum or Mother or Mummy.

Since this is the first time we've seen anything like this from you, you're just going to be placed on a two-day exclusion. But, let this serve as a very serious warning, Robyn.

Robyn wondered why these seats, that only got sat on for passing visits, were cushioned and the ones that they sat on all day, for fifty minutes at a time, were made from a hard, bobbly plastic that made her tights itch.

You'll be required to complete all your schoolwork at home and be completely up to date on your return, but hopefully it will give you some time to think about your actions. When you come back next week, you'll also be on report for a month, reporting to Mr Davies, your head of year, every day.

Watkins searched Robyn's face for any kind of emotion.

Do you understand, Robyn?

She shrugged.

I understand that your home life is not as straightforward, as most of your classmates,

Watkins appeared to blush.

And it's perfectly normal for that to throw up all sorts of feelings, perhaps anger, but it's important to talk about it, deal with it, in a responsible way, to save these sorts of outbursts.

Their silent stand-off was rescued by a knock at the door. Ms Watkins's assistant poked just her head in,

Mr. Anastas is here.

She did not look at Robyn.

Thank you, Theresa. Bring him in,

Ms Watkins shuffled papers on her desk.

Ron had been Robyn's guardian for nearly half a year. She'd moved into the Anastas home in the summer transition window between primary and secondary school, when everyone thought one upheaval could be masked by another. Ron and his wife, Mel, already had three children: Andreas, Nikolas and Toby. By the arrival of the third boy, Mel no longer disguised her desperation for a daughter. She refused to cut Toby's hair until he was seven and it began to catch in his waistband. And as the years passed, and her boys evolved into smelly, spotty, semeny savages, she'd longed more than ever for that extra X chromosome. Until one evening at the dinner table, as Andreas sat on his Gameboy and

Nikolas stuffed peas up Toby's nose, Mel had stood up, smashed her plate on the floor and screamed at Ron that she was going to suffocate if she did not have a daughter immediately. Ron had started the process the next morning.

A process which was surprisingly quick, and far less thorough than the charity who'd refused them a rescue dog. Quicker still was the realisation that Robyn would never fulfil Mel's daydreams of spa days and horseback riding. These days, Mel left most dinners with a ceramic smash.

Ms Watkins leaned across her desk to shake Ron's hand. Her height, and his lack thereof, made for a cartoonish picture.

Thank you for joining us, Mr Anastas. We're sorry to disturb you at work, we wouldn't if it wasn't,

Ms Watkins searched for the word,

urgent.

Ron ran a roof repair company with his brother, but in the months that Robyn had known him, he'd been on a roof only a handful of times. He'd damaged a vertebrae falling off a ladder a decade before, and the injury had returned to haunt him with a vengeance. He spent his days doing paperwork from their shipping container office, and his nights complaining about his days. Robyn thought he'd be relieved for the disturbance.

Earlier today, Robyn displayed some unacceptable behaviour.

Ron began to flush as if he was the one in trouble.

She was violent towards a classmate.

Θεέ μου,

Ron whispered.

He whipped his head towards Robyn, who absent-mindedly picked at peeling varnish on the chair arm. Ron clocked her swollen knuckles.

Θεέ μου,

he repeated, as he glanced skyward.

No no no, nonono,

he continued, shaking his head, as if he'd lost a child in a war.

Ms Watkins struggled to conceal a grimace at his reaction.

Robyn has shown no signs of aggression before now, and we're sure it was a one-off occurrence, she worked to mollify the small man.

But, as I'm sure you'll understand, as Robyn does, that we have a no-violence policy and therefore Robyn will be excluded for –

Ron threw himself back in the chair, before Ms Watkins could finish, flinging his hands up and slapping them down on his thighs in resigned despair.

Robyn's reaction was even less discreet than the headteacher's. She contorted her eyebrows and lips and stared at her guardian with such hearty disdain, it was almost intimidating. But Ron was too appalled to notice.

Why why why,

he muttered on.

Mr Anastas,

Ms Watkins sharpened her tone, trying to snap him back into the room.

I was just discussing with Robyn that having emotions, frustrations,

she stressed,

is perfectly understandable. And I don't want to encroach on your home life, but I suggest you and Robyn make space for discussions, or work together to find a healthy outlet where she can fully express herself.

Both adults looked at Robyn.

Do you have any hobbies you'd be interested in pursuing, Robyn?

Watkins tried to coax out a glimpse of something, anything.

Any of the afterschool clubs, perhaps? There's netball or girls football or there's music clubs, would you like to learn an instrument?

Or – or Mr Stone's drama club? They put a play on at the end of every year.

Or something outside of school perhaps, the local youth club has lots of events and things?

Ms Watkins became suddenly exhausted by Robyn's impenetrableness.

Right, well, I'm sure the pair of you can come up with some ideas.

She talked fast until they left her office.

I can't believe this,

Ron's pleather loafers squawked and squeaked as they scurried across the school car park. Robyn managed to keep up without any sign of exertion.

Not one of my boys has ever been excluded, ever, and now you, a girl.

Robyn had no idea what being a girl had to do with it. Nor where exactly the punishment was in being given two days away from her inane peers, who whined about what their mothers had packed in their lunch boxes.

Ron's little legs ground to a halt,

Do NOT tell Melissa about this. We'll tell her you're sick.

He looked at her with an uncertainty that undermined the imperative.

Twelve-year old Robyn was not yet aware that she made people feel uncomfortable, uneasy. It would be many years before she understood that her lack of facade was what made her difficult to read. That by taking no interest in the social cues designed to mask, distract, beguile, she was altogether more mystifying. And people did not like to be mystified, in general. She took too little interest in other people to realise that the way they looked at her, the way Ron looked at her in that moment, searching her for a recognisable expression, a sign of mutual agreement, or mild comprehension at the least, was not how they looked at everyone else.

For the next two days, Robyn sat in the shipping container office, staring at the clock and swinging her feet. The chair was just low enough that the toe of her shoes would scuff the floor on each swing. It was not until Robyn returned to school and Mel found the report book stuffed in a blazer pocket that Ron's plan of deception crumbled. A side plate and a salad bowl faced the consequences at dinner that evening. The three boys did not flinch at their mother's outburst. In fact, they took relief in her exit from the table to wail her woes loudly down the phone in her bedroom, since that meant that they too could get down, and slip off to shoot things or drive things or fight things.

Robyn pushed the last remaining peas onto her fork with her forefinger. She collected up the half-empty plates with her own and carried them to the sink. She squeezed a long tube of lime green washing up liquid into the water. *Far too much! Wasteful!* Mel would tell her, but she liked the sickly apple scent. Ron stayed sat at the head of the table, with his head in his hands. Robyn fished out wet peas and soapy mincemeat from the drain, then took a dustpan and brush to the scattered ceramic. The dining room was carpeted which made Mel's ability to smash crockery quite impressive. She'd honed her angles and learnt the necessary power after several underwhelming and unsuccessful *thmps*. Robyn scooped the big chunks into the plastic pan, but the smaller shards shimmied beneath the brush. She began to pick them up with her fingers.

Okay,

Ron was watching Robyn now, nodding to himself. It might be worth rescuing the girl they'd rescued to rescue themselves, but it also might be exhausting.

ELIZABETH. 1991.

Elizabeth tugged at her mother's arm. As a younger child, she'd liked to stroke this gently dimpled patch of skin, entranced by its softness,

but now she pinched the bingo wing tightly between her thumb and forefinger.

It was the only body part on show, draped over the low bedside, so that Mary's lifeless fingers nearly brushed the brown carpet. Elizabeth squeezed again, not noticing how her teeth also clamped together until she released.

The shape of Mary's body did not move beneath the pilled sheet as she slowly turned her head to face her daughter, swiping a line of drool across her pillow. She couldn't make sense of the purple vision before her. Everything was right, except not quite. The classic certainty and uncertainty of her dreams,

when it is her home   but not,
when it is her daughter   but not.

It's the first day of school,

Elizabeth said, quietly, not out of concern for her dozing mother, but out of embarrassment at having to announce the obvious. She fingered the cuffs of her shiny purple blazer, which was two sizes too big *so it would last.* She'd done four dress runs before today, feeling the fresh zip of the skirt, the thickness of unworn tights, the manufacturer's smell on the shirt. She'd paraded in the privacy of her bedroom, less trying on the uniform than the new girl who would be wearing it, who would have a locker and take the bus and sit on science stools. She'd paraded until the layers of polyester began to create a storm of friction and she got an electric shock from everything she touched.

Last night, she had hooked the hangers of her blazer and shirt to the outside of her wardrobe and lay the skirt and tights across the back of a chair. She'd folded the jumper neatly, and even lain her newest pair of pants on top, micromanaging her future self, diminishing her responsibilities. All she must do is remember to put on her shoes, which were by the front door, humming with the fumes of fresh polish. Mother and daughter had spent the evening sat on the newspapered kitchen floor, shining the black leather. They were brand new shoes, since Elizabeth, already tall for her age, had grown even more over the summer, but still they shined them for hours. Mary had told tales of her brother as she buffed in the circular motion that he'd taught her. Elizabeth giggled at the spot of black polish on her mother's nose, and her mother giggled back when she told her. Elizabeth had gone to bed so giddy, from not just the fumes but from excitement for tomorrow and contentment for today, that she'd forgotten to listen for footsteps, for the soft padding of slippers up the stairs not long after her own lights out that promised a good day ahead. She'd tumbled too easily into sweet dreams to keep her ears tuned for the muffled clinks of cupboards and countertops, bottles and glassware.

Mary burst awake, gasping for air, resuscitated by reality. She still wore her satin bonnet as they raced for the bus. Elizabeth's shoes scuffed as they ran.

Polly's mother, Mrs Hopfield, stood with one foot on the bus, the other clutching the bus stop pole, as if she could anchor it there. *Here they come!* She pointed and squealed and beckoned and smiled to assuage the driver.

Elizabeth hopped on, squeezing past Polly's mother, who smelt like soap and soft knits. *Whey!* someone called from the back.

She dared only look up a fraction to find Polly, tapping the vacant seat next to her. Elizabeth had wanted to sit on the top deck, cementing this new chapter of independence. But she'd also imagined she would sashay past new schoolmates, not skulk past waiting crowds. So for that, she was grateful for her friend's insipidness.

The bus doors hissed shut. Polly waved at their mothers, adding to Elizabeth's embarrassment. She did not look up. As the bus rumbled underfoot and chatter erupted and Polly twittered into her ear, she tried to subtly fan air into her shirt and stem the sweat that bled down from her braids. She felt as dirty as the thick bus air around her.

The school corridors swarmed like the tunnels of the underground, only more disorientating. Everyone was a speck of purple in an aubergine blend. Very few naturally stood out, only those who'd had older siblings attend long enough ago that their hand-me-downs were of a brighter violet. Others made themselves known.

Elizabeth was unloading new workbooks into her locker, when a Year Nine with a lip piercing said,
Don't use that. People steal shit. They slice it open with a ruler.

She was late to third period because four Year Tens interlaced arms and blocked off a stairwell, and during an introductory orienteering game, in lieu of Geography, she heard a Year Eight call the head of maths a *monobrowed cunt* to his face.

By the final class of the day, History, the Year Sevens sat quietly like the shell-shocked soldiers they would one day study on their syllabus. Ms Taylor was the only teacher not to assign alphabetical seating and Elizabeth wished she had. She winced at the flowery design Polly was gluing to her workbook.

Mmhmm, she replied anytime Polly spoke, in the hope that she'd stop talking. The classroom was so quiet, anyone could hear her. Elizabeth stopped replying altogether and angled her body away from her, ever so slightly.

They were only friends by default. Her best friend, Desiree had left for the US in Year Four, leaving Elizabeth in limbo between the very distinct groups of their small class:

Football Boys
Sci-Fi Boys
Unicorn Girls
and the Two Independents, (one who threw chairs and one who wrote with a special pencil grip).

So she'd had to settle for the Unicorn Girls – Gemma, Lucy, Tayla-Jane and Polly – who had fairytale pencil cases and pretended to be horses at break time. They spent sleepovers watching cartoons, when Elizabeth wanted to talk about boys and learn how to kiss and read the magazines that gave away free lipgloss. They wore fancy dress and made silly voices but when Elizabeth suggested prank calls or Knock Down Ginger, they flushed at the thought of committing such a crime. And yet, for all their obedience, none of them were an academical match for Elizabeth.

Elizabeth just got things. She had an awareness beyond her peers. She could read the patronising tone with which teachers simplified information, and detect the way they steered pupils towards answers with a subtlety that made them think they'd got there alone. She was more often unable to understand how her classmates couldn't understand, than not understand the class itself. She excelled in tests because she gave the answer they wanted. She understood the assignment and framed her thoughts, her voice, her opinions accordingly.

So she just had to withstand one term until classes would be reshuffled into tiers of intelligence and she could snake away from Polly, the only other Unicorn Girl to attend the lowest rated high school in their catchment area. Polly was harmless, sweet even. She didn't whisper when Elizabeth's mum fell off her chair at the nativity play or laugh when she was given two plain pieces of bread in her lunchbox. Instead, she'd split her egg mayo sandwich and home-baked brownie down the middle. She was the perfectly formed apple that fell, nay floated, from her mother's tree of well-meaning, guilt-driven philanthropy. Elizabeth liked to sting her own mother by recounting Mrs Hopfield's charity. But in truth, Elizabeth hated when Polly's mum gave her a pound coin to spend at the fete and waited with her at school collection in case Mary didn't show. Her life only seemed darker against the glow. The Hopfields lived in a detached house and holidayed in France but chose to send their children to the rundown state school because it was *character-building*, with disregard for the characters they were building in the friends who slept over in a home with more bathrooms than they had bedrooms. If they'd met here, Polly would be the type of delicate book worm that Elizabeth would choose not to make fun of despite the other popular girls doing so. Polly was the type of girl she should take pity on, not the other way around.

Did you see we have double science tomorrow morning? A double period, that's so grown up. I hope we get to wear lab coats, like proper scientists. Elizabeth had actually hoped for the same thing, but it just sounded lamer when Polly said it.

The queue for the bus was not a queue, but a chaotic crowd, pulsing with the energy of the free. Boys in backpacks sprinted to nowhere. Couples held hands as if tethered to one another for survival. Girls still sporting holiday hairstyles, twirled beaded braids as they gossiped about whose boobs had come in over summer.

CHUDS! CHUDS! CHUDS!

A chant erupted, aimed at a boy who was apparently Year Ten, but shorter than most Year Eights. He lapped it up, either in on the joke or trying to be. Elizabeth and Polly felt outnumbered by those who had things to shout about, but actually they belonged to the bigger party, of the quiet and awkward and invisible.

The bus pulled up and all energy funnelled towards the passenger doors, much to the dismay of the two unlucky civilians who sat on board already. No individual felt as though they themselves were physically pushing to get on, they were swept in the pushes of others, carried forward by a pooled push. The smell of cheap antiperspirant and warm rucksacks swarmed around them. Elizabeth came up to most people's shoulders, Polly only to their torsos. One by one, students beat the pack and made it onto the bus, like an air bubble escaping in a cherry soda.

Let's get the next one,

Elizabeth started to pull the reigns on her forward energy.

We can't, my mum will be waiting for this one.

Polly's panic was that of a first-class passenger on a sinking ship, tinged with entitlement.

We have to get this one.

She gripped Elizabeth's wrist and pressed on.

They were the last on. The doors creaked close behind them, snapping at Elizabeth's skirt. The bus lurched forward and Elizabeth got a mouthful of Polly's hair, who was standing on her tiptoes, trying to spot a free seat.

Come on, let's go upstairs,

Elizabeth was already on the bottom step.

She clutched the hand rails and raced upwards before she could fall. The top deck was full. Students sat backwards or stretched across the aisle or didn't sit at all. Polly tugged at the hem of Elizabeth's skirt, begging to go back downstairs. A dirty tennis ball rolled all the way down the central alley. Elizabeth stopped it with her once-polished shoe.

The only thing more embarrassing than sitting downstairs, was a failed attempt at sitting upstairs.

She picked up the ball and headed towards the back of the bus, just as the intrepid explorer knows sometimes they must venture further into the cave to find the way out. The spread of belongings and bodies made it hard to distinguish vacant seats. Her hands clutched from headrest to headrest like monkey bars, daring not leave herself unsupported for a second. There was a spare seat next to a large boy who was plugged into a walkman. It was occupied only by his rucksack and the spill of half his thigh, but she kept walking. One row from the back, a boy stood up and held his hand out for the tennis ball. Even with the coating of angry pustules, he was good looking.

Cheers,

he took the ball and sat down.

You can sit here, babe.

Elizabeth had been too focused on the boy to notice the empty space in front of him. The blonde girl chewed gum and looked up at her. Her lips were gently glossed and she wore a silver eyeshadow that made the whites of her eyes glisten.

Thanks,

Elizabeth slid into the aisle seat.

She caught sight of Polly, stranded halfway down the bus. She nodded towards the headphoned boy. Polly winced as she lowered herself to the very edge of the chair, trying her hardest not to disturb her neighbour.

Was today your first day?

The girl was studying her. The sweet scent of bubblegum carried her question.

Elizabeth nodded.

N'aww,

she clicked her tongue.

The importance of this interaction was not lost on Elizabeth and she knew silent affirmations would not cut it.

I like your bag,

she pointed at the nylon backpack.

Thanks, babe. It's not real though. My uncle got it from Turkey. He goes there all the time, so I can get whatever I want, dirt cheap.

There was a slight sound of saliva around her words but it was somehow enticing, adult.

Even a Chanel Flap?

Elizabeth asked.

The girl angled towards her, glossy eyes widened.

You know about Chanel?

Elizabeth chose to discard the shell of patronisation and nourish only the nut of respect.

Yeah he can, babe, I've got like four or five. My sister's getting a real one for her sixteenth though, lucky bitch. But it does mean that I can get one when I turn sixteen, I might get a Lady Dior bag though cos it's a bit more classier, ain't it?

Elizabeth nodded again.

Yeah, definitely.

The bus swept in left. A smattering of passengers stood up for the first stop, a distance they could have walked from school.

Where do you get off?

Maplewood Av, you?

Same.

Aw, babe! Twins!

Elizabeth wanted to be sisters with and mothered by and the protégée of and the muse for this girl, who was a whole eleven months her senior.

Leesh Leesh Leesh!

A boy leant over two rows to shake the girl's shoulder, with an aggression that was both infantile and neanderthal, and quite shocking to see inflicted on someone so glamourous.

Stop Damien, I'm talking!

She owned her dismissal with the perfect blend of seriousness and flirtation.

With my new friend –

Elizabeth.

N'aww, like the Queen?

Elizabeth raised her brows as if she'd never made the connection before.

I'm Alisha,

the statement sounded rehearsed, to be bestowed upon those who deserved it.

Alright alright, but guess what?

Carl K fingered Hannah Mitchell in the disabled toilet!

Elizabeth didn't turn away from the gossip. She listened blatantly, cementing herself as part of the conversation.

Err disgusting! She's such a slag.

The messenger with floppy hair looked chuffed, with the story or the reaction it was unclear, but he lingered uncomfortably across the head of the boy between them.

You coming park?

he asked Alisha.

Elizabeth couldn't know exactly where Alisha's eyes darted to, for an instant that seemed to hold the answer to her decision, but she imagined it was to the Tennis Ball boy behind her.

Yeah, alright.

Another wave of passengers alighted. Polly tried to make herself small as her seat-neighbour edged out past her, brushing his bottom against her book bag. Once free of him, she searched for Elizabeth's attention, to invite her over so the two of them could finally feel secure in each other's company amongst this deck of deviants, but Elizabeth had turned her body towards the window.

You wanna come park, babe?

Elizabeth hesitated, fearful the excitement would bolt out of her.

It's ok, I'll look after you,

Alisha squeezed her knee, and she could feel the warm pads of Alisha's fingers even after she'd lifted them away.

Yeah, ok.

When the bus pulled into Maplewood Avenue, a hoard of passengers were flushed out. They all stood and inched along the gangway of the top deck, waiting for those below to file out first. Maplewood Avenue itself was a sparse street, not even home to maple trees. Not even home to any trees, except one skinny silver birch that had been haphazardly planted in recent years, making a hash of the pavement they'd excavated for it. Except for the birch and the metal pole that waved down buses, Maplewood only offered a convenient central location for the streets and estates that surrounded it. Outside of the four distinct drop offs and pick ups, (AM work commute, AM school run, PM school run, PM work commute), it was as soulless as its artificially cheery name.

Elizabeth let passengers funnel out before her, building the barrier between Polly and herself. As she shuffled down the bus, she could see the top of Polly's mother's head outside, waiting as kids swarmed round her. Perhaps the mother and daughter would walk on, too engrossed in Polly's first day to remember to wait. She hoped she'd managed to sever the tie between herself and her primary school friend with one separated bus journey. Elizabeth dragged her feet slowly to the front of the bus trying to buy herself time, to hide amongst the crowd, but her plan was foiled. She stepped off and Mrs Hopfield uncrossed one arm to wave, her long fingers spread far apart. She wore black sunglasses and an open smile. In Elizabeth's periphery, Alisha and Damien and Tennis Ball Boy and others were reconvening.

How was it, girls? Are you going to come back to ours, darling?

I bought a box of ice lollies to celebrate, and I've filled the paddling pool.

Polly squirmed with the excitement of a toddler and Elizabeth wanted to push her into a bush and arrest Mrs Hopfield for saying *paddling pool* in public.

Babe!

Alisha called over.

The swathes of school children were quickly dispersing, leaving Elizabeth exposed, caught in the open fields of no man's land between one life and another.

I'm going to the park,

Elizabeth said, hardly moving her mouth.

Mrs Hopfield looked over at Alisha and friends,

Oh how lovely! Of course, go go. Darling, do you want to go, too?

she asked Polly, and Elizabeth thought she might combust with rage, and humiliation.

But Polly looked at the ground and shook her head. Then she quietly reached for her mother's hand.

Come on. Bye, Elizabeth,

she flashed a brief smile as they walked off.

Elizabeth's tidal wave of relief crashed on her shores, and she stood a moment in a pool of debris,

of guilt and pity

and longing.

You coming yeah, babe?

Alisha looped an arm through Elizabeth's, threading her question mark so tightly through the crook of her elbow that there could be no other reply than,

Yeah, course!

And any whispers of doubt for her actions were forgotten in the swell of Alisha's vanilla scent and the way she squeezed Elizabeth's hand whenever she exclaimed – which was often – and how she rolled her eyes at the boys and they jogged about her like puppies and the way she fingered the cigarette packet with its Turkish writing.

Elizabeth held tightly onto her link to a new life.

ROBYN. 2004.

Robyn had only sat in the front seat of Ron's car once before, on the day they had driven her home for the first time. Mel had squeezed in the back with Nikolas and Toby (Andreas, being the eldest, missed out on a spot in the five-seater) and she'd played with Robyn's hair through the gap in the headrest, giggling that they'd *get this mess sorted out, won't we.* Robyn sat forward slightly now, in memory.

She had a ring-bound road map open on her lap. A futile exercise since she could not read it, nor was the venue they were headed to even identified on the map. But at every traffic stop, Ron glanced down at the crosshatch of coloured lines. Despite driving a fourth-hand estate car, he wore Italian leather driving gloves.

I've worked so hard to get you in here, so you can't be – you've got to be –

Although he only muttered, he was sat so close to the wheel that his breath fogged up the windscreen.

I don't want you letting me down. Many people have recommended this place, but it's not easy to just, get in, here, like this, so I want you to, remember that, and be thankful, for the opportunity.

They stopped at a zebra crossing as a swarm of maroon-uniformed children toddled across, each one paired with an adult. They wore felt blazers and carried smart book-bags, channelling the city business-types they would likely grow into. Robyn watched each one yank on the hand of their parent as tales of their day burst forth.

Come on, come on.

Ron began to inch across the walkway before the final child had reached the opposite kerb.

The suburban spaciousness subsided as they crawled towards a denser, greyer part of town. Even the splashes of colour in,

TENNESSEE FRIED CHICKEN

Diamondz Nail & Beauty Salon

AFRIKAN MARKET

Guido's Grill

HOTEL HOTEL

New Pak Hong FISH & CHIPS & CHINESE Takeaway were coated in an ashen sadness. Residential facades loomed above the shop fronts in white brick, with dirty tear stains crying down from net-curtained windows. Discarded plastic bags quivered in the wind like city blossom. They were caught mid-flight around a lamppost if lucky, mindlessly trampled on if not.

At a red light, they pulled up next to an open fishmonger, where silvery corpses were displayed on a bed of ice. The car filled with the fish fumes, but Ron was too preoccupied to notice and Robyn too disinterested to care. On the opposite pavement, two construction workers in high-vis body warmers and tanned work boots called out to a mother pushing a double buggy. Robyn couldn't hear the exchange from inside the car, nor could she see the mother's reaction, whose head was buried deep within the fur-lined hood of her parka coat, but from the men's twisted laughter she felt she'd heard every word. To keep her distance, the mother walked straight through a puddle in her ballerina pumps.

The gaps between buildings grew even smaller, and soon the road was hugged by long stretches of concrete office blocks that peaked so high up, Robyn could not see their full height from the angle of the car window. At the end of one block, which they seemed to have been driving past for whole minutes, Ron indicated left with new-found assurance. The side street led only to a multi-storey carpark.

Here we are,

Ron was visibly chuffed with his navigation.

We go down.

Nearly every parking bay on the entrance level was occupied. But Ron was not on the hunt for an empty space. He made a beeline for the downward slope on the far side of the carpark. Down here, although only one level lower, the cars were immediately more dispersed and natural light was suffocated. The open sides became smooth concrete and instead, fluorescent strip lights illuminated the way. Ron wasted no time and looped this level as fast as the first, desperate to get deeper underground.

He drove two further storeys down. The screech of tyres echoed out as the levels became devoid of cars. On the fourth level down, there were no longer painted lines marking bays or arrows to show direction of travel around the perimeter. Ron drove straight across the middle of the concrete plane, but he eased to a stop just before the entrance to the next level down, which sat like a dark gaping mouth with a tongue that spiralled out of sight. He glanced at the map.

I'm sure –

Robyn closed it. A silent protest. A loud message. Give it up, Ron.

Defiantly he crept onto the downwards ramp. Darkness edged up the bonnet like tar. It had engulfed half the car before Ron switched on the headlights. But as they rolled out onto the fifth subterranean level, it was pitch black and the bulbs of the ageing estate car did little to lighten the mass of nothingness.

Just the week before, Robyn's interest had been piqued in Mr. Willway's geography class as they'd studied the layers that existed beneath the Earth's crust. Robyn had actively looked at the textbook for once, at the image of the dissected Earth and imagined the mantle, the inner core, the outer core all burning and bubbling away, miles beneath her. Ready to bubble over and ravage the world at any point, she was sure.

But now she was here. Experiencing it for herself, and this seemed much more fitting. There was no vengeful magma below the surface, there was nothing at all.

Each of Ron's shallow breaths filled the car like a sonic boom. He drove slowly in regret, now hunting for an upwards ramp. He narrowly navigated the concrete trunks that held up the heavy ceiling, which was also a floor for the level above, which was also holding up a ceiling, which held up another ceiling, and another two on top of that, and that's before it even got to the floors and ceilings above ground where heavy cars and heavy people were walking around completely unaware of these two, miles deep, surely suffocating and definitely about to be crushed and –

the driver's wing mirror snapped against Ron's window.

He jumped as high as his seatbelt allowed him and veered wildly left, out of reach of the demonic concrete post he had clipped.

There's a light,

Robyn pointed vaguely at the windscreen.

Ron knew they could get stranded at sea for twelve days and Robyn would utter that sentence with as much nonchalance as she did now.

Where?

Ron strained his eyes.

Robyn gestured again, to the clearly visible source of light. Ron switched off the headlights in an impulsive huff. Fear had given way to being officially pissed off at the clusterfluck his good deed was amounting to.

Oh yeah.

Sheepishly, he drove towards the sliver of light.

It was not until they were a significant way onto the dimly lit slope that they realised it was coiling downwards, not up.

For fucks sake,

Ron gripped the wheel tighter.

They emerged from the grim helter-skelter and rolled out onto Level -6. They both moved millimetres closer to the windscreen, surprised by this new landscape.

It appeared far smaller than the rest of the levels. Wooden hoarding, painted black, enclosed them in the first fifth of car park. And there was a car. A white Audi parked at a casual 45-degree angle, next to the partition fencing. Even beneath the single working tube light, the sports car looked squeaky clean.

I knew it!

Ron slapped the dashboard.

He sat back and ran his fingers through his hair, follicles graciously parting to form sweaty tracks.

Ok we're here. Come on, come on.

He killed the engine and unbuckled his seat belt simultaneously.

Robyn's expression openly mocked this sudden display of authority and confidence and motivation, but he was already climbing out of the car. As he slammed the driver's door shut, the broken wing mirror bobbled against it, clinging on by threads of wire. He scanned the hoarding for a sign of entrance, and caught sight of a hefty padlock, swung open on its shackle.

Come onnnn, Robyn!

The man jittered around.

Robyn pulled the car door handle, releasing the seal, but paused a moment longer before conjuring the energy to open it and get out. The car park was cold. A final blow to decimate any whiff of faith she'd had in Mr Willway and his molten rock theory.

Did you bring your trainers?

Robyn walked around the front of the car until Ron could see her plimsolled feet for himself.

Good, and remember,

he ushered her towards the fence door,

I've pulled a lot of strings for this so, don't screw it up.

She nodded, but then made no attempt to hide the large yawn that rumbled up from deep inside her. Ron lifted the lock from where it hung freely,

Actually, maybe you should wait out here first.

Ron opened the doorway mere millimetres wider than his frame, wedged himself through,

then disappeared.

Robyn lent against the wooden wall. Rogue splinters scratched at her protruding shoulder blades, which were uncovered by the tank straps of her vest top. The same vest that she wore to bed and under her school uniform and to the table on a Sunday when Melissa insisted they must dress their best because *Ο θεός* was watching closely. The black under-layer had been part of a multipack, donated to Robyn in a hamper of essentialsby a woman whose face and name and purpose she could no longer remember, but could still smell the suffocating cloud of talcum powder as she'd held Robyn's hand too tightly. Robyn didn't objectively like many things, but she liked this soft cotton vest as a constant against her torso.

She stared at the tube light, chasing the disappearing worms that glided across her periphery, a focus broken only momentarily by visions playing on another screen somewhere in the depths of her mind,

a child pulling on the hand of his mother,

a woman stepping through a puddle.

Clu – clunk.

Ron popped his head out from behind the hoarding curtain. He beckoned her in.

It was brighter, this side of the fencing, with at least two thirds of the lights in working order. Perspective immediately drew Robyn's eye to the far side of the space, where a stage was erected. The blue boxed base with red ropes looked bright and artificial in the slice of muted air sandwiched between the two concrete layers.

Its boldness was clunky and inviting, like a plastic toy buried within bran flakes. Upon the canvas stage, danced two boys. They moved closer to one another, then apart, flirting with each other's personal space. Robyn watched the entomological study from across the vista: their skinny appendages that protracted as fast as they jabbed out, their light feet circling the space, their shared knowledge that they were honouring a common ritual and the pretence that they were not. These adolescent insects were falling in love or fighting to the death, Robyn could not tell which.

Besides the ring, the vast room was filled with little else. A few piles of collapsed plastic chairs. Upright canvas columns that looked battered and bruised. Abandoned water bottles with chewed teats. Two men huddled at the ring-side, like overgrown groupies. One, dressed in a full grey tracksuit, barked orders at the sparring boys. The other man, seemed to repeat these orders, with less conviction and more delay.

Ok, so he's agreed to see you,

The excitement and anxiety in Ron's manner were palpable in equal measures.

So, just, head on over.

He shooed her with a flap of his fingers.

Ok, ok, I'm going,

he said when she didn't move, accustomed to being a searing source of embarrassment to his biological children and assuming, wrongly, that Robyn cared enough for the opinions of others to share this shame.

I'll pick you up in half an hour,

he bleated before wedging himself back through the fence exit.

Robyn strolled towards the boxing arena. There was still the distinctive smell of rubber tyres in this portion of Level -6, enough to make your eyes water on the deepest inhale, but in here it was cloaked beneath a layer of stale sweat. She did not intentionally lighten her footsteps as one might when encroaching on new territory, she simply had such little weight that her plimsols did not cry out and the men did not notice her approaching, until she was close enough to see the erect nipples on the boys who boxed in the ring. To see the way mouth guards distorted their upper lips. To see that they were perhaps only one school-year older than her. Only then, did the tracksuit-clad man notice the approaching shadow,

Jesus fucking christ.

He dragged himself off the elasticated rope he'd been leaning on. The other man, the echo, twitched like an alerted meerkat to get a look at her.

You must be –

The meerkat muttered something in his ear.

Robyn?

Robyn stared at the gold chain that lay around the man's neck, amongst a forest of black hair.

Pleasure to meet you too, Robyn. I'm Darrell. This is Winston.

Winston flashed a smile and a snappy wave. A reaction incongruous with everything else in this tableau, which was working so hard to be uninviting.

Watch them,

Darrell muttered to Winston, who nodded violently in return.

Stop being a pussy, Miller!

He barked a final order at the boxers, whose feet scuffled against the canvas matting more slowly now, then walked over to Robyn. Darrell was not a tall man, but the monochrome outfit made it difficult to judge what part of his body betrayed his height the most. He was not even gifted with compensatory inches atop his head, which was barely coated in a dusting of stubble. No comparison for the length of hair on his chest.

So you want to learn how to box?

Robyn looked over her shoulder, as Darrell walked her to a darkened corner of the car-park-gym, back towards the dancing boys. She had no desire to do that.

You fucking deaf or just dumb?

Robyn turned back to Darrell and examined his face. One eye was more bloodshot than the other, he had a gold incisor, which looked at home amongst the neighbourhood of yellowed teeth, and hundreds of fine purple lines were etched across the bulb of his nose.

Just dumb then.

He dragged over a freestanding punchbag.

Go nuts, kid.

The black sack was contoured with an aggressive history. Its undulating surface whispered, without complaint, of the hours it had withstood someone's worst day.

It won't hurt you, love.

Darrell put his hands on his hips, dissecting his all-in-one image.

You want gloves?

He disappeared further into the shadows and squatted down to collect something from the floor. As he reemerged, he threw a padded mitten at Robyn. It hit her on the temple.

Fucking hell, look alive, kid.

She turned her head away from the punchbag just fast enough to catch sight of the second incoming glove. She snatched it out of the air with one hand.

So you wanna,

Darrell squared up to the bag, raising his fists,

transfer the weight all the way from the   back foot forward.

But, Robyn did not want to do that. Robyn did not want to do anything this man told her to. She burned the heels of her soul to a grinding halt. Her silence because there was nothing to say, became a silence because she did not want to say anything. A nuance that would fly far above the tracksuit man's bristly scalp.

She stared at him.

He stared back.

He did not fidget beneath her gaze like most adults.

I've heard you're an angry little fucker.

Robyn's chest moved against the glove she was still holding.

Don't you wanna take it out on something?

he goaded.

Pretend it's the kids at school? Or your dad fella? He's a weird prick.

Bet you'd like to punch him.

She could feel her molars. She could feel. She was existing in a new limbo in between her known states, of nothing and everything. Normally, when feeling arrived for Robyn, it arrived so fast, so furious, that she could not in fact feel it at all. But here she stood, feeling every nerve in her body slowly rise to attention.

Darrell smiled. He brought his hands to his knees and dropped his voice to a whisper,

What about your mum? Gotta be annoyed she abandoned you.

And then, all feeling disappeared.

It evacuated her body, sinking through her stubborn heels, through the concrete floor and the miles of geographic lies she stood upon. It surged downwards through every vein and capillary with such velocity that she was forced to stay upright, rooted to the spot, unable to hear through the rushing in her ears or pause the endless plummet of her stomach. She was a helpless bystander, waiting for the trauma to subside.

–yourself, you little cunt.

Robyn dropped the glove. She was back in the room.

Darrell's trainers squeaked off, somewhere behind her.

Robyn picked at a shard of skin that had lifted away from her nail bed. Mere minutes had passed since she'd been waiting on the other side of the hoarding. The boards were not painted on this side. It would have been futile to maintain any facade of presentation once inside this bare dungeon. She tried to tweeze the skin between two other nails, but couldn't get the grip. So she took it between her teeth. It came away, and ran like a ladder, down into real skin, where it stung as it lifted.

Oi. Oi. My mate fancies you –

Fuck off –

He thinks your well fit –

Fuckoffyouprick

Robyn moved only her eyes towards the boys, still chewing on her cuticle.

Do you want his number?

This one's face still flushed red with the afterglow of exercise. The other one made a weak pounce for a headlock but red-face squirmed away, cackling. They both carried drawstring backpacks with oversized logos that had begun to disintegrate.

You've got bigger tits than her. Shit, maybe it's not a girl –

Oi, are you even a girl?

Oi, we're talking to you,

and he grew close enough that the soft blonde hairs on his upper lip came into focus.

I said, are you even a girl?

Robyn spat the speck of cuticle skin on the floor.

The visible edge he had on her, in height and weight, was minimal. But his contextual edge, in testosterone and technique and self-worth, was substantial. But Robyn did not care for context. She shoved his shoulders with her full force. He stumbled backwards, further than his contextual advantages would have anticipated.

You fucking what? Come on then,

he pushed her back.

Her shoulder blades and the base of her skull slammed against the wooden wall. He smiled, first with his puce face, then with his whole body as adrenaline reignited his spent muscles. A fight outside of the ring, where rules did not apply, was far more fun.

Robyn shoved him again, but this time she followed through, marching him backwards, until he regained his senses, and his stability, and became immoveable. At this standstill, she threw the first punch. It was wobbly, catching him on the cheekbone, injuring his pride and her knuckles more than his face. But it had elevated the fight in intensity, if not in damage. His mate circled around them, gauging his role in this interaction. Punching a (presumed) girl had just become fair game, but was two-on-one still vetoed? Would diving in to defend his friend's honour actually have the converse effect? His pondering ceased when a solid fist landed square on Robyn's nose.

Ooooooooh,

he was to be only a spectator.

Smack her again!

And a hype man.

Blood gushed from Robyn's nostrils and she blinked fast, trying to bat away the water that obscured her sight. But not in time to spot the incoming hook. This one connected with her jaw, sending her lower teeth on a different trajectory to her uppers. The force ricocheted through her head. Her plimsols tapped against the floor as she stumbled around.

Then she stood up straight.

There was a vague comfort in the all-encompassing pain occurring inside her skull. The throb of her nose, the sting of her eyes, the pulse of her gums, the stench of her blood, together it functioned like white noise. No thoughts were loud enough to be heard above it. Nor were the murmurs of these perplexed boys, about howonearth this skinnybitch was still standing. She returned to the boundless ring for more. She tried to land a punch through sheer quantity, firing her fists with machine gun speed. The aggressive flurry called for backup, and the spectator half-tackled her, clinging around her waist. Robyn continued to flail her body with mania. A foot or forearm connected with soft tissue here and there, but it was more effective as a defence than an offence. Until, her knee connected with a pair of precious, developing testes and Spectator was sidelined once more.

Unlike her remaining opponent, Robyn didn't need to catch her breath. She was too wired to stop and take stock of the blows she'd absorbed to the kidneys and gut and eyebrow. She ran towards him and he stuck out a foot, a last-minute reaction and desperate attempt to keep the skinnybitch at bay.

It caught her between the legs.

Robyn was aware of the shooting pain that fizzed up inside her from vagina to navel. But it bore the same weight as a light stomach rumble, a periphery occurrence, a body signal that could be both clocked and ignored. It didn't bear enough to alter her course, or to succumb to it. She pushed on, resorting once more to a shove, and this time, perplexity weakening his base, he fell to the floor. Before he could even establish his new level, Robyn was on him. She scaled his horizontal body and straddled him. The flurry began again. Spectator, who still half-keeled over, made a single step forward to intervene but his canteen lunch resurfaced, in splatters against the floor.

Despite the entirety of Robyn's combat experience being a singular punch to an unsuspecting classmate, and despite the fact that usually her muscles' code of conduct followed that of her tongue: move only when absolutely necessary, despite all this, she was not even on the fringes of fatigue. Fury was her fuel, and she was only beginning to scrape thimbles from her untapped reservoirs. The organic compounds of her short life had been relentlessly suffocated and compressed and now the fossils of her trauma had transformed into something volatile enough to spark a flame, and spread like wildfire. Fanned by pain, engulfing the knock-backs as kindling. Her fire whipped up, ferocious, dangerous, laughing at man's puny attempts to contain it.

Until suddenly, the boy was zooming away from her, further and further out of reach.

She was being dragged backwards by four hands, wrapped tightly over her shoulders and under her armpits. The rubber heel of her plimsols drew drunk tracks across the concrete.

Pussying out again, Miller?

The boy lay on the floor, dazed and dizzied but still stirring. A victim of repetition rather than strength.

And Bolton you fucking clear that up now.

Darrell stood up, hands on hips.

Winston stayed crouched next to Robyn, loosening his grip only a fraction, but the shackles were no longer necessary. Robyn was finished. She dislodged a clot of blood from a nostril and found her light touch reverberated across her whole face. Pain was seeping back into her consciousness.

And you,

Darrell turned to Robyn,

what did I say about transferring the weight forward? Not a single one of those landed because there was no transfer, no follow through.

She could only just about hear him over the thud that had begun to pulse through her brain, slow and steady.

The *clonk* of an open padlock preceded Ron's entry, where he was greeted by a young boy rolling around on his back, another who shepherded a pile of vomit with his shoe, and Robyn walking towards him with blood, of all shades in the crimson spectrum, smeared and splattered across her face.

Same time next week then,

Darrell called out, just in time for Robyn to hear him before she crossed the threshold.

In the car, Ron and Robyn began the twisted ascent back up to the outside world.

So, how was it?

Yeah,

Robyn slowly rotated her jaw.

it was good.

THE LAKE.

It was nearly two o'clock in the afternoon when Layla blinked open her eyes.

Delilah pulled back the damp flannel she was dabbing against the child's forehead. The two of them stared at one another.

Delilah did not say anything, because Delilah did not ever say anything. She'd been living at the site for four years without uttering a word. Nor did she sign, nor did she write. And yet the generosity of her spirit was so loud. She comforted and contributed, and taught the others a different depth of communication. She peered across the bed at Maria, who was sat on the other side, using her wet cloth to sponge away the dried blood from Robyn's face. She too pulled away her flannel, when she realised the child was awake.

Hello Layla.

Hello,

she whispered.

It's ok. You're safe here.

Layla did not move for a moment.

Only her eyes shifted slowly around, so as not to disturb the ethereal scene in which she'd awoken: inside a bright white womb with two angelic figures tending to her and –

she quickly rolled over.

Robyn was there.

Lying on her back, pale skin almost translucent in the tent's lighting.

She's ok, she's just sleeping,

Maria watched the child sink slightly in relief.

Do you feel ok, Layla? Are you hurt?

Layla looked down at herself, as if she wasn't sure.

She shook her head,

but her mind had drifted elsewhere.

My name is Maria, and this is Delilah.

Maria tried to coax her back from whatever horrors she was reliving.

Are you hungry?

Yes.

There was no pause this time.

Maria laughed, fighting the tears that threatened once again to overwhelm her.

Delilah did not have to be asked to fetch food for the girl, she was up and on her way in an instant. By the time she returned with a tray full of freshly baked sourdough and blackberry jam and raspberry jam and sliced apples and poached figs and pear juice, pressed this morning, Layla was sat fully up in bed, resting gently against the hand-crafted headboard and Maria had moved to sit next to her.

In their minutes alone together, besides Robyn's motionless body, Maria had removed Layla's sandals. She'd spotted hours ago how Layla's feet were deeply blistered around the velcro straps, which had once been adorned with rhinestones, but she'd wanted Layla's permission before removing them. As she'd slipped the sandals from the child's feet, she'd found the soles were also completely worn. Layla's heels were black with dirt, even on the raw layers of freshly exposed skin.

Layla welcomed the food tray onto her lap and stuffed a hunk of squidgy bread straight into her mouth. She hovered the next slice over a jam jar, famine still made way for manners.

You can dip it,

Maria motioned, and Layla dunked the dough so deep into the pressed raspberries that they coated her fingers, too.

Is that better?

Layla nodded and crunched down on an apple slice. Maria and Delilah watched on in delight, as if being nourished themselves. The tent flap *swwwsshed* open. Anna had been biding her time since seeing Delilah waltzing out of the kitchen with the tray, knowing it could only mean one of their new guests was awake. But since she'd been the one to suggest they do not crowd the patients, she had tried to remain invested in raking a spot of soil. She'd persevered long enough to maintain the facade of a well-timed check-in.

How are we getting on? Oh hello,

Anna was the picture of surprise, that someone was awake.

Layla glanced up, but swiftly returned her focus to the food.

Layla, this is Anna.

Hello, Layla.

Layla tried hard to swallow,
but the sticky bread took one –
two –
three attempts to get down,
and a small gasp for air.

Hello.

Layla's very hungry.

I'm not surprised.

Anna saw the pair of half sized sandals, worn to death, but neatly lined on the floor.

Have you travelled far?

With no answer, Anna directed her question onto Maria, using just her eyes.

Maria gave a small shake of the head. They had not reached that ground yet.

Layla chugged the juice in one go. Two pears, just like that.

brrrrrrrrp

She looked taken aback by the depth of her own belch.

Only Delilah was watching Robyn when she opened her eyes a sliver.

ROBYN. 2006.

pup

pup

pup

pup

pup-pup

pup

pup

pup

Robyn's gloves hit the pads with a rhythm more intrinsic than her own heartbeat, and a sound more recognisable. No matter how Winston danced and darted, her fists found the mitts every time, drawn to the target circle like magnets.

Left,

right,

left,

right,

Winston muttered, for his own guidance, because in Robyn's trance there was no left or right, no median line by which her body was split. Everything worked in unison. Each punch was holistically choreographed. Though the impact funnelled through four knuckles, its foundations were in the feet, where bodyweight was deliberately biased, balancing on the ball of the rear foot, employing each toe as a launchpad when the time came. Each connection was preceded by a pivot of the hips. The crest of one ilium sent in first, to announce the arrival, sweep the perimeter. All whilst the opposite shoulder drew backwards, peeling away to create space. There was no conscious isolation of fibre or tissue or muscle or bone, no hierarchy of contribution in their communal endeavour. Robyn moved with the fluidity of water and the spectacle of the ocean.

Double it up, Robyn, don't be fucking lazy,

Darrell didn't stop as he walked past the ring.

It's ok, you don't have to,

Winston spoke quietly, once Darrell was out of earshot.

It's been a long –

pup

pup

pup

pup

pup-pup

pup

Winston solidified his base for the double-time barrage. Every twelve counts, he shot a mitt out horizontally, which Robyn ducked beneath. She sprung back to standing before he'd fully retracted it.

They solved each step of their puzzle routine. Throwing antagonist shapes and finding harmony in their contrast. Robyn's focus was drawn away for a mere millisecond, over Winston's shoulder, to where Darrell talked to a woman in a trouser suit. But her concentration did not lapse long enough to interrupt the rhythm, or for Winston to even notice. Sweat ran off her nose and chin, dripping onto the canvas below, marking her path like a trail on a map. Winston sweated too, but his remained trapped inside his brown velour tracksuit.

Robyn!

Winston lowered the pads, but Robyn, too entranced to hear Darrell's call, finished the follow through of her jab and clocked Winston on the shoulder. He smiled, and waved a mitt to bat away the apology she hadn't offered.

Great session, Robyn, well done, well worked,

he puffed, and raced to remove the gloves and finally unzip his velvet casing.

Robyn got down from the ring, grabbed a wad of blue paper towels and hopped back up, in the time it took Winston to manoeuvre himself between the elasticated ropes.

Janet, in her trouser suit, waited in the shadows whilst Robyn mopped up sweat on her hands and knees, in the only well-lit portion of the gym. She crawled across the spotlit stage, a political statement to which she was the most dedicated activist. The last one standing of all those who'd been in attendance when she'd arrived hours earlier, straight off the first direct bus from school. There'd be a second wave of adult men later that night, but she'd outlasted her peers. It was always this way on a Wednesday, the busiest day in the gym, when frazzled mums across South London, desperate for mid-week respite, entrusted Darrell with their unruly boys and Robyn was left to train with Winston. On Mondays, she sparred with the boys, and on Fridays, she was at the centre of Darrell's focus, but on Wednesdays, she pummelled his right-hand man until someone called it a day, and it was never her.

Janet stood awkwardly. She was both tall and broad and her arms were crossed so tightly that her car keys were nestled into an armpit. On weekdays she still wore the uniform of a deputy headteacher, dark suit atop a cashmere crew neck and sensible shoes, despite having been retired for nearly three years. She'd still not reached her state pension age, but her only-child inheritance after the death of both her parents in quick succession and a particularly testing summer term had propelled her to pitch an umbrella and explore the rainy day she'd been saving for, which had turned out to be nothing more than deceiving grey skies and a disappointing drizzle.

Robyn was Janet's first foster child, and first child or consort of any description, apart from Bill, her partially-blind Jack Russell. Fostering had seemed a non-committal way to dip her toe back into mentorship, waters for which she'd always felt ill-fit until they'd dried up completely and her identity had vanished like a grain of sand across the vast desert of possibilities. What a heaviness it would have been to discover that the muzzle of mundanity had actually been her oxygen mask all along. Instead, she chose to believe it was the absence of disinterested teens in her life that was making her newfound freedom feel so incredibly suffocating.

Janet was initially intimidated by the pale fourteen-year old, as one might be of a spider: illogical, for she was by far the smallest being in the room, perhaps even squashable with a thumb, and yet, as she'd sat there at their first meeting four months ago, silent and spindly-limbed, her presence had seemed remarkably menacing. But there was a familiarity for Janet in feeling ill at ease, and wildly uncool, around a school child.

And at least she was quiet.

Janet had self-diagnosed her debilitating disease at a young age. Quietness choked her, weakened her, marred her life and bred a greedy bitterness. Constantly she yearned for others to stop talking, to not ask questions, to settle down. It was not a condition that could be cured by exposure, nor rehabilitated by mere determination. And the benign ailment somehow overshadowed all of her other functioning features. She'd found the sum of her facts on paper,

rescuing a one-eyed dog

+

a career in underprivileged schools

+

fostering a child in need,

would never be enough for outsiders, it would never amount to being a good person in the eyes of others, because none of it was gift wrapped in charisma. Shyness was the loudest part of her personality.

Janet and Robyn left Darrell's gym and got into the car, without exchanging a word.

They sat across from one another at the square dining table, which was dressed in a floral, wipe-clean cloth. Though a chair sat at all four faces, no more than three had ever been used at once (and no more than two since the death of Janet's parents). They ate macaroni cheese, because it was a Wednesday, and neither of them bothered to pick out the melted black specks of ready meal container. Bill lay beneath the table, across one of Robyn's feet. His warm belly smothered the bridge of her bare foot and his wiry coat ran slick against her ankle. He liked to stay within touching distance, a privileged proximity afforded to no others.

What were you talking to Darrell about.

It was a question in content alone, punctuated with a forkful of pasta.

Janet chewed her response, and the soft macaroni, as a bird prepares to feed its young, hoping she could regurgitate something more palatable. She lay down her cutlery.

The school phoned me about your scuffle, today.

Robyn struggled to recall events of the day. She'd seen a seagull with a canteen pasta pot stuck on its head. In assembly, the guest speaker had tripped up the steps to a makeshift lectern. Someone had engraved KYLE SUKED JACOBS DICK with a compass into her desk in the maths classroom. She had ripped the pocket off a boy's blazer as he ran away after calling her a *dyke.* Robyn didn't know what the word meant, but she'd had it thrown at her a few times and always by boys or girls whose manner made the pit of her stomach rise into her throat. The grab had been instinctual, reactive, a grasp at capturing the fleeing coward.

The blazer?

Robyn asked, this time.

Yes, the boy's blazer. And the boy in the blazer.

I didn't touch him.

She spoke with such nonchalance that dozing Bill was unaware of any tension above the table.

Janet exhaled.

It's only been a month, Robyn. And they were, hesitant to have you as it was. They're giving you a real chance here, you know you're on thin ice.

I didn't fight him.

Robyn scraped sticky cheese and tomato ketchup with the edge of her fork.

They're setting you up with a councillor, they want to help you.

Robyn turned her fork upside down and slid the gummy mixture into her mouth. She did not ask, *help with what,* just as she had never asked all the people before, who claimed this as their mission statement. They all wanted to help. Ron and Mel had wanted to help, Mzzz Watkins had wanted to help, the two schools between then and now, the three intermediary homes before this one, the social services, the countless councillors, Janet (though she'd never said it aloud), they all wanted to help, until they didn't. Until they realised, as Robyn had known all along, that their goal was fruitless because there was nothing to help in the first place. Of course, one grows tired of hunting for a solution to a question that has not been posed.

So you'll have to miss training on Friday.

At this, Robyn twitched and Bill was shaken awake. He waited a moment, before determining that his resting spot was officially compromised. His relaxed fleshy cushion was now ridged with tensed tendons.

I don't want to.

Well, you have to,

Janet looked down at a plastic peony.

They've been understanding and forgiving and you're not being excluded but they – this is their condition and they're trying to help and otherwise, you might not – you'll have to – we'll stop you boxing altogether.

She'd found match point.

If this is going to carry on.

Janet didn't specify if *this* meant her guardianship, or the bouts of violence that had seen Robyn tossed from every establishment that had vowed to better her. Including those of Ron and Ms Watkins, who had introduced Robyn to boxing then abandoned her when it transpired not to be the *healthy outlet for her complicated emotions* that they'd hoped for, but rather an estuary by which all passions could pour. It had chiselled her rage into more effective uppercuts, fine-tuned her anger into having greater physical impact and given her the reflexes to avoid any thump or thought that came within touching distance. Whenever Darrell was employed to insist that fighting was to be confined to the ring, it was half-hearted at best. Who was he to stop his prized student from gaining real life experience? To stop the girl with unthinkable resilience from thickening her armour even more? And who were the guardians, to forbid a hobby that kept Robyn out of the house for an extra nine hours a week? No one dared even threaten it, until now.

Their unusually comprehensive conversation was called to a close there.

The house looked like it had been extracted from a seaside cul-de-sac and dropped onto the suburban street as a social experiment. How might an ocean-breather survive in a capital city? Even on the peripheries, in subdued New Malden. The speed-bumped street was a mixture of modest homes. Terraced and detached, shiplap and roughcast, plastic double-glazing and shaky single. But this was the only bungalow. Painted white with lead-lined windows. A suitably nautical house number, in a pale blue stripe, confirmed that she was in the right place. Of all the councillors Robyn had met with before, this was the first one she'd attended as a result of coercion, rather than pure apathy. It was also the first time she'd had to travel to a home address and not an office block where hearty sniffles could be heard from the corridor. When Sarah opened the door, Robyn realised why.

Robyn? Lovely to meet you, I'm Sarah.

Robyn skirted around her and into the house. Not that Robyn ever indulged in pleasantries, but today she was particularly keen to press through the prescribed session so they could all arrive at the repeated conclusion of these meetings. Conclusions that were sent spiralling down telephone cords or branded onto paper, deconstructed and permanent. Conclusions that belonged to anyone but the subject matter herself.

Did Janet drop you off,   or did you get the bus?

Sarah was quick to disarm a non-verbal response.

Janet.

The hallway was void of furniture, but the walls hosted an array of artwork. Abstract acrylics on canvas, saturated landscape prints, watercolour scenes of quaint towns, each one in competition to mismatch their neighbour the most. The photographic pieces were presumably the stock imagery given away with the frame. Quotes were carved into cheap wood, or calligraphed in italics, telling onlookers

SMILE *And* THE **WORLD** *Smiles* WITH *You*

HOME IS WHERE THE CAT IS

collect *MOMENTS* not things

They lacked conviction, hanging hopelessly from wonky wire, but together, the exhibition worked to detract from the faded yellow walls that they haphazardly plastered over. There were five doors leading off from the gallery, three of which were deliberately pinned open by kitsch doorstops.

Aww good. In here.

Sarah directed her through the first doorway on the left, made passable by a gingham piglet.

An armchair was positioned purposefully to half-face the criss-crossed windows, and half-face a low coffee table. On which sat a box of tissues and a heart shaped coaster:

You're braver than you Know, stronger than you Feel and smarter than you Think.

Robyn took in what little else the room had to offer. Net curtains, shelves filled with academic textbooks, a collection of stuffed animals in a woven basket.

Thank you for coming, Robyn. I don't want you to feel like you're on my territory. This is neutral ground and a completely safe space. I like to invite people here, into my home, to make the sessions a little less one-sided. You might feel like you're doing all the sharing, so this is my way of offering up a little insight into my life.

It was a rare ability, to regurgitate a speech so often and still feel every word.

Also,

she tapped the arms of her wheelchair,

it is a bit easier for me.

Sarah wore rimless rectangular glasses, with black metal arms and a bridge that dug a little too tightly into her nose, and a paisley-print cardigan that served as a totem to all Sarahs past and future. To the kindly school girl she once was and the conscientious Masters student she'd been and the patient forty-year-old she'd soon become and the endearing eighty-year-old she would one day end up as.

Please, take a seat or look around if you'd like. Get settled. Would you like a drink? I've got water, squash, tea,

she spoke softly, through a smile.

Squash.

Robyn sunk into the armchair. Sarah excused herself to the kitchen, too imbibed in empathy to demand courtesy from the damaged teenager. When she returned, with a cold drink and a plate of biscuits, Robyn's thirst to reject and hunger to leave were temporarily quenched.

So why do you think the school and Janet have wanted us to have a chat today, Robyn?

Robyn ploughed through her second custard cream.

Well, truthfully it doesn't really matter. We don't have to talk about anything they want us to talk about. We can talk about anything at all, anything you want.

The wet biscuit began to lodge on her back teeth.

Sarah was comfortable with silence, for if she was listening she could not offend. But for someone whose career relied on the curation of tranquil valleys where others could meander through their own minds, she had an anxious aura. It was as if she absorbed all the nervous energy around her and took it on herself. So much so that her fine blonde hair fizzed with static, wisping this way and that, and in her martyrdom, others were free to feel calm.

The sweet, cold tidal wave of orange squash cleansed Robyn's palette, before she reached for a jammy dodger.

Anything you tell me in here Robyn, doesn't go any further than these four walls. It's just between us. Equally, if you just want a place to hang out every week and eat biscuits, that's fine by me, too.

I'm not coming every week.

A jammy crumb clung to her bottom lip.

Ok, why's that?

Boxing.

You box? Wow, that's impressive.

Robyn wiped her mouth with the back of her hand.

I'm missing training to be here.

Oh, I'm so sorry,

Sarah's great fear, of being an inconvenience, realised.

I didn't know that. We can always rearrange our session time.

Robyn's fingers, powdered in biscuit dust, began to pick at the woven arms of the chairs.

How long have you been boxing for?

A beam of sun streamed across Sarah's eye-line and she repositioned her chair.

Robyn could remember her first proper training session. It was a week after she'd met Darrell, and made that one boy vomit, and the purple bruises smattered across her face were ripening green. The gashes along her knuckles still prised open when she closed her fists. In that week, before she returned, her mind had wandered back to the underground gym, multiple times. An unfamiliar pull to be anywhere. Then the instant she'd met Darrell again, the cloud of anticipation had dispersed. She hated the way he walked fast. Talked faster. Clipped imperatives, in a gruff voice. As if he had somewhere to be. As if he was doing her a reluctant favour. She hated the way he made expletive asides to no-one. *Fuckin hell, alright then.* She hated how he chewed gum loudly, squelching it against his saliva. She hated that he hosted an arena for boys and men to stew in their own testosterone.

But then she'd slid the gloves over her broken hands that first time and the circuit switch closed. Currents could flow freely. Filaments deep within her buzzed at full voltage. She could feel her breath branching through each bronchiole in her lungs. It burned, but it did not choke her. She expanded her chest and made way for it, inhaling deeper and deeper. Even when fatigue began to gnaw at her shoulders, then forearms, then abdomen, then thighs, some force within her sank down, shook off a layer and powered through. And everything else, outside of this electric channel between her and the punchbag, seemed faraway,

inconsequential.

Even Darrell. Who'd circled her, fully captivated, betraying his facade of indifference. As all her energy poured into the flow of her fists, she had no surplus supply to hate Darrell with. No strength to barricade against his coaching comments, so they infiltrated her and she listened.

She tucked her chin down.

She softened her knees.

She tightened her fists on impact.

And a secondary channel had began to surge. From brain to body to movement. From textbook to student to essay. From hypothesis to experiment to outcome.

Robyn could remember all of this. The day it felt like she'd suddenly found whole rooms in her own home that she never knew existed, and gone exploring, switching on every light, opening every curtain. But just as she didn't know how long that first training session had lasted, she didn't know how long ago it was either. The demarkations along the timeline of her life were different to other people's. School years and term times were dissected by expulsions. Homes were so transitory, start lines were drawn in the wet sand at high tide. Robyn existed. Guided by the certainty of sunrises and sunsets, and little else. She was not moving towards anything, so why the need to remember a date? What was she meant to be counting down from? Or to?

I dunno,

she shrugged.

Do you compete in games? Or just for the fun of it?

Matches.

Matches, of course, not games, silly me.

I'm not very up to date on my sports,

Sarah smiled, hoping they could collectively wallow in her silliness.

Only sparring in training. Darrell won't let me fight anyone properly until I'm fifteen.

Robyn showed a hint of chagrin for the rule she'd stewed over many times.

Is Darrell your coa – teacher-trainer-coach?

Yeah.

In her hunt for a noun, Sarah had abandoned open-endedness.

When are you fifteen, Robyn?

She tried to claw it back.

Robyn scratched a little harder at the armchair. Birthdays were no exemption to her blank calendar. There could be no anniversaries when time unfolded in an infinite line, instead of the cyclical loop that humans confined themselves to. Also, the entire concept of celebrating a day of birth was somewhat undermined when it had been arbitrarily assigned to you. The date, which Robyn had not cared to keep memory of, was not the date that Emily had given birth on the floor of a leisure centre changing rooms long after closing time, surrounded by no one but a fellow cleaner, a mother of four who spoke no English, who'd held her hand and quietly added the bloodied towels to the industrial laundry load. The date, whenever it was, was an estimation, scribbled across a certificate along with the name of a German woman. Robyn was not aware of the degree to which the markers of her existence were mere guesses, mere to-do list items that were rushed through so a clerk could clock off and get to the shops before closing. But even if she had been, it wouldn't have mattered too much to her. After all, everyone was subject to the biologist's classification in one way or another. Born as rare insects in a petri dish, wriggling around, carefree, with no need for the identity that someone else was assigning them. At least Robyn had had longer than most to exist, before being stamped and labelled.

Soon,

but she swallowed as she spoke so the word sounded bubbly and alien.

She no longer listened when adults filled out paperwork in front of her, filling out the eight figures without consulting her. She'd lived with Ron and Melissa for sixteen months and no one had questioned that she'd not had a birthday.

I could beat them all already anyway.

The other students? Boxers?

The boys, yeah.

You fight with boys? That's –you must be tough. Not that boys are stronger than girls or,

her strained throat began to flush.

This room, her home office, was the one place where Sarah was usually free from her permanent state of fluster. Within the familiarity of the cream walls and creaky floorboards, an unfamiliar confidence could flourish. All she had to do was be still, empathise, give space to the young and vulnerable and tortured. Sarah didn't believe she was good at much, but she hoped she was good at that. And yet here was Robyn, beginning to scratch away that confidence, as unconsciously and definitely as she picked at the armchair threads.

How do you feel when you box, Robyn?

She shifted her focus with purpose and urged the embarrassment out of her body.

Robyn considered the question, so intensely that her fingers lay still.

Good,

she answered.

I think.

Sarah waited.

I don't really

know

how I feel.

Sometimes I don't want to stop.

Sarah's nod was barely visible, but it was enough to interrupt.

Robyn rushed to the surface, gulping in air. She began rub her knuckles against the fabric again.

Darrell doesn't tell me I'm the best but I know he thinks it, otherwise he wouldn't bother.

Is it important to you, to be the best?

Robyn shrugged.

Sarah watched the teenager, who was swamped by the sunken chair, as she stared around the room and through the window and retreated back into her own world. Sarah felt a heavy nausea swell in her stomach and rise to heartburn in her chest. She subtly gripped the handles of her wheelchair, trying to steady the overwhelming desire to reach out to Robyn, to tie a string around the abandoned kite, which tossed and turned at the will of the wind, and anchor it to safety. But now she knew there was no margin for error.

Care, to the uninitiated, was more daunting than disregard.

ELIZABETH. 1996.

Again we're talking about the individual versus the whole, here, these bigger, societal structures that are far bigger, or far more powerful, than two teens being in love. Or are they?

And that's the question we're asking here, can the desire of an individual bear more weight than a historical institution? Who am I kidding, you're a bunch of hormone-riddled teens, I know your answer.

A wave of half-hearted laughs shimmied around the classroom. It was not that Mr Williams's youthful approachability had worn thin, but rather the spirits of those in the final stretch before exams season.

But in a way that's exactly happens in the play, too. They put their love before anything else. They renounce their names as a big screw you to their family systems, they begin to think of each other in blasphemous ways, a big screw you to the church, and their suicide is the ultimate screw you to everyone. They choose themselves above everyone else, and all of society's structures. So, let's hone in on particular scenes and motifs where their personal struggles might represent a wider fight against institutions.

He sat down behind his desk.

Yes, Cat?

Cat's hand was barely held up. She had to support it by the elbow, weighed down by incomprehensible literature and the sociopolitical pressures of teenage-hood and a whole morning of being awake and impending life altering assessments.

I just don't get it, sir.

H'ohhh, Cat,

he mimicked her fatigue.

Which bit? Shakespeare? Life?

Yeah, just, Shakespeare I guess,

Mr Williams's playful mocking was not lost on Cat, she just couldn't be fucked with it today.

There were general groans of agreement across the desks. They were the top set class and Mr Williams, being on his third year of teaching GCSE English, knew well enough that it wasn't comprehension that was today's issue. He just had to navigate their collective dip in self-esteem and synchronised hormonal exhaustion.

Listen, I get that it's not always the easiest text to dive into, and sometimes we can overcomplicate it, or read too much into it, but what he writes about, at the heart of all of it, is the pure human experience. Ok, maybe witches aside, but it's all about love and jealousy and family honour and loneliness and he's put on paper, situations we're still experiencing hundreds of years later. There's a reason it has survived so many generations.

Elizabeth, the only student to not share a desk, vocalised her thoughts with no more than a sarcastic,

Uh.

She continued to doodle biro patterns in the margins of her exercise book.

Sorry, Miss Ojo, do you not agree?

She placed down her pen and sat up, sideways in her seat, leaning against the classroom wall.

No, I don't.

Mr Williams placed the lid on his whiteboard pen and leant back in his own chair.

Ok, give me your take then, hit me.

I think, it's bullshit.

Another, slightly more animated, wave of reaction echoed from the students. Only Elizabeth Ojo could get away with cursing in class. She could confront without being confrontational. She had the mind and the maturity to delude her peers and elders alike into thinking that her choice of vocabulary was artistic, and vital.

Would you care to expand on that sentiment?

Mr Williams asked, lips playfully pursed.

I think Shakespeare's dominance across the canon is the result of perpetual reinforcement from the patriarchy and scholars and is the greatest example of how even at the heart of art and literature, which are meant to be the most liberating elements of human existence, that it's actually still dictated by the arbitrary opinions of the few, and always the western white man of course, so that when someone disagrees or dislikes the work of a celebrated genius figure, it's a reflection of their poor taste or intellectualism, or lack of, no offence Cat. I also think it plays into a common misconception that to be enlightening it has to impenetrable, it has to be inaccessible to the uninitiated, in order to gatekeep high literature, when wouldn't the most poignant art be one that can move the everyday man?

I dunno, maybe he was a maverick in his own era, if he did even write his own work, which is a whole other conversation, but I think we should we be learning about contemporary writers and representatives of the world in which we live now, instead of trying to relentlessly, decipher and re-decipher the work of someone who existed in a time so oppressive to so many.

I mean, props to the guy for laying some literary foundations and being good at writing, sure, but are we not, like, over it?

What she said, laughed Trey Davidson, and Harry Gadford let out a small *woop* from the other side of the classroom. Cat sat taller in her chair, energised by being at the heart of Elizabeth's point, which she didn't fully understand, but it sounded like a valid one.

Ok ok ok,

Mr Williams smiled.

I mean, I completely disagree and the exam board will definitely disagree, so don't anyone dare write that on their paper, but fair enough, Miss Ojo, convincing in your conviction.

The bell rang and Mr Williams held the door open for the students who trudged out. Lunchtime was not quite the source of excitement it had once been.

Have you picked English for next year yet?

Mr Williams asked Elizabeth, as she filed out behind her classmates.

We study Gatsby *and you'll have a feminist field day.*

She gave a single hearty laugh,

I look forward to it.

The cafeteria queue was minimal by the time she got there. Some of the silver trays sat empty beneath the heat lamps, remnants of lasagne or cottage pie smeared round the edges. She selected a shrivelled jacket potato with baked beans and plastic strips of unmelted cheese. Two Years Sevens lined up behind her, both sweating profusely, carrying about seven bags between them, having rushed in from PE. Elizabeth could tell that they hushed their voices around her. It was more likely that they shrunk themselves for all Year Elevens than for Elizabeth in particular, but it was a periphery reaction she was used to at school. Sometimes she tested the limits to which a teacher or classmate would bend to please her or adopt her views as their own.

She slid the polystyrene carton in front of the dinner lady at the till.

I like your earrings, aren't they pretty,

she pointed a gloved finger at Elizabeth's gold hoops.

That's two pounds then please love.

Elizabeth handed over her canteen payment card. The dinner lady swiped it.

It's not coming up with anything. I'll try again. They're so temperamental,

she swiped again.

What was wrong with the good old system I'll never know. Always having to update and that aren't we,

and again.

Why can't we just leave well alone? If it ain't broke,

and again,

don't fix it. No it's not liking it, my love, have you topped up?

Yeah, my mum –

Elizabeth didn't finish.

Sorry love. Have you got cash on you instead?

Erm,

she exhaled.

She tried to think inside her purse, hesitant to rummage around for coins for a half-baked potato. The Year Sevens watched on in silence.

It's fine, I won't,

she started to back away from the till.

Go on, love, just have it,

the hair-netted lady whispered loudly, looking around.

No thanks,

Elizabeth recoiled at the offer.

She sat on the ramp of the sports hall's rear exit and hand-rolled a cigarette. She'd spent hours alone in her bedroom practicing to be able to nonchalantly shimmy tobacco into the perfect baton. And it all paid off when Matis said, *fuck you look so sexy when you roll.* She was glad the smoking quarters were empty of other kids. A teacher must have already done the lunchtime flush out. Her stomach rumbled. *The Bell Jar* poked its slim spine out of her handbag, but she couldn't muster the energy to open it. It was not a misconception that she was well read, or enjoyed reading, but her motivation was less organic than fans may have believed. Without an audience present, or without the necessity to escape at home, whichever highbrow text was on rotation often remained closed. She smoked in silence, and fiddled with her thumb ring.

Elizabeth dipped in and out of consciousness of, and care for, the fact that the only thing separating her from any other student who spent their lunchtimes alone and read a lot of books was the fragile perception of others. A result of a persona she had meticulously carved since the day she chose the park over Polly five years ago. She had not stayed friends with Alisha for longer than a year, but Alisha had been her gateway to the year above. To a friendship group where every boy or girl was either objectively good looking or proved their worth in wit. They set aesthetic trends that took three terms to filter down the school, and by then they were on to the next hairstyle or handbag or school shoe. They were affectionate and loyal and could tell one another *that top is fucking ugly*. They called each other's parents by their first names and played each other's alibis. They took each other's virginities and got into physical scraps. They talked about everything and nothing at all, they knew each other inside out, and then one day,

they were gone.

All but Elizabeth sat their exams and moved onto colleges and apprenticeships and promised that nothing would change, until the seamless age gap suddenly stuck out like a purple-blazered thumb. She had too much dignity to become the only thing holding back these plain-clothed young adults from getting served in the off-license. After four years of elevating herself to a higher importance by association, the glaring flaw in her plan became obvious. But still, she clung onto the elusive figurehead her peers expected of her. She embodied who they wanted her to be, who they wanted.

Elizabeth lingered at the lay-by railings after school. She'd reapplied her makeup and missed the mass exodus at the final bell. Very few students were still around, very few cars entered the school ground, but with each one that did she glanced up, hoping to see Matis in his red Ford Escort. She smoked two cigarettes, and would have rolled a third but she was running low on tobacco. She tapped her fingers against the barrier and heard it echo up the rest of the railing. There was a nostalgia in the waiting. She ached for her younger self, who she could still feel when the world was this quiet, when it left her waiting.

Teachers started to appear in the car park, clocking off for the day, but still she stayed. It was only at the pupils in sports kits, having finished their after-school activities, did she say,

Oh fuck off then,

under her breath and begin to walk home.

At which the beaten vehicle finally turned into the premises, indie rock and smoke plumes escaping from the driver's window. He honked for her attention and she flipped him a middle finger without stopping.

She heard the clunks of a three-point turn, and then he crawled alongside her,

I'm sorry I'm late, baby,

he turned down the stereo and crouched to call across the car. Elizabeth kept walking.

I forgot.

Ha! You For Got,

she enunciated each letter.

Fuck I'm sorry, baby, get in the car. Come on.

She shook her head, performative disbelief rather than rejection.

Fuck you.

Come on, I said I'm sorry?

he rolled straight over a zebra crossing.

Fuck off, Matis.

She heard his heavy sigh above music's ebb, then he accelerated off.

But already she knew she would forgive him. The threads of her reputation couldn't afford not to.

Elizabeth stood inside the front door for a quiet moment, as was her unconscious routine, before she took off her shoes. She listened for the television or the radio or a stirring sound of life that suggested her mother had not made it through a full workday, but the house was quiet. She heeled off her pumps.

She found an unopened pack of biscuits, a miraculous oasis in a deserted cupboard. She laid out two to have with her tea, but ate them both whilst the kettle boiled. So she took two more. The sofa didn't move as she slumped onto it. All air had already been compressed out of the world-weary cushions, but the brown corduroy was a comfort nonetheless. She opened *The Bell Jar*, ready to free-fall into someone else's world.

At the end of each chapter, she mindlessly went to the empty fridge, in case she'd missed something on the previous visit. She didn't realise how the low the light had gotten for reading, until her fifth return to the living room. She switched on a lamp but didn't check a clock, so as not to dislodge the possibility that her mother was doing a food shop on her way home from work. On the book's penultimate chapter, she heard a noise from upstairs. The type of noise that's so distinct, so definite, there is no ambiguity to its realness. The type to bring your heart's silent beat to the foreground before you have even registered fear. She stayed so still, her forefingers lay as limp bookmarks. She'd always wondered how she would react in the face of danger, and now she would live,

or not live,   in the knowledge that she was powerless. That her strength was fraudulent. That perhaps she'd not been a survivor of life's cruelties, but weak enough to be subject to them in the first place.

As the noises grew more constant, Elizabeth found a reassurance in their boldness. Surely no intruder would be so blatant. She heard a bedroom door open, then slippers on the stairs. Her heart rate didn't settle, but rather it beat to the rhythm of resentment. Mary appeared in the living room doorframe. Her dressing gown was grubby round the cuffs.

Oh hello, I didn't hear you come in,

she held onto the doorframe.

Elizabeth looked at her book page, eyes glazing over sentences she'd already read. She heard the floor creaking beneath her mother's soft swaying.

I need to talk to you-

Didn't go to work?

They spoke over one another.

Why didn't you go to work?

Elizabeth snatched at dominance.

I didn't feel very well.

Ha. Ok.

I need to talk to –

You didn't top up my canteen card.

The accusation lay heavy on Mary's tangled brow.

Oh, oh sorry, my dear. I forgot.

The anger snapped out of Elizabeth in the *SLAP* of her book shut. She jumped up from the sofa.

I need to talk –

I don't want to talk to you,

she pushed past her mother with a force that may have made even the sober lose balance.

I'm hungry, but there's nothing in the house.

Elizabeth sat down at the kitchen table with her school handbag. She unpacked her tobacco pouch and papers and began her nicotine origami. Mary's slippers scuffed onto the linoleum floor.

I will go to the shops.

No you won't. No you won't, because you'd have to get dressed for that, or have money for that, or be able to walk in a straight line for that.

I will go, Eliz –

Just don't. Don't pretend to –

Elizabeth licked the thin paper in lieu of finding the words. She was surprised to find emotion blocking her nose out of nowhere, why this interaction out of all its many exhausted versions should evoke feeling.

I went to a doctor.

Mary's accent was still strong, even after twelve years in which her only contact with her homeland were the Nigerian stamps on Charles's cheques, which brushed through the letterbox from time to time. He didn't know that in the beginning she'd worked solidly enough to secure a home with an upstairs and a separate bedroom for her daughter, he didn't know she had a daughter, but he knew that she cashed them and that she was alive.

Elizabeth,

Elizabeth rummaged in the dark depths of her bag for a lighter. Crumbs caught in her fingernails.

I am talking to you.

She had to peer into the bag. She waded through cosmetics and pens and wrappers.

Listen to your mother, I am trying to –

She found it. She placed an end of the thin cigarette between her curled lips.

Do not light that in here.

Her thumb pressed down and a timid flame appeared.

Elizabeth, don't you dare,

Mary walked towards the table.

The flame began to singe the paper end.

You do not –

she lurched a clawed hand towards the cigarette, and snatched it from her daughter's mouth. Mary's rough fingers scraped Elizabeth's chin, and a long nail scratched her upper lip. Mary dropped the cigarette to the floor and searched for it with her slipper as if blind.

You listen to your mother.

You're not my mother.

Elizabeth stood up abruptly, her chair toppled backwards only to be caught by the tight kitchen wall.

You don't get to call yourself my mother when you have not raised me. You haven't done a single thing for me except make my life harder.

Elizabeth had to force her voice out loudly to keep from crying.

You are a fucking failure, you're a disgrace, you're a burden.

I fucking hate you,

liberation gave way to realisation,

I fucking hate you,

which gave to way to liberation,

so much. Do you know that?

She genuinely asked the question.

She looked for the acknowledgement, for the pain, for the answer in her mother's eyes,

but they did not betray her thoughts,

they did not forewarn her of what came next.

Your father's name is Tristan Coles.

The name often came back to Mary in dreams, where faceless men introduced themselves, or she just knew with no introduction at all. But Mary had not said his name aloud to someone else, perhaps ever. For he had been born her secret lover and evolved into a mirage of memories. She may have doubted his existence completely, had she not lived with a piece of him for fifteen years.
He was from Leeds. He was rich.
Mary could remember the arch of his thick eyebrows and his gold cufflinks and the melody of his voice that was so deep it stirred her chest, but this hollow description of him, these two facts, were the only things she really knew to be true.
He is your father.
It was accusatory, explanative, and wholly numb.

She stood as the shell of someone whose purpose had evaporated.

Elizabeth stared at the trampled cigarette.

Where's your purse? I'm going to get food,

she collected her bag from the table.

The slam of the front door reverberated through every bone in the house.

For days, Elizabeth turned the name over in her head. She thought of nothing else or nothing at all. She did not finish the final chapters of Plath's plight. She did not counter Mr Williams's provocative argument that Shakespeare was a sixteenth-century feminist. And it was only on the fifth night, as her eyes stayed open to the pitch black of her room, when she realised that Matis had not tried to reach her, that she cried.

She sobbed so violently that she woke the next morning to a charred throat and the sensation of a bruise deep within her nose and a headache that pulled at her eye sockets.

Elizabeth had not been to the public library since Yari Lopez had proclaimed it was *only for people who shit themselves: the infants, the stupid and the homeless.* Instead, she loaned her books from school. So the public library card she used to take out the phone directory was still decorated with butterflies and cartoon figures.

Excuse me, you can't take that away.

At first, Elizabeth assumed the bald man with spectacles on a string was not talking to her.

The phone directories can't be borrowed.

His voice was startlingly loud. She didn't acknowledge him, only turned around and marched back to the aisle of thick paper catalogues. It was one of the thicker copies and she tried to wedge it back into a random space to spite the jobsworth. She had just slid it all the way in when she removed it again, and opened it.

She thumbed past businesses in chunks to reach the residential listings. Thousands of lives reduced to a line of minute font. She flicked over page after delicate page.

CABBERLEY
CABBERY
CABBETT

The crackling sound and woody smell of the paper leaves did not comfort her like usual.

CELMAN
CELMER
CELMONT

Her finger pad squeaked as it traced a smudge of grease down the columns.

CODDARD
CODDEN
CODDERINGTON

The lines began to blur.

COLDWICK
COLDWILL

COLE

She could feel her pulse in her fingertips.

David
Eugene
Joel & Amy
John
R

Elizabeth reread the five lines over and over until she could recall their postcodes by rote. She checked the front cover and the spine. Leeds. 1996/97. She became aware of how she was stood half buried into the bookshelf and how her breath bounced off the valley between the pages and how her fingers ached from holding open the heavy encyclopaedia and how it was absurd to think her mother would have offered her this clarity or that he wouldn't have moved in sixteen years or that she may have found a father in Tristan Coles.

Tristan Cole s.

Her eyes and fingers scanned again.

COLE-BARKER
COLE-CLARK
COLERISO
COLERTON
COLERY
COLERYRIDGE
COLES

Dale
George
Glenn
K
Robert G
Stephen & Carol
Theodore
Tristan

The greatest fiction of her life lay in published print.

Unlike the other, lesser, Coles of Leeds, Tristan Coles had two phone numbers listed. She'd scribbled them both on the biography page of *The Bell Jar* and rushed to a telephone box before she could change her mind. She chose the one outside the railed gardens of Eaton Mews, where only wealthy families lived and no one needed a public telephone.

The first telephone number rang and rang and, she hung up before it went to an answering machine.

The second telephone number rang –
GoodafternoonTColesandSonshowmayIdirectyourcall?

Elizabeth was winded by the lightning speed, before she could even begin to untangle the accent.

Erm, hi, err, I, erm, I I I wanted to send a lette –

Towhominthecompanyisitreferring?

Erm, just, just, erm, generally, I suppose,

I'mafraidwedon'tacceptroundrobinsflyersorunsolicitedcvs

She closed her eyes and held the receiver against her forehead. She was frustrated at herself for not preparing before her time was costing coins, and even more frustrated to being having this realisation whilst still on coin time,

I, I, just the office address please. I need to deliver something.

You from London?

Elizabeth had only caught coaches for school trips, when the rows were rife with gossip and paper notes slipped between headrests. There was no head count for this journey. The driver loaded large suitcases in the cavern beneath their feet and eased them out of the station as the sun was rising. She closed her eyes but still heard the muttering of passengers and the heaving of the bus engine. Her mind, for once, too daunted by what lay ahead, refused to travel anywhere but the present moment.

Elizabeth's first lived experience of other families was at nursery and it did not make her question her own. Classmates had both parents or one parent or only grandparents. The permutations were so fluid and varied that the three-year-olds were shown how flexible functional could be. But slowly this freedom became freakish with each storybook that showed another smiling family of four. *Where is my daddy?* Elizabeth had asked once. *I don't know*, her mother had replied. *Who is my daddy?* Elizabeth had asked a while later, once she'd grasped that parents were people in their own right. *Finish your peas,* her mother had replied. When others asked her who or where her father was, she pursed her lips to one side and shrugged. *Is my dad in prison?* she'd asked, later still, when she learnt that that's where Caitlin Jasper's was. *No,* her mother had replied, with an offended scowl. Then in Year Five, Tyrone Purser said he was going to rape one of the Unicorn Girls and Mrs Harper had sat them all down and explained why that was not ok to say. It was then, aged nine and three quarters, that Elizabeth decided her father must be a rapist. He was an anonymous thug who'd driven her mother to her sickness, and she never asked about him again.

But now he had a name and an address and a company. He could still be a monster, and a part of her still needed that to be true. To understand her mother's inability to love her. To understand why she kept this secret for sixteen years, even when she'd unravelled and allowed all other dregs of herself, all shreds of her decency, to weep out of her. But a bigger part needed it to be a lie. To know that she'd lived a lie, and only now, on the laces of motorway towards West Yorkshire, was her real life beginning.

The Leeds city map was haphazardly folded in her handbag. She'd bought it (stolen it) from a niche travel shop in a back street of Hackney. It was the type of indie store that would survive gentrification. The owner's peculiar passion for the ordnance survey would be deemed quaint, kooky, trendy. Elizabeth had memorised the route from the bus station,

George Street >
Vicar Lane >
The Headrow >
Calverley Street >
South Parade.

She knew all surrounding streets by heart too, for emergency points of reference, but she still felt the urge to reach for the paper map. The magnetic pull of her internal compass began to quiver this far north of London.

The fact that spring would soon be yielding to summer seemed not to be known here. A sharp breeze whistled down side streets. The ornate spires of the city's centrepieces pierced into a cotton blanket sky. Elizabeth didn't pay much attention to the red brick of the buildings that hugged the wide pavements, until they were gone. Until she could see more sky above and between buildings, and worried she'd walked too far. She stopped on a street corner to consult the map, and noticed the metal sign attached to black railings. South Parade.

The building was immediately obvious. It was beige and smooth, like unpainted plaster. Rows of rectangular windows recessed with the same characterless obedience. Elizabeth pulled the long vertical handle of the main door, before she could fathom the enormity of this everyday action.

The lobby was underwhelming. It had a plastic butterfly palm plant, a low seat, that no one would sit on, and a coffee table, strewn with today's papers, that no one would read. It was a cramped entrance for such a large building. It encouraged regulars to step straight into a lift and visitors to pause only to read the embossed menu of companies:

6th: AltTrust Ltd
5th: T. Coles & Sons
4th: T. Coles & Sons
3rd: The Belvue Society
2nd: Fenhurst Capital
1st: Drayton Insurance
Ground: The Ink Collective

The lift creaked from deep within, like the bows of a ship moaning against a changing tide. But it rose nonetheless. Elizabeth steadied herself against the perimeter handle, long after they'd arrived at the fifth floor.

In amongst her cyclone of fear she felt a droplet of relief, to see it was a man behind the reception desk and not the fast-talking lady from the phone. This entrance space was only marginally bigger than the one downstairs.

Hi.

Oh, dear lord!

She'd startled the svelte man, despite the lift having clearly announced her arrival.

Hiya, sorry, how can I help?

He had beautiful curls, side swept across his forehead.

The air conditioning seemed unnecessary. She shivered, quaked, from her gut. It made her knees want to buckle.

Is Tristan Coles here?

As innnn, Mr Coles?

He pursed his lips as he hung the question in the air.

The set of copper letters above his head doubled down on the patronisation of his confusion. Each slender line and curve of T. Coles & Sons glared at Elizabeth.

He's my uncle.

Ohhhhhhhhh,

even as his demeanour changed, and he came alive, he still looked her up and down.

Yeah, it's – I'm from out of town. It's an emergency.

His expression changed again, and she'd worried that her lie had become too much. To wield the word *emergency* in vain. And to give it no feeling, no sense of urgency. She judged her performance whilst still on stage. Like playing critique and actor at once, with different lobes of the brain. She told herself she was unconvincing, that this was all an absurd farce,

and yet someone was carrying on the show.

Oh, ok,

he didn't seem too ruffled by the *emergency* either.

Well, you're in luck, cause he only comes in once or twice a week now. I'll walk you down to his office,

He stood up from his swivel chair, but left his fingertips on the desk.

Elizabeth's heart began to thump in her ears. She winced, trying to hear over it, trying to grasp her surroundings, as if her consciousness were pulsing awake, trying to unravel the situation she'd sleepwalked into.

Actually –

at first he spoke to himself,

I'll call ahead, just in case, he's not there or, on the phone or,

then added poor excuses for her benefit.

Elizabeth nodded, a small, *emergency* nod.

She could hear the long *mrrrrrrm mrrrrrrm* on the other end of the receiver. He watched her, twirling the cord between his delicate fingers. Was he studying a face that looked a spitting image of his boss, or bore no resemblance at all?

Hiya,

this voice was different,   upbeat.

I've got Mr Coles's niece at reception–

his eyes widened at his own ineptitude.

Elizabeth,

she saved him.

Her name sounded ill-fitting all of a sudden. She blushed. Perhaps her lie would crumble with its only truth.

Elizabeth. Shall I bring her down?

Elizabeth turned away slightly. She angled towards the lift for a swift exit when the obscured voice on the line would certainly betray her. She looked at the carpet, which sent red loops swirling around her patent shoes and it dizzied her. Her arm hairs stood against the air conditioning, but her torso was hot. It burned beneath her maroon top and under her arms and she didn't know why she'd chosen to wear long sleeves. The armpit that clamped her handbag smelt strongly now. She felt as if the boundaries of her being were vibrating, buzzing as they began to disappear –

Great!

His voice electrocuted her.

Ok, thank you. Will do.

He rested the phone back on its base.

Right this way, Elizabeth.

She followed him down a corridor, through a frosted glass door and across a big open room filled with felt cubicles. They walked past row upon row of grey and white lives. The snippets of telephone voices and computer keyboards and the swish of her jeans became an orchestra, building the tension, pushing Elizabeth and her guide down the channel, towards a closed door.

The blinds on the slim windows either side of the door were drawn.

Mr. T. Coles - CEO

This plaque, small and bold, was even more intimidating than the one in the lobby.

Elizabeth watched the receptionist knock on the door. A physical pulse waved down through her body. It rumbled in her ears and drained the blood from her face. It dragged her stomach through her bowels and her thighs through her knees. It felt like the intense drawback before a tidal wave surged forwards, upwards, to cause devastation.

The door opened, inwards. An empty portal,

then in stepped Tristan Coles.

Elizabeth was formed from one being, in her mind.

She'd grown to know herself as the product of a single soul, moulded in the knowledge that she was asexual offspring, ovum alone. Some of her features were accounted for, reflected in her single parent, and those that weren't were natural mutations, expected in evolution,

then in stepped Tristan Coles.

She'd tried, and failed, to imagine the ways she might see herself reflected in a middle-aged man. Although it was a phenomenon that occurred the world over, it seemed absurd that two humans of polar opposite sizes and ages and genders could bear any resemblance. And perhaps to no one else they did.

But Elizabeth was struck by a height that she understood, and skin in the shade that she knew by heart, and how his nostrils arched into a v-shape, like the wings of a distant bird in flight, like her very own. The evidence of shared genes would seem too diluted to outsiders, but to Elizabeth, who'd lived in half a body, they were glaring.

Thank you, Scott,

his voice was deep enough to quake the earth if he chose to. He looked at her.

Elizabeth, hi.

He smiled wide, a hint of perspiration on his lip.

Come in.

Elizabeth wouldn't recall walking the ten feet into his office. How she had got from the spot where she'd been rooted, in the room filled with telephone calls and busy bodies, to inside the stillness of that office, where he quietly clicked the door shut behind her, she would never remember. It was dimly lit by desk lamps and had no external windows. It gave the casino illusion of eternal night-time. In here, one could lose hours in documents with no time reference to draw them back to reality. However, there were not piles of paperwork and bursting filing cabinets to be seen, and no heavy-set computer whirring away. Only one thin folder of loose papers was on the desk. There were shelves of leather-bound books with no wrinkles in their spines, and a large canvas of abstract artwork. It was the office of someone with a personal assistant, of someone who came in once a week to sign on the dotted line.

I have one sister, older than me,

his voice was slightly hurried, thinking as he spoke, and she was genuinely unsure whether she had asked a question.

She has two sons, twins as well in fact,

he gestured to a chair.

Lovely boys, lovely nephews. One of them is in Nicaragua at the moment actually, on a research project, botany. I believe.

He sat down opposite her, a thick mahogany desk between them.

Yes, great boys, great nephews. My sister is very proud.

He leant forward, his forearms propped against the desk edge.

But no nieces.

She realised she had not asked anything.

So,

he sat back again, a shadow of amusement on his face,

do you want to tell me who you really are?

The weight of the question sat on her chest. She struggled to breathe against it. Ringing telephones couldn't quite penetrate the office, but they threatened to, like shots on bulletproof glass.

I think you know, knew, my mum, Mary Ojo.

Speaking only worsened her nerves, it gave them something to take hold of, to run with.

She said – she's not very well – but she said,

and the longer she left gaps the more the nerves infiltrated the empty spaces,

she thinks you,

they were ceasing her whole body, trying to suffocate her,

I've never met my dad and –

and she thinks you are him.

She slumped into the chaotic silence of her own creation.

Tristan's existence was already grounded in composure, but his broad frame appeared to unclench a millimetre more beneath his suit jacket. He wiped his facial hair, three times, in quick succession. He alluded such control, it was not farfetched to assume he'd made a conscious choice to begin to grey.

How old are you, Elizabeth?

Fifteen, about to be sixteen,

she added, for timeline context, but cringed at how it sounded so childlike, boasting about her years.

Fifteen, ok,

he was graciously serious.

I have a wife, who I love very much, and we've been married for twenty-seven years,

but there was no grace in the lack of privacy he gave her, with his eyes fixed upon hers.

I have two sons, twins, who are twenty.

He edged a framed photograph towards her, spinning it round with just his forefinger so she could see the family of four. Their smiles stood out against the nondescript backdrop. It looked fit for a catalogue, for a children's storybook. The young, mixed-race men looked scholarly and sporty and kind-natured all at once. The cool air of irritation began to chill her nerves.

That doesn't answer the question, but ok. Are you sure?

It was too tinged with annoyance to sound like a beg.

You said your mother was sick? I'm very sorry to hear that.

Only rarely are you aware of the significance of a moment within the moment itself. Elizabeth knew instantly she would forever regret sewing that seed of doubt and planting the perfect alibi. She could already feel her future self, the woman she'd become, scorning the girl she was today, for having fumbled such a delicate moment, for having attacked it with the conflicting confidence of a teenager: blind boldness and skewed self-worth.

I'm sorry to disappoint you.

She was not crying, but water gathered on her lash line.

I'm sure it wasn't easy to make this trip. I'm sorry I can't be more help.

He stood, and then she stood, and the situation was getting away from her. It was hurtling towards a close before it had begun. He had a hand on the door handle, and against her will, she was moving towards him.

What does your company do?

He released the handle, and let out a sigh, that took the shine off his forced smile as he spoke next,

We're a private equity firm. We invest in companies, help them to restructure or to grow.

She could not be patronised by his necessary simplification,

It's very satisfying work.

A snappy quote, fit for an article.

He reached for the door again,

Well, it was lovely to meet you Elizabeth, and I do hope –

Would you take a paternity test?

His mouth stayed open ajar.

In his stillness, as she saw the possibility of a thousand responses fizz through his mind, she became aware for the first time, that she was alone with a stranger. She did not know this man.

Sure,

he narrowed his eyes and tried to squeeze out a smile.

And yet, she did not need a paternity test to know that he was her father. She felt satisfied at his surrender, but knew she would not follow through. Only less than she needed confirmation, did she need further rejection. He opened the office door and the sounds private equity at work rushed into the room.

Have a safe journey,

but he looked around the office and not at her.

She took a step out of his lair and into the brightly lit bustle, and then turned back,

Is Coles Nigerian?

He did not feign courtesy with this next pause.

No,

he said, short and sharp.

How was it?

Mr Williams had his shirt sleeves rolled up, exposing his forearms.

Yeah it was alright,

she nodded.

Come off it, so chilled! I'm sure you aced it. You're out early.

They were alone on the sunny courtyard. Her peers were still squirrelling away in the sports hall, squeezing every last drop of time to write and rewrite and erase and start sentences that had no direction.

Yeah, I just wrote: Shakespeare is shit.

He laughed.

It felt almost theatrical, to hear the echo of their voices in the empty space. And intimate, to share this speck of time together.

Nah, it was good. I'm happy with how it went,

she squinted one eye closed to look up at him.

I'm sure you did excellently.

Cheers, sir.

See you in September,

he saluted at her,

and she saluted back, unable to find the words to tell him that she'd changed her options to Maths and Business.

ROBYN. 2006.

It's officially happening.
It's allowed now, right?
I think so.
For sure! it's December!
Ok, here we go then.
Bells began to drown out the DJs.

Janet turned the car radio up by a whole, single notch. She drummed her fingers against the steering wheel, with timing closer to a nervous twitch than the beat of the festive song. She braked suddenly at a junction, and the passenger seatbelt dug into Robyn's throat.

Oop, sorry,

Janet looked in the rear-view mirror.

Bill, who was spread across the back seats, pushed up onto his front paws with the same rush as a drunkard waking suddenly at a wave of nausea. He bolted to attention.

Sorry, Bill.

Robyn pulled her seatbelt and twisted round to reach out to the startled lapdog. He saw her coming with his good eye and nuzzled his coarse head towards her palm. Robyn kept facing away from the windscreen, comforting Bill, until she felt the familiar rise and fall of speed bumps underneath. She started to open the car door before Janet had fully pulled into the pavement.

Thankyou,

Robyn threw the words behind her, followed by a *THMP* of the door.

Janet raised her eyebrows in the mirror to Bill.

The security light flashed on as Robyn skipped up the concrete, and rapped on the front door. Deadened clunks and clicks came from the other side, before it swung open.

Robyn, are you not freezing?

She looked down at her vest top and the goosebumps that bobbled across her own arms. Maybe she was. She hadn't noticed.

Come in, come in,

Sarah reversed her chair to make space.

It's so dark in the afternoons now,

she said, pulling on the light cord of her home office. The eco bulb came on with a dimness that somehow made the room feel darker. Robyn climbed into the armchair and sat cross-legged.

I've only got blackcurrant squash today I'm afraid, haven't had a chance to get out.

Ok.

Robyn waited alone, listening to the processes happening in the kitchen over the way: cupboard-tap-counter-cupboard-plate-cupboard. There was a green tinge over her sight as the room brightened imperceptibly. The glass and plate of biscuits barely kissed the coffee table before Robyn swept them into her clutches.

thnkyo

she said, muffled by a Bourbon.

So, how was it?

Robyn stared at her, chomping, like a ruminating cow eyeballing a countryside onlooker.

The English exam?

Oh,

she cast her mind back six hours, and shrugged,

it was ok.

Did the question you wanted come up, about, about Salome?

No.

Oh, that's a shame. Well, it's only a mock. Maybe that means it will come up in the real paper. I'm sure you did great, well done for doing it.

The quiet crunching of biscuit.

How has the rest of your week been?

Fine.

Sarah cleared her throat, and crept with trepidation,

Just fine?

She made the words sound breezy.

Just normal.

Sarah felt the vague warmth of a win. It had been two months worth of Tuesdays, of steady progress. Graphically, the incline was barely worth registering, but to Sarah it was steep enough.

Ok.

Bill pooed in my bedroom.

Sarah blinked.

Oh no?

It's ok. Janet said it was because he was confused because the plumber was blocking the kitchen so he couldn't get outside.

Right, oh bless him.

I don't know why he didn't poo in Janet's bedroom though. Maybe because it smells weird in there.

Yes, maybe he feels more comfortable in your room, which is nice, even if it is to go to the bathroom. Am I right in thinking you've been with Janet and Bill for about six months now? Did you want to – maybe we could talk about how you're settling in?

At first, when Sarah had slipped questions like these into their conversations, just as a parent would hide vegetables in an infant's meal, Robyn had wanted to lash out or snap shut, to make it known that she had not taken the bait. But she'd come to learn that if she refused to answer, Sarah would simply leave it. She didn't press it, or circle back to it, or disguise it in new semantics. It did not create a shadow that darkened with each swerved conversation. Instead, it dispersed, evaporated, and Robyn retained the freedom to stand up straight. To talk or think, without a weight of expectation.

If you're comfortable with that,

Sarah added, as she always did.

Soft headlights beamed into the room at intervals, drawing peaks like a heart monitor as they traversed the road humps outside.

Ok,

Robyn hugged her knees into her chest.

Ok,

Sarah swallowed her jubilation.

We could start by talking about anything that you enjoy about living with Janet? Is there anything that makes you feel particularly happy, or comfortable? Any reason you're glad Janet is your guardian?

Robyn watched Sarah until she'd finished talking. She was the only person Robyn knew who honoured the permanence of words. Who put consideration and craft into that gap between thought and sound. She cared for them as she cared for all things, completely, fragilely. Robyn found it respectable, and a bit irritating. After an endless gestation, the questions were finally birthed and Robyn was forced to turn her head away from them. A tall man bobbed passed the window. A learner's moped moaned up the

road. She dropped her chin to her knees and didn't lift it as she spoke,
I like Bill.

I like taking him for walks.

And when he sleeps on my bed, I like it, I guess.

And Janet is –she's old, but it's fine.

She lets me box and takes me here and she doesn't really annoy me or anything.

The hum of a refrigerator and the erratic clicks of a pipe somewhere and the song of a stray blackbird scored Sarah's wait for an adjective that she could hold on to: *happy, comfortable, safe.* A word that she could replay when panic gripped her at night, or in the supermarket, or watching a film, when anxiety would grab her by the shoulders and ask: what will become of Robyn? But her desire would not be satiated today.

Instead, she suppressed the unprofessional lump in her throat and asked,

Ok and is there anything you think could be improved? Anything you're maybe not, particularly, happy with?

Robyn closed further in on herself, bringing her forehead onto her knees and chin tucked towards her chest. She kept her eyes open, intrigued by the macro view of her own thighs. Fine hair lay flattened and tousled, like a wheat field after a storm. Some upright strands shivered beneath the exhales of her breath, which felt warm and moist trapped within this makeshift cave. Calmness and clarity could pervade here, as her physical world reflected the psychical, external mirrored internal, it was all her. Enveloped by her own being she was guarded from the incomprehension of her own incomprehension. In here, there was no hunt for unattainable answers. *Anything you're not particularly happy with.* A baby could not comment on what it feels like not to talk. Nor was there space for distant dreams. *Anything you think could be improved.* As Robyn hugged herself, confronted so closely by the present moment and her place in it that she could not be tempted to explore the vague dreams that lived somewhere unknowable. The ethereal visions of a life where –

She sat up.

No.

Ok. Well, that's good.

They discussed the perfect ratio of squash to water for the rest of the prescribed hour.

The students lounged across their desks like wilted lilies, lit by the blue flicker of the television screen. Matilda plaited Jessica's hair. Kaz pretended not to notice Matthew's pinky finger brushing hers beneath the desk. Tobias, out for the count, drooled on his blazer arm. One might have assumed the film was a treat, since it was the last class of the day, and the last Religious Studies lesson of the year, but it was actually the third time they'd watched it that term. Mrs Knapp had chosen the film hastily one day, when a deathly hangover made the lesson plan unbearable, for its themes of Sikhism and cultural integration. She hadn't realised at first that she had stumbled upon the elixir, that its more prevalent plot lines of football and lesbians would focus the Year Ten class like nothing else.

The triple showing worked well for Robyn, who had slept through the first viewing and spent the second viewing watching the wind drag a drinks can around the playground outside. This time, she watched the film, keeping her chin propped up by her fists. She didn't laugh at the prescribed points, but it maintained her interest. Until Jake Gresham leant adjacently across the aisle and whispered in her ear,

I bet this gets you right off.

He then retracted back to his side, balancing on the rear two legs of his chair and mimed rubbing his crotch frantically with his fat tongue hanging out. Before Robyn could react, the chair legs swept underneath him and Jake thudded to the floor. The glimpse of embarrassing horror in his face served enough retribution for Robyn, and she returned to the football film.

Robyn arrived at Sarah's that afternoon with a surplus of energy, and a peculiar desire to talk. Questions and thoughts bounced around inside her, with such vigour that they might have tumbled out if she opened her mouth. On the drive over, she'd even pointed out a dog that looked like Bill, to Janet. *He looks like Bill*, she'd said.

Robyn bounded up to the front door. It opened before she'd had a chance to knock. A woman and a young boy came out from Sarah's house. They crowded the doorway, facing away from her.

What do you say, Rory?

Shall we say 'bye Sarah, see you soon, Sarah'?

The woman held Rory's wrist, rather than his hand.

Bye Suhuh,

he twirled his hips from side to side.

The parade of questions and thoughts fell quiet.

Oop, sorry,

The woman nearly trod on Robyn's foot.

Oh hi, Robyn, sorry, didn't see you there,

Sarah clutched the front door. Her face reddened slightly. Rory looked up at Robyn with a dusting of fear.

Come on, Rory, bye Sarah, I'll call you tomorrow or yeah, tomorrow sometime probably.

The woman wore flat mules that clapped against her feet as they walked away.

So sorry about that, Robyn, just another client, we overran and –

Sarah talked with even more fluster than normal, as she followed Robyn to the room.

Robyn wanted her to feel embarrassed. To feel shamed that the farce of their set-up had been exposed. To be reminded that Robyn knew full well that this was all a contractual arrangement, that each interchange was formulated by textbooks, not genuine concern or intrigue. Sarah was paid to listen to Robyn. Their "conversations" paid for the artwork on the walls, and the biscuits and the squash.

It was a last-minute rearrangement, because obviously normally I don't like to – I try to leave plenty of time, so there's no overlap between clients.

Robyn clenched her fists. She could smash the lamp in the corner that was made from seashells. It was probably her right, as her *client*, she probably paid for it.

Anyway, make yourself comfy, I'll be back in a moment.

Robyn imagined walking back down the corridor, waltzing out of the front door and being halfway down the street before Sarah returned with her sorry plate of biscuits. She ran the vision over and over in her head,

but her feet stayed planted to the floor.

Happy Birthday To You,
Happy Birthday To You,
sorryI'mterribleatsinging,
Happy Birthday Dear Ro-byn,
Happy Birthday To You!

Sarah had one hand on a wheel and one hand guarding the flames, as she edged into the room. In her lap, on a plate with a ceramic floral rim, was a homemade chocolate cake. But the cocoa sponge and rich cream filling could barely be seen beneath the decoration: an assortment of biscuits. Custard creams and jammy dodgers and ginger nuts and shortbreads were intricately arranged and stuck on with icing. A bourbon biscuit took centre stage, from which the others seemed to cascade out.

It was the most impressive thing Robyn had ever seen.

And it was for her.

I know it's not until the weekend, but –
(more than Robyn knew)
I couldn't fit fifteen candles on, completely forgot after decorating, but –

She lifted the burning cake up towards Robyn, who took it with both hands.

You can just,   you can just blow the candles out if you like.

Sarah cut them both a slice. Robyn ignored the miniature fork that Sarah chose to eat with, and worked with her hands until she was squidging crumbs into moist clumps. Then Sarah cut her a second slice.

Thanks, Sarah,
Robyn sat back in the armchair, crossed legs, her belly pressing into the waist band of her shorts.

You are welcome, Robyn.
A different silence than usual filled the room, one thick with contentment. A pause which no one was trying to scramble away

from or fill, a pause that wasn't pointed in its lack, a pause simply because the moment needed nothing else to feel complete.

Sarah sighed gently, and lay her cake fork down.

I hope you don't mind that I – I just happened to come across the date in your file and realised it was this week and we couldn't not celebrate it! But I hope that, that I haven't overstepped a mark or –

Robyn shook her head,

Thanks.

Sarah greedily lapped up the gratification Robyn was so generously pouring out today. No matter how much cake she consumed, this was a separate, insatiable appetite.

Have you got any plans with Janet? And Bill? For the big day?

We're going to the cinema.

It was the first lie that Robyn had ever told. She'd never cared enough to lie before. The generic reasons for lying – protecting pride, boosting ego, evading punishment, diminishing offence to others – were not cause for concern to her. But the falsehood had just appeared. Her subconscious had gone in search of an excuse and plucked a memory, the time at an interim home when they'd all gone to the cinema for a girl's birthday and they'd watched an animation and one boy threw up from too many fizzy laces on the minibus back home, and decided it would suffice as a lie before she'd even decided to lie. Before she'd even realised that it was not her pride she wished to preserve but her councillor, with the soul of porcelain, who wouldn't be able to hide her sadness at the forgotten birthday or her embarrassment at overstepping the mark with a client.

Oh how lovely! What are you going to watch?

I don't know.

A less clear-cut individual would likely spiral at the stain on their clean sheet, but Robyn was able to move swiftly on from this anomalistic occurrence.

And so you must be able to – you said that you can – are you looking forward to boxing against others, now that you're fifteen?

Robyn almost gasped. The elusive threshold had finally become tangible, and it had nearly been overshadowed by cake.

Robyn slid into the passenger seat, clutching an old biscuit tin.

Hi, love,

Janet's mumble went unheard beneath the rain hammering the windscreen, the squeak of a lazy wiper and the steady click of the indicator.

What's in there?

She flicked the indictor the other way and pulled off the kerb. Janet preferred conversation when driving, when eye contact was frowned upon and there was a definite place to put her hands.

Cake.

Is it Sarah's birthday?

She thanked a driver with a flat palm. The question was merely the appropriate integer in the conversational equation. She was not particularly interested. Although, she was vaguely pleased that the tin did actually contain sweet treats.

No,

Robyn's voice slightly strained from where she contorted herself to reach back and stroke Bill. He licked dried icing from her fingernails.

It's mine, at the weekend.

Janet's cheeks coloured. She turned off the wipers in a panic, then immediately back on.

Oh right, yes,

she fiddled with the heat controllers.

Darrell's gym was as underground in operation as it was in location. The governing bodies of amateur boxing would identify a dozen violations before the second light tube had buzzed on (admittedly, this did take some time). Their Health & Safety measures were largely a penknife and an antibacterial spray and the closest it had ever come to a tax return was putting elastic bands round wads of cash in the safe. It did have a fire exit (a prerequisite of a council-built car park) and they had once owned a fire extinguisher, but that had had to be destroyed as evidence, after Pitbull Pete had gone awry and used it as a weapon and put a man in a coma for three days. However, sometimes Darrell would be momentarily gripped by the desire to professionalise the establishment. One season, he hired an accountant who quit after three days. The next year, he hired a secretary, who quit after two. But always, within a few days, the glistening vision of a fresh slate and a reputable company would tarnish, and turning a blind eye to the skin indents from a hacked-off ankle tag and accepting a questionable stack of fifties just seemed a lot less effort.

Perhaps Darrell had been in the throes of one of those detoxifying spells when he'd randomly plucked fifteen as the age that Robyn could start fighting. Child welfare wasn't a renowned concern of the coach who let underage boys batter each other without any legally-required head gear. They wore it at their own discretion, and truthfully, if a new boy turned up with a headguard they were likely to get double the battering and decide to ditch the helmet for their own protection. And yet, Darrell had decided to implement this arbitrary age rule on the most relentless youth boxer he'd ever seen. And more shockingly, he'd stuck it. His decision had remained long after all other attempts at professionalism had melted away. He'd toyed with abolishing it when it dawned on him that once Robyn was unleashed on the circuit, faithless gamblers would bet against her in their droves, laughing her out of the ring and piling cash into his tracksuit pockets. But for some reason, he had not faltered. And on the Monday that Robyn walked into the gym and said, *I'm fifteen now,* a shard of Darrell wanted to move the goal post and keep the young girl out of the ring a second longer. But instead he said,

Glove up, then. Standing around like that. Jesus fucking christ.

Twenty-eight seconds into the second round, Robyn was knocked out. Her opponent, Yosef, was a year younger than her but had the body mass and moustache of a grown man. Unlike most of their peers, Yosef didn't have a particularly aggressive streak or a delinquent attitude, he merely had a mother who wanted him to shift a few pounds. Robyn's punches barely made his blubber ripple.

You're not sparring now, Robyn. It's not just shots on fucking target, where's the power?

Darrell called out, draped over the ropes.

The fight had been cobbled together quickly. Darrell had clicked his fingers at Yosef, *you, get in the ring,* and insisted they start before Winston had even finished stringing the referee's whistle around his neck. Robyn was vaguely surprised how mundane it felt, even as crowds started to gravitate towards the ring. All the boys wanted a look at who'd been lucky enough to fight the skinnybitch first, and how he'd get on.

But she'd imagined a proper fight would feel proper. Robyn buzzed around Yosef for the first three minutes. Mosquito versus elephant. And after the break (in which she received only the flash of a forbidden thumbs up from Winston), she returned with the same zeal and same game plan. Dipping and ducking. Dippinganddducking so fast that she came back up whilst he was still mid swing.

Robyn realised then that she had never felt a proper force to the head.

Yosef looked around as the girl dropped to the mat, terrified of his own mittens. A few onlookers lingered to wallow in the joy of seeing the star pupil out cold, before shuffling back to their training. Yosef fumbled to help her up with his padded hands. The pair of them sat cross-legged on the ring floor for Darrell's debrief. Robyn clicked her mouth guard in and out with her tongue.

Well, that was a shit show, wasn't it? How disappointing. Nearly three years you've been slagging my ear off to get you in the ring. What a fucking disappointment. You know why I put you against him? Because he's a fucking idiot – no offence, lad, but you are, you're fucking slow,

Yosef nodded, apologetically.

Should have been a walk in the fucking park. There was no power, no fire. Maybe you let the glory of the ring get to you, coming up here, few kids watching, thinking you're Billy Big Bollocks and look what happened.

The metronome of her mouth guard stayed steady.

Have you been wasting my time all this time? Hours of training for nothing. I don't like wasting my time, Robyn. Pull your fucking finger out.

He walked off into his office (oversized cupboard for the trip switch). Robyn jumped to her feet, wincing as her brain reverberated inside her skull. Yosef stood up too, after a couple of failed attempts.

Whether she was being chased by Darrell's criticism or hunting down a win, Robyn charged through her campaign to improve. And opponents threw themselves into her path. Boys clambered over one another to be picked by Darrell to face the girl. No one else felt the satisfaction of a knockout blow (a satisfaction that, admittedly, Yosef had not felt himself), as Robyn grew more resilient in only a matter of weeks. But the losses still piled up. Despite her strength being impressive for her size, it was still rarely a comparison for her male counterparts. An ant can lift fifty times its bodyweight but still be crushed by a pinky finger.

So she strengthened her awareness. She bettered her brain power. Most of her oppositions and their weaknesses were known to her already, from around the gym, and if they weren't, she began to sniff them out within seconds after the first bell.

Raymond didn't retract quickly.

Addy had no power in his left.

Kyle's lateral movement was slow.

Dan sniffed every time before he sent a cross.

and Mikey– Mikey, Mikey, Mikey and his piss poor balance.

It took Robyn until the third round to take full advantage of Mikey's instability. She lured him into attempting big glory punches, which she dodged, then attacked whilst he still wobbled around, making enough contact that it was her arm that Winston raised once the whistle was blown. Their peers had not stayed to watch the fight.

Finally,

Darrell muttered, as he walked off.

Robyn stood alone on the stage, chest heaving.

And then I did two double jabs which he didn't block because I was too fast and I went for a hook with my left, but he got his hands up in time. He did land an uppercut,

she lifted her chin to show off the emerging scab to Sarah.

So then I slowed down, as my counterattack, and he didn't know what to do. He thought he was pushing me to the ropes, but I was walking there. He left himself wide open and I landed three jabs, a cross and a body blow.

Sarah fought to contain a wince,

Congratulations,

she whispered.

Did you decide whether to go on the field trip yet? To the Celtic camp?

No.

No you're not going? Or no you haven't decided?

Barely a morsel of impatience was detectable.

I don't care.

Well, that's a shame.

There was the shadow of a tremor as Sarah took a sip of her tea with two sugars.

Robyn shrugged.

She bit her thumb.

Darrell said –

You never know if it will help with your exams. I find it far easier to remember information if I've actually experienced it, rather than just in the classroom. And you're very lucky that you can go on these trips, I missed out on a lot at school when places didn't have wheelchair access.

Sarah's face burned impossibly red, heat being a by-product where anger and embarrassment clashed. Robyn did not honour the common courtesy of looking away. She watched Sarah's eyes become pale oases in a red-hot desert. She watched her take another drink, trying to lap up composure.

I'm sorry, Robyn, that was out of order, and unprofessional. I shouldn't have said that, that was unfair, and unfair of me to imply that you, erm, she fumbled to pick back up the gauntlet she had wildly thrown down in a contest of disadvantages,

that you haven't faced your own difficulties in accessing school trips and, experiences.

Robyn didn't care for her apology; she hadn't been offended.

Why are you in a wheelchair?

Sarah looked at her wheelchair, as if noticing it for the first time.

Erm, well, ok. When I was born – there were some difficulties when I was born – which resulted in damage to my spinal cord, which controls the movement in your legs, and that meant I, I have never been able to walk, or move my legs independently. I suppose in a way, I'm lucky because it's all I've ever known. I've never had to adapt,

It was a line she'd fed pseudo-sympathetic quizzers many times.

I just live without my legs,

only this time, it felt less convincing.

Robyn glanced down at her own legs. They lay still, crossed in the lap of the armchair, knees resting against the sides. For a moment, they seemed independent. That they would never raise on her command again.

Anyway, again, I'm sorry Robyn, this is not about me. I mean, I'm happy to talk about it, me, if you find it helps you, but, yes, I shouldn't have.

Robyn stretched her legs out deliberately and crossed her feet on the coffee table.

It's entirely up to you whether you go on the field trip, of course – I'm sorry that you can't walk,

Robyn interrupted.

I've never thought about it before, but I guess it feels good to walk and run.

Sarah stayed quite still.

I think I could walk forever without stopping.

It kind of feels like, like everything's right when I'm walking or running or moving.

Like that's how it's meant to be. And when I'm sat down or stood still it's like I'm sleeping, even if I'm not.

Well,

her voice croaked,

that's great Robyn. And that's a freedom that no one can ever take away from you. But sometimes, sometimes it's important to stand still, even if it's uncomfortable, and to try to understand why it's uncomfortable. That's what we do in here, isn't it? We sit still and we think about things instead of running away from them or, or covering them up. Sometimes you have to ask yourself whether something actually makes you feel better, or whether it just covers it up for a while.

Robyn distractedly brushed a thumb over her chin wound.

Bill barked at the television. It was a pitiful bark, as if he didn't want to alarm anyone, but he could definitely hear a chorus of distressed dogs. Janet raced to turn off the undercover panorama on abusive animal shelters.

Robyn! Dinner!

she called out, as pitifully as Bill's bark.

Robyn began to leave her bedroom, when she spotted the damp towel on her bed and remembered Janet's awkward intervention a few days prior about this practice. She hung it up in the bathroom on her way downstairs. Her sopping hair trickled down the back of her vest. A plate of ready-meal Shepherd's Pie sat waiting for her.

Janet tried not to look at the teenager's nipples that stood alert, like two push pins on a flat cork board. She looked only at the potato and mince, and heard only the clink of cutlery on ceramic, but thought only of how she could address the subject. Admittedly, Robyn did not need one for the support, but for social decency. Janet still toyed between using the mature *brassiere* or the more colloquial *bra* or whether she could bypass it altogether with an ambiguous suggestion of *support*, when Robyn clattered her knife and fork down against her plate and stood up.

Thanks.

She put them in the sink. She paused in the doorway,

I'm not going to training tomorrow,

then ran up the stairs, two at a time.

THE LAKE.

Robyn still hadn't said a word when she took the tumbler of water from Delilah, who held the icy carafe like an obedient waitress. As she sat up to drink, Maria winced in anticipation, but Robyn didn't flinch. Perhaps the broken ribs diagnosis was wrong.

Robyn didn't seem too interested in her surroundings, but she did keep glancing down at Layla, as if to check that she was still there.

It's ok, Robyn,

Layla placed a mature hand on Robyn's thigh.

They're nice ladies.

Hi Robyn,

Anna tried to garner whether Robyn remembered her from the cabin hours before, but her expression gave away nothing.

My name's Anna. You collapsed back up at our cabin, so we took you in – we took you here to rest,

she corrected herself.

This is Maria, she's a trained doctor.

Maria looked pained.

How are you feeling?

Robyn looked past Maria. There was another double bed, similar in structure but with its own unique carvings, and a single, also hand-crafted, and yet the bell tent remained spacious. The canvas ceiling draped way above their heads.

Do you want some bread?

Layla held out a slice.

Robyn took it from her.

They all watched her devour the thick slab of sourdough, showing little concern for her swollen lip. As she swallowed, the choker of purple skin across her throat danced up and down. A light breeze shimmied through the tent, gently flapping the tent's entrance. Robyn caught sight of something outside.

Is that a lake?

Anna, Maria and Delilah all whipped their heads towards the exit, as if they didn't know themselves exactly where this tent stood.

Yes,

Anna encouraged.

Robyn gave the shadow of a nod. A hint of relief, perhaps.

Would you like to go and see it?

I think you should wait, there's no rush, regain your strength,

Maria tried to dissuade.

But Robyn didn't take her eyes off the curtain entrance, which had now settled closed again. Then she took another slice of bread from Layla's tray.

You want to go see it?

she asked the child.

Layla nodded, then slid from the bed.

Her wounded feet landed on the coir matting and her legs buckled. Maria instinctively swooped in, catching Layla under her armpits.

Don't,

Robyn's voice barely raised a notch, and yet it sliced through the tent.

she can stand.

I can stand,

Layla said to herself,

and to Robyn, and to the other three women and Maria backed off a little. But as she pressed her feet into the ground, her eyes welled up and she sank back down into a squat. Again, Maria made a small, reflexive step towards the child.

I'll carry her just to the grass,

Maria pleaded with her eyes.

Robyn's nod was only slightly clearer this time.

If that's ok with you, Layla?

Maria checked.

Yes please,

she whispered.

Anna led the way. Someone had smudged a thumb of white wisps across the pastel blue sky. The afternoon sun beat down, but it was a crisper heat out here than the muggy warmth of the tent. There were three more tents, slightly smaller in size, and together they curved like an amphitheatre, focused on the glistening main attraction down below. A selection of horizontal trunks were arranged to be benches with the best view in the house. This semi-circular campsite clearing was naturally encased by fir trees, and although the woodland was only metres deep, it was dense enough to hide any view of the main buildings.

As they padded across the grass towards the water's edge, Maria still carrying Layla, there were whisperings of movement from other women. All perfectly occupied changing bed linen or carrying cushions from the main house or collecting kindling from the fringe of the forest floor, but not too busy to steal a glance at the two new guests, alive and well.

A short distance from the water's edge, Robyn stopped.

How deep is it?

From the very edge here it's shallow for about twenty feet, standing depth. Then it gets deep pretty quickly.

Robyn watched the water as Anna spoke.

Lake Fripstow. But I'm sure you already knew that.

The dark pool sat impossibly still. From where they stood, neither end of the lake could be seen, as it coyly snaked through the valley, winding behind wooded banks. The water's edge gently mirrored the land it hugged, glinting a myriad of greens. Each bank-side tree had a twin, inverted and ever-so slightly blurred, so as not to outshine the real thing. But, like an artist's palette, whilst the perimeter was alive, blending from colour to colour,

the centre sat untouched.

Shaded by the mountain that swelled up from the opposite bank, it did not even reflect the light blues of the day's sky. The distance from this bank to that one was immeasurable. There was no person or boat to act as a size guide in the stretch of water that shimmered like black liquorice.

And what lay beneath was even less knowable.

Long had Lake Fripstow's waters been unmarred by fishermen. The body of water, sanctuary in name and in nature, possessed a tranquillity that even the most tenacious hunters did not wish to disturb. Those who existed in the depths of this underworld could do so without a shadow of concern for what lay above their rippling ceiling. Perhaps three-spined sticklebacks were hunting tadpoles and rainbow trout were showing off their colourful flanks and endangered schelly reproduced in thousands,

but no one could know for certain.

It's not too cold this time of year, it's had all summer to heat up.

Robyn's gaze was near the shoreline, where the water was shallow enough and clear enough to see the pebbles beneath.
I can't swim.

Anna searched the strange young woman's face.
She didn't sound embarrassed or fearful, it was more like a fact that she'd plucked from somewhere forgotten.

That's ok, dear. No one's making you go in.
Robyn exhaled loudly,

then began to heel off her trainers.
She walked the last few lengths of grass in her bare feet and stepped down into the water. The lake sealed itself around her ankles. Maria gently lowered Layla down and she tiptoed to the edge, lifting the hems of her leggings. She winced as she entered, feeling the sting of cool water and uneven rocks beneath her sore feet. The two guests stood with their backs to the bank.

Maria began to slip off her sandals, when Anna rest a gentle hand on her arm.

Let them be alone, together.
Robyn waded further into the water until it made her shorts billow up like sky lanterns. Layla wobbled a few steps before launching forward, still fully dressed, her belly slapping the surface and a shriek crying out.

Robyn quickly whipped around,

but it was a wail of joy.
She kicked her arms and legs with fervour, a puppy paddle, bouncing off one tip-toe or other, as she stayed just within her depth. Robyn copied her small friend, lowering herself fully into the healing waters. With the lake taking her weight, she lowered deeper and deeper until the crown of her head dipped below the surface.

Layla's splashing simmered slightly,

then stopped altogether,

as she waited for the re-emergence.
Anna and Maria watched on. Delilah unconsciously held her breath.

Layla began to move towards her guardian, as assertively as one can against a body of water, when Robyn thrust out of the water, gasping. Her darkened hair was slicked against her head, showing the smallness of her skull. Layla followed suit, sinking under the surface, but bobbed straight back up again, her curls falling fully free from her wayward buns. The afternoon light glinted off the soft waves that rippled away from them. They dipped and dunked and splashed and glided in their shallow pool, without so much as a tremor disturbing the darker distances of the lake. All the women on the bank, some more outwardly than others, watched on.

Robyn beckoned Layla to the shallowest point, where she lay down on her back, propped up on her elbows so that the inches of water could just about cover her belly button but not her face. Robyn took one of Layla's feet and began to scrub.

Schhh –

her sharp inhale could be heard back from the grass. Robyn paused. Then, with a small consenting nod from Layla, she continued, more gently.

We'll let them have the Bell to themselves tonight too,
Anna said to Maria, but she still looked towards the bathers.
Whoever was meant to be in there can sleep up in the main house for a night or two.

Who knows what they've been through.

ELIZABETH. 1998.

Anita Cheong wore twenty denier tights and gold hoops in both helixes, hidden by black hair that fell to her waist. She smoked vogues that were as delicate as her long feminine fingernails and could disseminate the audit team's misogyny with a single quip. But, as was often the ironic case for someone who could quote passages from *The Second Sex* and *The Female Eunuch* by heart, it took her a week to warm to the new girl.

Their temporary receptionists were usually middle-aged women in catalogue trouser suits that sat too high above their ankles and too tight around their sprawling behinds. Elizabeth was their youngest hire ever. Anita could either ignore the beautiful eighteen-year-old and wait for her to disappear off to university (which she did for the first week), or she could choose to unite with her.

Elizabeth had spent the best part of three years feigning her independence as a choice. Her classmates assumed she had older, cooler friends, waiting for her somewhere on the outside, filling her evenings and weekends, so she simply had no capacity, or desire, for school friends. She even convinced herself of this, and in a way, they were waiting for her. She had companions, lovers, soul mates all waiting for her, at university. She'd resigned herself so strongly to the fantasy that it was within the next chapter of her life that her loneliness would be resolved, that she never dreamt of meeting someone in her summer job. And never someone as alluring as Anita.

They spent long lunches smoking on the pavement outside the fire exit of an Indian restaurant. They drank black coffee in the kitchen, and exchanged loud looks that made colleagues aware they were being judged, even in the silence. They disappeared from their desks half an hour early on Fridays to get changed in the bathroom, spritzing perfume and compliments, such as *shut the fuck up you look so skinny*, and their absences were somehow always overlooked by managers, but never colleagues.

Elizabeth smelt Anita's blood orange shampoo before she saw her step out of the lift. Anita was wearing a trench coat, even though it was not cold. She had recently invested in an authentic second-hand Burberry and took every overcast opportunity to wear it. Anita walked straight up to the reception desk,

Eurgh one day, that saxophone man is going to kill me. I swear to god, if I have to hear his rendition of –

Elizabeth just stared back urgently, eyes ludicrously wide.

What? Oh FUCK! Is that today? Have you got them?

She pincered a brown envelope between her forefingers and thumbs.

Anita sucked in her lips and widened her eyes too.

Bathroom,

and she held out her hand.

Elizabeth's attention fell outside of herself for the first time that morning, to the softness of Anita's palm.

The ladies' loos were always spotless. They were cleaned an extravagant three times a day, so that the mirrored wall was never smeared and the red gloss tiles shone like freshly manicured nails. There were five cubicles, nearly a toilet for every female employee in the company, and Elizabeth had her favourite. Second from the end. Far enough into the bathroom to show restraint and composure, but not at the very end, which reeked of shame, figuratively, and sometimes, literally.

She sat with her tights down, too distracted to care that her hands were wrapped around the seat of a semi-public loo. She was not sure how the reputation she'd built for herself had stayed standing. Her fraudulent performance was pushing boundaries of mere social perception and beginning to make marked changes to her life. Her economics teacher had been so fooled that she had championed her university application and single-handedly secured her the largest grant possible. The office manager of a top accountancy firm had been blinded enough to offer her this administrative summer job that should require at least some experience. She was an imposter. She'd managed to dupe and scam and it was all about to crumble, she was sure of it.

Hurry up, Bess!

In all her life, Elizabeth had never had a nickname. Anita had been theatrically stunned by this on their third interaction. *Liz, Beth, Eliza, Lizzie, take your pick*, she had said, *but no Elizabeth is actually called Elizabeth.* In their next exchange, Anita had called her *Baby*

Bessy and it had stuck. It still felt like an unexpected embrace every time she heard it.

I can't go, I'm too nervous,

she pulled her knickers up and flushed water on top of water. In the brief blink before she unlocked the cubicle, she saw her father's face. Tristan Coles, sat at his desk.

Anita was inspecting her invisible pores in the mirror. She held the brown envelope in a hand by her side.

You've got this baby,

she passed the envelope over.

Elizabeth took a breath.

Her eyes could not focus straight away on the three As.

My baby's going to Oxford!!!!!

For minutes they embraced and squealed and laughed, and Elizabeth even punched the air like nobody (and especially not Anita) was watching. As they left the bathroom, still breathing in that exasperated way after a fit of heavenly hysteria, to begin their working days thirty-seven minutes late, Elizabeth stopped,

I actually need to piss now.

Ok, babe,

Anita blew a kiss and disappeared into the office.

Elizabeth sat on the closed toilet lid, second from the end, and cried and cried.

That evening, despite being a Tuesday, the women returned to the bathroom to reapply deodorant and face powder and switch court heels for heels heels. They drank wine bought for them by strangers and shouted *OXFORD BABY!!!!* beneath the boom of speakers. They became entangled in other parties but always found their way back to each other, spilling stories of where they'd been and who they'd met, that the other could not make sense of in the noise and haze.

On Wednesday mid-morning, they sat on their smoking stoop. Anita leant against the restaurant exit, alternating between a black coffee and a cigarette. Elizabeth lay with her head in Anita's lap. When she lay perfectly still, eyes closed and warm sun on her cheeks, the hangover was silenced for a sweet second.

Do you want to move in with me?

Anita asked at the end of a long, smoky exhale.

Hmm?

Elizabeth thought she may have drifted completely into a dream.

I know you're going to uni in a bit, but John's moving out, he's going to start a drag agency in Brighton or something, so his room will be free and I don't really need a flatmate now, money-wise, but you could come and stay until you leave. Get out of your mum's. Then whenever you're back from uni you can stay. Like a spare room, but it's yours. The Bess Room.

Elizabeth sat up quickly, and the walls of her brain punched against her skull.

Are you serious?

Yeah, why not?

Anita fingered a strand of Elizabeth's hair.

It was not rooted in her scalp but she could almost feel the touch. She collapsed back into the lap, for fear that she would cry.

Thankyou,

it was muffled.

Anita leant in close to Elizabeth's ear,

Rooooomies,

she whispered and kissed her on the cheek.

Elizabeth had packed all her belongings within twenty-four hours. Her books were in boxes and her clothes in bin bags. She had little other possessions, for what she lacked in disposable income was not supplemented by sentimentalism. She had a folder of old essays and handwritten stories that she reread from time to time, impressed by her own eloquence. She read them one last time, cross-legged on the floor of her childhood bedroom, then threw them in the bin along with old mascara wands and holed socks.

Why do you have to leave now?

Mary asked, but it was no longer a question. She'd been loudly puzzling over the same point since she'd learned she was losing her daughter a month earlier than planned. She was sat at the kitchen table in her dressing gown, as Elizabeth boldly raided the cupboards for tinned goods.

You cannot wait one more month. One more month for your mother.

Elizabeth tried to ignore the dripping tap of slow words, the torturous stream that trickled once more each time she thought it had finished.

Elizabeth,

this tone was new, laced with vulnerability.

I'm not very well.

Elizabeth left her head in the cupboard. A blend of spilled spices tickled her nose.

She had wanted to hear these words as a confession, and not as an excuse for another bed-bound day, for so long, but this still didn't feel like the confession she'd hoped for. She began to feel choked by the blend of curry powder and ehuru and stray shards of dried thyme. She turned back into the room, leaning against the cupboards for support, and distance. Elizabeth had not properly looked at her mother for years, leaving rooms as swiftly as she entered, not bothering to enhance the blurry image of the woman in a stained housecoat that she held in her mind.

She could see now how she had aged and thinned.

Please don't leave me.

For her mother, Elizabeth buried her anger,

and for herself, she buried her guilt.

I'm sorry you're ill,

but I don't think me being here will make anything better.

The sound of soft whimpering beneath a refrigerator's whirr would forever disturb Elizabeth in silent moments.

And he set this man's, or this woman's, boob on fire, he threw it up in the air, this burning breast and threw it into the crowd. Someone said it burned a girl. Can you fucking IMAGINE getting third degree burns from a flaming fake tit? Anita's voice was so croaky that her laugh almost disappeared completely down the phone.

Elizabeth was sat in the large common room with the lights off. Before now, she'd only poked her head into this room on a guided tour on her first day, when she'd spied the telephone next to the armchair. She doubted anyone would ever actually use the phone. Who would want pool players and ping-pongers privy to their homesickness? But tonight, it was empty. She could hear the distant hubbub of a drinks reception in the cloisters.

She pictured Anita laying on the sofa with the receiver on her belly. Anita had not helped Elizabeth move into university halls like she had promised, because she had also promised John that she would attend his drag festival in Brighton. A subsequent, but apparently more binding, promise. Just as it dawned on Elizabeth that Anita had not asked how her first week had been—

Anyway, what's it LIKE? Tell me, tell me.

she realised she didn't want her to. A wedge in her throat caught her off guard.

Yeah, it's alright,

she squeezed her fingers and curled her toes as she spoke, trying to draw the tension anywhere but her voice. She had hardly spoken a word to anyone all week, and now she was unable to.

Are they all awful human beings?

She gave a fake laugh.

Have you fucked a choir boy yet?

Then a real one.

The laugh sparked a glimmer of relief in her, she was fine, she was overreacting, she would settle in soon, but as soon as it came, it went, and in the privacy of the darkness she wanted to tell Anita that loneliness had followed her here, and without the familiarities of home, it was a stranger she was scared of. She wanted to admit to how she was disappointing all previous versions of herself, who had imagined her here, time and time again. And she wanted to confess that she would trade her future to be a receptionist forever, that she would trade it all to be on the brown sofa of her mother's home.

Not yet,

she spoke without breathing.

What are you doing tonight?

Not fucking a choir boy.

Shame. Where are you going out?

Elizabeth wondered if Anita could sense the strain in her voice, and was pushing her on purpose.

I'm not tonight.

What? It's fucking Saturday in your first week at uni.

Elizabeth stared at a pile of board games, with names she couldn't make out in the dusk, until her eyes stung. Tears appeared, but stayed hugged to her eyes.

I've got to go,

she hung up and sat for a while. Still, the tears did not fall. Another disappointment.

Elizabeth was caught on the tight staircase up to her room, trying to let two girls past in the opposite direction, when a boy in a suit thundered between them. *PARTY ON WALTON STREET!* he called out, but did not stop.

The three girls shared a tentative giggle at the town crier who'd drunkenly remembered that he had not fulfilled his only duty.

Which one's Walton Street?

one of the girls asked.

I think it's like, over there,

the other pointed at a wall.

They didn't directly talk to Elizabeth, but they were still stationary on the stairs, giving the essence of an invite to the conversation, without exposing themselves to rejection.

I think it's like, the main one, not the main main one, but you know,

The pair looked strikingly alike. Long brown hair and freckles.

Oh yeah, I know.

She didn't sound as if she knew.

How are you meant to find the party then?

Just look for that dude I guess,

Elizabeth chimed in.

The twins laughed. Another indirect welcome, for it hadn't been that funny.

Shall we go?

One turned her head towards her lookalike, but flicked her eyes towards Elizabeth at the last second. A true invitation.

Elizabeth walked with Daisy and Margot to Walton Street. They had waited patiently for her at the bottom of the stairs, whilst she quickly got ready (stared at herself in the mirror, imagining telling them that she was suddenly unwell or had another party offer or could just never leave the room until they left without her) and re-emerged in a different pair of jeans and some oversized earrings.

Even without an inch of geographical understanding of the city, Elizabeth could tell they were taking a nonsensical route. *Oh nonono, it's this one, it's definitely up this one,* Margot said about four times, self-assurance sharper than her sense of direction. They were nice enough, but tremendously beige. Once they had covered the prerequisite topics with all the humanhood of a written questionnaire (*What are you reading? Where are you from? What A levels did you get? What societies are you joining?*), Elizabeth was glad that they slipped into their own conversation without her, about a girl who wore fake cat ears to the drinks reception. The sun had surrendered to dusk and she studied the buildings of the long Walton Street, as if she were in a simulation. It was as if someone had tried to recreate her world and just missed the mark. The architecture was familiar but not spot on. The pubs and off-licenses were accurate, but artificial. She was walking and breathing, but not for real.

Do you think it could be that one?

She interrupted them, and herself, and pointed up at two small balconies that overhung a darkened estate agent.

On one, a couple were talking, clutching beer cans.

On the other, a boy was stark naked wearing a welsh flag as a cape. The three girls joined the queue of silhouettes entering the front door below.

There was a strange liberation in the crowdedness of the flat. Crushed by the bodies and the music and the mood lighting, Elizabeth was finally free to feel suffocated. It made sense in a way that it didn't when she was in her spacious bedroom or the grand dining hall or the rolling college gardens. She wanted to sink into it, this feeling of being just another body in a room, with no capacity for thoughts, no space for loneliness.

The speakers played a song she barely knew but she found herself embracing it, letting the beat roll through her shoulders as she followed Daisy and Margot down a tight corridor. She began to move with a self-satisfaction that was alluring to watch – alluring to those unaware that such an absorption in one's own world is always performative – and let the rhythm rebuild the person she thought she'd lost.

They arrived in a kitchen, the only room with the main lights on. Rows of bottles and cans, upright and undulating like the pipes of a church organ, covered every inch of the countertops. Carriers bags clumped in piles on the floor, sticking to people's ankles as they popped in and out, to top up their drinks. Elizabeth's mind wandered to her mother's kitchen. She shook the thought away by agreeing vehemently with something Margot had said, something that she had not heard.

They rummaged through the stranger's cupboards for glasses, and settled for two mugs and a university sports bottle. Daisy poured a healthy base layer of vodka into each one, then watched them fizz to the top with cola. She did not add their bottles to the landscape of booze, but tied a knot in their carrier bag and hid it in a cupboard, behind a colander.

Remember it's in there, girls!

Daisy said, with a level of genuine concern that made Elizabeth's insides churn.

They passed a room which had a bed turned on its side, leant against the wall. The music was coming from in here. People were not dancing in the makeshift space, but moving loudly with their bodies. Doubled over with laughter or shaking someone's shoulders for attention or flinging their fingers to the furthermost extremity to make a point. Elizabeth knew she had been that person on nights before, free from inhibitions, basking in the boldness of living, but it was very annoying to watch.

The living room was teeming with people, spread across fly-tipped furniture. There was a three-seater sofa that had a large tear in the backboard and a two-seater on antique wheels. All the cushions had been tossed to the floor, offering sponge islands to sit upon. Some people perched on a paisley footstool, and others sat precariously on a low laminate table, reminiscent of a primary school desk. One partition wall away from the music, conversations flowed more easily in here. A boy moved onto the arm of the larger sofa, so the three delicate girls could sit down. They had to sit right on the edge, on one buttock each. Elizabeth drank from her mug, trying to tune into the conversations around her.

Nah nah fuck that.
Let me try them on.
Yeah, but have you TRIED the bacon flavour though.
It's set in like mid-century Rome.
Do they suit me?
I got three As and a B.
Have you seen the one with –
Everybody knows that's bullshit.
I had to drop maths because –
Do they actually?
Ready salted is for the demented.

She reached the potent portion of her drink, but didn't slow down.

Strawberry lace?

The chivalrous gentleman on the sofa arm offered Elizabeth a sweet. He had shoulder-length hair and wore a plaid shirt, and had an endearingly open face.

Thanks,

She ate the string, tearing an inch off at a time.

I'm going to get a drink. Save my space?

She asked the boy, in a way that made her aware the spirit was sinking in.

She felt foolish crouching to fetch the hidden vodka, so poured herself a triple and left it on the side out of spite. She leant on the Strawberry Lace boy to squeeze back in next to him. Half the room had opened up into a wider, collective conversation.

That's not always the case,

Margot directed at a boy on the low desk.

It is! It's so predictable. We're hard-wired egotists.

Individually, his features weren't handsome, but overall he gave the illusion of handsomeness.

Not everyone,

Daisy tried to defend her doppelgänger.

How many kids do you want?

A girl across the circle, with sunglasses on her head, asked.

Elizabeth physically recoiled at the invasive question, but no one else flinched.

Three,

Margot said.

And do you have two siblings?

No, one sister.
Then that's bullshit! You're trying to make a point.

Some people don't want any kids,
Elizabeth said into her mug.
That's true,
Strawberry Lace looked down at her. Only he had heard and his quiet agreement was so wholesome. The sweet cola was beginning to fur her tongue, and she rest her shoulder against his knee.
It's the same with careers,
a new boy contributed to the inane conversation.
Yes, that I agree with,
said Daisy.
Elizabeth rolled her eyes to no one. Daisy agreed with this boy's collared shirt and nothing more.
Yes, this is always so interesting! What do your parents do?
The sunglasses girl asked the shirt boy. Daisy had competition.
They're both in biomechanics.
And what are you reading? Sunglasses asked.
Physics, so not exactly the same, but yeah, I see myself getting into it.
So interesting, Daisy said.
SO interesting, Sunglasses agreed.
What does everyone else's parents do?
Margot tried to cool the battle for his attention.
They began to roll call high-flying careers. This group of teens, at an actual party, waited patiently for the conversation baton to reach them, to discuss the achievements of their parents. Elizabeth looked to Strawberry Lace, to unite against the vulgarity, but he was listening intently, nodding at the sons and daughters of lawyers and doctors and researchers. A few of them skirted embarrassedly around their mothers who were *just mums.* She cringed at the way their vowels dragged on for hours. Each of them had a bubble in their throat, that apparently made it impossible to ever close their mouths completely. As the conversation snaked closer to her, she scoffed loudly,
What the fuck is this?
She downed her drink and put the mug by her feet, knocking it over as she got up and crossed the room. She closed

the balcony door and was alone in the night air. The fizzy swell in her stomach was not as tantalising out here. She pulled a pack of straights and a lighter from her jacket pocket. As she smoked, she watched two men on the street below, one giving the other a piggyback. They dipped in and out of pockets of light from the streetlamps. She watched them until they did not re-emerge from one triangle of darkness.

Music and chatter grew loud for a moment, as the balcony door was opened behind her. She stayed leant over the railings, she would not turn for Strawberry Lace, he could come to her.

But he did not.

Hey.

Instead, it was the unhandsome handsome man.

He stood next to her, resting his forearms on the iron railing. They both looked along the length of the darkened road, eyes drawn to the same lit windows and shadowy chimneys. A smudge of artificial orange ran along the base of the sky. It gave them a perverse sense of community, to belong to something so bright and intrusive.

He swigged from a beer can. She watched his cheeks fill, then his jawline reappear as he swallowed. She studied his broad shoulders and the muscular arm nearest her, with a toned bicep poking out beneath his t-shirt sleeve, and decided that it was this mature physique that gave the impression of good looks. It naturally elevated him above his peers. With his conventionally stylish dress sense and thick dark hair, his audience were fooled. She almost admired the way he had deceptively repackaged his slightly-too-large nose and slightly-too-small eyes.

She knew he knew she was examining him, in the way that she always knew when people watched her and she pretended not to notice.

Are you ok?

He asked without looking at her.

Yeah, but that was a fucked-up conversation.

She stamped on her cigarette stub.

Doused in self-awareness, he slowly turned his back to the balcony railing.

Why? What do your parents do?

He asked, with a smirk.

She smirked back, deciding.

My mum's an alcoholic and I've only met my dad once.

It had been reactive, a taser shot intended to stun. One sentence to quantify the miles of distance between them. But it had caught herself off-guard instead.

To encapsulate her life's pain in one breath.

More surprising to her still was not that she'd revealed her deepest secret of abandonment to a stranger,

but that she had never called her mother an alcoholic before.

She felt nauseated by instant regret, not for sharing but for how, despite no desire for sympathy, that's all it became when vocalised. Her sad story, her beg for pity.

Shit,

his eyes widened.

I thought you were going to say your dad was a plumber or something.

Elizabeth laughed.

Full laughter that vibrated through her soul and dampened her eyes and had her gasping for breath. Her loud cackles ricocheted off the houses opposite, and little screams of sheer amusement filtered into the light-polluted sky. Each time she calmed, she recalled the shock in his face and the seriousness of his sentiment and flew off into hysterics again.

He chuckled, both chuffed and a bit confused.

Ahhhhh,

she began to compose herself.

Fuck. I hate it here.

She gave the last echo of a laugh. Her body buzzed, with a newfound freedom.

I'm Norman,

he said.

This would have been funny too, had she not drained herself of laughter.

Elizabeth.

By Christmas, Elizabeth had made three friends, close enough to warrant a goodbye before the holidays. Richie and Shravya were on her course and Danni lived in her halls. She'd overlooked Danni until a late October evening, when she'd overheard her telling Rufus Minch to *suckmydick, you misogynistic piece of shit* and suddenly, she'd respected her dungarees. The four of them had bonded over their peerless ability to talk about things other than other students. Richie had already set his sights on becoming the first mixed-race, openly gay student president. Shravya was a legitimate descendant of Indian royalty whose heart was with improving animal welfare. Danni was always arriving late, coming from chairing a petition for a skateboarding society or front-row cheerleading her busking girlfriend or lobbying for better female changing facilities for a sports team that she wasn't on. And after twenty-four hours back in London, Elizabeth was surprised how much she missed them. She didn't know whether Anita had deliberately sharpened her sting to punish her for becoming a cushioned Oxonian, or whether she had just become a cushioned Oxonian. But her anecdotes seemed louder, her judgements more disparaging.

On Elizabeth's second evening home, on their second bottle of red, she watched from the sofa as Anita sat on the floor, painting her toenails a deep maroon.

He's a centrist, he's so fucking straight, its personal power, I'm telling you. He wants a place on the world stage, that's all it is and he's picked the party line that will get him there.

Anita's soliloquy was only interrupted for a swig of tepid wine or to concentrate on a particularly key brush stroke.

Elizabeth felt her affirmations become less and less convincing, until she stopped *yeah*ing and *mm*ing altogether, and disappeared into the dialogue in her head, which was critiquing Anita's personality in real time. She realised now that with her uni mates, when they discussed politics and current affairs it was with a refreshingly positive purpose. The flaws of society were central to their conversations, but framed in a way that leaned towards action and change. They could establish the reality of a situation without wallowing in its negativity. Elizabeth thought of how Shravya would tell them about a cosmetics company that had been found to test on animals, in a single sentence, with her bottom lip pouting sadly, before moving on and asking about Elizabeth's day whilst she quietly drafted a letter to their MP and the cosmetics head office and national newspapers. And how Danni would arrive at dinner with paint-stained hands because *oh you know, the board are a bunch of wankers* but it didn't sour her mood or her fruit salad. Perhaps it was the optimism of the young, or the protection of the privileged, that allowed them to lend their head and heart to an issue without losing themselves in the process. Elizabeth couldn't deny that Anita still had her finger on the political pulse, but now it felt as though she was looking for signs of death, not life.

And referencing Boyzone? How embarrassingly transparent, what speechwriter thought – oh fuck,

a blob of polish landed on the sheepskin rug.

Elizabeth jumped up to assist. She was so energised by a possible break in Anita's sermon that wine sloshed over the side of her glass, soaking a diamond patch on her cream cable-knit jumper.

Oh shit.

Anita stayed on the floor, clawing her wet toes like a bird of prey, holding her hands out for a damp cloth. They both mopped at their pink stains.

This is my favourite jumper,

Elizabeth mumbled into her damp chest.

The jumper was slightly cropped, in a cut that cinched her waist and accentuated her hips. The sleeves clung to her arms all the way down, elongating them, and the ribbed body hugged her breasts in a way that showcased them as undeniably ample without being too much. The first time she'd worn it to a lecture with a plaid mini skirt, Shravya had actually, physically, applauded the outfit.

Really?

Anita arched one eyebrow.

Elizabeth dabbed at her jumper more slowly. Her uni mates had also begun to cast doubt over her long held belief that real friends were the ones who Told It How It Was. If brutal honesty was the hallmark of a better friend, then why did it feel so much better when Richie told her the spot on her chin wasn't noticeable? Sometimes she'd wondered if they were as unaccustomed as her to such religious support and they'd each just followed the other's lead until they'd accidentally bred a culture of unrelenting respect that no one dared disrupt. Nothing in their artistic, musical, fashion or cultural tastes overlapped, and yet, *Right on,* Danni told Richie as he belted out a pop song she'd never heard of, *So cute,* Richie told Shravya when she hand-drew a flowery border on an essay, *Love that*, Shravya told Danni when she heard the premise for her art installation, and maybe that was the mark of true friendship.

Or maybe Elizabeth really had become a cushioned Oxonian. She kept rubbing at the patch until it turned a murky grey and began to squeak, allowing a deliberate silence to stretch out between them.

Right, I'm running you a bath,

Anita stood up abruptly and walked to the bathroom on her heels.

At first, Elizabeth thought Anita was clueless. She had misinterpreted the silence as the easy type, that comes only with comfortability, and not the heavy, foreboding silence that is a conversation all on its own. But as Anita ran the bath and filled it with bubbles and described Elizabeth's small waist as *sickening* and consulted her on what background music she'd like, Elizabeth realised Anita was trying to apologise.

The confrontational had been confronted by no confrontation, and it had scared her.

Anita sat on the loo whilst Elizabeth bathed and she silently questioned her earlier theories that friendship was based on politeness, because she couldn't help but feel fucking cool that her best friend sees her naked.

And what about boyzzzz then,

Anita asked, scooping up a palmful of bubbles, still steering the conversation in a way that flattered and focused on Elizabeth.

She immediately thought of Norman.

Yes, I'm married to a priest and cheating on him with my lecturer, and cheating on HIM with the groundsman, and we had a threesome last week with the chancellor's wife. It's a fucking scandal,

she deflected and swished water over her knees.

Elizabeth feared the field day Anita would have over Norman's name alone.

Plus, there was nothing to tell.

She had not fancied Norman on the balcony. She went for boys that talked little and ate little and smoked a lot and had a mildly grubby aesthetic. All he shared with her previous boyfriends was an air of arrogance. And after that night, he'd become nothing more than a recognisable face around the college campus. He would smile when he passed her, and they'd share a brief moment of mutual recollection.

But slowly, without realising, she had begun to seek out that smile. She ran a constant background search for his broad shape and the echo of his rich voice. And if her senses fell upon what they were searching for, they dialled into a frequency of self-interrogation. She became acutely aware of her own hand movements and the arch of her back and the shape of her mouth as she spoke. God forbid she had eaten in the previous twelve hours, for it was undoubtedly still smeared across her teeth and pervading off her breath. And yet she craved, formulated even, these moments, for the chance to occupy a second of his day. She'd deliberately dropped her fork so that she could cut into the dining queue where he stood, pick up clean cutlery and maybe receive a *hiya.* She'd renounced her decline of Richie's invite to a pub quiz once she'd learnt he would be there. And she always packed her belongings up slowly at the end of a Tuesday morning lecture because once it had accidentally timed perfectly with crossing him in a hallway.

Elizabeth could not explain to Anita why she manipulated the mundane in this way, because she could not explain it to herself. She was certain it was not him, as such, that made the uneventful electric, but rather that she had manifested a game, a habit, in which she hunted the attention of someone,

without being sure if she actually wanted it.

Poor baby Bessy,

Anita blew the bubbles off her hand.

Christmas passed in a slew of rich wine and cheap meats. Sparkling friends sailed through the flat, remedying the blown bulbs in their multicoloured fairy lights. Most mornings, Anita and Elizabeth woke up together, but on New Year's Day Elizabeth woke up in her own bed, to the clunk of the room door opening. She stretched her legs and kicked someone's shin. Jack. James?

She didn't open her eyes until she felt the mattress sink at her feet. Anita had sat down. She was wearing a man's t-shirt. She squeezed her foot through the duvet.

Bess?

Mmmm,
Elizabeth gurgled a response in her throat.

Bess, it's your mum.

She passed away this morning.

Elizabeth rolled onto her back and stared at the ceiling.

I forgot to take my make up off,
she picked at dried mascara.

NORMAN. 1999.

Norman Sear was the youngest of four siblings and all their birthdays fell in September. This was not a coincidence but the result of an intricately calculated fertility plan, that ensured they would all begin school aged a full forty-seven months. They were then given the freedom to pursue any extra-curricular passions they wanted, until the age of six. At which point their interests were streamlined to one sport, one instrument and one language. This meant their energy would not be wasted on a thin spread of mediocre talents, nor would they be pigeon-holed to one skill. But their lives were not consumed by practice either, since the Sears recognised the cognitive importance of maintaining social interactions with peers. They also knew that the impressiveness of a skill was heightened when it was seasoned with nonchalance. The hard work occurred behind closed doors, so that in public Norman could casually converse with their summer neighbours on the Cote D'Azur, or step in last minute for an impromptu Christmas piano concerto. Nepotism secured Norman's place at secondary school before he could recite the alphabet, and his A Level choices were pencilled when he was aged thirteen. By the time the seed of a potential political career was sewn, he was already using hockey away games to network and understood that every Easter church service, every sailing regatta, every boys' sleepover could be viewed as an opportunity. He consciously chose to read Classics, as opposed to an overtly political degree, so that his career path would seem destined, not calculated. Nothing in Norman's life was coincidental. It was laced with strategic forethought,

except, his meeting with Elizabeth Ojo.

When Norman had stepped onto that balcony, his only premeditation was a night of sex. She seemed fiery and dominant and lonely. It was not until later that night, lying alone and sexually unsatisfied, that he had begun to consider how else she may slot into his life. And when he returned to university after the Christmas break, with a term's worth of patience under his belt, it was time to go in for the kill.

He found her, a sitting target, at a single desk hidden between two library stacks. But she was not focused on her textbooks. Instead, she stared at the snow that was falling outside the small window in front of her. An impeccably clean blanket soothing everything.

Hello.

She spun around.

It pleasured him to see a blink in her composure. To know that she could be ruffled by conventional surprise.

Hello,

but she hid it well.

How are you?

Another tiny flicker in her certainty.

I'm good. How are you?

I'm good.

He spread out a s m i l e , slowly, deliberately.

Good Christmas?

Yeah,

there was no hesitation this time.

Aren't you doing PPE?

He picked up the only open book on her desk, which was not a philosophy, politics or economics textbook, but a novel with antiqued pages.

She smiled, and closed it.

Who's Ruth?

He asked, reading the title.

Boy you ask a lot of questions,

she scowled, playfully.

Sorry,

he laughed and touched her shoulder. A purposeful action. He felt her flinch a little beneath him, where his forefingers lay upon her collarbone.

ELIZABETH. 1999.

Even the speed of campus gossip could not keep up pace with their relationship. By the time rumours broke that Norman Sear was no longer single and that it might be with Elizabeth, they were caught holding hands on the quad, *I'm pretty sure*, and then he was spotted high-fiving Richie, *but they could have been friends anyway,* then she was seen sitting on his lap in the common room, *it was quite in your face, actually,* and by the evening of the debate society's Valentine Ball, as they walked through the marquee, Elizabeth in a floor-length fuchsia gown that belonged to Shravya and Norman in a tux that made the suits of his schoolmates' look like infantile imitations, people did not look upon the couple in surprise, but in awe.

And the onlookers, dedicated devotees to debate, secretly hoped to see the couple dip into a disagreement. It wasn't a rare sight, given the differences in their fundamental politics, but it was an electric one. A firework display in which each explosion of opinion was magnificent. They gave a masterclass in eloquence and execution that couldn't not be topped, unless, they united.

Together, they formed an impenetrable, beautiful wall of intellect and lightning recall, off which others' arguments ricocheted and faced the fatal friendly fire of their own words. Their combined charm was invincible. Though Norman deployed his more often, Elizabeth's was more potent. At her first society function, attending as Norman's plus one, she had casually lulled the president of the union into a conversation about legalising sex work, and before he knew it, Ryo Yamaguchi, the honoured captain of civil debate, was stumbling over his words and retracting earlier statements on the immorality of the age-old profession.

Hello hot pink wonder woman goddess star,

Danni had something cream cheesy amusing her bouche.

Wow, holy shit,

she swallowed it, and gave Elizabeth a hug. Danni was wearing a blue-checked suit that sagged around her knees. She flicked her chin-length hair over to one side, forming the crest of a blonde wave.

I love the suit.

I get a builder's bum when I bend down, so, don't let me do that. Champagne?
Danni plucked two full flutes from the table next to her.
Suck the patriarchy dry.
They cheersed.

Elizabeth couldn't always decipher whether Danni was blind to the irony in her comfortable takedown of capitalism, or in on it. Someone's laugh rang out, clear above the general hubbub.
Where's Normy Norm?

Elizabeth nodded in his direction, with her nose and mouth muzzled by the thin glass. Norman was with a group of boys across the room. Body language alone determined he was the king of the conversation, and their open smiles hung on his every word.

Is Delilah coming?

No, she's performing in the morning. Big set. She's landed Cornmarket Street.
It always surprised Elizabeth that Danni's girlfriend could sing in front of strangers but could not ask for ketchup with her chips.
So you've got me all night – actually wait, I wanted to corner Adrian Hummel about the lacrosse team. I heard he's running for Sport's president next year and if he wants my vote, boy better earn it,
she took two more cheese bites,
let's see what he's made of,
and made a beeline for Adrian.

Go get him, babe.

Elizabeth watched Danni leave and smiled at the peculiar swell of love she felt for her peculiar friend.

Then she took two fresh champagnes and sashayed towards Norman and his audience. She liked the tickle of her long hair against her bare shoulders, and the way it shimmied as she walked.

Hello gorgeous,

he cut across an ongoing conversation, and turned every inch of his attention to her.

Elizabeth used to believe that there was a desirability in the apathy of her previous boyfriends, that there was an added realness by their objection to ostentation, that the rarity of compliments increased their value, and the reluctance in which they were wrapped only meant they were more painfully heartfelt.

Until Norman showed her what it was to be publicly wanted, and it became all she desired.

Watch out, Yamaguchi,

one of the boys teased the president.

She's coming for your title again.

Elizabeth bristled at the minimising pronoun. She felt a warm flush and she knew her tongue would be used as a whip tonight.

Good Evening, Elizabeth,

Ryo said with a dip of the head and extravagant maturity.

I think your reign is safe. Elizabeth doesn't see the point in the society,

Norman reached around and held her hip, in a way that deafened his words. He took a full handful at the widest point of her curve. It was bold and embracing and made her acutely aware of her womanhood, and her power.

No, I don't particularly. I find futile debate, for the sake of debate, largely pointless. I don't believe we should be building a society in which those with conversational skills win, over those with knowledge. If anything, I think we've stood upon that for too long. Just because you can win an argument, doesn't mean you're right,

but her sentiment lacked conviction and concentration. Her mind was with Norman's fingers. She wanted them to press deeper into her flesh.

Well, I would counter that by saying that's exactly what we're endeavouring to achieve here, to better everyone's chance at contributing to the conversation. And ultimately celebrating the central pillar of democracy,

Ryo spoke, but Elizabeth didn't listen to him, as Norman leant in close to her ear and whispered,

You're so fucking sexy.

Her pink dress and his black blazer were entwined on the floor like a stick of liquorice. Elizabeth lay on her back, heart rate still raised, feeling the gentle aftershocks of peak pleasure. Norman kissed her on the shoulder, and watched her watching the ceiling. He was too big for the university's single bed, even without her in it.

Your hair's so shiny,

his voice was small, and innocent.

She smiled as she surrendered to sleepiness, and then the thought crept to her, slowly at first, until it hung fully formed in her mind,

and she turned to ask,

You do know this isn't my real hair, right?

What?

It's a weave.

It's a what?

Norman clonked his elbow on the wall as he adjusted himself to sit up.

A weave. It's extensions.

He stared at her hair, the hair, which lay across the pillow.

Really? Have you always had it?

Since I've known you, yeah. I got this one re-sewn two weeks ago.

Sewn!

He clonked his elbow again.

Yeah, they're sewn in.

Into what?

Into my hair.

So where's, what's your hair?

It's braided underneath.

He drove a clumsy hand in towards her scalp and she snapped away, but, defiant, he didn't withdraw completely. He cupped the top of her head, then kissed it.

I want to see your real hair.

Elizabeth was so excited walking to class that she trotted every fifth step. She kept her hands in her pockets, out of the late winter chill, until she reached the lecture hall entrance. It was more of a classroom than a hall, as only a handful of students had opted for the Marxism module. But Richie and Shravya had, and that was all that mattered. They were already seated when she arrived. Shravya was cradling a thermos of tea.

Oh hey,

Elizabeth stood by their desk, and whipped off her beanie hat.

No WAY! The Big Chop!

Richie gasped.

Elizabeth!

Shravya looked like she was welling up.

You look amazing!

Elizabeth ran a hand over her tight coils, barely a centimetre in height, and playfully posed from side to side.

Their other classmates, all six of them, joined in with nods and smiles and hesitant compliments.

Thank you, thank you,

she sat down.

May I?

Richie asked.

You may.

He caressed her short hair.

Eurgh, so fresh, I love it.

Shravya rested her chin in her hands.

What inspired you?

she asked, looking adoringly at her friend,

As did everyone else. Those who usually tried to steal glances at her rejoiced in this opportunity to stare openly, to be a part of the conversation, twisting on their chairs for full, flagrant viewing.

Well, I was chatting with Norman and realised, I've been relaxing my hair since forever, and then weaves, and always long and straight, and subconsciously toeing the patriarchal line, and he suggested I go natural, and he loves it, and I love it, and, yeah.

She ran both hands over her head, beaming, unable to get enough.

Richie touched his heart.

I love that.

Shravya squeezed Elizabeth's hand. It was still warm from the flask.

I don't know but,

a new voice chimed in,

and like, you look amazing,

Katie always looked like she had a common cold, pale and clammy.

But like, I don't know but, isn't it just swapping a society of white men's opinions for the opinion of one white man?

Her sickly skin flushed.

The sixteen eyes stared a little harder.

You're right,

Elizabeth said,

you don't know.

ROBYN. 2007.

Janet had not enjoyed Parents Evening as a teacher. From her very first one, it had become apparent that what she'd assumed would be her opportunity for revenge and a chance to incriminate the ill-behaved was actually an occasion for her own performance to be scrutinised and asked *but WHY had Rikard been ALLOWED to go all term without turning in a single piece of homework?* This reversed assessment only worsened throughout her career, as the inflation rate of children's self-entitlement rocketed and the market's valuation of teachers diminished.

But here she sat on the other side for the first time, finally in control of gradation.

And she's really been getting to grips with the module content this term, I think in the mock exam you scored a,

the chemistry teacher rifled through leaves of paper,

a D, so that's, well that's – it's a foundation paper obviously, so remember the top grade is a C,

Janet nodded vigorously, trying to establish their educator mutuality.

And overall class participation we've seen a real improvement, too, you know, she's there, safety goggles on, ready to go, fully showing up to class, much more than last term. Perhaps it just took her a while to settle in, it can be –

Robyn looked around the sports hall, which was dotted with pop-up tables. It looked uncharacteristically rigid, much like the PE staff themselves, who were half-dressed in cheap suits. The two sets of fire doors were open, allowing a breeze to ruffle through the stuffy room. Early spring was rearing its head with certainty.

In each pocket of the desk patchwork sat a parent, or two, and their child. The clarity with which features were watered down in children was a marvel. Each pupil was drawn like an ode to the original, the essence was always there, with varying degrees of artistic interpretation. And in a way it infantilised the adults. These stretched out, sadder versions of their offspring looked to Robyn like overgrown children who'd got stuck playing dress-up and long forgotten the enjoyment of it. Overlapping conversations rose to the rafters, gathering amongst the forgotten basketballs.

Thanks so much, yes, yes, I'll make sure she does.

Janet was up, shaking the hand of Mrs. Thurlow in another act of role play. They moved onto Maths, then History, then PE, then one teacher who Robyn couldn't be sure if she'd ever actually met before, then English, then another Science teacher, all of them talking of *progress.* English and PE revelled in it, as if they'd paved the way for this *progression.* Maths mentioned it timidly, as if he might scare it away. History seemed almost annoyed by it.

Robyn and Janet edged their way to the sports hall exit, swerving clumps of chattering parents, who stood with mortified teens idle at their sides. Just as they reached the door, they were stopped by Ms Broadbridge, who opened her lipsticked mouth wide as if she couldn't BELIEVE the chances of bumping into them here.

Yeah, yeah, ok love,

Ms Broadbridge finished her conversation with a colleague, and turned her attention fully to them.

Well, hello!

Janet had never met her before and yet she felt a blushing pride at this faux recognition.

How's it going? You all done?

Broadbridge nodded, with her eyes and mouth open so wide that Janet couldn't help but nod along. A criminal would be coerced into a plea by this woman's assurance, surely.

Aww good good good,

she clutched the hefty collection of keys that hung from the lanyard around her neck.

And all good, I'm sure. I can't tell you,

she put a hand on Robyn's shoulder,

how much progress we've seen, haven't we?

Few little hiccups at the start,

she shook her shoulder now,

but we got there. You've settled right in. And I shouldn't say this, but,

she lowered to a stage whisper,

you've been talk of the staffroom,

everyone's been so impressed.

She was close enough that Robyn could smell the coffee, or smoke, or both, on her breath. She could see the threads of grey sewn into her harsh centre parting.

Uh ah yes ah uh huh,

Janet elaborated.

Good girl,

Broadbridge added an overzealous wink to the final shoulder squeeze.

Janet and Robyn crossed the school car park. The evening sky was at that crossover light when headlamps are lit at the driver's discretion.

Robyn, I just want to say,

the thighs of Janet's trouser suit chaffed together.

I'm really proud of you.

Swish-swish, swish-swish.

Well done.

Swish-swish.

Robyn had not actively paid more attention in class over the previous few months, nor had she applied herself better, or had more fun, or made a single friend. But she'd also not punched anyone, in or out of a ring. So presumably, this was the *progress* they were speaking of.

Shall we pick up some treats on the way home?

Janet almost skipped with giddiness.

Yeah,

please.

Robyn watched a plane score across the sky as she waited on the sloped doorstep. Its powdery trail was the only cloud in the blue expanse.

Hi, Robyn, sorry,

Sarah's hairline was dampened with sweat. The inner edges of her glasses steamed up.

Erm, I was thinking,

Robyn would have bulldozed past this awkward opening had Sarah not blocked the doorway with her wheelchair.

maybe we should, we could, it's such a nice day out, maybe we could go to the park instead? If you'd like that, if you – I know we'll be in public, so of course, not if you don't want, it's your privacy but –

Robyn squinted at the evaporating white line.

Ok.

Great, let me just –

Sarah disappeared back into the house.

They sauntered down the residential street. Baby plane trees lined the way, casting shadowed stepping stones along their path. Sometimes mischievous roots wormed up to the surface and Sarah's wheels juddered over uneven blocks. They spoke little as they eyed the array of front gardens. Along the stretch of terraced houses, the identical rectangles out front were blank pages on which the homes' forewords were written. Each with its own vocabulary as precursors to the stories that lay within: Hanging baskets and pungent geraniums in plastic tubs. A home for the dustbins. Suave black and white mosaic paving and wrought iron railings. A rusted bike. An overgrown, out of place, palm tree that tickled both adjacent neighbours. Immaculately pruned lavender bushes, which would not bloom for weeks yet. A junk yard (or a victim of fly tipping).

Like all domino runs, the blank tiles with their individual markings came to an abrupt end. The women turned down a smaller street, with larger houses. Tucked at the far end was a pedestrian entrance to the park. Sarah squeaked open the black metal gate and began to heave herself up the unwelcoming incline.

Without a word, Robyn began to push Sarah.

Neither her body, nor breath, thought much of the effort. Instead, she looked around at the park that began to unfold before them: empty goalposts that stuck out like white staples, the runner's trail that meandered around the perimeter, the colourful thin lines of a playground in the distance. As the hill evened out, and the whole park came into view, Robyn kept a grip on the handles of the wheelchair.

Sarah lay her hands in her lap, purposefully.

I can't believe how warm it is. It's only March.

Groups of boys were playing football on the green, shirts versus skins. The adolescents who mistook a lack of body fat for having a muscular physique had been quick to elect themselves onto the shirtless side. A child on a bike with stabilisers overtook Robyn and Sarah, wobbling across the uneven pathway. There was an air of frivolity across the park. Shared between strangers in a passing smile, in the extended patience holding gates open, in the way a teen boy rushed to hand back a toddler's dropped dummy. The gratitude for this glimpse of summer, gifted months early, was palpable.

Sarah knew well enough that this was counselling. This was therapy. She did not need to ask Robyn about her day, or her feelings. This simple shared experience was more telling, more healing than –

Did you have a nice day?

The wheelchair tyres buzzed.

Erm, yes, I did, thank you. It was, it was, yes it was nice, thank you. Did you?

Yeah,

Robyn kept them moving at a steady pace.

Good. Lovely sunshine.

They reached the far side of the park, where the trail ran close enough to the boundary fencing that children could be heard playing in the estate on the other side. The shade on this part of the path was denser, from the mature horse chestnuts that towered above. Even without yet fully blossoming, they created a thick canopy, and the air below was cool, untouched by the day's warmth.

It was the day he died, or, or, came back to life. Came back to life, I think. Maybe both. That's why there's a couple days of celebration, I suppose.

Why do we celebrate if he died?

Well, yes that is a good point. Maybe it's more celebrating his sacrifices, and things.

So why is there a rabbit?

They were pulled from their dissection of Easter by a loud laugh up ahead. The type of laugh that is twinged with mania, that's less reactive and more of a statement in itself. Three teens sat on a bench in the darkest part of the shaded path. Two boys, in white shirts, blazers stuffed into the backpacks by their feet, and a girl, who wore hers. The same cheap blue blazer that Robyn had worn earlier that day. One of the white shirts angled himself so closely to the blazered girl without any perception of the desperation in his body language.

The two groups – Robyn and Sarah, and the flirting teens – were so close to sailing past one another without noticing. But at the last moment, Robyn and Jake Gresham clocked each other.

The three school mates hushed as she walked by with her councillor. Robyn wasn't aware of the mortification that this brief interaction was supposed to bring. She wasn't aware that although she may pass them many times in a corridor during the thirty hours a week they spent confined to the same campus, that this was different. That in this situation, in the outside world, it was most natural to be filled with a holistic depletion in self-esteem, and far less natural to be distracted by a scampering squirrel before the onlookers had even erupted into flagrant whispers.

Robyn watched the squirrel scale a tree with enviable agility. The pathway curved back into the sun as they entered the return half of the large park loop. The central green was flecked with more spots of spontaneous revellers now. Office workers using suit jackets as makeshift picnic blankets, wiggling their toes free from leather cages. Clusters of friends encircling a panic-bought collection of crisp packets and cold meats. Lone relaxers reclining with headphones in, prolonging the time spent outside their airless flats.

Bill would like this park,

Robyn commented as they passed a Border Collie.

I like this park.

And,

just as a young lover barely dares breathe when their crush rests a head on their shoulder,

just as a flatmate removes a utilities bill from a pile of birthday cards,

just as Sarah did not offer to take over the pushing of her own wheels,

she did not respond to this revelation, for fear of ruining the moment. Instead, she let the sunshine seep into her bones and sat a little heavier in her chair.

By Monday, the city had awoken from its fever. Rain dampened all memories of the heat. As one wakes from a tumultuous night's sleep, collectively they asked, *did I imagine it?* At lunch time, pupils filled the assembly hall with gossip and litter. They sat in groups in the sports hall, each circle a conscious political division. They spilled into corridors and doorways and off-limit classrooms.

Robyn sat in the corner of the canteen. She watched puddles forming on the courtyard outside until the windows became too fogged up with the hot breath of those she was tuning out. Robyn sat at the far end of this long table every break time, every lunchtime. Today, as crowds sheltered from the weather, each seat in the canteen was precious and she was forced to share it with a group of Year Seven girls,

Nooo, Mollllly-ahh!

One snatched a yoghurt pot back from a friend.

Robyn had long finished her tuna and sweetcorn packet sandwich when the first bell rang out. She obediently sloped to clear away her tray. In a questionable spot, next to the overflowing bins and used tray rack, sat Jake Gresham and friends. The twelve-strong group, of boys and girls, still had tupperwares and pasta pots spread across the table with no hint of moving. As others began to pack up belongings, they were determinedly brazen in their statement that their lives were not dictated by a bell. They would stand their ground until the teacher on lunch duty shuffled them along, chuckling, as if he were in on the joke. Jake was sat on the table, seeking kinghood in the monarchy of rebels. He flicked his eyes towards Robyn.

Oi, oi,   OI,

he demanded the attention of a friend, slapping him on the shoulder.

Who am I?

He hopped down from the table and into a vacant chair.

Jake began a mime. He kept an eye on Robyn as he entertained his audience.

JaAAke,

one girl softly protested against his derogatory charade.

My nan's in a wheelchair, actually, Jake,

said another, without conviction.

Robyn felt the rush of heat that had evaded her for months.

She envisioned herself leaving the canteen, lining up outside maths, writing in her graphed workbook,

but she couldn't move.

She couldn't look away from Jake. The laughs of his companions pierced through the general noise and echoed inside her head. Her feet stayed rooted. He multiplied the vulgarity, intensified the stakes.

A small student bumped into her. It was all the nudge she needed to fly into action.

Mr Mansford was finishing an apple when the familiar feeling broke out. The contrasting rise of both silence and sound, stillness and scuffle. The slurry of blazers leaving the canteen slowed, as they were drawn towards something happening in a far corner, important enough to be a reasonable excuse for tardiness. Mansford would let it play out for a second, allow the feral young to be briefly unleashed before he'd rein them in. It happened every few days, and in truth, he didn't mind the paperwork. It was often the highlight of his banal week, listening to the teenage tensions that had boiled over into the physical. The previous Thursday, Shelley Andrews had yanked Tara Rowan's clip-in extensions and spat in her eye for sitting on her boyfriend's lap on the sports field. On the Tuesday, Jude Ferrari threw wayward punches in Craig Cox's direction, because he'd stolen and sold his bicycle.

But then Mr Mansford felt a shift.

The chorus at the back of the canteen simmered, and clearer, singular shrieks rang out. He binned his apple core and hastened over. The second red flag came in the way the kids cleared to let him through.

The third was a spread of blood that he'd never seen before.

Robyn thought the clock must be new.

Tick,

tock.

Tick,

tock.

She'd never noticed it fill the silences before.

Tick,

tock,

Tick,

tock,

Tick –

I don't understand Robyn. I thought we were making such progress.

Sarah said her name, but she wasn't really talking to her. There were no biscuits on the table today. Robyn's dry mouth could use a squash, but she didn't ask.

Tick,

tock.

Sarah had not looked directly at Robyn since she'd arrived, but Robyn could see she'd been crying. Robyn could see the giveaway red, even from behind the spectacles.

Sarah took a deep inhale, and Robyn could hear the air stick against her blocked nostrils.

The school informed me you'll be going to a secure home until things progress.

Robyn wasn't aware of this. The police had terminated their questioning at 17:36 the previous evening and no one had spoken to her since. Janet, who'd said minimal as her accompanying adult, had said nothing at all on the drive home. Or throughout the evening, until she'd gone to bed, taking Bill with her and locking the bedroom door. This morning she'd left a note:

Gone into the school. Will be back to take you to Sarah.

Again, she'd taken Bill with her.

From my understanding, Jake's parents are being extremely forgiving. They're not taking any action against the school, so they might – well, we'll have to wait and see. They just want their little boy to get better, understandably.

He's not little,
it was the first thing Robyn had said all day and her voice sounded faraway.

Robyn, please, do not make this – he is in hospital. This is very, very serious. You have to take responsibility for your actions here. Do you understand the severity of what you've done?

The flood of emotions was too much for Sarah's dam of professionalism to withstand.

You have seriously injured another human being, and even if – lets hope he makes a full recovery – but even still, for your own life, the repercussions are going to be a lot. If it gets taken to court, that could mean going to some sort of institute, and on your criminal record forever, and even if it doesn't, at the very least it means a new school, another new start, no more of these sessions,

Robyn jolted,
What? Why?

Because, Robyn, this is a school-provided service. No school, no counselling,

Sarah sagged.

I just don't understand where it came from, why all of a sudden – what happened?

Her bloodshot eyes pleaded with Robyn's.

Robyn covered her mouth with her fist.

What made you that angry?

She shrugged.

He was being annoying.
The words were muffled.

Sarah exhaled, this time through her mouth, loud and telling.

I can still come and see you.

Not if you're under a court order, or – or not if your new guardian doesn't want to.

That's not fair.
The clock sound had disappeared.

Well, you're paying the price for your actions, Robyn. It's not fair what you did to Jake, is it?

Robyn felt her cheeks flush. Her arms began to tingle in a way that demanded movement. She clenched and unclenched her fists trying to rid the sensation.

Ok, ok, let's cool off,

Sarah sighed again.

I'm going to make a cup of tea, then I'm going to come back and we will sort this out.

Sarah returned with a tea and a squash, having read Robyn's mind. She downed it in one. Seagulls squawked outside, navigating where to call home in this ever-changing season.

I'm sorry, Robyn, for losing my temper. It just made me so sad to hear the news. I really thought you were in a happier place and it made me question whether I am the right person to be helping you.

Sarah spoke more freely, as one does once emotion has released its tight grip and there's no fear of tears interrupting.

But of course, whatever happens, if you want me to be there for you, if you feel like this is beneficial, then I will be. We will work it out with whoever.

Robyn felt a different heat in her chest. A smoother, calmer warmth. The type she felt when Bill curled up in her lap, or when she heard rain at night on her bedroom window. She leaned back fully into the chair, and was hugged by musty feathers.

We will work it out,

Sarah affirmed to herself.

Things are going to be a little different, anyway, for a while,

she set her tea down.

As I actually have my own news.

Robyn thought she could fall asleep in this chair, if she looped her legs over one side. She threaded her fingers through a material rip in the seat pad. If only it were big enough to tuck her legs into. She could stay here forever.

I'm actually,   well,   becoming a mother I suppose.

I'm going to have a little boy.

Robyn bolted upright and stared at Sarah's stomach.

I'm adopting. I'm in the process of adopting. We're nearly there, nearly finalised. His name is Rory and I'm really excited and hopefully he is, too, and, and so yeah, my life is going to be a little topsy turvy too, and I'll be taking some time off, but it shouldn't affect us, I'll make sure that we –

Robyn stood up. Her legs felt like empty cases.

Robyn?

She left the room without stopping to absorb the scent of artificial lavender for the last time. Or to run her eyes once more over the memorised spines of psychology books. Or to squeeze a soft toy in her palm, not because she was a child, but because she liked its velvet skin against hers. She didn't pause to bask in the safety or tranquility for the last time.

Instead, she fled from the house and ran along the familiar pavements that she knew by heart from the passenger window. She ran until the buildings grew greyer and less inviting, and she kept running to find the fire exit and the endless spiral of stairs.

She ran
        down
    and
        down
    and
        down.

Jesus fucking christ. Look who's back.

ELIZABETH. 2011.

The tinkling of glasses rippled across the castle ruin, in fizzy, golden waves, as Norman stood up and straightened the tails of his suit jacket. *NO PRESSURE!* came the predictable heckle, and more waves, of fizzy, golden laughter.

Norman bowed his head, humbly defeated already. He adjusted the knot of his tie, waiting for the audience to simmer and willing them on at the same time.

Yes, if you'll all bear with me, this is completely new to me.

More laughs, the kind that erupt automatically from expectation and excitement.

No but it's true. Now I actually have to read my own words, I've become acutely aware how flippantly I've been writing floccinaucinihilipilification.

Laughs.

Writing speeches for others is far easier. Far, far easier. And not least because, as those of you in the trusted circle will know, I'm in fact blessed with a fantastic ghost writer, in my WIFE,

Cheers.

But, unfortunately, I couldn't consult her on this one, so we'll see how I get on. Before we do turn our attention to my goddess of a new wife, if I can pull your focus, and my own focus, for a few moments longer, there are some people royally deserving of a raucous round of applause.

Elizabeth felt her ribcage relax a little, as much as it could against the structured bodice of her silk dress.

She could stand the warmth of the spotlight how an actor can, once they've adorned their character. But a wedding, for all its rehearsals and costumes and scripts, felt far more exposing. There were no wings in which to escape the applause, because she did want to escape it. For even compliments were still unsolicited critiques. She'd not asked to be publicly lauded. She'd not asked for any of this at all.

And Blowfish, for a man who missed a flight because he mis-timed a shit, sorry Mémé, how you can miraculously pull such spectacular organisation out of your arse is beyond me, but I'm eternally grateful for it. The organisation, not your arse. Well.

A gentle breeze whispered through the glassless window behind her and rustled along their living ceiling of lush vines. She let it kiss the back of her neck, but no one else appeared to notice its touch.

Nor could they hear the sea lapping against the cliffside far below, or smell the dust on the eight-hundred-year-old bricks that encased them. Only Elizabeth.

She looked around the white tables that were wedged down upon the yielding grass. She searched only with her eyes, stealing quick glances, so no guests and no photographs would see anything beyond a wife looking up at her husband. A crowd of the familiar, not familial. Between a sea of heads and shoulders she caught glimpses of Shravya with her husband, and Richie with his boyfriend at a far table. She thought briefly of Danni. Would she have slipped into this setting with her open spirit, unashamed and authentic? Or would she have recognised when the time came to no longer support this union. Would she have made a stand, just as she had done so often for others? Elizabeth felt her eyes well up, as they had so easily all day, covered by the canopy of celebration.

We're absurdly fortunate to have you, we love you, I love you, thank you so much, Mum and Dad.

Clapping and stomping bought her attention back.

Norman's mother was crying, mouth fully downturned, no attempt at elegance, and his father was crying, too, in a fashion common to many men, where no tears are visible and yet they plug their tear ducts and scrunch their face as if they were in full flow. They were not sat at the top table, for there wasn't a top table. Norman had immediately rebuffed the idea to the wedding planner, without explaining that Elizabeth had no one to seat at such a table, and she had been filled with a nostalgic flush of love for him. Then later, when he had quietly whispered, *it'll just be us up there*, she'd asked herself how she could have overvalued his intentions, after all these years. Elizabeth was still watching his mother wipe tears with the back of her hand,

–me to my WIFE,

Cheers.

I don't think I'm ever going to tire of that, and honestly, it's exactly what my heart does every time I think about how this spectacular woman is going to be by my side for the rest of my life.

Norman looked down at her.

Sorry,

he paused.

And this woman, this woman deserves all the woos in the world.

Her eyes filled again. She tried not to swallow, or breathe, not to become his mother.

When I met Elizabeth, all those billions of years ago, I remember being struck by what an anomaly she was, and not just because she didn't own a pair of wellies, but because she was this fully formed, well-rounded human being, amongst a gaggle of weedy, acne-ridden teens who thought cooking spaghetti was the height of domestication. There she was, fiercely strong, delicately graceful, deeply caring, undeniably fuckably cool, and don't get me started on the supermodel packaging she came in, and I was floored. I was awestruck, intimidated, in love all at once, and I've still not got over it. I've still not got over you. Every single day, I am bowled over by the wholeness of your being, by how you handle yourself and how you care for those around you. Every single day, I am a proud witness to your boldness and brightness. Every single day, I am grateful to be a part of your world. I am grateful to live in your world, a sphere that makes any other life seem muted and colourless. I feel like we've lived a life together already, and if the past decade is anything to go by, in which you have educated me and encouraged me to be a better man, I might just about be your worthy equal by the time we're eighty. So, my beautiful, unbelievable wife,

he hyped up the cheers, and cheered along with them, and raised his glass,

here's to you, I love you.

She did not reach for his hand beneath the applause, as she had spent a life learning not to reach for anyone.

For years, she had shunned the institution of marriage, a plausible cover story for someone who dismissed most of society's constructs, knowing full well it was not marriage that she didn't believe in.

It was him.

She couldn't pinpoint when she had stopped believing in Norman because she'd hidden the truth from herself for so long, desperate not to topple the idea that she was finally, truly loved. Even as she had cut her hair and stopped smoking and traded friends, she'd remained the hypnotist's willing subject. She wanted to be fooled. Only someone, buried deep within the shell she lived in, was still awake, and had resisted being tied to him forever. But when he had eventually proposed, disregarding her wishes and her life plan, as he always had done, it had been her money, her social life, her home, everything in her existence, who had got down on one knee and asked her to commit.

He was the security blanket she knew she had outgrown, and yet, when Norman reached for her hand beneath the cheers, despite herself, she held on to it so tightly.

Only after they had made love that night, consummating their marriage in the darkness, did the tears that had threatened all day, finally fall, sloping silently across the bridge of her nose.

Elizabeth didn't feel pregnant.

She'd not had a period on her pill for years, so there was no red flag, or lack-of-red flag, and she now contested the claims that *you just know.*

Pregnancy denial is more common than you think,
Dr Medlock had a gentle South African accent.
I'm not fucking denying anything,
she was embarrassed that she'd cursed,
I'm just not fucking pregnant,
but didn't want to let on.
I mean,
Medlock shook a pot of urine,
you are.
Well, that's not fucking mine. You can do it again –
Ok, let's do it again,
I'm not fucking doing it again.
Elizabeth snatched her leather jacket from the chair, knocking over a leaflet display as she left.

For each one of the following 106 days, Elizabeth thought of her mother. She grew enlightened and understanding of how it would be possible to not love your own child. She dreaded the postpartum depression, certain it would debilitate her, since she had lived so many years on the cusp of everyday depression.

But on the 107th day, the thought finally disappeared. She experienced something closer to postpartum euphoria, in which her world was doused in a dazzling light.

And Layla, only minutes old, taught her what love felt like.

THE LAKE.

Anna was fully awake by the time light creeped into the tent. The type of cool blue light that seems bright compared to darkness and dim compared to daylight; that only makes itself known to the few who witness the sliver of dawn in a day. Even the birds were not privy to it yet this morning.

Anna lay in the silence. The absence of sound would have been all encompassing, thick enough to question reality, solid enough to give the sensation of drowning in air, had it not been broken only by the gentle breaths of her sleeping roommates.

It had been a while since she'd stayed in this tent, which slept six, the most of all the tents despite being the smallest by a slim margin. Though she encouraged, near insisted, upon moving beds and bedrooms regularly to prevent any ownership of spaces arising, Anna was starting to find the constant shifting less invigorating and refreshing, and more of an upheaval. She felt an inkling of desire to bed down somewhere familiar; to know what creeks of the homemade bed-frame to expect, and not be startled awake as a reminder. She'd chosen to stay in this one last night, since it was the closest to the bell tent and her new guests.

Everyone who arrived at the camp, arrived with their own story to tell, which might unfold in time, or quietly dissolve as they brush off past lives. Anna was not concerned with unearthing what had shaped someone, only with how she could best offer them solace now. How she could lighten the heaviness in their step. And yet, something about Robyn and Layla ignited a gluttonous intrigue. Perhaps it was their own apathy that sparked it in Anna instead. She wanted to listen to them, swaddle them, heal them. She wanted them to need her, like they needed each other.

Anna slid from the bed, trying to glide out in one controlled motion so as not to disturb Freddie, who slept on the other side. She quietly slipped from the tent, slinking under the entrance flap, without a pause or glance back or even a breath, until she reached the grass. Here she stood, allowing her bare feet to lap up the cool dew. She scrunched her toes to feel the spongy earth beneath her. The lake sat as still as a painting, but for the mist that whispered above its surface. Goosebumps shimmied across her arms, as she stood in her calf-length summer nightdress. She inhaled deeply, feeling her rib cage fully expand and the misty air reach the depths of her lungs, and she smiled, at the thought of this secret moment between her and the lake.

Then, as if to correct her, a blackbird began to call, and she smiled even wider.

Anna crept past the bell tent. Though she did not permit herself to stop completely, her ears strained for any hint of talking or movement from within. Disappointed, she continued on. But as she trod carefully through the strip of woodland and arrived at the main building, her ears still pined back towards their tent.

On occasion, in these brief moments where she stood alone in the kitchen, or when it was a hive activity playing host to a dozen women buzzing around, Anna experienced a ruffle of pride. The structure they had built over twenty years ago, equipped with only basic tools and even more basic knowledge, not only still stood, but still functioned with purpose, with life.

It had multiplied in its abilities and intricacies over time. What had started as a rudimentary shelter, clay plaster between oak pillars, now had counter tops made from wooden pallets and wall shelves just for display and a deep ceramic sink.

Anna dipped a saucepan into a barrel of fresh water, filling just enough for one cup, for no one else would want one at this hour. She found the embers of the wood stove still glowed amber from the night before, which called for pause: how early *is* it?

I made a cuppa about an hour ago.

Anna spun round so fast that the water slopped out of the pan.

Sorry, didn't mean to make you jump, dear. You were so in your own little world I didn't want to disturb you, but, alas, I did anyway.

Anna placed a hand on her racing heart.

V,

she panted,

I didn't see you there.

Violet gave a wicked chuckle. She was sat on the sofa, with mounds of material across her lap. Her grey hair fell about her face in every direction.

Sorry, dear,

she said, but she still chuckled.

Couldn't sleep?

Mmm,

Anna agreed, feeling a wave of tiredness. Perhaps she wasn't as awake as she thought. She refilled the saucepan, enough for both of them, and set it on the stove. Then began to feed the fire beneath.

What about you?

She asked, as she prodded the kindling.

I wanted to get these bits done for the ladies.

Violet was holding up a knitted jumper. The left sleeve was stopped around the elbow by a diamond of needles.

Aw, you didn't need to stay up to do that,

Anna walked over to the sofa.

Well, the bits I gave them yesterday were so tattered.

Violet inspected her own work.

Probably a bit warm for now, but with the cold weather around the corner, and they're both such tiny little things, I'm sure they feel the cold.

Well, we don't know if they'll be staying yet.

Violet lowered the jumper back to her lap,

No, I suppose not.

The renewed fire crackled softly from the other side of the room.

Oh, well, they'll need something more than what they came with, wherever they go,

and she began to tap the needles together, her fingers salsa dancing around one another.

Anna joined her on the sofa. She picked up a patchwork summer throw that had been reincarnated as a long-sleeved dress, evidently for Layla. Violet was the only woman older than Anna in the group, yet her spirit was impressively young. It almost made Anna feel fraudulent, to think of herself as a champion against how the world expected her to age, when in reality she wilted next to this woman. Violet had fled a suffocating marriage nearly twelve years ago, and settled in here with unrivalled ease. Within hours of her arrival, it had been impossible to imagine a time without her.

Have they talked much about their situation?

Anna gently folded the dress and placed it down.

No, and they might never. It's not for us to know, I suppose, she tried to sound at peace with idea, but Violet did not need to lift her head from her knitting to see through Anna's pretence. The quiet bubbling of water spilled into their foreground.

The women came in batches for breakfast once the sun had fully risen. Though there was no designated time for the morning meal, it was only natural that their body clocks were somewhat synced. The earliest risers would brew the lavender tea, press the juice, slice the bread, ready the jam, stir the oats. Most had been and eaten and gone, but Violet still made final stitches to her garments and Anna sat at the dining table, attempting to write the list she'd never gotten around to the day before. Delilah quietly washed up and Cynthia sat at the breakfast bar, which divided kitchen from living area, still sweating from her daily run.

Anna's concentration kept meandering away from her. She chased the tails of thoughts, and ended up running circles around her own brain, each time coming back to the blank page in front of her. And if she ever felt on the cusp of concentration, a bolt shot through her body, inexplicable nerves, that caused her to jump up and rearrange a shelf or pour another tea. She dotted the pencil on paper, staring out the window, across the courtyard.

Wan-me-to-shave-some-for,

Cynthia swallowed a mouthful of bread,

the others?

No, it's ok, my love,

Anna was snapped back into the room.

Delilah lifted a tea towel cloche on the sideboard next to her, revealing an array of reserved food.

Great,

Cynthia 'cheersed' another slice.

Maybe I should go and check on them,

Anna raised to the room the thought she'd be swallowing for hours. Violet lifted her eyebrows and Cynthia gave a *hm*, and it was all the encouragement Anna needed.

The community had naturally found a balance between having a shared experience and respecting privacy. They all knew each other's rhythms as well as they knew their own. They were as accustomed to the ebb and flow of each other as the shore is to the tide. It was a long time since Anna had felt unsure of another's boundaries. It was a long time since Anna had felt compelled to knock on a tent door.

She gave a feeble tap on the canvas, and peeled it open.

Layla gently shook Robyn, and they sat up in unison.

Sorry to wake you, I thought you might want some breakfast.

Did the two bleary faces showed a glimmer of disappointment that she'd not brought it with her?

It's up in the house. Take your time.

Robyn and Layla peeled themselves out of bed in synchronisation. They too knew each other's rhythms.

Maria's eyes lit up as Anna entered the kitchen with the new guests. She left the bunch of flowers she was arranging and approached them immediately.

Good morning!

How did you sleep?

Well, thank you,

Layla replied, impeccably.

Good! I'm glad. And,

Maria reigned in her beaming smile a touch,

how are you both feeling?

Fine, thank you.

Maria brushed a gentle hand across Layla's cheek.

Good,

she whispered,

once again caught off guard by a rising choke.

Breakfast!

Anna intervened.

Robyn and Layla sat next to each other on one of the tree trunk pews. It was too heavy to move, so they had to awkwardly manoeuvre their skinny legs under the table. Anna brought over a tray of breakfast items, only slightly less extravagant than the one they'd had delivered to bed the day before. There were no figs today. Delilah placed down two earthenware plates, hand-painted with abstract swirls of colour.

There's porridge too, if you'd rather,

Anna offered.

But they were already slathering jam across the squidgy bread.

What would you like to drink, water or juice, or tea?

Juice, please.

Layla bowed her head.

Juice,

please.

Cynthia still sat at the bar, blowing on hot tea, eying the diners over her mug, and Violet sat in the darkened corner frantically racing to the woollen finish line. Maria completed the posey, placed it on the centre of the table, then slid in next to Layla. Delilah had slipped from the room, and Anna flustered about with imaginary tasks.

Layla gently pushed her empty plate away from her an inch. She watched her bulging belly panting up and down. Then her eyes wandered across the room, taking in the rows of handblown glasses lined up on open shelves, and the mis-matching mosaic tiles surrounding the sink, and the colourful throws strewn across chairs.

This is a nice campsite,

she said quietly to herself. Perhaps to Maria, too.

You like it?

Yeah, me too.

Layla nodded, a little lost in thought.

I was meant to go camping in the summer holidays,

but then we stayed at Robyn's instead.

Robyn, who had been watching Layla, turned her eyes back to her own plate.

Oh really?

Maria asked calmly.

A saucepan lid crashed to the ground, as Anna fumbled to pick it up.

Well, you get to go camping now!

Layla gave a polite smile.

Although only for a couple more nights, because then weeee take the tents down and pack them away annnd come and sleep up here.

But that's not camping?

Maria smiled.

True. But we live here, Layla.

Here?

Layla was perplexed.

As was Robyn.

Anna gripped the saucepan tightly so as not to let it slip under the shock that Robyn had displayed a readable emotion for the first time since arriving. The young woman was not entirely impassive.

Yes,

Maria laughed.

We all do.

All of you? But,

Layla wrinkled her brows,

determining which of the many, many questions she should ask first.

Where do you go to work?

Cynthia failed to suppress a laugh, and Layla blushed. Maria couldn't help but reach out and stroke Layla's back, which was now dressed in an Indian tunic. It drowned her tiny body, but the kurti, which had belonged to Geeta, who had lived with them for three years in her late teens, was the smallest item of clothing they could find. Robyn waited for Maria to answer the reasonable question.

Weee go to work here,

Maria signalled with her slender fingers.

But you're a doctor?

Robyn cut through.

I trained as a doctor, yes, ermm, but I stopped a long time ago.

When weeee moved here.

Layla was on the cusp of understanding, when Robyn asked,
So what do you do here?

Wellll, all sorts. We have to farm the land annd grow our food annd build and make and continue living here.

Maria saw her answer deepen the furrows on their faces.

I suppose that's what's so good about living here. We don't need jobs, because we don't need money.

Robyn slouched, absorbing the idea with seeming approval.

So you get free time all the time?

That's cool,

Layla ruminated on the idea, too.

We can give you a tour of the site, show you all the things we do,
Anna could no longer watch from the wings.

The women determined they were well enough and intrigued enough to agree to a tour. Cynthia offered to clear away their empty dishes, an unspoken apology to Layla, but before they left, Violet finally stood up from her needlework post.

Here, ladies,

her arms were full of garments.

Here's a few extra pieces in case you want to change.

Robyn unconsciously itched around the neckline of the hemp t-shirt she'd been gifted the day before. She took the bundle from Violet with a muttered *thanks*, but shook her head at the second-hand sandals, staying true to her flat-soled trainers that looked worn beyond their years. Violet did not drift off to bed to finally rest, but instead to the lake for a refreshing swim.

The tour began in the courtyard. The space between the outbuildings was empty except for a small circular herb bed. Around the edges grew rosemary and thyme and sage and basil and dill, all invading each other's space, and in the middle was a statue of a woman with a bow slung across her.

Artemis. The huntress,

Anna said, catching Robyn gazing at the nude figurine.

Gail, who was here right from the start, was an excellent sculptor. She made that on our one-year anniversary of living here.

They both studied the figure, whose soft curves were moulded from hard stone. Moss gathered at her feet and she was dappled in dirt, but otherwise she was relatively pristine. When gifted the goddess, Anna had imagined how it would decay with time and become a mottled artefact, a chronicle of the length of their life here. And yet here she stood, outliving her creator with barely a dusting of age.

So you've seen the first thing we built, the main building,

Anna signalled behind them.

That's where we cook and eat and convene in the winter months, it's our main hub. There's also two bedrooms upstairs. They're mostly used as private rooms, if someone feels they need some privacy or alone time. Otherwise, all the other bedrooms, in these buildings, she gestured at two twin buildings,

are communal.

Anna lifted the stable door latch on the nearest bedroom building. Structurally, it closely resembled the main hub, made from oak and clay, only smaller in size. Robyn, Layla and Maria followed her over the threshold and were immediately in a bedroom. Three beds, one double, two singles, each immaculately made up with colourful quilts. They hadn't been slept in for weeks.

Like boarding,

Layla concluded what communal meant.

There's two more doubles upstairs,

Anna said before ushering them back outside.

That building's just the same,

she walked past the next building without stopping.

But with four singles downstairs. So all in all, we can sleep eighteen up here, twenty at a push. We're thirteen at the moment. In here,

Anna opened the door to a shorter, squatter outhouse,

is our store room.

The storeroom was perpetually cold. Not even the hottest of summers could penetrate these thick brick walls. Anna and Maria were so well adapted to the low light of the space that they knew the exact whereabouts of the potatoes and the fermenting goods with no need for any light at all. But to newcomers it was a cave: acquiring its treasures took courage and night-sight in equal measures. Robyn and Layla hung by the light of the door.

Kindling, oats, spare jugs and jars, it's all in here.

Stocked shelves ran away from them like an architect's drawing, perspective disappearing into the depths of the darkness.

If you see anything needs topping up just –

Anna stopped herself. This was not a settler's introduction.

I must,

she mumbled the nothingness as a coverup.

They all hurried back beneath the sun. The final building, and the second-longest standing, was a tetris of washing facilities. On the north side were two cubicles. The doors were decorated with feathers and shells and pebbles and finger-painted hearts, deceptively inviting for the faecal buckets that waited behind them. Anna once again found herself teetering on the unfamiliar edges of embarrassment. She chose to slap a hand on a decorated door and say, *loo,* rather than explain their dunny system. Then she led them inside the building through the courtyard-facing door. The floor was a mismatch of ceramic tiles, haphazardly grouted together. In the centre, a large cauldron of water sat over an unlit fire. Though the logs were arranged perfectly, ready to be lit at a moment's notice.

In there is where we do our laundry,

Anna stressed the correct pronoun, and pointed at the saloon shutters ahead. Through gaps above and below the outback-style doors came wafts of dried lavender pouches and water infused with rose petals.

And here's the showers.

Along the south wall, four empty sacks were strung from hooks, like dehydrated carcasses. Each had a small shower-head at the bottom, controlled by a valve. Anna dipped her hand in the cauldron, then flicked off the cold droplets.

It's been so hot the past few weeks, we haven't needed it, but usually this water is kept warm pretty constantly and scooped out to fill the shower bags or a tub for washing. Anything not used is put back in the pot. We try to conserve as much water as possible. I'll show you the rainwater butts dotted around the place that we use for waste water. Fresh stuff comes from the river, which is quite a task to transport so we try to be conservative,

with a small c.

Anna looked at Robyn and Layla and worried they were now expecting a small sea hidden within the grounds, so she forged on.

And out here,

she opened a door on the far wall, to the outside.

This is my favourite part of all,

Maria whispered to Layla and squeezed her little shoulder and saw a flash of the excitement that should be constant in a young child's eyes.

The backdoor opened straight onto a panel of brushwood fencing. The vertical twigs and branches, tightly packed together, gave nothing away of what lay behind. They stuck close to the fencing

as it curved

round

to reveal

a bath tub.

Copper in colour, it stood alone on the earth flooring. This nook felt transcendent. A jungle love letter slipped inside a provincial envelope. Artemis herself could have bathed here, beneath the treetop canvas, amid the birdsong soundtrack, finches unflinching at nature's second truest act.

Maria looked to Layla, hoping for a picture of enchantment,
but the child began to weep.
She tucked her chin to her chest,
trying to hide it,
as her shoulders shook up and down.

Maria and Anna froze.

Robyn was the last to notice. When she did, she silently slipped her hand into Layla's, and they stood there a while.

Come on,

she said eventually, and tugged Layla's hand, leading them back out the way they had come.

The tour continued through the grounds, inspecting the raised vegetable patches, and manicured rows of rich soil as Anna spoke of the forthcoming harvest, and dashing into the steaming greenhouses where they ate tomatoes from the vine, through the cool of the shaded forest, until they emerged back at the lakeside.

Tonight is our harvest festival,

Anna nodded towards the women piling high the foundations of a bonfire, in view of the trunk benches.

We eat and sing and dance and make the most of our last evening sleeping out here, it's great fun. It seems a shame to be packing up when the weather is still so warm,

she almost talked to herself.

But we always do it when the blackberries are ripe, or else the weather changes like,

she clicked her fingers,

and we miss all chance of a party.

Maria nodded alongside her,

And we can't miss a party! It's our favourite night. So fun that you're both here to see it!

She winced at her own insensitivity,

Of course, only if you feel up to it, you don't have to join us.

I know the harvest festival,
Layla confirmed.
but it wasn't a party at my school,
we only brought in baked beans.

Oh, I know the one,

Anna chuckled at a faint memory from childhood, a clip she didn't know she possessed.

Your party sounds more fun.
We like dancing,
Layla spoke with such oxymoronic solemnity, it drained the life from Anna and Maria.

Shall we sit down?

Anna had already begun crouching.

I think Betty was making apple juice. I will get us some glasses,

Maria excused herself, desperate to comfort, lighten, mend.

They sat on the grass. The silence that simmered between them went unnoticed. Each looked out at the body of water which sat still beneath the high sun.

Their eyes fixated; their minds less so.

But once Anna became aware of the silence it began to billow like clouds of dark smoke, choking her, yet willing her to say something.

I've just got to,

she stood up, brushing grass from her backside.

But neither of them looked at her. She started to leave when,

How do they all find you? All the people that live here.

Robyn looked up at Anna, shading her eyes from the sun.

Anna felt a familiar calm return.

The same way you found us.

The same way anyone finds anyone in life, by chance.

PART 2

2018.

ROBYN.

Ermmmmm and this one.
NO this – No, oh no, I don't know, sorry.
Erm, erm, erm – No, I'll go for the –
I'll go for the Kit-Kat. Nope, no, the Twirl. Is it too early?
Nope, I'll go for the Twirl, final answer.
I'll take the Twirl.   Love a Twirl.

Robyn scanned the chocolate bar.

Fuel?

Oh yes, duh, of course, erm, yes, pump number – number…

The small woman craned her neck.

Number four? That's mine, the Fiat.

There were no other cars on the forecourt.

So is that pump number four? Or number three?

Robyn selected the pump and took payment. She daren't ask if the woman needed a carrier bag.

Thank you for stopping and shopping with us today!

Eddie called after the indecisive woman.

Morning morning morning, Robyn! Another warm one today! I'm sweating already! If you need me, I'll be in the backroom fridge! No, I'm joking. But if you do need to cool off, feel free, my love.

Eddie was loading newspapers into the stand as they spoke. Robyn stretched her arms way up high until her body shuddered. She had worked full time at the station for nine and a half years, starting exactly a month after her seventeenth birthday, and each week, twice a week, she worked an early morning shift which still felt as unnatural to her senses as it had on her probation period. She slumped back onto the till and watched Eddie flit around the store.

Eddie's personality was so great it seemed to swell out of them. It burst forth through corkscrew curls, puffed up cheeks and a large bottom that merged their legs all the way down to the knee where they

split
like a
mermaid's tale.

Oh, bless Kate,

Eddie paused to fawn over a headline.

Robyn cracked her knuckles, then her neck in both directions.

Oh, Robyn! You know that gives me the heebyjeebies!

It was a routine act she couldn't remember the origins of.

Sorry,

she bit her thumbnail instead.

Oh! They've bought back Vanillaroma!

Eddie inhaled a car freshener through its packaging.

My favourite!

These few hours in a shift, when Really Early Morning sloped into Early Morning, were Robyn's favourite. The trickle of customers was slow enough and she and Eddie were the only ones working. She liked to watch Eddie potter about the station, arranging and rearranging, asking themselves in what way could they make the shop – nay, the world – a better place. Sometimes it was merely colour-coding the soft drinks. Eddie went above their duty to help drivers get from A to B and asked how else they could flavour someone's journey, with de-icer, an energy drink or a sleazy tabloid. It was what made them the youngest store manager of all petrol stations along the South Circular. Eddie had been hired four years after Robyn, but her responsibilities hadn't evolved since she'd been entrusted to dispense lottery tickets. Her salary had followed the slow incline of minimum wage and no more.

The shop door dinged open.

A construction worker approached the counter with heavy footsteps. His steel-toed boots rattled the shelves of confectionary.

Number two.

Fifty pounds, three pee.

He unfurled a loose banknote from his back pocket and slid it across the counter. His fingernails were stained with grime. Robyn waited.

Fucks sake,

he whispered and hunted again in the pocket for a coin. She fished out seven pence change from the till, and sent him on his merry way.

Have a great day, sir!

Fuck off.

Oh,

Eddie watched the man cross the forecourt,

Not a happy bunny!

But they'd already returned to restocking head-torches. Robyn and Eddie's physiques and dispositions were so opposed that they belonged on different spectrums, but together, the clashing creatures harmonised to the sweet tune of non-judgment. Though one arrived through apathy and the other through empathy, they met at the crossroad of the uncritical. Robyn was the only colleague to never have questioned why Eddie wore nail varnish, or sneer at the concept of having an 'Edie' day. And Eddie had never pried beyond what little personal information Robyn comfortably offered up or balked when a new chunk was cut into her mullet. They were as jarring and matching as their electric blue polo top uniforms. They'd not spent a second together off the petrol station premises and yet, they were the most unquestioning, supporting, loyal friends.

I think we should put those little fans next to the till, they say it's only going to get hotter! A heat wave! Don't we love the drama! What do you think? Little fans?

Yeah?

Yeah? Yeah, I think so!

Robyn lounged behind the till as Eddie went about their sprucing until rush hour bought the commuters streaming in, needing expensive petrol and cheap coffee. Linda, the eldest employee, turned up mid-morning to half help.

Robyn, love! Mr Peters is here, pump 2!

Eddie burst into the store, carrying a bag of barbecue coal from the outside display that changed year-round to match the seasonal demands. Robyn abandoned a customer, mid-payment, and sloped out onto the forecourt.

Eddie's branch was the only station in the region to not have received updated pumps in a recent overhaul that allowed a customer to preselect the value of fuel they would like to dispense. Despite being a head office oversight, Eddie liked to claim it was because they had no need for it, they had Robyn, who could rival any machine for precision reaction speeds.

Alright, Peter.

I I I I'd like fifteen pounds annnd twenty-eight pence please,

Mr Peters still wore an anorak despite the warm weather. He handed her the single key to his three-door. Robyn undid the petrol cap and began filling. She leant casually against the car, eyes on the counter that began to tick up.

Mr Peters kept his hands in his pockets. His skinny legs drowned in baggy jeans and he wore black boots, miles too big, that began to shuffle in excitement. His tongue poked at the remnants of cauliflower soup that clung to his grey, straggly beard. Robyn held the trigger all the way in, as petrol poured into double figures. Mr Peters was practically skipping as they thundered into the £12s, then £13s, with no sense of slowing down. Robyn still lounged nonchalantly against the dented car body as they approached the £14s and the rectangular numbers ticked faster than ever. For a long time, Mr Peters had shouted at her when they'd got close to the mark, rattled with concern that she'd forgotten the amount or was duping him out of pocket. But, not unlike Darrell, Mr Peters had learned to nearly trust, and fully utilise, her talents.

They reached £15 and her fingers began to lift,

ever so slightly.

She watched the pence racking up. Too self-assured for premature evacuation. She stayed still, as Peters lost his shit around her. Her heart rate was steady and breathing smooth.

CLICK.

She dropped the trigger.

Mr Peters peered at the counter with trepidation.

15.28.

He was astonished, as if he hadn't watched her hit the mark bang on, twice a week, for years.

At 12pm on the dot Robyn clocked off, leaving Linda fussing over a till transaction and a long line of impatient customers.

Coming! Coming! Coming!

Eddie called to the queue, skipping along and scooting behind the till.

See ya, Eddie,

Robyn called out from the shop doorway, over the heads of those waiting.

See you, my love! Good luck tonight!
Warmth bounced off the forecourt tarmac. She weaved between the thirsty cars, immune to the flammable stench.

No one saw Robyn come in through the fire exit. The gym was packed, as it always was on the third Friday of the month, and all eyes were on centre stage. The warm-up act. A legally-blind boy against Vlad, who was missing his left forearm. Darrell liked to ease in touring crowds with a spectacle exhibition match. It set the tone of the night: crude and unlawful. Audiences could settle in under a playful pretence, loading up on substances and loosening their wallets.

The two men fumbled around the boxing ring, off-balance and disorientated. Winston darted in between them, soaking up his role as referee. He'd polished his whistle for the event, despite knowing full well there would come a point that night when his authority would be overthrown and an organised match would dissipate into a platformed brawl. Robyn picked her way through the crowd, searching for Darrell. She was invisible between the low-lighting and high volume. Thankfully, the summer heat could not penetrate this far underground. For if it had, the fragile men and their boiling tempers would have cracked completely. But the air was still thick with bodily warmth, laden with egos, overflowing with ill-intent. It was suffocating.

Robyn was weaving through the third side of the in-the-round audience, when everyone leapt to their feet. Vlad's punch had only come into the opposition's focus centimetres before it knocked him out cold. Spectators cheered or jeered dependent on the fate of their stake. Activists against the legitimacy of such a fight suddenly sprung from the depths of their defeat. Robyn's path became even more obstructed as everyone scrambled to collect winnings and settle debts. Only then did Darrell appear, a relative stillness amongst the chaos. He stood, wiping his brow, talking to a man who looked almost classy in such a context, in a white t-shirt and belted trousers. Robyn appeared silently at Darrell's side.

Jesus fucking christ,

he jolted.

Alright, alright, Benny, I'll catch you later.

He shook the man's hand then shoved Robyn away from the crowd. They huddled in a quiet corner, as quiet as quiet could be in the raucous cavern.

You're on last.

Robyn slicked her dark hair back with clammy palms, gathering what of it would reach into a ponytail. Last meant that she had a tough fight ahead of her. Last meant that Darrell wanted the audience to be intoxicated enough to take one look at her, and her opponent, and bet their life savings against her.

He slid on some pads,

Czech guy. Big fucker. But you've got him.

Robyn flew light flurries at Darrell's hands, easing her body up to speed. Finally waking up, seventeen hours after getting out of bed. She wore her second uniform of the day: flat-soled trainers, football shorts and a sports bra. She only lived in one of these two outfits, she only lived as one of these two.

You know the drill, don't let him touch you in the first few, by the third or fourth round he'll be fucking knackered, then just, fucking bang it home.

Aesthetically, old age had only begun to tiptoe into Darrell's features. Grey sprinkles appeared when he left his stubble for a few days and delicate lines scratched at the crease of his eyes, like pencil sketches yet to be fixed. Perhaps he had not been as old as Robyn had assumed when she'd met him fourteen years ago. Or perhaps it was the consistency of the never-changing tracksuit that gave the illusion of frozen ageing. Or perhaps he had prematurely carved himself into a figure of upper-middle age back then, with the shaved head and yellowed teeth, and therefore had successfully plateaued ever since.

But in his character, a weariness was more evident.

It was difficult to assess which was the catalyst and which was the product in Darrell's withering enthusiasm and the slowing intake of young boxers. These days, those from families with an inch of integrity chose to train in above-board (and above-ground) centres, where there was funding and drinking water and the constant hunt for Olympic medallists. It was only the dregs who still chose Darrell's as their stop gap residence before a more permanent place behind bars. The same battered equipment got knocked around, the same nondescript stains got avoided, the same instructions got yelled with less rage. Darrell spent more hours in his office and less on the gym floor. Coach evolved from verb to noun, and the once-sporadic attempts to professionalise ceased completely. Whispers blamed Robyn for Darrell's downfall. Who continues to sift through the silt when they've found a fistful of gold?

But he could still pull a crowd on a Friday night. Darrell owned one of the last spots in the city where card machines didn't exist and laundered money could pass between unwashed hands. On these tertiary Fridays, the crowds came from distant lands beyond the M25 – Luton, Dover, Kettering. Away teams were brought in by brothers he hadn't seen in years. Those who were bound for life by unspeakable acts in the invincible days of youth. Blood bonds that could withstand years of silence then drop into town with a parade of thugs in tow for an evening's entertainment.

But yeah, don't let him get contact 'cause…

he glanced towards the ring.

The next two boxers were parading the perimeter, giving punters a chance to assess their nags.

Well, just fucking don't. Don't be an idiot.

Truthfully, Darrell had no more wisdom to impart. He'd totalled more contact hours with Robyn than he had with at least three of his five children, and she'd shucked and shined every possible pearl he had to offer.

But he was not redundant.

Darrell existed to rile or placate when necessary. It had taken Robyn years to find a gear besides fifth. To understand the purpose of warm-ups and the impracticality of going full throttle at every opportunity. Darrell coiled his prize snake in his basket, only bringing her out to new audiences who could still be duped. He could charm her with the right tunes, or make her attack with the whisper of an opponent's darkest deeds.

The crowds began to roar as the bell rang out. Robyn instinctively picked up the pace.

Alright, alright, rein it in.

She pulled her punches back to a steady patter, bouncing from one foot to another.

Six more men took to the stage, three of them leaving victorious, before it was Robyn's turn. Darrell had slipped back to the party, which had grown more boisterous with each fight. How contrastingly the crowd's passion multiplied as their awareness declined. Robyn retied her laces, pulling each rung on the frayed ladder tighter. She heard her name announced in the distance. Some cash blindly wagered on name alone, as if she were a racehorse named Velvet Logic or Solar Boss and it just felt lucky. She slipped her mouth guard out from her sock and ventured towards the masses.

Winston, who'd greyed dramatically in comparison to Darrell, remained as spritely as ever. He was the man unlocking the doors every morning, and switching the lights off every evening, and coaching each pupil as if he were being assessed by a board. On these Friday Night Fights, he played referee and judge and MC. Although he functioned more as a figurehead, since there were no official scorecards or points systems or declaring stoppage on medical grounds, so the crowd could get what they really came for: a knock-out. But he embraced his multirole with gusto, and headed into the sixth match of the night with fresh enthusiasm, brushing off racial slurs as he spoke into the chaotic abyss.

So let's get to it! Our final contest of the evening, the headline event.
Introducing, in the Away Corner, is Rost –
Rost – Rostivlav –
Rost i slav –
Rostislav Tome ček, Tomeček.

Rostislav climbed up between the ropes on the far side of the ring. He wore his forehead like a visor, so protruding it shadowed his deadened eyes. He was topless, but not bare, for jet black hair covered his chest, belly, back, arms. He knocked his own fists together, then pumped up the crowd. They went wild for the bear.

TIME TO GET ROASTED,
he shouted.

Some could not make out the complete catchphrase through his thick accent and gum-shield lisp, and others could not comprehend its nominal relevance, but still, they understood the sentiment and cheered along.

And in the Home Corner, it's our very own, homegrown...
Robyn!

Winston's obvious affection would have ignited claims of bias, were the scales not vastly weighted the other way.

What the fuck?

There was the first drop of quiet in the commotion. Robyn appeared like a stick drawing next to a fully fleshed statue. She cracked her neck, out of habit, not showmanship. Men strained their own necks in search of the actual opponent.

Fuck off, Robin's a boy's name!

A man clambered across laps to snatch back a blind bet he'd made.

This is fucked, even for you, Daz!

A toothless man hooted.

Disorder erupted once again as they raced to place their solid bet before the first bell. But those in the know sat quietly. They offered up reckless odds. They nodded along to claims they were blind drunk and senseless, and yielded to those who took advantage with a suppressed smile. Winston ushered the fighters to their respective corners, and rung a handheld bell like a town crier.

Robyn inflated her lungs until all background noise dulled and her focus fell like a spotlight upon her opponent. Her eyes dissected him until he no longer stood before her as a man, but as a collection of flaws. A tower block to be toppled by nudging the correct brick.

He hopped towards her, somewhat light on his feet. Often her opponents took a moment to acclimatise to their diminished target. (Surprisingly few took any time at all to question the ethics). He threw a hefty hook that whistled just past her ear. The wave of invisible impact made sense of Darrell's vague advice, *don't let him get contact 'cause…*

Robyn kept her guard high. He jabbed at her twice. She flinched back from the first, but underestimated his reach and the second kissed her on the breastbone. Only a clip, it was still enough to jolt her ribcage and shock an extra beat into her heart. Winston danced in and out of her periphery, but couldn't be afforded her full focus.

Rostislav lurched towards Robyn again. His gloved hand rivalled her whole head for size. He would cement his superiority with a showcase of textbook punches in a glorious combination, enough to seal his win immediately and never have his calibre underestimated again by facing such a ludicrously unworthy opponent.

Only he didn't.

Instead he proffered on a canvas platter a welcomed test of her body language literacy. She skirted around each blow as slickly as oil evades water. Her boxing intellect and lightning reflexes were a blur to the crowd. How she'd escaped the combination unscathed was incomprehensible, a fluke. Rostislav responded in the same tone as pressing an unresponsive remote slower and harder, when annoyance overrides sense. He made slower, heavier hits, which were all the more avoidable. She continued to dance around him. She flinched out of reach with magical foresight. He sulked back to his corner when the bell rang.

Two more rounds passed in which the opponents played different sports. Their aims and actions were so at odds, competition was the only loser (and the impatient spectators). Rostislav swiped at the nuisance fly to no avail, but he didn't tire.

On the third break, he stomped back to his corner. He roared and shook the ropes. His coach slapped him square across the face and he roared even louder.

Robyn sat alone in the opposing corner, trying to blink a salty bead of sweat from her eye. Darrell, as the impartial tournament host with no financial interest, could of course not coach, but he sat in the front row. Winston was still panting when the sixty seconds on his watch ticked up. His tongue felt fat and furry with dehydration. He took his place and began to lift the bell–

when Rostislav threw a punch.

It landed just off-centre of Robyn's face and she fell flat to the floor. Winston's shock delayed the start of his count.

One.

He could not really be heard beneath the boom of the crowd.

Two.

Her pale body blended into the white canvas.

Three.

Rostislav spread his arms to the sky, absorbing the cheer with his chest.

Four.

His back was still turned when there was the first flicker of movement.

F – five.

Darrell edged forward in his seat, each thumb and finger pad digging into the flesh above his knees.

Six.

Winston was unsure whether to slow down or speed up the count, to will her to move or to stay down.

Seven.

She dragged one knee up. Then both.

Eight.

Rostislav flared his nostrils as the girl unfurled herself.

Nine.

Robyn stood on her feet, unaided.

There was a collective pause,

before Rostislav thundered back towards her.

His limbs were heavy from the peaks and troughs of adrenaline. Lactic acid had flooded his muscles at the false finish, but still the chemical handicap was not equal to the effects of a knock-out blow. His next slow throw caught Robyn's cheekbone.

Her whole body twisted with the momentum and she caught herself on all fours. She had still been trying to reorientate herself from the last punch, and now the world shifted again. Matting beneath her knees, lights somewhere up above her. Her eyes were open but the link between vision and thought was missing.

One.

She just had to get the soles of her feet flat.

Two.

The rubber bottoms searched for an even surface. Tapping around as if she were on a rock face.

Three.

She found her footing and rocked into a low squat.

Four.

Fluorescent light overhead. The shoes of someone stood next to her.

Five.

A chorus was chanting.

SIX!

She could sit back down if she wanted to. She could lie down and never get up.

SEVEN!

Her mouth guard felt too big for her jaw. She parted her lips to breathe.

EIGHT!

Then her body moved of its own accord.

She pressed through her trainers and stood up. She stepped backwards, feeling for the ropes.

The ring floor waved as spectators drummed their hands against it. They were out of their seats, banging on the animal cage, demanding action. Robyn's eyes searched for her opponent, across the ring. As he came towards her, she moved just in time, relying on the ropes like a novice ice skater. Though everything spun and blurred, someone kept her moving. She was both the drunk passenger and the designated driver. Her eyebrows couldn't stem the flow of hot sweat from her forehead. She wiped them with her glove, and dark blood appeared across the blue leather.

Stop using the ropes, you slut!

She lurched away from the supports. Rostislav retreated away from her. Robyn followed towards him, regaining confidence, when Winston swept in and ushered her towards her corner for the fourth break. She hadn't heard the bell.

Robyn, are you ok? If you need to stop,

Winston whispered.

She sat with her back against the corner-post. The clawing crowds were enough to shield Darrell pouring water into her mouth. As soon as it reached her stomach it bounced back up, along with a slew of bloodied saliva, splattering over the side of the ring. He squirted the water across her forehead, and she felt her breath return to normal. Robyn could make out the ceiling and the floor and the heaving chest of the Czech who sat in the opposite corner.

Winston put out a hand to help her up –

Don't.

Darrell said.

She can stand.

The external belief soothed her like an anaesthetic. She stood up, unassisted, just as Darrell had predicted. She trialled two punches on the air, reclaiming the movement.

When the fifth-round bell rang, it was clear as day.

She started towards Rostislav. And for the first time, in the thirteenth minute of fighting, Robyn landed a punch. Then two, then three. Though her power didn't come close to that of his usual counterparts, it was bolstered by the element of surprise and fortified by fatigue on his part. He'd never gone more than three rounds. It was in this red zone, when usually quiet capillaries begged for oxygen, when a boxer began fighting with themselves, that Robyn thrived. The question of endurance became fatal.

She would either pull something from the depths to survive,

or she wouldn't.

A noise escaped her mouth as she continued to hunt him down with her fists. Her forearms began to sieze up, her knuckles started uncurling themselves. Rostislav took each shot to the body and head, absorption was all he could rely on now, the energy for dodging had drained away. He made one last attacking attempt. A jab, possible by muscle memory alone. As much power as he could muster was in it. It made contact with her left temple.

But not enough.

He'd followed through with his whole body leaving his head close to her chest. She curled uppercuts to his face.

Left,

right,

left,

right.

He collapsed onto his knees.

One.

Winston raced.

Two.

He looked from Rostislav, to Robyn, to Darrell to double check what he was seeing.

Three.

The crowd did not count along this time.

Four.

The Czech planted his gloves on the mat.

Five.

Robyn stared with all her energy.

Six.

Any lapse in focus and she would vomit or collapse.

Seven.

Winston struggled to keep the steady pace.

Eight.

Rostislav began to shift his weight.

Nine

His foot slipped and he tumbled forward onto his hairy chest.

Ten.

TEN!

Robyn vomited so forcefully that her mouth guard flew out.

Winston was collapsing the plastic chairs and carrying them to designated piles along the edges of the room. He envied the chairs, folding up and lying down for the night. Only a few stray spectators remained. The most intoxicated, unaware the evening had ended. A small group talking in hushed tones. Two picking an echoey fight in the emergency stairwell.

Robyn sat in Darrell's office with a wad of blue paper towels held to her forehead. The cupboard space could only fit one chair and a filing cabinet which doubled as a desk, so Darrell stood, leaning against the doorframe.

Other than the royal fuck up at the start of the third –

He threw before the bell went.

So fucking what? If he marched in here now, you'd –

I'd beat him again.

By the skin of your fucking teeth maybe.

Still won,

Robyn nodded towards a banded roll of notes Darrell clutched in his crossed arms.

He slid it into a tracksuit pocket.

Alright, you fucking smart arse,

and stood up straight.

Dark ink began to seep through the paper towels. Robyn still lived for this state of existence. When her body thumped and burned and pierced and she felt human. These glimpses of proof that she lived in the same corporeal world as everyone else. When the heat of a fractured chin connected her to the woes of her neighbours. When the sting of a slit septum bonded her with the vulnerability of strangers. When her body vibrated with pain, demanding her attention and anchoring her to the physical world, for a while.

Darrell wafted his hand, signalling for a glimpse at her eyebrow. She lifted the towels, but a piece of tissue stuck to the open wound.

Get me a – get me, in there, the bandage roll,

Darrell tried not to look directly at it.

Robyn opened the top drawer of the filing cabinet. The tight space meant she couldn't open it fully so rummaged around blindly with one hand, spreading bloodied fingerprints across final demand letters. She fumbled in the second drawer down. But her hand paused over an unmistakeable object.

A cold metal grip. A deceptively lightweight trigger.

Robyn looked at Darrell, but he stared over her head, then back over his shoulder. He fidgeted his arms and cleared his throat.

Come on, hurry up.

Robyn slipped her hand away, and into the final drawer for the gauze roll.

You can still be with the wizard,
what you've worked and waited for,
you can have all you ever wanted –

I know, but I don't want it.   *No –*

Eddie closed their eyes.

I can't want it, an - y - moreeee.

They spread their arms wide enough to graze both sides of the aisle.

Eddie and Linda had next to nothing in common. Eddie was a joy-spreading, people-loving, enthusiast for life, and Linda had left one-star online reviews for nearly every purchase or trip she'd made in the internet era. Cruise holidays, buffet restaurants, bed linen, Accident & Emergency wards. The only experience to escape a scathing review and the demand for a refund was the West End musical, 'Wicked'. Linda had seen it thirty-one times. For nearly eleven years, she'd gone for every birthday and Christmas and whenever else husband Gary would pay for a ticket. Eddie had seen 'Wicked' a measly two times, preferring to spread their theatre experience and expenditure, but on a Saturday shift, in gaps between customers, Eddie preyed on this thread of common ground to bring Linda out of her shell. Each week, they performed the soundtrack in the correct chronological order, with grave sincerity. Eddie's manager role did not afford them immunity from Linda's infamous critical nature. This Saturday afternoon, Linda had a stuffy nose so Eddie landed the role of Elphaba in the climactic duet.

And nobody in all of Oz,
No wizard that there is or was
Is ev-er gon-na bring meeeeee down!

They sang up towards Linda, who used the counter like a Juilet balcony.

I hope you're happy!
Look at her! She's wicked! Get her!

She concentrated hard on her multirole.

Bring meee down!

No one mourns the wicked!
So we've got to bring her,

Eddie puffed their lungs for the crescendo,
OHHohhhOhhOhhhhhhhh

Oh god,
Linda recoiled.
Oh no! Really? That one felt good!
Eddie deflated.
Not you,
she nodded behind him.

Robyn had slipped into the store, unheard beneath the dramatic chorus.

Oh, Robyn!
Eddie gasped.

Are you ok, my love?

Robyn had a bandage wound diagonally across her head. A brown stain marred it over the one eyebrow it covered. Her dark hair poked out in tufts around the tight wrapping, and the exposed parts of her face were swollen.

Alright,

It was neither a question nor answer.

I didn't mean to – you can,

she vaguely gestured for the show to continue.

No, my shift's done,

Linda was already logging out of the till.

Robyn grabbed a fizzy drink from the fridge, which Eddie pretended not to see, and settled in for her night shift behind the register.

One woman tutted sympathetically, one woman wished her good luck with the results, one man seemed genuinely oblivious, one man *eurgh*ed out loud. And for each different customer, Robyn and Eddie's reactions remained the same. Robyn said nothing and Eddie said,

You should have seen the other guy!

The lingering summer sun had officially faded, and the petrol station became the only place open on the street. The fluorescent shop lights cast shadows across the dark forecourt, which became a hive of less and less activity. At home, Robyn didn't own a television. So at work, the small CCTV monitor behind the till proved top entertainment. She watched an Uber driver pull away silently, with a full tank, on the grainy screen.

My love, are you sure I can't get you some antiseptic?

Eddie asked again.

It looks like it might be a little nasty under there!

Nah, I'm fine,

She walked a loop of the store, to stretch her legs. Then she took a Curly Wurly from the display, and tucked into her dinner, watching the live black and white feed.

I still can't believe you won! Well, no, I can believe it!

Eddie restocked the chewing gums.

Because you're so strong and awesome, obviously! But, a big man? My goodness, I'd be flattened!

Robyn stopped eating, eyes glued to the CCTV screen.

I know I'm a lover not a fighter, but it is concerning. Maybe I should take a self-defence class actually. You could teach me! I'd be dreadful, but you could –

Robyn stepped out from behind the till and left through the shop's exit, without saying a word.

ELIZABETH.

The third smallest room in the house, after the pantry and the cloakroom, was a joyful echo chamber in which giggles bounced off the tiled walls. Even their walk-in wardrobe and the guest's en-suite had more square footage than Layla's bathroom, but it was Elizabeth's favourite space. She chose to forget her initial reaction when Norman had suggested their baby should have her own bathroom. She could no longer hear her words, *she will not be a product of privilege, she will not be a product of you–* beneath the gushing tap. The warm waterfall poured into the tub. White bubbles rose in peaks, forming a mountain range across the water's surface. Elizabeth turned off the tap and they were plunged into quiet,

save for Layla's gentle splashing.

The sound of water swilling around was so enticing it was almost edible.

I would like to do a spelling bee,

Layla stared intently at a handful of bubbles.

A spelling bee?

Yes. I am good at spelling, in fact.

How do you know what a spelling bee is?

I don't know.

She clenched her fist and watched the bubbles squeeze between her fingers.

You are good at spelling, that's true. Do they run spelling bees at school then?

No,

she sighed.

Ok. How, do you spell, tap?

Tap. Tuh Ah Puh. Tap.

Elizabeth laughed at the official recital.

Where did you learn that?

Did I get it right?

You did, yes, well done.

How do you spell, tub?

Tub. Tuh Uh Buh. Tub.

This words are eeeeasy, Mummy!

Ok ok, clever clogs.

How do you spell water?

Water. Wuh.

She silently mouthed vowels, trying them on for size.

UhhAh,

Ah, yes.

Tuh, wart, Uh Ruh. Water.

Ee, arh, yes. Well done.

Layla exhaled the weight of performing.

Elizabeth watched concern, relief, pride wash over her daughter's face. The emotions invaded her delicate features with no care for concealment. Her eyes reflected Elizabeth's, her long neck was Norman's and her skin the perfect blend of both, but this openness, this honesty was not learned from either of them.

Elizabeth lurched forward and kissed her damp cheek. This love was still ferocious.

Oh, thank you, Mummy, and one for you,

she thread her wet fingers through the coils at her base of her mother's neck,

and planted a kiss on her lips.

Thank you,

Elizabeth whispered. This love was still overwhelming.

Are you getting in?

Not today,

Elizabeth went to check her watch, forgetting she'd taken it off.

They'd bathed together since Layla was born, Elizabeth being unable to resist the inviting water and the feel of her baby's skin on her own. It was always too cool and too shallow, and yet her favourite way to bathe. But Layla had only begun to ask if she were joining, every time, after a particular incident over a year ago, when Elizabeth had stepped into the bath fully clothed. She'd been giddy on Norman's absence and heady soap fumes and committed to proving her point, that she loved bath time more, and climbed into the tub, soaking her cotton cigarette pants and satin shirt, an irreversible decision that she would not have chosen to reverse anyway, for Layla's hysterics still rang in her ears.

I love bath time with you, Mummy.

Layla might have been trying to incite another a comedic dip, but the sentiment was still stirring.

I love it, too,

she kissed her tiny knuckles.

There was a tap at the door.

Iss juss me,

came from behind the wood.

Elizabeth scrambled awkwardly on her knees to open the door.

Amelia!

For weeks, Elizabeth had corrected Layla, *A-meel-ia not A-mell-ia,* only to learn that her six-year-old was in fact correctly pronouncing the name of the Catalonian nanny.

Hello Layla Loo! Hello Mrs Sear,

Amelia's hair was shoulder length, thrown in a casual side part. As effortlessly beautiful as her undressed eyes and the natural prominence of her cupid's bow.

Hi,

Elizabeth started clambering to her feet, feeling old and ungainly by comparison.

Can we do a spelling bee?

Layla asked.

Of course! Sorry, I'm a little early,

Amelia rolled up her sleeves.

No, not at all. No worries, I need to get ready anyway.

Elizabeth tried to swallow the stab of betrayal as she left the bathroom and Amelia had slipped so easily into her place, knelt next to the tub.

As she unwrapped the navy velvet dress from the dry cleaner's plastic covering, she resisted glancing at her reflection in the mirrored wardrobe doors. She didn't have the strength this evening to gamble on how she would feel about the woman looking back at her.

She was knocking on the door for ages.

Norman sat on a footstool in the centre of the closet (full-sized room), horning on a patent loafer. He too seemed to avoid looking his wife who was dressed only in underwear designed to support not seduce.

Sorry, I didn't hear,

she slipped the dress over her head. The heavy material fell just above her ankles.

Poor girl,

his heel slid into the sole.

Well, she was early. And you answered, so that's ok, isn't it?

I was rehearsing my speech.

Elizabeth pretended not to hear. She zipped herself up to just below her shoulder blades, but it would budge no higher. She didn't have the angle to inch it over the width of her ribcage.

Can you?

she signalled.

Norman stood up and straightened the hem of his suit trousers. He pulled at his cufflinks and slowly smoothed the lapels of his jacket, guided by his mirror image. Elizabeth was about to ask again, when he came over.

He pulled the material away from her skin with one hand, and slid the zip up to the nape of her neck with the other. He had sealed the dress but he didn't let it go.

So if I fuck it up,

he leant in close,

it's your fault.

He held the velvet pinched between his fingers, watching the hairs on her bare shoulders stand up.

She stayed looking down.

He released his grip, and rubbed her upper arms.

You look gorgeous,

he said, full volume, looking over her shoulder at their reflection.

We'll leave in ten,

and he left.

Only then, did she look up, drawn not to the fit of the dress, but the lifeless eyes of a coward.

Here she is! Twit twoo!

Norman called as she descended the stairs.

Layla gasped and clapped at her mother, then Amelia joined in.

Beautiful!

Elizabeth clutched the bannister and feigned concentration on her block heels.

Oh, please,

She rolled her eyes as she reached them, all clustered around the newel post of the grand staircase.

Layla was in her favourite pyjama set, leggings striped in two shades of pink and a long-sleeved top adorned with a sequinned unicorn. Amelia still looked flushed from the warmth of bath time on a summer's evening.

Right, goodnight, Lay,

Norman crouched down.

Be a good girl for Amelia.

Layla wrapped her arms around him.

I am a good girl,

she poked her tongue through a gap in her teeth.

Yes, you are,

he smiled, and she giggled.

Elizabeth slid her hands in between them, picking Layla up. She inhaled the smell of her clean skin.

Night night, baby,

she kissed her daughter's temple.

Night night, Mummy, I love you,

she whispered the secret,

with wet lips and bubblegum breath.

Amelia started climbing the stairs behind Layla, then she twisted round suddenly.

Oh Mrs Sear! Did you take your job?

Elizabeth opened her mouth to respond, before the answer had reached her.

Erm,

she searched for it,

Not yet, I haven't decided yet.

Come on,

Norman opened the front door.

Norman always chose to drive, not taxi, to events. It gave him total control over the route and a method by which to immediately flea when the time came. He was not required to wait for anybody, nor compelled to curb the freedom of his speech for any eavesdropper. But the car made Elizabeth nauseated. So much so, that her body began to pre-empt it, rocked by queasiness before they'd even made it through the electronic gates. It was either the stop-start motion of capital traffic or his sickening acceleration on clear roads or the stench of polish from its weekly valeting or the fact that she was locked in with her husband.

Angela keeps ringing me, I had two missed calls from her this afternoon. They're getting impatient, they want an answer. I think I—

Can we not talk about this now actually?

Norman pulled out of a queue, and sped up the empty oncoming lane.

Waiters in tails lined the perimeter of the patio, holding platters of champagne. For over an hour they had stood as statues. Statues who sweated beneath their waistcoats and jackets and thick white gloves, as the summer evening sun lowered at a torturous speed. It had sunk to eye level for most, blinding them from knowing which Very Important Person chose a flute from their tray. One head waiter, in the heavenly shade of the pillared building, stood watch for the slightest sign of unbalance. He'd only missed one wobble so far, and swept in too late to save the fountain of falling glass. Between the guests, there was not a conversation that didn't start,

Gorgeous evening!

Gorgeous!

or,

Beautiful evening!

Beautiful!

And their ever-ruddied faces were more puce than usual, as the concoction of a June heatwave and bottomless bubbles and outrageous banter raced to exorcise itself through their flushed complexions. Elizabeth would have been lost at Red Sea had Norman not navigated, using her lower back as the rudder for she deliberately kept her hands occupied by a glass and her clutch bag. In all the years she had been attending such functions, she'd not yet learned to identify one suited, overweight, grey-haired patron from another. They still appeared to her like fungi, round and beige and impossible to determine which to avoid.

Norman Sear!

One mushroom slid his hand into Norman's.

Andrew.

Stunning evening!

Stunning!

Hello, dear,

he stood on tiptoes to kiss both of Elizabeth's cheeks. As his pursed mouth passed her nose, she got a waft of something far stronger than champagne.

Man of the hour, I hear. Aren't you a lucky lady?

He squeezed himself against her, and she was grateful for the foot of height she had on him.

Definitely not me, tonight's all about Bernard,

Norman bowed with humility.

Yes, yes, Berny, of course,

but Andrew still looked up at Elizabeth.

We better go find out about proceedings actually.

Norman pulled Elizabeth away and she was saved, as helpless and passive as the already drowned.

As she followed Norman between the swell of conversations, she felt the final shreds of her pretence drop away.

She was exhausted.

Her whole life she'd sculpted herself into a masterpiece, glazing over the cracks so that no one would spot the forgery. But it was not the world who she could no longer deceive, it was herself. The nights in which she silently promised tomorrow would be approached with a strength that never surfaced. The arguments prepared in private only to evaporate in public. She was done.

The curated person was to be collapsed.

Ladies and gentleman, if you'd like to make your way inside, dinner will be served shortly.

They funnelled into a great hall where wineglasses outnumbered guests and chandeliers outsized tables.

Even after all these years, all these invitations, Elizabeth still wondered whether she may bump into Tristan Coles at one of these events. She was unsure whether it was with hope or fear that she pictured her father, never aged more than the day they had met, standing out amongst the mushroomed guests. Only once had she searched for him again, on the internet. She'd locked herself in the bathroom, thumb pads drunk and clumsy, and scoured pictures and articles and video clips of her half-brothers. She'd consumed all the information too quickly, too greedily, then felt sick in the aftermath of her binge. She'd never looked again, but still clung to an absurd hope that he might miraculously decipher her married name that appeared, squat and bold, in bylines and determine that she was his after all.

Norman pulled out Elizabeth's chair, and she obediently slid into her spot. She ate the medallion of beef and the carrots with their tops still on, for something to do besides socialise. She wished for another bloodied steak when Norman took to the stage.

And the amount of alumni here tonight offers some insight into the degree to which Bernard was the pinnacle of inspiration for so many. To have had the privilege of your mentorship throughout –

Elizabeth slipped off to the bathroom before he made it back to the table.

On the loo, she allowed her vision to blur over, succumbing to eternal capitulation, until,

Did you see Elizabeth Ojo's here?

she was snapped back to reality.

She silently pulled up her knickers, heart thumping, interest piqued.

Yeah.

God, we used to be so intimidated by her at uni.

Elizabeth rolled her lips in, sucking in a smile.

Did you hear she was offered political editor at The Guardian*?*

Deputy.

Well deputy, yeah but, she turned it down.

Then her heart beat harder.

Yeah, she turned it down.

What do you mean? You think Norman made her?

She wished her chest would quieten so she could hear them fully.

I mean, how would it look if he's gunning for spad and she's spewing a leftist agenda?

But that's their whole thing. Always been their thing. The perfect new age political peace couple. Crossing racial and political boundaries, uniting the world one mixed race baby at a time.

There was a silence, which she knew was being filled by a look. She was sure they must be able to hear the thud of her chest.

I'm pretty sure she's a Tory anyway.

And then her toes began to tingle, as if she were emerging from hibernation,

Really riding that champagne socialist wave.

and she could feel her pulse in her fingertips, relearning what it felt like to exist.

Good for her, fighting for the poor in her Gabbana velvet, I mean, come off it, darling –

She opened the door to two women she'd never seen before.

One sent her lipstick skidding onto her chin, the other remained quite still. Elizabeth's heels echoed as she walked to the marble basin between the frozen women.

Slowly, she lathered and rinsed her hands and dried them on a cotton flannel. She studied her reflection and scrunched the tips of her afro. The velvet took on a precious sapphire tone in this bright bathroom. She took a deep inhale, and exhale, flaunting the ability to breathe freely in front of her choked critics. She paused a moment longer, toying with the will of her beating heart. Then she left.

Norman was still not back at his seat, but caught in conversation over the back of someone's chair.

I'm going home,

she walked past him.

There was panic in his eyes. Actual panic and she almost laughed, and almost cried. How had she relinquished every speck of her power to a man who could be shaken by the mere prospect of social embarrassment. As she weaved between tables, heading for the entrance where the epic front doors were still open to encourage a draught, she regretted forewarning him at all. She should have just left.

She should have just left.

Can I get a taxi please?

she asked a startled waiter.

Startled because transport was nowhere within his weekend catering job remit, and startled because her voice had come out shrill, strangled by a rising panic.

Quickly, please.

He nodded and placed a dirty tray down on an antique mantlepiece.

The hard soles of Norman's loafers clapped against the tiled floor, ringing up into the decadent gallery above. He clutched his suit jacket in one hand.

You can stay, it's fine,

she started backing away from him.

No, no,

he steered her again, this time by a tight grip around her elbow.

She was flooded by too much else to notice the familiar nausea as she got into the passenger seat.

I did it FOR YOU, for fucks sake, you couldn't make up your mind.

I COULD make up my mind! I wanted to do it, I wanted to take the job, but you wouldn't let me!

Her voice bounced back off the windscreen.

Wouldn't let you!

He kept his eyes on the road.

Listen to yourself, Elizabeth.

Hedgerows zoomed past. The car headlights lit up hidden worlds for a split second at a time. They were hurtling back towards the city. Snot streamed from both her nostrils and thick, hot tears from both eyes. She let them fall and stain her velvet lap. She wiped away oceans with the back of her hand, but still they poured. In the dark, and at that speed, the point at which green hedges gave way to brick buildings was imperceptible.

I hate you,

she whispered, the sobs having stolen her voice.

I hate you so much.

There was a comfort in its completeness, but it sounded juvenile. Somehow, over the years, the worst words possible had lost their weight.

No, you don't,

Norman reached a hand out to her knee.

Don't touch me!

She flinched away.

But he pressed down harder.

You are my wife. I will touch you if I want to touch you.

She squealed against his pressure, and her cries became whimpers. He let go of her to steer them onto a main road that cut between tower blocks and shops and dipped under railway lines. He sped past cars in the outer lane, as green traffic lights bowed to let him past.

You don't throw a paddy because you can't get what everything you want,

The automatic gears shifted for him.

I don't get anything I want.

He laughed, flinging back against the head rest.

She'd never had such little control over her own language, she was speaking authentically for the first time ever and it turned out to be a spew of pathetic sentiments.

Jesus christ, yeah you've only got a four-bedroom house in Kensington and a beautiful, healthy daughter and a loving husband and great career prospects and job security, fucking hell, Elizabeth.

His mouth was still ajar with theatrical offence, and disbelief. He didn't indicate as he turned off onto a straighter, emptier road.

You need to stop this woe is me attitude. You had a tough childhood, we get it, so do lots of people, you need to drop that now, drop that bullshit and realise how lucky you are. A lot of people would be incredibly grateful to be in your position. You could have fucking nothing to your name but I gave you –

Elizabeth grabbed the wheel.

She yanked it hard towards her side.

They began to spin,

twice,

and again,

maybe a fourth.

She was pinned back against the seat,

all air squeezed out of her being,

until a low brick wall stopped them.

The right-hand side of the car absorbed the brick barrier. The full length of the black metal cushioned the blow, crumpling inches in on itself at the impact. Elizabeth's mind still spun for moments after they'd entered stillness.

Rattled breathing was all that reverberated off the windscreen now.

Her feet were still pressed hard against the floor mat, clenching her calves, thighs, buttocks. She stayed braced as she scanned herself, by sight alone, too disconnected to trust sensation. She saw only the salt stains that were beginning to crust on her navy lap.

Slowly,

she looked at Norman.

His hands still gripped the wheel.

His shoulders rose and fell with life.

When he too turned, to look at his wife, her eyes were fixed upon his right thigh, which was compressed against his left and closely hugged by the car interior. The whole inner door had moulded against the side of his body.

The broad man, forced to shrink himself.

Their eyes met, and all at once,

they were strangers who had survived adjacent storms,
they were children who knew no better,
they were inextricably bound,
they were in love,
they had died.

Elizabeth unbuckled her seatbelt, eyes still fixed upon her crushed husband and the way he watched her back. The face she had looked at more than any other, the face she had fallen for, created with, been sickened by, seen warped by age and anger, looked new once more. He was at the mercy of her move, unable to dictate what would come next. He was powerless, scared and hopeful,

until she pulled her door handle.

Her numb arms fizzed against the weight of the door, and she took a final look at his eyes, drowning in weakness. As she pulled herself from the car, his arms snatched out towards her, but seconds too late, she was on the deserted road. The night air was still warm. The orange streetlights threw a dusty haze across segments of the tarmac. She began to walk, then run, her heels calling out into the apocalypse. She watched the white lines run and break and run beneath her. A car passed in the opposite direction, paying no heed to the sapphire vision trespassing on vehicle territory. Then she was alone again. The shadowed buildings set back from the road sat like silent spectators as she continued running to nowhere, hearing nothing but the pant of her breath and the

CLAT,

CLUT,

CLAT,

CLUT

of her shoes,

and,

another set of footsteps.

PLUMB,

cshhhhhh,

PLUMB,

cshhhhhh,

PLUMB.

Norman was emerging from the nothingness, dragging his right ankle.

Breath punched in and out of her, going no deeper than her throat. Her voice strained chords of desperation, like tuneless notes dragged on a violin. She tried to speed up but it was as if the air willed otherwise, hidden hands pushed against her and the uneven footsteps grew louder. She did not look behind her, but instead as far as she could see up ahead, willing two beacons of hope to speed towards her. Her own noises of fear and wheezing began to drown out her hunter. She looked only for headlights.

Please, please, please,

she said aloud, or in her head,

and white light appeared.

But it was on her side of the road. A petrol station. She ran past the pumps, but not into the shop.

She hid herself around its side, in the pitch black.

NORMAN.

Norman paused in the shadows of the forecourt. He watched the two workers through the windows of the petrol station, like a scene upon a cinema screen, an illuminated rectangle against a black backdrop. One stacked a shelf and the other waited behind the till. Nothing out of the ordinary. It was an opening scene, a before. Neither looked rattled by an unannounced visitor, but he was sure she'd turned in here. His head pounded and his neck burned and his ankle howled with pain, but he was sure.

From his vantage point he ran his eyes over the pumps and the bags of barbecue coal and the fire extinguishers. He could taste blood. He squinted into the darkness. The lit shop lent some light to the tableau. Empty newspaper stands and full dustbins were all dimmed the same dark grey. Only down the side of the building, hidden from the windows, did it look free from any colour,

and then he knew.

He walked, limped, towards the abyss, and paused again, this time to summon his fury

and bask in his victory.

Hey.

He spun around.

DAY ONE.

It was difficult enough to decipher the man's exact outline, stepping from such artificial brightness into the trueness of night, but Robyn's bandage also forced one eye half shut. She could just about tell he was faced away from her, feet spread but only the left was fully planted.

Hey,

she spoke.

When he turned he was still a faceless silhouette. He jerked around unsteadily on one ankle.

Help – help – help me,

came from somewhere beyond him, in the deluding depths of darkness.

He turned towards the voice, then back to Robyn.

We're fine,

he said.

It was odd, to hear a voice with such clarity emerge from nothingness.

Help,

this other voice was barely an arrangement of air.

We're fine. Go back inside. My wife isn't well.

Robyn wondered if this man were etching features on to her invisible face, as she was to him. He would likely be imagining eyes that were filled with fear or the naive smile of someone who was about to mind their own business,   and how wrong he would be.

She drove her trainer into his right ankle. His metatarsals scattered like pearls finally breaking free from a worn necklace. He caught himself on the concrete with the heels of his hands.

You fucking,

he crawled towards her, swiping a hand at her legs.

As he inched out into the lit forecourt, she could begin to make out a jawline, then a nose (larger than she had imagined) and the collar of a shirt. The shirt was a light colour, baby blue maybe, and it moved towards her like a large body of water. She edged backwards, coaxing him onto the lay of land she knew so well, pump 2.

Elizabeth crept back towards the light. She felt along the building, steadying herself against the bricks, fixated on the bizarre episode playing out on the forecourt. Her husband gone feral, on his hands and knees, stalking his prey, a tall child, who only added another layer of peculiarity to this wild spectacle. She tried to untangle the moment, make sense it of it, but still felt as if she were trapped in a spinning car.

She reached the end of the building's wall. Her fingers wrapped around the corner but she hesitated to bring any more of herself into the open. She watched the petrol station worker slowly backing away from crawling Norman. It was insane to imagine these two beings were the same species. How did this person fit all the same organs into their body as Norman. Perhaps their heart was even smaller. They looked light on their feet but their face was too mangled and squashed behind a lop-sided dressing to tell if they backed away in fear, or bravery. Elizabeth didn't know who was playing with who, but in her intrigue, she had edged out into the light, next to the station's seasonal display.

Robyn wasn't sure how long this man was going to keep up his futile quest for power, or what she was going to do with him, so she bided her time, staying only millimetres out of his reach. It was a tool she often used in the perimeters of the ring, where she preyed on opponents' underestimation of her and overestimation of themselves, to keep their stamina quietly ticking down. But out here, not bound by time or ropes, this child's play could be infinite and her shift was nearly over and she wanted to get to the out-of-date sandwiches before Eddie binned them. Real-life fights demanded a purpose, and in truth, she had no idea what her purpose was here.

The man clawed at her laces and she shook him off. Then sent a soft kick to his nose. Not even enough to draw blood, just a sparring shot to keep him in check. They were nearly at pump 4 now. Eddie would already be examining the sell-by dates on the Ham & Cheese, she just knew it. She searched for them through the station window, but her eyes fell upon someone else, a woman on the edge of the shadows.

She wore a midnight blue gown that dripped down her body like a moonlit waterfall.

She stood across the court from Robyn like a waiting train passenger, a fleeting vision, with a story, dressed for a destination, but her eyes, they looked unsure if she would wait for the train to stop before stepping off the platform. Robyn saw light glinting off her wet cheeks –

then an orb of bright white.

The bulb above pump 4 had only been replaced last week and its glow was very intense. She was on her back. Her elbows had taken the brunt of the fall, having tripped or been tripped.

You broke my ankle, you psychopath.

The suited man was on her. He pulled both her ankles towards him. The drag lifted her top up and grazed her back against the ground.

You have no idea who I am,

he straddled her,

and you're going to fucking pay,

and covered her mouth, despite her making no attempt at noise.

Do you understand that? I'm going to take you to the fucking cleaners.

His hand spanned right the way around her jaw.

As he pressed down harder, Robyn could feel shards of broken tarmac indenting into the back of her skull.

But she didn't fight back, or even wriggle, and she didn't know why.

I'm going to fucking rape you of your life.

She could not see fully out of both eyes so instead she closed them. The bright station lights still wavered behind her eyelids. She did not push against his hand with her swollen jaw, only let it sink deeper into her face. Her rib cage struggled to fully expand against his thighs, but she drew as much breath as she could.

Fucking ruin you,

With each syllable he jabbed his hand down harder.

It wouldn't be losing if she didn't know what she was fighting against, or for. It would be like crawling back into bed at the end of a long day. How easily she could slip under the covers of unknowing, unbeing. Its comfort was so enticing that she wondered why she had ever stayed awake so long. What had been the point of enduring each day? She couldn't feel one single thing, only a mass of weight pressing her body down into the earth. Her heels, her calves, her back, her skull. She was dipping below the surface, sinking into the concrete,

deeper

and

deeper,

then a force landed on her nose and she was back on the floor of pump 4.

She'd long since become immune to the scent of unleaded, but she could smell it now. The man was slumped on top of her, and towering above them both was the blue mirage.

Elizabeth held the fire extinguisher out in front of her as if he might spring back into action at any second. Then talons of maroon began to seep from his crown and she lowered it an inch.

Oh my god,

she kept watching the blood as it crawled into his collar. She didn't notice the person beneath him slip out, or how the extinguisher was gently slid out of her hands, all she could see was Norman, face down, in a position not destined for him. This was the motionless figure of nightmares and dramas and rubber models with no lives to leave behind. He was not meant to break.

She was being guided away from him.

I need to,

but she couldn't be sure if she was speaking aloud,

Wait here.

She didn't know where here was. *DING.* A breeze of cool air blew across her skin.

Oh, hi Robyn! You're still here! I thought you'd just clocked off early!

The voice was muffled, behind a glass door.

Lock yourself in. Call the police. Maybe an ambulance.

Elizabeth looked at her hands in the light that bled out from the windowed door. *DING.* She was surprised not to be holding an extinguisher. She couldn't remember putting it down.

Come on.

Elizabeth's feet were moving again. She watched the scuffed suede on her square toes march further and further away from the light and take on an orange glow. She was back on the streetlamped road, except this time it ran parallel to her. She was on a pavement. Sporadic beech trees hung over head. Shadows of their circular leaves dotted the floor, like a haunting disco ball. She could not hear another pair of footsteps, but the swish of baggy material between thighs.

Wait, wait, wait, my daughter.

Elizabeth had not thought the thought, the words had simply tumbled out and stopped her in her tracks, as if some other version of herself had been thinking this whole time, whilst she had barely been present in body alone. But she was here now.

Her guide looked back towards the station, confused.

She's at home,

Elizabeth clarified.

Where are we going anyway?

She hurtled into the realisation at how far they had walked. The person looked like one of Layla's drawings come to life, with jagged hair and limbs that were a single line and a swollen face of inaccurate proportions.

Where do you live?

Her voice was young.

Elizabeth was now alert enough to hesitate in giving her address to this stranger. One whom she was following to nowhere and had witnessed her crime and who looked like the runt of humanity's litter, but not quite alert enough to fill her hesitance with something convincing,

Erm, *I can go alone.*

But as soon as the cogs began to turn, they jammed. She clutched her sides,

Shit.

Elizabeth's stomach sank, and she felt weightless, unanchored by a beaded clutch bag underneath her armpit. Her mind presented false polaroids, snapshots of the purse stranded in the dark corner of the petrol station, or on the floor mat of the mangled car, or abandoned on the marble countertop of a restroom she had walked away from with composure in a different lifetime.

She tried to think, but it was impossible. It was as if she were trying to solve a problem when on the cusp falling asleep. Her mind drifted somewhere untraceable for seconds, maybe minutes, at a time, then circled back suddenly to the question, that sat as open and intimidating as when she'd left it.

The station's just up here.

Elizabeth had no choice but to accept this solution.

In the back of a cab, her chaperone rode backwards, on a fold out seat.

You want some?

and she held out an anaemic looking sandwich.

The security light automatically blinked on and Robyn stood a few steps behind the woman who banged on the emerald front door. The stained-glass panels, geometric shapes of sludgy colours, rattled in protest to each knock. A young woman answered.

Mrs Sear,

her voice was hoarse.

I'm so sorry, you're later than I thought,

and thick with an accent,

I must have fallen asleep.

As the cape of sleep began to dissolve, her face changed,

What's wrong?

Mrs Sear kept her head down and pushed her way into the house. Robyn waited next to the chugging taxi in the driveway, then the floodlight snapped off and she was drawn through the inviting front door that had been left wide open. The entrance hall was empty. It reminded her of one of the last homes she'd lived in before her flat. A Victorian townhouse with high ceilings and hallways that had got narrower with each storey. She could still hear the creak of floorboards beneath worn carpet as other kids had scurried around at night. *Halfway house,* they'd called it, but she'd never learned where it was halfway to. Everything in this house looked more polished. The carpet on the sweeping staircase, pinned to each step with a brass rod, had no sign of wear at all.

There was a muffled sound of movement upstairs. Rushing muted by thick ply rugs.

Robyn caught sight of herself in a large mirror. The puffy face who stared back at her from behind a discoloured bandage was bordered by ornate carvings in brushed gold. She stepped back from the mirror and a floorboard groaned beneath her.

Gently she shifted her weight from side to side, playing the creaking instrument.

The younger woman was the first to fly back down the stairs. She wore mismatching spotty socks that would not mark the immaculate staircase, and held a brown leather holdall. As she placed it down at the bottom of the stairs, Robyn saw it was stuffed with clothes and wash bags and the corner of a book poked out. The woman didn't look at Robyn as she fled off into another room.

Then Mrs Sear, in her navy gown, came downstairs. She was still wearing her heels, that were certain to muddy the carpet. She descended more steadily, clutching the bannister for balance, for in her other arm,

she held a small child.

The other woman rushed back in, holding a biscuit tin.

Is this the one?

She held up the tin.

It was deep and round and decorated with images of holly leaves. The metal was dented in several places.

Yes, that's it,

Mrs Sear glanced up for a second, still carefully navigating her way down. The child clung to her mother. Her bare feet hung limply and as they reached the bottom of the stairs, Robyn could see the tiny toenails that stuck to each tiny toe.

Thank you, Amelia. You get yourself off, I'll contact you in –

oh, the phone. There's a spare phone in top kitchen drawer.

Amelia darted off down a passage before even being asked. The mother, in her stained velvet dress, looked completely different to how she had done in the unflinching lights of the petrol station. Here she looked purposeful, and strong.

Where are we going, Mummy?

the dozing child asked.

And then a glimpse of the lost woman returned.

Erm,

Got it,

Amelia re-entered.

I don't know,

Elizabeth realised.

To a, to a, to a hotel, I suppose.

Amelia threw the mobile into the unzipped holdall and held it up. Robyn watched as the mother began to slip back into uncertainty. The panic was physically visible, building with each breath. She was becoming engulfed by a suffocating cyclone. Robyn was sure she would drop the child,

You can come to mine.

The child picked her head up off her mother's shoulder.

Amelia noticed her for the first time, too.

Are you the,   taxi?

Ok,

The mother cut across.

Thank you.

Elizabeth searched in the biscuit tin for the taxi fare. She hid the expired twenty note on the bottom of the pile and hoped the driver wouldn't notice in the dim light. By the time she'd climbed out of the car, still holding Layla, their host was across the road, carrying their brown leather bag, bypassing a defunct buzzer system and heaving open the entrance door.

Elizabeth looked up at the derelict block of flats. It had been years since she'd been in a corner of the city where these structures existed, or paid attention to them. Even in the cover of night, she could see how each window was filled with a wire meshing. The small woman held the heavy door open with her back. Its corrugated metal sheeting looked fit for a prison. Elizabeth felt Layla tense up as they crossed the threshold,

or maybe she was the one who tensed.

A square light flickered overhead. *BUNG. BUNG.* Its electrics twanged somewhere within. Small puddles had gathered on the tiled floor, despite the weeks of dry weather. Some flyers drowned in the wet patches and others poked out like tongues from a wall of pigeonhole slots. The entrance space had a complete chill. It wasn't the directional blast that came from a machine, but a well-rounded cool that came from the thick concrete walls that warmth could not conquer.

Without looking back, the slight woman had begun climbing the stairs,   two at a time.

Elizabeth followed. She felt her toes squash against the tips of the shoes that she'd been running in for hours now. The sound of the hard heels clattered off the bare walls and echoed up and up and up. The weight of Layla began to crush her right arm. She looked up to see an endless zigzag of flights above her, and the woman's head traversing them like a pin ball. Elizabeth gripped the rubber bannister and used it to pull herself up step by step. Her adrenaline was diminishing with altitude. She kept looking at Layla's bare feet. With each flight she grew more confident that they'd be fine on the questionable floor, until she was absolutely certain and –

she nearly collided with the tour guide, who had stopped and held her arms out without saying anything.

Elizabeth handed Layla over to the stranger, with no strength but to trust she'd be safe in her hands. The woman wrapped a spindly arm around her daughter, still holding the leather bag with the other, and continued to take the stairs, two at a time. The pace and the strength of the stranger seemed absurd.

She handed back Layla when they finally reached her front door.

The entirety of the flat would have fit within Elizabeth's downstairs living room. The woman didn't turn on a light and Elizabeth didn't know whether it was to save embarrassment, or hide horrors, or because it was the middle of the night, or because it simply didn't have electrical capabilities.

You guys can have the bed if you want,
I normally fall asleep on the sofa anyway.
She nodded to the door behind Elizabeth.

Elizabeth pushed on the paper-light pine to find a single bed, dressed with one pillow, a crumpled blanket and no top sheet.

Thanks,

it was voiceless, unconvincing.

She let Layla slide down to the floor.

I'm Robyn, by the way.

Elizabeth couldn't see her properly, but she sensed she wasn't talking to her.

Elizabeth.

And I'm Layla.

Elizabeth only fell asleep for seconds at a time, before being thrown awake by a forceful spinning or the clunk of metal on skull.

DAY TWO.

Robyn could doze through the sounds of her building waking up. The routine neighbourhood noises had become as conducive to sleep as silence:

the corridor lights buzzing to attention as Reg sloped off for his postal shift,

the whirr of next-door's shower heaving up warm water,

the distant beeps of the green man hurrying pedestrians along outside,

the *CLNK-click-CLNK* as Bharti locked, unlocked and relocked her door,

the hollow screams from the stairwell of the child who protested school every day,

the thud of drum and bass from the parked minibus that clanked open its wheelchair ramp.

So although they were only whispers, Robyn was acutely aware of the high-pitched muttering that was disturbing the usual soundscape. She rolled onto her side and stared at the bedroom door from the sofa.

And then they go beeboop for the lady please,

Elizabeth awoke to the sounds of Layla's imagination. She presumed it had been only minutes since exhaustion had defeated her and she'd sunk into unconsciousness, but then Layla also seemed to be quite far into an intricate storyline. The bedroom was only marginally lighter than it had been hours before, as a sliver of natural light crept in beneath the door. There was a wire hanging from the centre of the low ceiling, with a pendant attached but no bulb.

Mummy, do horseys like going for rides?

Elizabeth didn't know whether her daughter had detected she'd woken, or if she had just been asking her questions this whole time.

Erm,

her nose was blocked,

yes, I think so,

and her jaw ached from clenching her molars.

Mummy,

Layla rolled onto her side so that her face was inches from her mother's.

Elizabeth sweltered beneath her velvet dress, it seemed to pulse out from her core, and sweat was cooling across her back, but still she pulled her warm-blooded baby in towards her and didn't let go.

Is this a sleepover?

A sleepover,

she jumped too quickly at the lifebuoy,

yes.

Why are we sleeping over here?

She wrinkled her nose.

A mattress spring had coiled free and pierced through the surface by her feet. The musty pillow contained a compact history of sweaty nights. Elizabeth felt tears surge up.

Mummy and daddy had a fight.

Mummy and daddy had a fight,

Layla repeated,

and Elizabeth heard the words reverberate from a witness box or in an interrogation or as an officer knelt by her daughter's side coaxing answers out of her and,

No, no, we didn't. Not really. We just – we needed some space.

Who is Robyn?

She's,

the centre of Elizabeth's chest began to burn. With each breath a band of acid stretched up and down, and yet she continued to breathe, continued to test it, to hope she might breathe deep enough for it to snap, but it burned on. She tried to focus instead on the way the bare mattress scratched the back of her arm, or how the clammy skin behind her knees was stuck together, but she couldn't escape the fire. She was losing the fight against it and started to succumb to tiny breaths, only hoping not to disturb it or deepen it,

Mummy, I said I need a wee.

A wee?   *Oh, a wee,*

Elizabeth sat up quickly,   and the fire petered out.

She opened the bedroom door to see their host, curled on the sofa. Robyn made no attempt to disguise that she'd been staring at the closed door, nor looked away now that it was open.

She needs a wee,

Elizabeth said.

Ok,

Robyn said.

Is it –

she pointed, even though it was evident, she hoped, that a bathroom would be behind the only other door off the compact living-eating-cooking-sleeping area. She pushed it open. A shower, toilet and sink were squeezed into the impossibly small space. The sanitary ware and shower cubicle overlapped with almost-ingenuity, leaving no space for mother and daughter to fit in at the same time. Elizabeth looked around the bathroom (that had neither a bath nor room), for any razor blades or needles but it was bare, of everything, except a lime green bottle of 3-in-1 wash on the floor of the shower. Standing outside the bathroom, she helped Layla onto the loo, then pulled the door to.

Robyn still watched her from the sofa. Her eyelids were swollen, but with the bandage removed and in the light of morning, Elizabeth could see her irises were not the solid black she'd sworn they were the night before. There were flecks of light brown in the darkness, specks of humanity within the deadpan gaze.

Elizabeth cleared her throat and fidgeted on her bare feet. She could feel crumbs and shards of grit squashed beneath her soft soles. She looked too closely at a streak of mould across the ceiling and shivered, she felt as if the mould were running down her spine and sitting on her lungs.

I –

The door swung open,

I watered my hands but there was no soap,

Layla scrunched the sides of her leggings, leaving wet handprints.

That's ok, good girl.

Oh,

Layla looked at Robyn.

You've got a,

she pointed.

Robyn touched her own mangled eyebrow.
Yeah,
she agreed.

Lay, can you – can you go do some drawing in the bedroom? Your colouring book's in the bag, can you – would you mind?
I just need to have a grown-ups chat with Robyn.

Elizabeth wasn't sure if Robyn even was a grown-up. Layla obediently scampered back into the cavernous bedroom. Robyn didn't sit up.

I,

Elizabeth closed her eyes, and pressed her fingers to her forehead.

I need to,

she pressed them harder, trying to detract from her trembling voice.

I need to figure out what –

Mummy, there's no pens!

Elizabeth snapped her eyes open.

What?

There's no colouring pens, in the bag or anywhere.

Oh, erm, maybe, Robyn do you have,

she couldn't finish the question. The woman didn't even have a bed sheet or a lightbulb or a separate shampoo from body wash. The chances of colouring pens were slim. But Robyn raised herself off the sofa. She walked around the kitchen counter and rummaged in a drawer that sounded filled with loose cutlery. Elizabeth instinctively reached for Layla,

when Robyn pulled out a pen. A biro. She clicked and un-clicked the spring mechanism, and handed it to Layla, who accepted the pen, with its snapped clip and *J & M Construction* logo, as if it were an ornate multicoloured quill, and she scurried back to the bedroom.

Thank you,

Elizabeth whispered.

So, erm, yeah, I need to sort out someone to look after her,

she tried to push the words out now, faster and stronger, to expel them before they choked her.

And then I will, I will go and, erm, figure this out and turn myself– turn myself in. It was insanely irresponsible of me to come here, I appreciate you taking us in, but to get her involved and you involved and – yeah, I appreciate it, but I obviously can't do this, I can't hide.

Robyn crossed her arms and leant against the kitchen counter. Elizabeth didn't lift her eyes as she talked. Her speech sounded unplanned, yet spoken with such decidedness. The morning sun fell upon her shoulders in the soft crisscross pattern of the window's meshing. Still in her navy dress, even with its crusted stains and dark patches beneath the armpits, she looked like a polished droplet in the decaying flat, like an exquisite glitch in the system.

Robyn yawned. The skin around her mouth felt bruised, in the shape of heavy fingers.

Sorry, am I keeping you?

Elizabeth didn't scowl at the floor now, but at Robyn. Her body language changed. Robyn became aware of the point of her chin, the sharpness of her elbows.

No?

Elizabeth stared at her, with newfound horror.

What have I,

she muttered to herself, shrinking into her own body.

You don't have to stay here?

Robyn believed she was offering what the woman wanted.

Yeah, thanks, we won't be,

but her reply only became sharper.

Ok?

Elizabeth stayed rooted opposite her for a moment, before she rushed the three steps to the bathroom. Robyn stared at the tail of the blue dress and the soles of bare feet, as she listened to the sound of vomiting.

Elizabeth clutched the cold ceramic of the toilet pan. Her nose burned and her eyeballs pulsated and a whisper of realisation began to talk more loudly to her.

Her only witness was her only alibi.

She should not bite the hand that feeds her: an excuse to use reasonable force. Only Robyn could validate that she'd acted in defence at all, the poor, mentally-challenged stranger whose life she had valiantly saved.

Elizabeth spat the last strings of bile into the bowl and flushed. Robyn was waiting for her with a plastic cup of water. Elizabeth, distracted by surprise at the gesture and intense dehydration, did not dwell on how many times the single-use cup had likely been reused. She drank the tepid water.

Were you sick, Mummy?

Layla was hovering in the bedroom doorway.

Yes, sorry, baby, I'm just feeling a bit poorly, but much better now.

It might be a tummy bug.

Maybe,

the innocence stung more than the acid that still scorched her nostrils.

You didn't kill him, by the way.

Robyn announced, so nonchalantly.

Layla's eyes bulged from her tiny face.

Elizabeth pounced to sweep up her daughter, twisted her by the shoulders and shoved her back into the bedroom.

Finish your drawing, baby,

she shut the door with an unsatisfying lightness.

What the fuck!

she snapped at Robyn, but only mouthing, so it was a blend of salivary consonants.

You fucking psychopath, she's six years old!

her lips smacked on *path*

and her teeth hissed on *six*.

She was starting to remind Robyn of the women who shouted at her across the till when they'd had to wait behind two other cars for fuel on the school run. Hostility didn't phase Robyn, it just felt more intrusive in her own home. No one else had ever even stepped foot inside the flat in the eight years she'd lived there.

She scratched the back of her neck and waited for the onslaught to subside, as it always did, and for Elizabeth to be left panting in the comedown of her own tantrum, as they always were.

I thought you thought you had, and that's why you –
Robyn pointed at the bathroom.
But yeah, you didn't kill him.
Her stomach was rumbling and she wanted a shower. She could feel a thick warmth at the back of her head, but as she reached into her matted hair, she was reminded of the loose tarmac. It was too tender back there to work out what were clumps of grease and what was blood.

What do you – how do you know?

Elizabeth was still panting.
'Cause he was breathing, I guess.

Those fire things, I've never seen them fight a fire, only seen them nearly kill a guy – not your guy, another guy – but he was like in a coma for bit. He survived though, I think, and you only used a small one,   so.

Elizabeth held a hand out, fingers loosely splayed,

Are you sure?
There was something in her face that bought Robyn's mind all the way back to Sarah, just for a second.
Yeah, you definitely used a small one.

Elizabeth snatched her fingers into a fist. It was the desperation to know, to understand.

I mean about him breathing.

Oh, yeah. Yeah, I think he was.

Elizabeth's face crumpled. It looked like a melting candle as her mouth and brows drooped downwards and lines appeared in her forehead and at the corners of her damp eyes.

You think? You need to, you need to, you need to know.

She still had one hand on the bedroom door handle, locking her child into the dark airless cupboard.

You need to tell me what happened.

Elizabeth could hardly contain the concoction of chaos that swirled inside her. It was as if every switch on her control panel had been flicked on. She wanted to sit on the floor and she wanted to run and she needed silence but her ears rumbled and her heart raced and she wanted to vomit and her body shivered and her palms sweated and her mouth was dry but she could taste blood and she felt like she was falling and her eyes might close and she wanted to scream but she didn't know how,

so she remained as still as she could,

holding the cold handle and focusing only on Robyn.

There were voices on the street below, one friend calling out to another. Loudly, to be heard from up here. Maybe it was a rare enough run-in that they'd tell their spouses about it later, or maybe it was such a routine interaction that they'd have forgotten it happened at all by dinner time. How did the hands of time dictate for whom it was a second and for whom it was a lifetime?

Well, I didn't see it happen, but he was out, 'cause you hit him, with the thing, and then you were just stood there, and when I pushed him off, he started like gurgling a bit so I didn't want him to get up and start everything, so we left.

Elizabeth could feel the metal in her hand. She saw the back of his head, thick hair she used to run her hands through. Then the judder of hard against harder. She shivered the thought away, and warm saliva swarmed her mouth.

So he was – he was ok?

Then she could hear a gargle, and her whole body began to shake.

Yeah, it was just a knock-out.

All the sirens in Elizabeth's body screeched to a silence. She sunk down onto the floor.

Robyn squatted in front of her with a refill of water. Layla emerged from the bedroom, as the unlocked door yawned open.

This is for you because you're poorly, Mummy,

she climbed into Elizabeth's lap.

It was dark in there so I couldn't stay inside all the lines.

And it's not too pretty colours, in fact.

Once she took the plastic cup, Robyn got up and walked away. Elizabeth held her baby close.

Robyn was never usually fussed enough to wait for hot water, nor patient enough to fully rinse the soap out under the shower's dribble. But this morning, the temperature had crept all the way up and the crown of her head squeaked before she turned it off. She stood for a moment in the cubicle, feeling the water drip off her, inhaling the sweet lime air. The vapour tingled across her skin and cleansed her lungs. It was a refreshing sensation, like stepping into a brand new body, trying its nervous system on for size. She did not use a towel, but pulled on her shorts and polo top.

She opened the bathroom door in a cloud of moisture. The limey particles dispersed into the room, their freshness quickly eaten up by the stale and stagnant. Elizabeth and Layla were on the sofa now, huddled together. Layla talked animatedly, whilst her mother, faraway in mind, was as close as she could possibly be in body. She held her and stroked her and pressed her lips to her head.

Robyn watched them, another glitch. Such unimaginable intimacy.

She hung upside down and dried her hair roughly with a tea towel, gritting her teeth as she rubbed the back of her head. When she stood up straight, Elizabeth was in her kitchen with her.

I need to check he's ok.

Robyn threw the dish towel on the counter and opened the fridge.
Ok.
She drunk whole milk from a pint-sized carton,

He might be in hospital, somewhere,

Elizabeth kept her voice so low that Robyn could hardly hear it beneath her glugging.

And even if he's ok, I crashed our car, that's why we were there, at the petrol station, and so they'll be looking for that anyway, and even if he's fine, there's so much that I've done and, I don't know – I don't know if he'll be with them or, what he wants.

Robyn finished the pint and wiped her upper lip.
I can check with Eddie?
and she let out a small dairy-fuelled burp.

Who's Eddie?

At work.

You're going to work?

Elizabeth looked at the bright blue polo top for the first time.

I'll ask what happened to your man after we left. You can stay here if you want. Then once you know you can go find him.

Or not find him,
she shrugged.

Elizabeth was still in the corner of kitchen, trying to hunt out the inevitable flaw in the overly simple plan, when Robyn opened the front door to leave.

Wait, wait, you're going already? What do we – what do we do?

Elizabeth grouped herself with her six-year-old, who was still shading a tiger's head with a black biro. Robyn shrugged again.

What's your number, in case we need you?

I don't have a phone.

You don't have a television,

Layla added.

Well, how long will you be?

Elizabeth felt her dignity disintegrating. How many times in the past twelve hours had she not recognised the vulnerability, the pathetic nature, of her own voice.

I finish at six.

What about food?

Robyn came away from the door.

Give me some money,

and she held out her hand. It was neither threatening, nor vulgar, but oddly maternal. Said with such a sigh of surrender and the want for an easy life, that Elizabeth found herself rummaging in the biscuit tin immediately. Elizabeth handed Robyn two twenties and she slammed the door behind her.

The irregular ends of Robyn's hair were still wet as she strode towards work. The mid-morning sun was strong already, beating harshly upon her pale skin. It stirred up a heavy, acidic smell from sweaty bin bags on the pavement that had been put out too late to be collected. Robyn had walked this commute, from station to station, train to petrol, enough times that she could have skirted the pharmacy's sandwich boards blindfolded and timed the traffic light crossings to the millisecond. But this morning she watched her step more closely, as if showing someone else the way.

An estate car was parked at pump 4. Somewhere beneath its rear differential had her skull been crushed against the ground the night before. She weaved between the suckling cars, and *DING*. The shop smelt of bleach.

Eurgh,

Bex rolled her whole face.

I was meant to have my break twelve minutes ago, Robyn, and I was meant to ring my nan and now she's going to be all deteriorated for the rest of the day.

She came out from behind the till, rolling a cigarette.

She's eighty-six, so thanks for that.

Bex had a silver ball bearing pierced through her lip that Robyn couldn't help watching every time she spoke. She also had purple hair and inch-long fingernails (except the left middle and right index which had snapped) that she boasted about growing herself. Whenever she dispensed fuel, eight pointed tips pierced through the latex gloves.

Bex left through the door marked Staff Only.

DING, the estate driver, a silver-haired man in a checked shirt walked to the desk.

Mornin'. Pump 4 please. Oh erm,

he coyly placed a Kit-Kat Chunky onto the counter.

Hot out there already, isn't it? Nice and cool in here, though.

Fifty pounds and seventy pence.

Oh, I thought I got it bang on the mark. Oh damn, I was chuffed,

he slid a flattened wallet from his back pocket.

It's for the chocolate.

Oh, of course! So I did get it bang on. Woohoo!

He pointed a finger to the sky.

Thanks very much. Have a lovely day.

Robyn watched the man walk back to his car, buckle his seat belt and turn on the engine. But when he drove off, she looked away from the empty space that he left behind. There was a vague sense of community amongst those who travelled the high street at this modest hour. These people did not have to squeeze their errands into a lunch break or buy groceries when the checkout queues were backed up into the aisles. They were a collective of kids skipping school, discovering the slow pace of daytime television.

Eddie entered through the Staff Only door.

Huh!

They gasped and grabbed both their cheeks.

Robyn! RobynRobynRobyn love.

They swished quickly towards the till, a lanyard of keys jangling around their neck.

What are you doing here?

I thought I was on ten til six?

Eddie looked around, a full half-turn one way,

then the other.

I mean, after last night,

they whispered.

DING.

Oh! Hello! Welcome welcome!

Eddie's puffy cheeks flushed.

Pump 2.

EXcellent choice of pump! Well done, you! I just need to – I just needed to erm – If you'll excuse me. Ex-cu-say-Mwah!

Neither Robyn nor the customer paid attention to Eddie's little bow, or their power walk back through the staff door. Eddie poked their head out minutes later, to check the coast was clear of customers.

This is a violation of my rights to work actually,

Bex followed Eddie into the shop.

I could faint from exhaustion or dehydration and you're going to have to pay me millions.

Oh I know, I know, love!

Eddie was only half-listening, effectively dragging her to the till.

Just five mins, five mins, my love! I just need to have a convo with Robyn!

Are you firing her? Because you should.

Well, move then!

Bex twitched her silver ball at Robyn.

Robyn followed Eddie down the backstage corridor, past the stock room and the walk-in fridge and the disabled toilet that smelt so strongly of stale urine it made most people's eyes water, into Eddie's office. Loose papers were strewn across the plank of wood nailed to the wall that served as a desk. Eddie cleared a pile of boxed wiper blades off a chair, and Robyn sat. They shut the door.

Robyn, my love, what HAPpened last night? Who WAS that man?

I don't know.

You, you don't know? Well, why did you, why did you hit him, my love?

Concern was furrowed so deeply across their brow. Eddie, a self-confessed hugger, would have taken both Robyn's hands if they hadn't known better.

I didn't hit him.

Well not badly.

It was quite bad, my love,

Eddie grimaced.

No I didn't do the –

Robyn mimed a clonking.

The fire thing. That was someone else.

She saw the lost lady in blue, waiting for a train. Eddie's grimace didn't budge as they stared at her. The rumble of a hand-dryer whirred through the back wall of the office. They sat for a few moments in a stalemate.

You can check the CCTV,

Robyn pointed behind Eddie.

The small square box was switched off, showing nothing more than a blue-grey screen, convex and opaque. It was sat on top of a heavy duty safe, made of textured black metal, where bags of sorted coins hid in the dark. Eddie's expression sunk a little, and flushed a lot.

I got rid of it,

they clamped a hand over their mouth, modelling five baby blue painted nails.

I just saw the blood! And the police were coming! So I gave the extinguisher a quick once over and cleared the tape and told them it had been glitching! Oh my giddy aunt! I'm a stone-cold criminal, Robyn!

All ten blue nails were over their mouth now.

Why did you do that? It looks like you did it.

I don't know! I thought you'd had an altercation, and I didn't want you to get in trouble!

Robyn reached out and put her hand on Eddie's shoulder. The gesture was not premeditated. It was a jerk reaction, like catching something that's falling. She felt the cotton of Eddie's polo, softer than hers, beneath her palm for a second, then pulled away, left with the memory of it in her hand and a strangely violent urge towards this person who she didn't want to hurt at all.

Eddie took a deep breath in, sweeping the air up with their hands.

It's ok,

they exhaled the air away.

The man actually ruled me out to the police straightaway anyway.

He was awake?

Oh yeah! Yes! By the time the ambulance arrived, he was pretty much fully with it!

Robyn thought of Elizabeth, vomiting in her flat. It had sounded so loud, another person existing in her private space.

Listen Robyn, I think I even heard him say he wasn't going to press charges. I mean, he was probably very concussed at the time, but if you did, if something happened, I think you're going to be ok.

Eddie reached for their own knees, the furthermost point of their body and the closest point to Robyn.

I didn't do it.

Ok, my love,

and Eddie did not nod like a disbelieving teacher or a patronising guardian or a social worker searching for clues. They nodded like a friend with full faith.

Well, then! We're all in the clear. What a peculiar night of events! He was a bit of a handsome devil, even with all the blood,

Eddie stuck their tongue out.

Robyn got up and walked out.

Yes, yes, completely, back to work! Righty-ho!

Elizabeth had stayed curled on one end of the sofa, feeling her need to wee evolve from the very first shadow of a notion, to the desperate stabs and squeezes of her bladder, but still, she didn't move. Though her eyes were on Layla, she wasn't really watching her. The child was laying on her back, squirming around on the tiled floor as she played games on the spare mobile. The phone that could contact a different continent in seconds and recognise a thumbprint and tell you the weather forecast if you asked it nicely and had been sat in a kitchen drawer for months.

Ohhh, I died!

Layla blew a raspberry and splatted her limbs at awkward angles. She was still wearing her pyjamas, but the top had ridden up, crumpling the sequinned unicorn, and her round brown belly was exposed. She lay just beyond the angled square of sun that was cast on the ceramic floor. She let her toes dance in and out of the edges of the warm box. This time, she didn't return straight away to the game, with its addictive pathways and tinny soundtrack, but stared up at the ceiling.

Mummy, when are we leaving?
It's not very fun here, in fact.

Elizabeth had been charmed the first time Layla had added *in fact* to her vernacular. But when she'd later heard Amelia using the expression, with the same slight clunkiness, she'd felt an exaggerated fear for her daughter's future. A future in which her greatest obstacle would be weeding out minute phrasal misuses, learned from her loving au pair.

I don't know,
the words came out heavy.

It's a weird sleepover.
There's not any giggles or games and never even midnight snacks,
and it is the daytime now.

I don't know, Layla!

Layla rolled onto her front and buried her embarrassed face in her arm.

Elizabeth would have welled up with guilt at her outburst, at her everything, but every drop of liquid inside her had accumulated in her bladder, pushing the walls, ready to burst. She planted her feet on the cold floor, and the sense of urgency finally took hold. Her head pounded with each rushed step to the bathroom.

She sat on the toilet, folds of velvet, her second skin now, hiked up around her waist. It was a credit to the muscle memory of bodily functions that she was able to urinate when her mind was lost somewhere in a thick fog. The wee was pungent. At first, she didn't notice the knocking.

Then she presumed it was Layla, fidgeting on the hard surface.

Then she heard it. Distinct, purposeful rapping on a door. She didn't flush the loo. Layla was still on her stomach, but with her chin resting on her arm now, eyes fixed on the front door.

Is that Robyn?

Layla asked.

Probably,

Elizabeth said, hiding a slight quiver.

She tried to quieten her rational brain, that told her Robyn had a key. Elizabeth stepped over her daughter and approached the door. It was light grey, painted so thickly it was almost grooved with slapdash drips. She held the metal latch, and could feel Layla's eyes burning into her back. They were forcing courage. But was it more courageous to not be afraid of cowardice, to hide and protect with no care of judgment?

Elizabeth had never been that brave.

She opened the door.

And a small boy stood there.

Woah, nice dress, lady. I respect.

His hair was in straight braids and he wore a white tank top.

Got your shopping.

He held up two carrier bags.

The striped blue plastic had turned white in places, where heavy items inside threaten to split it open and spill out. He squeezed between Elizabeth and the door frame, before her shock had subsided enough to stop him.

I'll put them up here, I guess.

He heaved the bags to his shoulder height, standing on tip toes to rest them onto the kitchen counter. Then he slapped his hands together like a middle-aged baker, satisfied with his work.

Robyn didn't tell me what you wanted, so I just got a bit of this, a bit of that. I've never had to spend forty before. I did get you some of these guys,

He pulled a Tupperware lunch box from the bag.

Always useful,

he knocked on the plastic box.

Then just the usual really. Potatoes, tomatoes, chocolate milk.

Layla had sat up on the floor, watching their new guest, her interest piqued by the mention of chocolate milk.

Oh, I did get myself –

As he rummaged in another carrier, a tin of baked bins fell out and rolled across the counter. Elizabeth stopped it just before it fell.

This,

He lifted up a sour lollipop.

Hope you don't mind. For the troubles and that.

Thank you, for this, erm, sorry, who, who are you?

I'm Vinny,

he said, as if that were all explanation necessary, and slid the sweet stick into his mouth.

Thank you, Vinn – how old are you?

Elizabeth couldn't not ask the question.

I'm nine.

And you're a friend of Robyn's?

I live down the hall with my grandma,

Vinny puffed on his sugar cigar.

I cut Robyn's hair sometimes.

At least something finally made sense in the slew of absurdities of the past day.

I can cut yours if you want?

We're fine, thank you.

Vinny hadn't noticed a second person until then. He peeped round the counter corner.

Unicorn. I respect.

Layla checked out the magical creature on her own top, but was ambushed into an unusual coyness.

Well, you ladies need anything, you know where to find me.

He might as well have doffed his cap as he left.

Elizabeth was still processing the flying visit from the middle-aged nine-year-old, when Layla starting hovering round her feet, trying to nosy in the shopping bags.

We don't know where to find him, in fact.

Robyn slid the loose, single key from her shorts pocket into the front door lock. It was so satisfying, how the deliberate cuts slotted between their matching walls, but she didn't turn it right away. She listened for signs of life behind the door and felt a vague dullness when she was met with silence.

But when she opened it, four eyes, mirrors of each other, darted straight towards her.

Elizabeth was in the kitchen, preparing food, whilst Layla sat on the countertop, an observant sous chef. The evening sun was a match for midday, streaming through the window, barely shifting the reflective dial on the floor, but they had a light on. A white bulb below the cooker hood that Robyn never knew existed. Elizabeth lay down an eating knife that was halfway through a raw potato.

Hi.

Hi.

Hello Robyn.

The flat smelt of watered-down tomatoes, like the canteen pasta at school. Robyn wondered whether Elizabeth had been sick again.

Come on then, Lay, get down.

Elizabeth picked her daughter up and placed her on the floor.

She stayed hugged to her mother's thigh.

How was, work?

Elizabeth returned to seesawing through the potato.

Fine.

She looked up, studying Robyn, her bloodshot eyes hunting for a deeper meaning, a clarification, and Robyn understood that they were in a silent conversation.

It was fine,

she repeated. She watched Elizabeth's fingers trembling with the blunt blade.

We met a boy called Vinny,

Layla announced, flirting around her mother's skirt.

Robyn nodded.

Yes, thank you for sorting that.

And she nodded again.

Robyn swapped her polo top for a tank top in the bedroom. Picking up from one spot on the floor and throwing down onto another, then headed back for the front door.

Where are you going?

The knife was still not all the way through the potato.

Training.

Training for what?

Boxing.

It was as if Elizabeth had adopted, very quickly, Robyn's disinterest in hiding any expression, for her own face was hung with perplexity.

I'll be back at eleven, maybe twelve.

Twelve?

Elizabeth lifted the potato on its metal handle.

No. No, Robyn. We're not staying. We need to talk, and then we need to leave.

Robyn looked out of the window. From this angle, she could only see sky. The portion where pastel blue faded into white. Winston didn't come to the gym on Sundays. He never had, for as long as she'd known him. So she usually trained alone, which meant simply going against a canvas sack until she stopped, or was stopped. There was an off-duty atmosphere on Sunday evenings. She was a background mechanism, whirring away, whilst Darrell pottered in his office, maybe a couple sparred in the ring. She'd only ever missed a couple of Sundays, when she broke her femur and couldn't get down the stairs. She considered how the blue sky would be black by the time she returned tonight, and Elizabeth and Layla would be gone, and decided she could miss one more.

Ok.

Ok,

Elizabeth slapped the potato down and it fell in half.

There'd been a phase when Elizabeth had taken a perverse pride in her inability to cook. When the truth (that home-cooked meals had been a rarity in her childhood), was overtaken by a new truth (that she'd been consistently catered for by university staff and restaurant chefs), she lounged in the fact that she'd never needed the rudimentary skill. She was a woman so revered she needn't get her hands dirty. Others took care of the basics so that she could dedicate her intellect to the intellectual, on a full stomach. And now, the intellect was roasting potato chunks with no oil.

Lay,

Layla looked up at her from the colouring book, which was now densely covered in shiny black scratches.

Do not touch anything, ok? ANYthing.

She nodded furiously.

We'll just be out here.

Elizabeth opened the front door for Robyn. The corridor lights staggered on, and she closed the door behind them, so it just nudged the frame, without locking shut. Robyn leant against the opposite wall, with her arms behind her back, like a sulking pupil exiled from the classroom.

So?

Elizabeth was growing impatient with Robyn's oddities, edging closer to believing her nonchalance was affected and her whole existence somewhat intentionally weird. No one dries their hair with a tea towel.

So your man's fine.

Elizabeth bit the walls of her mouth. She'd only just regained dominance over this situation, she couldn't afford to let it slip away with more vulnerability. She let the answers come to her.

Apparently, he was awake and talking and said he didn't want the police.

She clamped down harder on the flesh.

Eddie got rid of the CCTV, and yeah,

she shrugged,

it's all fine. You can go home.

Her eyes filled.

Good,

she spoke without breathing,

that's good.

As soon as the tears escaped, she brushed them away. The lights timed out and neither of them moved to motion them back on. They stood in the near darkness of the windowless corridor, their outlines only alluded to by the light that came from the stairwell at the far end. Slow footsteps echoed up the stairwell shaft, the sluggish thuds of a worker returning home from a long day.

You can stay if you want though,

came from the darkness.

Robyn sat on the floor and Elizabeth and Layla were on the sofa, all eating their dinner in silence, except for the sound of Layla smacking her tongue against the roof of her mouth, grimacing her way through the chalky potato wedges and homemade tomato sauce. She ate out of a plastic bowl that had come free with a carton of cereal. Robyn and Elizabeth's meals were served in lunchboxes,   always useful.

A siren pierced through the closed window. It did not softly announce its presence and grow louder, it suddenly blurted out, on the street below, making Elizabeth jump. She had hardly touched the potato that tasted like an unsweetened apple.

Thank you, Mummy,

Layla breathed a sigh of relief at her empty bowl.

She had a watery red moustache.

What time have you got work tomorrow, Robyn?

Elizabeth asked.

Tomorrow's my day off,

she drunk the last of the tomato juice from the corner of the lunchbox.

Is it Sunday tomorrow?

Monday.

Monday?

On a Monday, I have gymnastics after school.

I can do three roly-polys, one two three,

Shall I show you?

Layla asked Robyn, already getting up.

Just,

Elizabeth held out her arm,

let your food go down.

Oh yes, or I might be sick,

like Mummy.

Maybe you did too many roly-polys?

She got very close to her mother's face.

Robyn got up and rinsed out her Tupperware box. She left the flat without a word, paying no attention to anything but the intense need to move. Before she'd even reached the bottom of the stairs, she was starting to feel more   correct. The cogs of her machine began turning, and they didn't stop until she'd walked to Stockwell and Oval and Elephant and Castle, to Shadwell and Mile End, watching the sun kiss the city goodnight.

DAY THREE.

Robyn once again woke to whispers. But these were quieter, yet louder. They were only hushed lisps and concentrated breathing, but this time they were in the room with her. Robyn kept her eyes closed, trying to arrange the sounds into a scene: the peeling open of the fridge's rubber seal, the stickiness of bare heels against the tiles, the soft *waitwaitwait,* the rattle of a drawer being eased closed on its tracks.

She gave up and looked.

Layla had both hands wrapped around a chocolate milkshake bottle and Elizabeth covered her own lips as she chewed through a mouthful of plain bread roll. They looked different.

Where's your dress?

Robyn asked.

Elizabeth nearly choked on the white dough. She'd been so glued to their mission of not waking Robyn, that she'd not noticed when they'd failed. Layla lowered the milkshake with a hearty *t'ahhhhh.* There was a semi-circular indent from the bottle lip upon her own.

We had a shower last night when you went out,

the crust scratched her throat.

I hope that's ok.

In Robyn's unannounced absence, Elizabeth had seized control in the most matriarchal way known:

by declaring Bath Time.

Only it was Shower Time, and although it barely qualified as that, the trickle of water and sickly soap had felt more rejuvenating than the rainfall power shower in her en-suite ever had. She'd washed away the dried tears that were still encrusted under her jaw. When they'd been lost for a towel, she'd used the navy dress, soaking each spiky, shiny strand of rich material, taking pleasure in knowing it was being ruined for life, rubbing hard between her toes and under her armpits. Then she'd plaited Layla's hair into two thick braids, and dressed her in fresh clothes, white leggings and a floral t-shirt. Layla had outgrown the top by a few months, but it was all Amelia had packed in the rush. And Elizabeth had also changed, into a cotton t-shirt and loose black trousers, that were cropped just above the ankle. Her clothes smelled of home. Of the warm utility room that constantly murmured with the cycle of the tumble dryer, where she sat sometimes, soundproofed by the folded stacks of linen, wishing the softness of it all would swallow her whole.

Do you want some?

Layla held the chocolate bottle out to Robyn.

Elizabeth sometimes, shamefully, feared that Layla was performing around her. That she thought of her more as a Head Teacher figure than as a mother, one who bore influence and was worth impressing and could give out gold stars for acts of generosity. Perhaps it was a deep-rooted disbelief that someone raised on so much could genuinely care for others.

Perhaps it was because she'd fallen for it once before.

Robyn stretched out fully on the sofa, pushing her fingertips and toes in opposite directions, until her body shuddered. She got up and took a swig of the milkshake.

Hm,

she nodded with approval then handed it back.

That's enough now,

Elizabeth intercepted and placed it back in the fridge. The shelves were mostly empty, apart from cold water that had gathered across them and a six pack of five bread rolls. Vinny had probably spent too much on the lunchboxes in hindsight.

Have some water.

Then am I getting ready for school?

Elizabeth pretended not to hear. Robyn knew Elizabeth was pretending because Robyn had heard it and she was much further away.

Robyn would you –

do you mind watching Layla?

I need to make a phone call outside.

The child looked up at her, softly panting from lapping up water. Robyn was used to being stared at expectantly, but rarely was it entwined with a glimmer of wishfulness.

Ok.

Robyn sat back down on the sofa.

Elizabeth half-closed the front door and crept into the corridor. The lights were already on. Her heart began to thump and her stomach fizzed as she clutched the mobile awkwardly by her side. She slipped onto the landing at the top of the stairwell, knowing that she couldn't risk being any further, nor closer, to the flat.

She trembled as she tried to operate the smartphone, her clammy thumbprint being denied more than once. She scrolled in the contacts list. *N.* In the decades since she'd nervously scanned through a library phonebook, so much had changed

and so much hadn't.

Her finger barely tapped the symbol.

brrrrrrrr

brrr –

She hung up.

A door opened on some level below her. Feet pattered down the stairs. She backed away from the bannister so as not to see or be seen.

She tapped at the phone again, swiping into unnecessary apps, until her brain caught up.

Brrrrr –

Good Morning, St. Catherine's Preparatory, you're through to reception.

Hi, good morning. It's Mrs Sear, Layla's mother. I'm afraid she's not well this morning, so won't be in.

Elizabeth shouldered her way through an abrupt conversation, only to be left in the creaky silence of the damp landing. The corridor lights flicked off behind her, the automatic timer running out, but she was still in the fluorescence of the stairwell. She wished she were in the dark too. She leant over the rubber-topped railing, dizzying herself with the zigzag of flights below. She scrolled and tapped before she could think.

brrrrrrrr

brrrrrrrr

Her heart trampolined between stomach and throat.

Bm. Bm. Bm. Bm.

brrrrrrrr

brrrrrrrr

She felt sick.

bm. bm. bm.

brrrrrrrr

brrrr

Hello?

bm. bm. bm. bm.

Hi.

bm. bm. bm. bm.

I just wanted to say that we're fine. I've got Layla and we're at a hotel and we're fine, she's fine.

The fuzz on the line sounded alive, charged.

I'm sure you understand that we won't be coming back, until we've figured things out –

What is there to figure out?
his voice sounded constricted.

You tried to kill me. Twice,
yet crystal clear.

bm. bm. bm. bm.

You crashed my car. You kidnapped my child. All because you didn't get a job you wanted.

bm. bm. bm. bm.

I think all we need to figure out here is how you get your hands off my child.

Norman was loosening up now, exorcising the anger, cracking his knuckles, giving free rein to the rage.

And how we get you some serious psychiatric help.

That's not –

That's not what? True? Let's let a professional decide, shall we? They'll have a field day with you. The daughter of an alcoholic who never knew her father? It's understandable, I suppose. Not permissible – but it sure makes sense, of course you'd be fucked up, of course you'd be angry –

That's not –

That's not WHAT, Elizabeth? You can't debate away the facts here. You wanted the father of your child to die, you left your husband to die. You're unhinged.

But at that moment, it felt as if her bolts were tightening.

And as they wound, slower and slower, securing into place, her anger became something stable and reliable. It became a force for courage, a trusted friend she knew she could fall back on. Her vision focused.

I will go public.

She didn't listen to his laugh. It was unconvincing.

With everything. I will go straight to Angela and it will be everywhere. The tunnel in Italy. My 30th birthday. The waiter whose scholarship you secretly got revoked because he gave me a priced menu. The waiter whose career you secretly finished because he gave me a look. The job, the joint account, tying your fucking shoelaces. The time you spat in my face while I had Layla strapped to my chest. The miscarriage.

BM. BM. BM. BM.

And in this current climate? You're just the next in a long line of men who had it coming, only no one gives a FUCK about a politician. Everything will be over in an instant. Your career, your life, your future, everything you've spent your whole fucking life plotting, Norman.

BM. BM. BM. BM.

So if you want me to go quietly, you will sign the divorce papers as soon as I send them and you will not fucking see or talk to me or Layla ever again.

Elizabeth dropped the phone over the bannister and watched it fall with precision through the narrow gap.

When it smashed on the bottom floor, all it sounded like was a gentle knock.

Robyn did watch the child. She watched the child, sat on the floor, scrawling her name over and over in the blank spaces of her colouring book, the corners of white paper that were not already filled by printed lines or amateur shading. Her tongue poked out in concentration.

She swiped away a loose strand of hair with a flat palm, then sat back to admire her work.

How do you spell Robyn, Robyn?

she asked suddenly.

Robyn held her hands out for the biro and book.

The plastic felt brittle between her fingers. She pincered it tightly around the nib and pressed down hard against the paper. She took her time with the curve of each letter.

Ruh

Oh

Buh

Yuh

Nuh,

Layla spoke as she wrote.

She was stood so close, Robyn could feel her warm breath. Robyn looked at the letters on the page, the arbitrary bundle of shapes.

How did you hurt your eye?

Layla was watching her now.

Boxing,

Robyn handed back the pen and paper.

Ouch.

She was fixated on the wound that was beginning to stitch itself together.

When I was in pre-prep a boy in my class called Arthur fell off the monkey bars and his tooth went through his lip.

She climbed onto the sofa.

The sofa still held the heat of Robyn's sleeping body in its flattened cushions. The sofa had been thrown in with the flat, after neither the previous tenant nor landlord had any desire to attempt getting it down the stairs. The faded yellow material had turned waxy with years of use, and was dotted with brown spots of aged blood, trophies of various matches, that had wept and oozed in deep sleeps.

What's pre-prep?

You don't know what pre-prep is?

Robyn was not embarrassed, nor patronised, by the child's disbelief. To Robyn, it seemed a bizarre contradiction, that one was expected to feel embarrassed if they didn't know something, and yet if that something is that someone else doesn't know something, it was considered a place of power.

However, Layla did not linger in this place, she rallied round to enlighten her friend.

Pre-prep is the school you go to when you're little,
for nursery and reception. Sometimes they do lessons,
but also some of them are babies and have to take naps.
I'm in Year One now so I'm in Main School
but after the summer holidays I'll be in Year Two.
Did you never go to school then?

She pulled at her t-shirt sleeves that hugged a little too tightly around the upper arm.

I went to school.

Which school did you go to?

Different ones.

Were you in home school?

Adelaide is a new girl in my class and she never went to school, only to home school, in fact. But she's not very clever so her mummy is probably not a very good teacher, and she always forgets to put her hand up. But I gave her my unicorn pencil. I didn't really want it anymore, because it is a little bit hard to write with because it's all wobbly, but I could have thrown it in the bin, but I gave it to her because she doesn't have any fun pencils.

She just has the normal ones.

She rested her chin in her hand, thoughtfully.

The information fell upon Robyn like a stream of confetti: although each piece was not distinguishable, overall, it appeared bright and colourful.

Do you know, Robyn, I like your house, in fact.

It's like a bedroom but with a kitchen in it,

and it is high up.

Sarah had once told Robyn that she liked her trainers, and Eddie had told her that they liked her name when they'd first met. Robyn had never minded having little to offer, or little to like, but now these confetti words stuck to her skin.

Layla raced off to the sofa, over to the window. Robyn watched her struggling on her tiptoes to get her eyes just above the sill that was only an inch wide and that she clawed at with her fingertips. Her tiny calves bulged beneath her white leggings, trying to edge herself millimetres taller. Her heels tapped back down for a breather, then she lifted straight back up, determined to see the skyline from the tall building that she liked, in fact.

Robyn felt if she kept watching, if she silently willed her from the sidelines, she would see Layla grow tall enough. Minutes passed and then Robyn got up. She lifted Layla from behind, wrapping her arms around the child's abdomen with her fists clenched, like how Darrell made her carry weighted sacks sometimes for strength training. Only Layla was far lighter, and her soft clothes smelt almost edible. The window's glass panels were already warm to the touch. The sun had risen with an agenda today. The only cloud in the sky was the one Layla breathed out, with her open mouth so close to the glass as she inspected the city below.

So many little bits,

her cloud blew bigger.

Robyn looked out at all the little bits. All the teeny tiny lives.

And windows windows windows.

Elizabeth wasn't sure how much time had passed on the landing. How long she'd sat on cold ground, gripping the metal bars of the bannister, waiting for her anger to subside. And as it did, in its wake, came a thrilling sense of winning, and freedom. It was in this buzz that she finally walked back along the corridor, excited to collect her daughter and her things and begin a new life.

She pushed the open door with more force than needed, but Layla and Robyn didn't hear her come in. They were at the window, counting something. Elizabeth held off waltzing into the future, to watch them for a moment. Robyn's arms were wrapped around Layla, uncomfortable yet protective.

As she stood there, a bold voyeur, Elizabeth's high was interrupted by an inner voice of rationale, who chastised her impulsivity for having smashed the mobile phone. Their one remaining shard of normality, of luxury, of connection. She thought about who may try to contact her, who may be worried about their sudden disappearance but came up with no one. All her friends, her family, were Norman's. Her virtual diary was micromanaged by his assistant. There wasn't a meeting or smear test that he didn't know about. And her prescribed squares of free time were allocated by him, neatly outlined on their shared gridded screen.

Thirty-three, thirty-four.

Layla was tapping on the window, greasing it with her prints.

Thirty-five.

Robyn pointed, too.

Elizabeth had been her daughter once. To trust those who she shared nothing with except a moral compass, to overlook peculiarities in the name of a good heart. And they'd been the greatest friends she'd ever known. She'd spent only a split second with them in the hour of her damned life, and maybe now she could turn back the clock. Maybe now she could do whatever she wanted, outside of all gridded lines.

Elizabeth joined them by the window.

What are we counting?

she whispered.

Windows. *Windows.*

The sun was burning through the glass, but she stayed with them in its glare.

Hey, Robyn,

Elizabeth hadn't looked this closely at the young woman's face. Her pale complexion was flecked with the small white lines of half-healed scars, and her dark eyes, with their traces of light, sat like sunken saucers, buried alive except for in that brief moment, when they were called to attention, and gave away just a flash of connection, enough for the impromptu request to tumble out.

Would you mind if we stayed a little longer?

Layla twisted herself to await the response.

Sure,

Robyn said, but the disconnect had returned, and she put Layla down.

Robyn had never used a trolley before. She'd never even used a basket before, since she only ever bought an armful of groceries at a time. A loaf of white bread and a jar of peanut butter could last her a week (particularly when supplemented by petrol station confectionaries).

Layla looked too big for the trolley seat, but her mother wedged her in, clearly believing thigh bruises would be less eternally damaging to the child than a potential run-in with someone who shopped in the discount supermarket. Robyn followed the cart up and down the freezer aisles, marvelling at the host of meals that lay in icy waiting, perfectly packaged and ready to go. Elizabeth was slow to add to the trolley at first, wincing at the products on display, but after the first pepperoni pizza landed a spot, and Layla nearly combusted with excitement, she began to stock up. Soon Layla was the conductor of a carriage full of potato waffles and chicken nuggets and spaghetti hoops and chocolate biscuits and sweet cereal. Both Robyn and Layla dimmed a little as they ventured down the fruit aisle, Elizabeth adding apples and satsumas to the pile out of shame if nothing else.

They snaked through the stocked lanes. Where other shoppers whizzed round for essentials, these three meandered amongst the goods, fully absorbing the magnitude of what was on offer when not restricted by money or rules or the judgement of others. The shelves were a vista of brightly wrapped gifts, and they could have anything they wanted.

In the toiletries section, Elizabeth loaded up on bottles of hand soap and three separate bottles of shampoo and conditioner and body wash. Away from the main aisles, they pulled into the comparative calm of the clothes corner, where their overloaded senses could pause a moment.

We need a couple bits,

Elizabeth said to herself, pushing the trolley into the muted zone of hanging material.

Robyn watched her finger fabrics, and pick up and reject items, just by the hanger. She rifled through a line of wireless bras, like a filing cabinet, selecting the right fit. She placed a multipack of knickers on top of their multipack of crisps, and a pair of rubber sliders. In the children's section, Layla chose two t-shirts with delicate floral patterns, not unlike the one she was already wearing. Then she gasped at a pair of pink sandals, with foam soles and bejewelled straps, and Elizabeth added them to the trolley.

Would you like anything?

Elizabeth asked Robyn,

who had been loitering by a rail of jumpers. Robyn's wardrobe still only consisted of her work polos or boxing kit, items gifted over the years by guardians trying to make a good first impression or donated as part of someone's charitable drive. She owned one hoodie, two vests, two shorts and a handful of holed underwear. The vests looked tie-dyed with old sweat and any socks with the heels still intact were stained a grubby grey that couldn't be reversed with washing up liquid in the sink. Robyn thought that maybe she would like to wear something that smelled like Elizabeth and Layla, that filled her nose with such a delicate landscape and had a softness that she wanted to rub her lips against.

No,

she shook her head.

At the till, Elizabeth kept her purse inside her bag as she counted out notes.

As they walked back home, all three of them contended with a rapidly melting choc ice. The sun was beating down furiously overhead, at the exact point where no one left a shadow behind. Elizabeth could feel her t-shirt sticking to her stomach, and the backs of her ears were becoming uncomfortably hot, but she wouldn't complain. Robyn was carrying all three heavy duty shopping bags. All Elizabeth was holding were the five precious fingers of her favourite person on the planet. She held on tightly as they navigated the pavements, filled with swathes of people. Human body heat rose like steam from a stew, thick and pungent.

Brixton always reminded Elizabeth of Anita, of the feminist lecture they'd attended in Lambeth Town Hall and the man who sold them weed who lived in the doorway of a wig shop. Elizabeth still thought of Anita often, living in her memories far longer than she'd actually existed in her life. Some days it was only a flash of a scene, smoking on their stoop or ladling mulled wine on their gas stove, and it was batted away within milliseconds. Other days she spent longer, contemplating where Anita was now and wondering how she would judge the woman Elizabeth had become. Elizabeth could simultaneously know that she outgrew Anita even before their year of friendship fizzled out, and still feel an intense need to impress her.

These memories flitted somewhere in Elizabeth's mind, disjointed and ethereal, whilst she was confronted by the reality of their town, two decades later. It was unlike central London where every pedestrian had a clear purpose. Here, the people wandered and chatted and played instruments and waited. Some of them waited in the middle of the pavement, with no evidence as to what they were waiting for. Perhaps they didn't know themselves.

But Robyn sped through the crowds, and Elizabeth and Layla struggled to stay on her tail. The space between pedestrians grew even smaller as they passed the entrance to the underground. Elizabeth looked down at Layla. Though she could feel her hand in hers, she still needed proof that she was there, that she was safe. Layla looked back at her, with chocolate smeared around her mouth, and eyes filled with uneasiness at the swarm of hips around her. Elizabeth didn't move to comfort her, in the hope that no comfort would be a comfort in itself. That there was nothing to worry about. That this was London, that this was how Mummy had grown up.

But in truth, she could only recognise Layla's uneasiness, because she felt it herself. For years, she had jumped to the defence of these communities, without stepping foot in one. She'd tutted when Norman locked the car doors as they drove through certain neighbourhoods, but it was easy to tut, with her safety belt on. She used to thrive off being a part of something. And she'd always thought she still was. But now, amongst the vendors and the players and the waiters, she wondered if the fear of strangers was only natural once you'd shrugged off the invincibility of youth, or had she shrugged off more than that? She flushed at the thought of the women in the bathroom. Perhaps they had not been frozen with embarrassment for themselves, but at the *champagne socialist* with no self-awareness.

The pavement opened up and they could see more,

but not Robyn.

Elizabeth stopped next to a flower stall. She whipped her head around, scanning the bodies for the skinny white limbs. She squinted into the distance, how far could she have gone. It felt like her eyes weren't working, scanning letters over and over without reading a word. *flowers for you miss*, said a man with no teeth and she shook her head. A bus pulled up and passengers alighted and flooded the pavement again. Someone knocked into Layla. She'd have fallen to the ground if Elizabeth wasn't holding her hand so tightly. She swept her up into her arms, trying not to panic, but the hot bodies felt claustrophobic. Perhaps they'd missed a turn? Elizabeth looked back down the street, more people pouring out of the station. She tried to look for shopping bags. Three large shopping bags. Three large shopping bags, filled with free food.

Elizabeth's stomach sank further.

Where's Robyn, Mummy?

Layla asked.

Elizabeth's eyes were drawn to the same spots, the same shop fronts and sections of pavement, again and again. She thought she was looking for a black vest top, but now she doubted that's what she was wearing. She doubted she knew anything about her at all. *Please miss, flowers, roses roses.* Elizabeth pulled her handbag in tighter. She tried to think of their journey to the supermarket. They hadn't come this way, they'd never passed the station before. Why had they been led somewhere new, why had she darted off. The movement of people around her was dizzying. She held onto a wing of the flower stall's gazebo, as if pinching the thin plastic sheet would steady her. She looked down at her new sandals, the poolside shoes, trying to think, struggling to breathe. She had cash, for a cab, but to where? Her eyes began to prickle, and the weight of it all,

There she is!

Layla pointed at the small person, laden with bags, weaving back towards them.

Why did you stop? Where did you go?

Robyn asked.

Where did YOU go?

Elizabeth still guarded herself, and Layla.

Robyn struggled to find her pocket, as she clutched the shopping handles. She pulled out a single, silver key.

I got you a key. So you can go in and out.

Elizabeth's heart still pounded.

Did you want,

Robyn pointed awkwardly towards the bunches of flowers.

Elizabeth shook her head, and the three of them continued home.

Robyn was polishing off her third slice of pepperoni pizza, grease shining across her lips, whilst Elizabeth and Layla still worked their way through their first. Elizabeth dabbed at the corners of her mouth with a tissue before any mess even appeared. Tonight, they all sat on the floor, encircling the pizza, like a sacred ceremony. The brown tiles were still putting a cool fight up against the growing heatwave.

As Layla reached for her second slice,

Uh,

Elizabeth paused her,

Let the first one go down first. It's not a race.

If it was, they'd be losing, thought Robyn, as she reached for a fourth.

Layla sat on her hands.

It is a race at school.

To eat your food? I hope not,

Elizabeth covered her mouth as she spoke.

No, sports day race!

I was on the blue team in reception

and we lost because Oscar dropped the bean bag,

so I don't want him on my team this time.
Losing one time is ok,
But, but,
losing two times is –
it's too much.
She bounced up and down on her hands.
I love sports day because you wear PE kit alllll day,
and there's no lessons, and I like lessons, but sometimes,
sometimes I like no lessons, too.

Robyn could only remember attending one sports day, at a school she didn't know the name of, even at the time. She'd only joined the week before the end of term event, and a clerical error assigned her to the boy's register. She was picked by random to compete in a middle-distance run, and the sunbathing teens on the sports field had laughed as she stepped onto the boy's start line. Teachers had tried to amend their mistake, to usher her out of the race, but she'd run anyway. She sprinted until her lungs burnt, and wiped seconds off the school record.

Are you going to watch me again, Mummy?
You saw me run really fast, didn't you?
And now I'm bigger and run faster, in fact.

She still kept obedient self-control from the next pizza slice (by squashing her hands).

Well, actually, Lay,
Elizabeth cleared a chunk of crust from her throat.
You might have to miss sports day this year.

Oh,
Layla's shoulders sunk,
followed by her whole body.

Just because, because we're here, and we're quite far from your school. So we might have to, we might have to start summer holidays early?
Elizabeth placed a hand on her daughter's slumped back.

And not go to school at all?
Not even for the disco party?

Layla's cheeks and chin began to bulge. Thick droplets appeared on her lashes.

Robyn had never seen tears emerge so slowly on a child. The ones she grew up around, the ones she passed in the street, seemed to erupt into wailing in an instant. But Layla's face changed slowly, as if she were trying to sit on her tears like she sat on her hands. And she started to resemble Elizabeth more, in this compressed pain.

I'm so sorry, baby, you're such a good girl, such a good good girl, and we'll do lots of fun things here, I promise,

Elizabeth had leant right down, so that her lips pressed to Layla's head as she spoke.

Why are we here?

Layla whispered,

with a runaway tear rolling next to her nose.

Robyn had forgotten about her fifth slice. She watched Elizabeth sit up straight and draw breath, the greasy tissue still balled between her fingers. Footsteps and clunking came from the corridor, and a purr of traffic from where the window was open at its widest possible slit, and a gentle sniffing from Layla.

Well, baby, me and daddy had a fight. Daddy wasn't very nice, and he scared me.

Robyn thought of the black and white figure limping towards the darkness on the CCTV, of the faceless man telling her to leave.

And I don't really want to be around him.

Elizabeth's voice changed, it drew upwards and inwards.

I don't want to be scared,

She rubbed Layla's back again.

Daddy scares me too, sometimes,

it was even quieter.

Elizabeth stopped rubbing.

Robyn thought of the man with his hand over her mouth. How she had just closed her eyes and lain there.

Well then,

Elizabeth cleared her throat.

We won't let that ever happen again. We won't let him ever scare you again.

The *we* rang in Robyn's ears as she picked up a fifth slice, and passed it to Layla, who wiped her nose and graciously accepted.

Do you want us to have the sofa tonight?

Elizabeth asked, as she carried a sleeping Layla towards the bedroom.

Robyn shook her head.

She bedded down on the sofa. She didn't feel the need to walk tonight. She drifted to sleep, in a silence that wasn't empty.

DAY FOUR.

Layla already had her new sandals on for breakfast. She sat with her legs dangling off the sofa, swinging the pink shoes back and forth, as she ate a bowl of cereal. Milk threatened to slop over the sides, as she kept her gaze on the jewelled straps, floating in and out of her vision.

What shall we do today, baby? Anything you want.

Elizabeth also had her new shoes on. She wasn't so dazzled by their style, but did appreciate their comfort, and their protection from the crumby floor. Robyn had left for work, and the sky was a blistering blue and Elizabeth felt positively positive. She'd had a dreamless sleep, and today she felt as new as her supermarket bra and knickers.

Ermmmmm,

Layla swung her legs.

We could go tooo the Natural History Museum? Orrrr the aquarium? Or the cinema – no it's too hot for the cinema –

We could go to the park?

Layla pinged like her lightbulb idea.

The park?

We could get ice cream,

she poked her tongue between her teeth.

That sounds wonderful!

Elizabeth zoomed in towards her, dodging giggles and soggy cereal to plant kisses wherever she could.

On their way out of the building, the loose front door key safely zipped inside Elizabeth's purse, they passed Vinny, sat on the top step of the stairs.

Oh, excuse me, ladies,

he scooted to one side.

Lovely morning out there.

Elizabeth swallowed a laugh that bubbled up.

Good morning, Vinny.

They squeezed past the boy, Layla hugging her mother's side.

Shouldn't you be at school?

Elizabeth turned back to ask, aware that she was shepherding her truant daughter.

Oh no, not really,

he was holding a ball of blu-tack.

Where's your grandma?

She's at work. Hotels don't clean themselves!

So you're by yourself all day?

Elizabeth noticed the dry skin around his eyes that she hadn't seen on his flying introduction. It had turned his lower lids darker, with small flakes gathering in the creases.

I go with her sometimes. I stand with Jeffrey the doorman, carry suitcases for him.

Well, we're going to the park, if you'd like to come with us? If you don't think your grandma would mind.

The innocence flashed across his face, and the eczema became that of a baby, not an old man.

And we're getting ice cream,

Layla was still half hidden by her mother's legs.

You can show us the way, Vinny.

The three of them travelled the long road to the park. Vinny stood on the outside of the pavement, shielding the women from the bus lane, and let them pass through the park gate first, all whilst recounting neighbourhood tales with warm-hearted nostalgia. Layla's attention was drawn only sporadically from the boy to admire her pink sandals slapping against the hot ground.

The park did not yawn out in front of them like the one behind their house. This one opened up slowly, a trail rolling through soft hills, that passed yellowed slopes and basketball courts and arrived at the prized play park.

Robyn watched heat bouncing off the ground with a stinging fury, blurring a mirage across the empty forecourt. She sat alone at the till. On Eddie's day off, Bex was acting manager, who acted nothing like a manager. She'd been in the back office for half the afternoon, stocktaking with Sanjay. Robyn worked her way through an entire packet of bubblegum. It was always quieter on hot days, as if drivers daren't risk being around such flammable liquids.

She didn't notice the small car splutter into pump 1 at first. Then Mr Peters caught her eye, waving manically next to his vehicle. Robyn left the store completely unattended.

I I I I'd like twelve pounds annnd thirty-nine pence please.

Robyn started filling. She knew to allow for the slightly jammy trigger on pump 1. She watched the counter, and Mr Peters watched her, a ploughman's sandwich caught in the beard today. Her eyes drifted past the trunk of the dispenser, from where fuel hoses snaked out like roots, towards the high street. Emptier than usual, as pedestrians tried not to linger in the sun. Her eyes flicked back to the counter, marching its way up in value. And back to the high street, where shoppers darted from the air-conditioned pharmacy opposite. The petrol chugged loudly, and beneath it, the wheels of a buggy. A woman in denim shorts and sunglasses pushed it along the jagged pavement. She had hair like Elizabeth's. And from the pram, stuck out two little brown shins,

HEY HEY HEY, I said twelve!

Robyn let go of the handle. 13.09.

Stupid, stupid girl! I'm not paying for that.

The woman and buggy had disappeared.

Robyn pulled the handle and dispensed a glug more.

Stupid, stupid girl!

Mr Peters drove off and Robyn returned inside. Bex was still backstage and would learn nothing of the £13.15 stolen petrol until she cashed up. Robyn sat in line of the air conditioning unit, counting down the minutes of her shift. When the hour did arrive, Sanjay finally sloped out to cover the till.

On her way out, the spread of magazines caught Robyn's eye. She'd never stopped to look at them before, and definitely never read one. En masse, they all blurred into one. Even the glossy rows of shiny homes and smooth faces alongside the bold typefaces and amateur snapshots, it was all a blur of faux content. Like seeing poster after brightly-coloured-poster on the underpass, how they fused into one artificial wallpaper. But today, on the bottom shelf, Robyn picked out a distinct shape: a unicorn. It was purple, with a white smile of square teeth and a rainbow-coloured horn.

FREE COLOURING PENS! It said next to it, in a star banner. And, sure enough, attached was plastic wallet of four felt-tips.

Robyn knelt down and snatched it up.

I'm taking this,

she said to Sanjay without turning around, and left the store before he'd found a voice to question her.

Elizabeth felt a slight rush of relief hearing Robyn's key in the door. Not that she'd known there was anything to be relieved from. The day had been joyous and she'd loved every second of its escapism, but still anxiety had bedded down within her nervous system, so quietly that she'd not noticed it was sleeping there,

until Robyn came in and shooed it away.

There were chicken nuggets in the oven and she was sterilising every crockery and cutlery item in hot soapy water. Layla was choreographing a routine in the sliver of floor space, occasionally incorporating the sofa as a raised stage or cushioned tumble mat for the more elaborate manoeuvres. It was the picture of domesticity.

Elizabeth had found herself gathering questions for Robyn throughout the day, about Vinny and his grandmother, and how Robyn came to live here and her family background. With each hour that passed, Elizabeth tumbled into an almost nostalgia, a rose-tinted remembrance of the creature who could frustrate her, potentially endanger her. With distance, came intrigue and a desire to study. To unlock and to understand. She'd also collected anecdotes from their afternoon – of Vinny and an ice cream vendor, of a near collision at the traffic lights, of a cocksure rat on the stairs – and hoped Robyn could provide a place to lay her souvenirs.

Hi,

Elizabeth found herself stirring the washing up.

But Robyn lingered by the door, and the anxiety barged its way back in. It was noticeable this time, like a once-docile wasp now disturbed and enraged.

Everything ok?

The hot water stung her hands.

Robyn still didn't move. She had her arms behind her back.

Elizabeth clutched a handle beneath the water line.

Erm,

Robyn scowled, then marched towards Layla.

Elizabeth pulled up the metal item, a useless spoon.

Here you go.

She handed a magazine to Layla.

Layla gasped,

A magathine!

A UNICORN!

Look, Mummy, it has a unicorn on it!

Her legs were planted wide apart, as wide as her agape jaw.

It has pens, so I thought you could colour. If you wanted.

Elizabeth plunged the spoon back into the sink with a splash.

Layla gasped again.

It even has purple,

oh my goodness,

she shook her head in disbelief.

Thank you, Robyn, thankyouthankyou.

In Layla's bedroom at home, she had a hand-carved oak desk, and above it, attached to the wall, was a pen holder, designed like an over-sized harmonica and filled with every shade of felt-tip pen imaginable. They were always meticulously arranged by Amelia to smoothly blend from one colour to the next. Layla also had a climbing frame in their garden, personalised with princess-style turrets, but today she'd gushed over a rusted see-saw in a public playground. And last month, she'd attended an ice-cream birthday party, where they'd had bottomless access to sprinkles and sauces and cones, but earlier she'd listened intently as Vinny described all three experiences he'd had with soft-serve. Elizabeth saw her daughter's gratitude appear like a miraculous, self-seeded flower. She knew she'd done nothing to cultivate its growth, but here it was. And now that she'd noticed it, she would tend to it, and nourish it, and be thankful for its existence every day. It had grown as a resilient weed, and now it was her prized showstopper.

That's very thoughtful, thank you, Robyn,

Elizabeth wiped her hands on a towel.

Robyn disappeared into the bedroom. Elizabeth crouched to peek at the nuggets through the stained black gauze of the oven door. As she watched their crispy skins sizzle, and heard Layla's animated muttering over articles, she felt a strong wave of giddiness. Not the type of contentment that one wishes to live with permanently, but the momentary, electrocuting shock of pure joy, that shimmies up your spine and flutters across your ribcage. The sensation that is as fleeting as a sneeze, but marks you like a scar.

She dished up the chicken nuggets with baked beans and potato waffles, using packaging scraps as placemats on Layla's dance floor. The caged window was open an inch, but the evening air was too heavy with its own heat to heave itself into a breeze. Elizabeth fanned herself with her hand, then Layla helped, flapping her new magazine, as they waited for Robyn to come out of the bedroom.

When she did appear, she looked as if she were headed straight for the front door, only drawn off course by the spread of party food on the floor. She hesitated and sat down.

How was work?

Elizabeth ate a waffle with her fingers, tearing off one dainty corner of latticed potato at a time.

Ok,

Robyn put an entire nugget in her mouth.

We went to the park and Vinny did a flip over and onto the slide.
He was holding the pole and then, and then went upside down,
and just like,

Layla rolled one hand (with a nugget) over the other (with a waffle).

I was going to do it, too,
but I think I'm too little
and also, I think I'm not a daredevil.

Elizabeth was too busy fawning over Layla to notice how Robyn had finished her meal already. Suddenly she was on her feet and at the front door,

I'll be back later.

A draught of warm air wafted towards them as the door slammed shut.

Oh, here she fucking is, the queen of fucking England.

Robyn didn't look at Darrell across the ring as she strapped up her hands.

Jesus fucking christ, haven't seen you in two days, thought you'd died. Or finally got a fucking life.

A couple of new guys sniggered.

Robyn sprinted on the spot, then tuck jumped high in the air, sending oxygen knocking on the walls of her muscles, like battering rams trying to smash through the lethargy.

You all good, Robyn?

Winston gave her a thumbs up, with both thumbs.

She nodded. Then cracked her neck and knuckles. She hopped up onto the mat, teetering on the edge, on the outside of the ropes.

Nope,

Darrell didn't look at her, but pointed.

You're off.

It's a Tuesday?

He turned to her now.

I don't care if it's Christmas fucking day. You don't turn up, you lose your slot.

Robyn scissored over the ropes and marched towards him.

That's not the rules, I'm here every day.

Were you here yesterday?

Were they here yesterday?

She flung a strapped hand towards the two pretty men loitering next to Darrell.

Were you here the day before that?

Were they?

Get out of my ring, Robyn.

The white light beat down over her head. She couldn't see into the bowels of the gym, but could hear the squeak of trainers and the patter of fists against unsuspecting rubber. Only the mask of Darrell was lit, where he leant against the ropes, and it darkened under his eyes and nose with evil shadows.

Get out of my fucking ring, Robyn.

She looked him dead in his half-lit eyes, because she didn't have the energy to catch a pretty boy smirking.

She slowly climbed back over the ropes, and disappeared into the background, becoming just another pair of hands battling against a lifeless bag.

And it did not feel familiar.

Perhaps the two days away had been enough to sever her innate tie with the exercise. Because she did not feel like a saltwater fish gliding back into the ocean, finally able to breathe and move with full freedom. Instead, it was as if she was sinking further into a thick bog with each stroke. All she wanted to do was stop.

stop

stop

stop

stop-stop

stop

Each punch called out to her.

Even in the delirious depths of a twelve-round match, her instincts had never been so loud in their want to surrender, and never been so tempting to listen to. And here, with no knock-out blow awaiting, the possibility was so easy. Those around her, who fought their own demons, would surely not even notice.

And then it dawned on her,

whilst her arms still,

Pup

Pup

Pup

Pup-pup,

that she had been here before. Just days earlier. She'd nearly been seduced by surrender, as the man had suffocated her own sounds and pushed her into the earth.

She felt his hand over her mouth again.

Pup

Pup

Pup

And saw his face, contorted by her own blurred vision.

Pup

Pup-pup

pup

Then she watched him, following Elizabeth into the dark,

Pup

Pup

Pup

and her throttled whisper for help.

Pup-Pup

Pup
Then she imagined him straddled over her navy dress,
Pup
Pup
his hand over her mouth instead,
Pup
Pup
Pup
and then Layla,
watching on,
trying to contain her slow tears.
Pup
Pup
Pup
Pup

DAY SEVEN.

Robyn sat on the countertop, eating cereal, from a bowl, with a spoon.

Have you got work today?

Layla turned away from the window.

No,

she dribbled milk as she spoke.

Boxing?

Layla herself had a smudge of toothpaste around her lips. Her hair was down. Loose coils still frizzed and fuzzed from pillow friction.

Uh uh,

she shook her head and dribbled again.

So are you with us today?

The three of them had slipped into a routine, by which Robyn was in the flat as little as possible, at work or at the gym, and Elizabeth and Layla were in the flat as little as possible, at the park or buying new household essentials, but they would all convene at some point for an oven-cooked dinner on the floor.

I'm working tonight,

Robyn said, then drank the milky dregs straight from the bowl.

So you can come to the park if you want to?

With us?

In the daytime?

She drowned each word in hope.

Ok,

Robyn hopped down from the counter.

My god,

Elizabeth opened the bedroom door. She wore the same top and slacks as the past few days.

How does it keep getting hotter?

She fanned herself with the fridge door, and the room with a vague hint of forgotten vegetables.

Robyn's coming to the park with us, Mummy!

Robyn couldn't see Elizabeth's face, hidden in the cool cupboard. But Layla was far bolder in hunting a reaction, skipping up to her mother's side.

You love that park, don't you?

Elizabeth squeezed Layla's cheeks.

They collected Vinny along the corridor and walked as a peculiar band to the park. It was surprising to Elizabeth how quickly complete freedom had taken on a schedule. Each day was a blank canvas by which they could paint the most abstract of worlds, and yet, their meals and showers and bedtimes were as linear as graph paper. This walk to the park, that they could run or skip or snake backwards should they choose, had become a commute. Their footsteps adopted unnecessary purpose, marching towards a destination, forgetting that each stride was as much a part of their day, if not more, than the imagined lands that lay ahead.

Except for Layla, who found something in every step to

look at,
laugh at,
comment on,
step on,
step over,
whilst the rest of them forged ahead.

The park's grass was keeled over in exhaustion, dehydrated and desperate and not even halfway through the summer months. It crackled beneath picnic blankets and makeshift football pitches, that were already out. It was not lunchtime yet, nor the weekend, but it teetered on the cusp of both, and such a cusp could be conquered when the sun was this hot. College kids could play truant and colleagues could work from home, in the unspoken agreement of exceptional circumstances.

They walked past the playground that buzzed with children. Sun-creamed grips and sticky handprints clung and swung and slid from every item, trying not singe themselves on boiling metal.

We'll come back when it's quieter,

Elizabeth tugged Layla's limp hand.

They drifted past waves of tinny music and beverages not brewed for this hour and found quiet shelter beneath a common lime tree, but Layla was not ready for rest.

Mummy, will you time me to run to that tree?

Elizabeth hadn't put her watch on in days.

Why don't you race Vinny?

Layla stared at her new friend, the eloquent storyteller with pungent manliness.

But, he's a boy?

That doesn't matter. Does it, Robyn?

Elizabeth instantly regretted the question.

It sounded like she was attempting to lean on a coparent or corner her into agreement or insinuating that Robyn believed herself to be on par with boys or maybe it questioned her gender identity altogether or brought back visions of their collective defeat of Norman or –

No. I'm faster than all the boys.

Layla squinted into the sun.

All of them?

Yeah.

Elizabeth felt a punch of pride in her gut, and it trickled over her lips. She had to bite down to stop a smile spreading.

Ladies, ladies, ladies,

Vinny cooled them.

I'm pretty speedy.

Elizabeth stayed beneath the dappled shade, watching the makeshift sports day unfold. She slid off her sandals and pumiced her hard heels against a patch of dried earth and squeaked yellowed blades between her toes. She leant back on her hands until her shoulders ached and she was frozen in position. No longer able to flick off the insects that adventured across her, she let them trespass in peace.

She spectated the competition dramas from afar: the false start that demanded a rerun, the change of the finishing tree, the English Setter that joined as a stray competitor, the decision to reform the challenge completely as a relay race. And as she watched on, a nuisance tear kept appearing, tickling the corner of her eye. It was as unconsidered as tears caused by the wind. She kept dabbing it away, forcing her focus to remain on the races. Soon the troops returned, shining with sweat.

Have some water,

Elizabeth passed round a bottle from her bag.

We were,

really fast,

Layla panted.

Layla and Vinny supplied an in-depth debrief and Elizabeth dutifully filled each pause for breath:

Oh really,

uh huh,

yes, I saw that,

until the commentary dried up and they all reflected silently on their own performances.

The four of them lay beneath the lime tree, gazing at the pinpricks of blue that edged their way between the green leaves. The gnarled trunk was wrinkled with wisdom and stood as certain as the solid blue sky behind it. Even the branches did not quiver, for there was no breeze to yield to. Only when a bird landed somewhere unseen, in the heights of the dense tree, did the leaves dance a little.

Mumma?

Elizabeth felt the weight of the air press down upon her. In the shade the heat did not pierce the skin, but lay thickly on top, compressing the will to move, to talk. Perhaps she would not respond.

Yes, baby,

Who was she kidding?

Why do birds sing?

Elizabeth inhaled to answer,

then stopped.

It was as if her tongue looked around to see her brain had abandoned the plan. Instead, she listened. To the bird above them, and then to the others. She tuned in, to the calls and caws and cheeps and tweets. And as she dialled into their station, the rest of the park became nothing but peripheral static. It was like walking into a room full of people, hearing the clashing conversations of all pitches and tones and speeds and yet, somehow, there was an overall rhythmic pulse, the need to converse, to be heard. Why did these birds converse, what did they have to say? Was every call a danger warning? A celebration? A mundane passing thought? Did they sing in fear or pain or jubilation? Did they know someone was listening or call out anyway?

Did they know she was listening?

Elizabeth couldn't tell her daughter for sure, so she didn't tell her at all.

I don't know,

and the tear reappeared.

That's ok,

Layla felt for her mother's hand.

Answers had allowed Elizabeth to transcend the life she was given and take the life she wanted. Knowing them all was her greatest illusion.

This time she let the tear slope across her cheekbone, before she wiped it away. Her hand accidentally brushed Robyn's on the way back down. She'd forgotten she was listening.

Perhaps just as the birds had.

Early afternoon, they travelled back home. They stopped in a store, for rubber gloves and kitchen roll and a blast of air conditioning to revitalise them for the rest of the journey. The high street was fairly empty and Robyn and Elizabeth walked just behind the children. Robyn found it hard to follow their sluggish footsteps.

I got pudding for dessert today, I reckon. Grandma always says, blue sky at night, angel's delight. Butterscotch, I'm feeling it,

Vinny carried a four-pack of kitchen roll beneath one arm.

It's nice you live with your grandma,

mine is all the way in France, in fact,

Layla spoke to Vinny, but was focused on avoiding cracks in the pavement.

Ooh la la,

Vinny joked.

I only,

she made a big step,

have one,

and another,

because my mummy doesn't have a mummy.

Robyn was sure Elizabeth would drop into conversation here, but she didn't.

Vinny swapped the rolls to the other arm.

I don't have a mum either, actually,

his bravado had diminished, revealing a young boy who Robyn hadn't seen before.

The different rhythms of their gaits beat upon the same drum of the hot pavement. Soft sandals skipped cracks and tired trainers marched on and reluctant sliders slapped out a constant base.
I don't have one either.

All three of them glanced back at Robyn, but did not break their stride. They continued on in their tuneless melody. Not even the jet that blast across the sky had a lyric to contribute.

It's my birthday tomorrow,

Elizabeth finally spoke.

DAY EIGHT.

Robyn waited for Eddie to alarm the main doors, not out of politeness but the contractual obligation that required at least two staff members to oversee the station lock-up in the early hours of the morning. She stood eating a Crunchie that she'd pocketed on her way out, whilst Eddie went about their managerial duties.

The alarm code changed every fortnight and it never failed to be a source of hypertension for Eddie.

Four nine six two –

Eddie?

Yes, my love! Three four one.

What do you do on someone's birthday?

She dug out a chunk of honeycomb with a fingernail.

Birthday? Oh darn, four five six –

Yeah, people do things, don't they?

Two four, No! Two three, oh dammit! Sorry, my love, birthdays, yes people celebrate birthdays, four nine six two three –

They whipped around to Robyn, aghast.

It's not your birthday is it, my love? I know you don't celebrate, but it's never too late to change! Oh, I wish you'd said, you can get your free sausage roll!

It's not my birthday,

she pocketed the wrapper.

People go to the cinema for birthdays.

Eddie surveyed her, checking for signs of a birthday martyr.

Yes, I suppose they do,

but it didn't seem very Robyn.

You can do all sorts! Whatever you like! Eat cake, drink wine, go out to dinner!

Go out to dinner?

Four-nine-six-two-three-four-one-four,

they hurried, then turned their full attention to Robyn.

Yes! A nice meal! Well, doesn't even have to be a nice one, really. Paulo took me to a crappy buffet last year, but it was just heavenly to be out of the house! Is it – is it someone special's birthday?

Robyn dislodged another bit of honeycomb.

She waited for the alarm to settle, then disappeared across the forecourt with a wave.

Elizabeth woke before Layla for the first time in their single bed, which was now complete with a bottom sheet. It was not sunlight that beamed in below the door, only the idea of light. Light by comparison. She had no way of knowing the time, but she could picture the empty streets outside, in that civil twilight, when it looked as if the sleeping world had accidentally left a light on.

Elizabeth had awoken to hands around her oesophagus. They had slipped quietly into this shelter and strangled her in the night. She could still feel their pressure now. The ten familiar fingers of anxiety choking her. She could feel their shadow in her stomach, flapping dark wings each time she inhaled. How foolish to forget about them, to think that she could hide in a new life. She lay in the almost-darkness, permitted to a few normal breaths, natural and reassuring, before one would jump up and throttle her,

and she gripped helplessly at the mattress.

In the ebb between these ferocious tides, despite herself, she thought of Norman. The abandonment and isolation that had been her own doing, and had masqueraded as freedom, now seemed so obviously ripe for ambush. Where was he, what was he doing, what was he planning? Her self-imposed exile had become overwhelmingly claustrophobic. She tried to pant quietly and compress the panic from punching out of her body, to avoid waking Layla.

She was so glaringly out of her depth. She'd made no moves for a divorce, she didn't know where to start, she didn't even have her own bank account. And he would have known. He would have seen through her sham strength, the way he had all those years ago, when he'd picked the weakest prey to feast on for life. He'd never not got what he wanted. *You're unhinged.* How could she still be fooling herself?

Her nails dug into the bed.

She tried to listen for Layla's breath, but it was not enough. She gently squeezed her daughter awake. In the months after Layla was born, Elizabeth had often woken her up, purely for reassurance that she was not alone, that she was still needed, that Layla was not too good to be true.

Layla chewed on air.

Elizabeth kissed her sweaty forehead.

Hello, Mummy,

She wrapped her clammy hands around Elizabeth's arm.

Hello,

and suddenly they became the only fingers wrapped around her person. After a moment, Layla sat up abruptly and scuttled out to the toilet. She left the door open and in the cool light, Elizabeth subtly checked the corners of the bedroom for hidden shadows. When Layla came back in, she jumped on the bed.

Happy birthday, Mummy!

she waggled a drawing in her face.

That evening, Robyn waited on the sofa. Her hearing floated in its perspective, alternating from the faraway sounds of the world down below, hearing the traffic through the window crack, to the noises just behind the bedroom door, of mother and daughter readying themselves for dinner. They seemed to take hours.

Robyn started to fidget, and second-guess her level of preparation for the occasion. She dampened a sponge (Elizabeth's latest purchase) and rubbed at the salt stains on her top. She watched the swirling estuary of old sweat across her vest disappear momentarily, then creep back.

Finally, the door opened.

Layla's hair fell about her shoulders. Each spiral looked smoother, coaxed into the coil with conditioner. She wore today's supermarket special, a sky-blue dress printed with a hundred rainbows. The jersey cotton danced at her knees, as she twirled bashfully from side to side. Robyn would have hardly recognised the new child, had she not had on the pink foam sandals.

Elizabeth lingered behind Layla. She wore blue jeans and a white linen blouse, that was gently creased. She wore the suede shoes from the night they'd met. The heels she had run a mile, and more, in. Her lips looked shiny.

Haven't put jeans on in ages,

Elizabeth covered her hips, wriggling under Robyn's gaze.

The restaurant was heaving. Waiters darted between the diner-style tables, with a momentum that kept the baskets of food and embellished cocktails stuck to their circular trays. All that could be heard of the blues soundtrack was a distant bass, all else was drowned by diners dining. Elizabeth couldn't place the intention of the decor: the floor was lined to look like black and white tiles, each table had a green banker's lamp, and motorcycle magazine covers decorated the walls. Whatever the desired aesthetic, it was all abandoned for the sake of survival with large free-standing fan units placed throughout the restaurant. Red paper napkins quivered in the path of recycled air. They were led to a table booth on a mezzanine floor.

The menu of chips and burgers and wings still excited her, even after a week of similar stodge. Even more exciting was the prospect of someone else preparing it, in a kitchen that was required to meet a hygiene standard.

It's Mummy's birthday,

Layla told the waitress that took their drinks order.

Oh no. No, no.

Elizabeth was haunted by a vision of sparklers and someone playing the triangle.

What are you going to have, Lay?

She changed the subject.

Corn.

Corn?

It says corn

on

the

cob?

You can't just have sweetcorn.

Corn like unicorn.

Layla smiled so wide her cheeks could have plugged her ears, and Elizabeth could have melted on the spot.

Why do you like unicorns so much?

Robyn crossed her arms and leant her elbows on the table.

Because, they're magical.

And they're always friendly.

Robyn stayed pulled into the conversation, wanting more.

My favourite place in the whole wide world is Unicorn Hill,

Layla obliged.

Its a big, big hill, and you have to walk and walk,
and at the top you can see so so far away,
like all the whole world,
and there is a brick bit, on top, that is like a unicorn horn,
so it's called Unicorn Hill,
she was kicking her heels against the bench seat.
Me and Mummy and Daddy have been there,
three times, no NO,
four times.

They'd first discovered it when Layla was two years old. Norman had carried her up the steep hill, strapped to his back. The weekend away had been wedged into their schedules, as formulaically familial as their annual trip to his relatives on the Cote D'Azur or their additional   proper   holiday to somewhere hot and unconventional enough to arouse interest: Zimbabwe, Indonesia, Costa Rica. This was ticking a box, a symbol of functionality and privilege, not a genuine grasp at respite or adventure or alone time.

However, they had stumbled upon it.

Between the dramatic rise and fall of green curves that held them like a secret in their valleys, the cuddles of dark trees that came together to form forests they wanted to be a part of, the rugged crags in the earth that were buffed smooth by water fresh enough to drink, the dry stone walls that guided their way like an ancient prophet, the way the sun lit up as it spoke to them, shining a spotlight on where to focus, and the bodies of water,

so still that it halted everything else in their lives.

It's amazing.

It is,

Elizabeth could feel the fresh air of the lakes in the roots of her hair, and the possibility of peace that they carried, buried within her bones. A long-lost freedom she had forgotten about.

Robyn was still drawn in when their drinks arrived.

They ate their way through chicken burgers and curly fries and sticky ribs and corn on the cob, until the plastic baskets sat empty, except for grease-soaked paper and shards of fried nothing.

It was still warm as they left the restaurant, in a way that was less threatening, and more exciting, after dusk. The sun had signed off and they were left to their own devices in the ripples of its heat. There was also something apocalyptic about the foreign night air. People walked down the middle of the road, as if, since the laws of British weather had been abandoned, then so was everything else. There was greater awareness of, and tolerance of, other people. They were all existing within the same breezeless bell-jar.

I'm so full,

Elizabeth said, multiple times.

Layla was dragging her feet, also weighed down by the large meal. A group of young women, in denim shorts and high heels, consumed the whole pavement as they walked. The white streetlight picked out glitter on their earrings and acrylic nails and clutch bags, as they approached with no sign of dispersing.

Robyn grabbed Layla and placed her on her shoulders, just in time to weave between the armada of women. Layla looked around, baffled at her new height, then gripped onto Robyn's forehead.

Thank you,

Elizabeth smiled, as they emerged on the other side of the glittery gaggle.

Thank you for everything, really,

she went on as the path quietened down ahead of them.

For letting us stay. And for, helping me, the other night. It was very brave of you to come to the defence of a stranger,

she only stole quick glances at Robyn as she spoke.

To risk your own safety for someone you don't know, that's, you clearly have a very strong moral compass.

Either that, or you just like getting in fights,

she crossed her arms and huffed at her own joke.

They passed a dry cleaners that was closed, and a laundrette that was open. Robyn could feel Layla twisting her neck around, surveying the town from her new perspective. The pink sandals dangled by her ribs.

Do you?

Elizabeth asked the question to the ground first.

Like getting in fights?

then looked up as she clarified.

Robyn liked the weight on her shoulders, it felt grounding.

I don't know,

I don't really think about it at the time.

The half-moon watched over them, slung back in a hammock. It was soft in position, and sharp in clarity.

About the consequences?

Elizabeth's arms were still crossed.

Layla's sit bones squashed a shrug. They passed a pub that was crammed into a single shopfront. Patrons stood outside, talking and chatting and balancing drinks on narrow ledges.

Layla said you went to different schools,

Robyn's rider shifted balance at the mention of her name.

Did you get in trouble for fighting?

She held on to Layla's ankles.

Yeah, I guess so. I didn't really care, though. I didn't care about moving schools or homes or whatever. One time, they said I would go away somewhere, and I didn't, because the boy was fine, but I don't think I would have really minded that, either.

I don't think I would have missed anything.

Robyn felt like she wanted to say more, she wanted to watch the pavement absorbing her words, as if they'd be locked away in this moment, in these stones, forever a part of this balmy evening, but she didn't know what. So she would become the listening stones instead.

When I was younger – really young, still at primary school – there was a fire,

Layla gasped, somewhere above Robyn's head,

but Elizabeth continued.

At a factory, just up the road from my school and where I lived. It was a fabric factory I think, only small, they made clothes of some sort. And it was a big news story and everyone talked about it for weeks, and the main tale that came out of it was about a mother who worked there, who had saved her daughter who also worked there. Apparently, when she realised her daughter was missing, she had ignored the firemen and run straight back into the burning building looking for her. And she found her, and she got her out, and it was a miracle, and everyone knew about it, and for years, ever since I can remember, ever since then, that has been my way of judging my relationships. With anyone. I always thought, would they save me from a burning building? And for a moment, I suppose I thought I had found that, with Norman, but I hadn't. And it turns out it's a very scary, very lonely thing, to realise that there is no one in the world who would save you. To know that you don't mean enough to anyone for them to risk their own life, or that their world wouldn't be worth living in without you in it. And it's fu– mucked up, I know, probably extremely egotistical and twisted, but also, I think it's even scarier, even lonelier to realise that there is no one who you would save, either. When I realised there was no one I cared about that much, it can make you think like, what's the point? In all this.

Then obviously, Layla was born and suddenly I had that. And I would run into a burning building, in the middle of a war zone, in a fu– bloody typhoon to save her.

I think we can underestimate how much people are our purpose.

And what I mean is, in your case, it might be kind of the opposite. It's not about you finding someone you care enough about to fight for, it's about finding someone you care enough about not to fight for.

Robyn's feet struck the pavement like the hands of a clock, like the one in Sarah's office that had ticked down as she'd sat there, a disappointment. She wrapped her hands tighter around the pink foam sandals in front of her.

Sorry. I don't know.

Elizabeth exhaled and her belly was strangled by the waist of her jeans.

A disco party!

Layla took one hand off the reins of Robyn's hair to point at a building up ahead.

Red, green and blue lights whirled across a section of the pavement, like a kaleidoscopic doormat, daring passers-by to cross the threshold. Music didn't escape so boldly from the venue. It maintained more mystique, alluded to only by soft thuds. The women stood in front of the open entrance, staring at the motion of the cheap lights that obscured a straightforward staircase, which led down to the unknown.

You going in?

A man stood outside. His t-shirt didn't cover his biceps, but an armband that read [ECRUIT] did.

Uh,

Elizabeth snorted. She motioned obviously at her child.

Is it a disco party?

Layla, on her person platform, was the same height as the security guard.

Ain't no party right now,

he had a Jamaican accent, as warm as this summer night.

You going to start it for me, miss lady?

She's six, so,

Elizabeth scrunched her eyebrows.

You can help her then,

he smiled, and Elizabeth subtly held her stomach away from the denim waistband.

I don't think so.

Just one dance,

Please, Mummy!

Not only did Layla twist towards her, but Robyn also turned, awaiting her response, as she held onto Layla's ankles. Elizabeth stared back down the staircase that led to some psychedelic underworld. She couldn't deny its pull. To be lost once more amongst moving lights and consuming music.

One dance.

They ventured into the basement.

The brick walls were lit sporadically by stretches of green, then yawns of blue, then sweeps of red, and the whole space was masked by a contrived haze. Even through the visual veils, it was clear that the place was empty. A silhouette or two lounged behind a small bar, and a DJ two-stepped in a makeshift booth, headphones half-on and eyes fully averted from the dead dance floor.

The three women stood, underground, allowing their senses to be warped. One song juddered into a fresh one,

and then Layla began to dance.

It started in her knees, bouncing and bending,

and soon her whole body followed, with every joint flinching and flexing to the beat. Her hair floated through the vaporous air, fanning the faux smoke, as delight shook through her head and rolled through her shoulders. Unplanned moves burst from her body, intwined with the sharp elbows of precision choreography.

It was a firework display. A spectacle of pure, unfiltered humanhood. The others watched on.

Then Elizabeth began to rock in the wavelets of Layla's ocean, pulled into her joyful tide. The music crawled up her legs and through her hips. The beat in her chest moulded to that of the song, and she became a conduit for its rhythm. Her limbs flowed wherever it took her. She floated low, with the sway of a feather and the pull of a magic trick. She'd forgotten her body could move in this way, and it did so without instruction. She cracked open the can of life and danced in its satisfying fizz.

Robyn watched the dancing shadows. It was as if happiness saturated their bodies and it had to be exorcised, it had to be twirled and shook and stomped out of them. It had to be shared with the world. Robyn knew the stillness that movement could bring. But the way that they moved, with no purpose but movement itself, with such fearless freedom, made her question if she had ever truly moved at all.

She closed her eyes,   and began.

And the three of them danced,
and danced,
and
danced.
They spun in and out of each other's worlds, sharing every
moment and treasuring it for themselves.

Elizabeth walked barefoot up the many tiled stairs, holding her shoes with her forefingers. She kept on Robyn's heels for once, who attacked the flights with less speed than usual as Layla lay conked out in her arms.

Robyn lowered Layla onto the bed.

In the darkness, she began to speak,

I was thinking about what you said and, you saved me, too. You didn't know who I was, either, and you came to my defence.

So thanks and, I think you're brave, too.
Then she slipped from the room.

Robyn,
Elizabeth whispered after her.
I think I need to go home.

Will you come with me?

DAY TEN.

Elizabeth felt the familiar stick of her key in the lock. They'd bought the most expensive brass latch available and yet their keys had always caught like dodgy replicas. But she was relieved to find it still stuck, it still fit.

Coming in from the relentless sunshine, the house felt dark in a way that she'd never noticed before. The mahogany floorboards and moss-coloured walls closed in like the thickets of a swamp. What creatures could survive in such dankness? Robyn and Layla both stood upon their lily pads, eyes wide and feet afraid.

Well,

Elizabeth spoke timidly into the silence.

I need to gather some bits, and sort some things. Lay, why don't you show Robyn around?

Robyn and Layla looked at each other.

Go on, show her your playroom.

Elizabeth watched them disappear into the playroom, comforted that they'd be just next door. Even though it was a Monday, and it would be empty, she still pushed open the office door with trepidation. Jolts of nerves kept jumping out of nowhere. One shocked her so violently that for a second she saw Norman looming over the desk, his body filling the large leather chair. She stared at the empty brown seat, blinking away the vision.

Then began to rifle. She wasn't sure what for.

She'd retracted her initial belief that she was ready to see him. Instead, she would dip her toe back into his waters. She would gather and prepare and build watertight foundations for her escape.

Mummy!

She was electrocuted again.

I'm going to show Robyn my bedroom!

Layla was talking, constantly, as they ascended the stairs. Robyn had long zoned out of her tour. She was wearing her work polo top, despite taking today off. Eddie had been overjoyed to hear she was finally using her untouched annual leave, having accumulated some 207 days over her nine years of employment. She watched her trainers leave their imprint on the immaculate carpet. She hadn't given Darrell the same forewarning of her absence. She ran a hand along the wall that curved along with them. The green paint looked smooth from afar, but it felt like pimpled skin beneath her touch.

On the landing was a gallery of photos. So many smiles framed. Babies and mountains and weddings and beaches and Christmas trees, and Elizabeth and Layla and him.

And that's my own bathroom, but you can use it if you like.

Layla's bedroom was the size of whole living rooms, of whole flats. It was wallpapered in a candy-stripe of pink and white, and her double bed was draped in a netted curtain. The room was filled with drawers and shelves and soft boxes and plastic boxes and a wooden desk and full-sized wardrobe, and still it was not full. Robyn stood in the middle of the overwhelming space, on a soft rug, whilst Layla fiddled with something under her bed.

Just a minute,

Layla had a new hairstyle today. Her long curls where slicked into two tight buns. It felt like the child was zooming away from Robyn, hurtling through a thousand changes that made her unrecognisable, and if Robyn were to reach out and grab her, she would slip through her fingers like smoke.

There we go.

Fairy lights lit up around the bedhead.

There were drawings pinned to a cork board that were the work of a different artist. These freehand, colourful creations of people and places weren't constricted by predetermined lines. They had all the space, all the materials they could wish for. There was one, of a house, that wobbled into the sky in thick red lines, taller than the cotton bud trees beside it and she wanted to rip it down –

Robyn,

we can look out of my window, but it's not as high up as yours.

She looked down to see Layla by her side.

She followed her, cautiously, to the sash window. The glass felt antiquely thin in such a large frame. Below them was a garden, modest in context, overrun by an ornate climbing frame. The grass around it had kept its chlorophyll-green, seemingly untouched by the drought, and the whole space was bordered by lush bushes. Pops of colour announced themselves here and there, flaunting their full bloom. And what lay beyond these pruned borders, over a high fence and through thin-trunked trees, was unmistakeable. Even with only a dissected view, Robyn could instantly recognise the low-lying gaps and the pigmented palette. It was a park.

There's not so many windows,
but we can count trees if you like.

Layla didn't begin the count straight away.

She didn't take her own suggestion as a dictation. She let it hang in the air, as an offering should.

One, two,

Robyn tapped against the fragile glass, pointing at two fir trees.

Elizabeth paused, unnoticed, in the doorframe. Her arrival was sworn to secrecy by the carpet. She watched them, once more with their faces pressed to the window, counting over the top of one another. The backs of their knees had the same skeletal shape. But all else was different. The lay of their hair, the colour on their arms, the spirit with which they counted, and yet, she could believe that they were the same species. They were simply innocence and good intentions encased.

She wanted to pick up the scene and relocate it back to the flat, way up high where no one could touch them. She would choose to spend a lifetime confined to that tower, over incarceration in this so-called freedom.

Mummy, we're counting trees, look!

Layla spotted her.

Elizabeth knelt down next to her, and pulled her in, close enough to feel her cheek on hers.

There's sooo many.
Who even grew all of them?

That's a good question, a very thoughtful question.

Elizabeth gazed at Layla, who gazed at the many trees,

and she was awash with pride.

She took a rare moment to gloat, that her prized possession had not been bought or gifted or found by luck, she had created it. She had not fooled or flirted anyone to better its merit. Elizabeth paused at the top of an inhale, suffocating all inner voices that told her that this was a fluke, that this was not her doing, that one day her daughter would abandon her as everyone else did, and for a brief quiet moment,

Elizabeth did not feel fraudulent or fearful.

She felt what it was to be loved by herself.

She kissed Layla's perfect cheek, and felt Robyn awkwardly shuffle beside her. She'd turned away from the window. Elizabeth stood up, thrown back into self-awareness, or other-awareness, horrified that she may have become Mrs Hopfield, flaunting her maternal love in front of those who were most lacking. But Robyn didn't look as Elizabeth had as a child, masking longing and envy with a face full of disdain. She looked concerned.

Erm,

was all she said and Elizabeth's heart began to race.

Then she heard it. The mechanical creak of electric gates. Opening with sickening sloth.

Take Layla,

she said, without hesitation.

Where?

Layla chirped.

There's a balcony, from our bedroom, with steps down to the garden,

she still spoke to Robyn.

I don't want him to see her.

She daren't use her daughter as bait for reason. She'd seen her own rage, her own will for revenge, produce unspeakable acts that bore no thought for Layla's life.

She could feel Layla yearning next to her for an explanation, only restrained by perceptiveness.

We'll all go,

Robyn said, as cool as ever. As cool as she had been the last time she was in this house. When her straightness, her simplicity, had sliced through the hysteria, and offered Elizabeth a way out.

A car door opened.

And her coolness was as inviting now. How easy it would be to bathe in that oasis, forgetting the heat of the sun.

But Elizabeth would not today.

No, I need to. I need to do this.

A car door slammed.

I'll stay, too. I can beat him,
her voice was still so assured.

A key sticking in an expensive lock.

Layla held onto Elizabeth's leg.

The sunshine beamed into her brown eyes.

Elizabeth shook her head.

So can I. I'll be fine, I am brave, remember?
Something beneath the surface of Robyn's face shifted a touch.

And I need you to look after Lay.

A front door squeaked open.
Robyn nodded. It wasn't so assured, but it was a promise.

Ok, go go, I'll meet you back at the flat.

Elizabeth whispered. She ushered them off, then pulled Layla back at the last second,

I love you.

I love you, too.

A door latch closed.
She watched them disappear down the corridor, holding hands, hurried footsteps silenced by the carpet.

Robyn headed straight for the glass doors on the far side of the bed. She turned the brass key, fit for a treasure chest, that waited patiently in its hole. She held Layla by one shoulder, who was twitching her head around nervously.
It's ok,
Robyn steadied the small shoulder, unsure why she had just told the second lie of her life.

The glass-panelled door had hinges that had rusted to a copper colour, and groaned loudly as she opened them.

GBRRRRRRRP.

Hello?

it was faraway, but Layla recognised the voice.
Robyn battled with the rising sensation inside her. Through the open door, she could hear a bird flapping in the arms of a tree and the faint whistles of park people beyond the fence, but she was only really listening back down the corridor. She could creep along it, unheard and unexpected and defeat the man who deserved to lose. Or just lay in wait, as a backup. Every fibre began to ignite, ready to spark a thousand flames, and she knew that that wouldn't

be possible. She wouldn't be able to stay back. Her breath began to slip into the same focused rise and fall that took hold just before the first bell of a fight went, when each inhale and exhale edged her closer to her present moment, and dimmed the light on any future.

Hello?

it called again,

and she stepped away from the balcony, back towards the bedroom opening to the hallway. Each heartbeat was a punch to her own chest.

Robyn,

I'm scared.

The small whisper settled as snowflakes upon her fire.

Robyn had learned that people didn't say what they meant. They fluffed and finessed and skirted around the truth for no reason. But each day with Layla, she was unlearning. She was an archaeologist unearthing forgotten possibilities of humanity.

Layla scrunched the hem of her dress,

and bit down on the threat of tears.

Robyn faltered in the centre of the room,

then marched back to the window and scooped her up.

They clattered onto the metal gridded balcony, down the spiral stairs and into the green garden.

Hello?

Hi,

Elizabeth came out onto the landing, clutching a cardigan of Layla's.

Norman stopped on the stairs, and looked up.

His face was grey. Dark half-moons eclipsed under his eyes, so sunken and defined that they looked drawn on. His hair was unkempt, and longer than she remembered. He had withered faster than an unloved houseplant.

His eyes stared up at her, reddening with strain, glazing with tears.

Sorry I didn't mean to shock you, I just came to collect some things.

He didn't move.

He wore an open-collared shirt and navy trousers, with the right leg tucked into an oversized boot. The ankle support looked embarrassingly clunky on a man who built his image on expensive cuts and clean lines. Elizabeth imagined the tailored linen awkwardly squashed beneath the five velcro straps.

She pinched at the knitted cardigan, trying to hide her trembling hands. In their heavy silence, the electronic gates whirring back into place sounded like a military procession. Elizabeth glanced towards the noise.

Taxi,

Norman found his footing, in the glimpse of her unknowing. The shift from surprised to surpriser fed action back into his sallow face.

I had to get a taxi because I can't drive,

he heaved himself up one step.

Because I broke my ankle in two places. And, because my car was written off,

he limped up one more.

I don't want to –

Elizabeth held her hands up, scrunching the cardigan.

I'm not here to talk about anything, I just want to gather some bits.

Where's Layla?

As Elizabeth had heard them clattering onto the escape route, her heart had run after them. Her knees had buckled under the will to be with them, to be with Layla. But she knew that that was her body's plea for her own protection, not Layla's.

She's fine.

That's great, but that's not what I asked. Where is she?

She pulled the cardigan close to her chest.

I'm not going to disclose that.

Disclose? Fuck! Elizabeth,

his phoney laugh echoed up the curved wall. He pincered the bridge of his nose, hanging his head in amusement.

What is this?

Sincerity had returned when he looked up.

Aren't we done now? Just come home. I know you want to be here.

He climbed another step.

We can just put it all behind us, it's over, it happened.

She smelled a hint of Layla.

I was thinking and,

he climbed another,

and I think we needed that, you know. We've been together so long and we needed that burst, we needed to kick and scream and have our space for a second. We needed to clear the air. You needed to say your part, you wanted to hit me, and you did. You got it out your system. I know this life can be a lot sometimes. I know I can be a lot sometimes. I can be a fucking arsehole sometimes. But, I only do it because I'm so fucking in love with you.

He took another step, round the crux of the bend.

I need you and want you so much, it scares me. The past week has been the worst week of my life, not having you here. I just missed you so fucking much. I don't care about all the other stuff, I really don't.

He was on the home straight, three from the top.

We can put that all behind us and move on, a fresh start,

two from the top,

and I really fucking mean it,

one from the top,

I just need you to come home.

Their eyes were level and Elizabeth didn't step back.

You look like shit.

His hand wrapped tighter around the smooth bannister. Photographs peppered the wall next to them, in gilded frames worth more than the memories within them: of groups of people she called family who she felt nothing for, of designer outfits that had to be dry-cleaned for the tear stains, of a smiling couple in gowns and mortarboards. If she looked at that picture close enough, she could see the uncertainty in girl graduate's eyes. It was only the photos of Layla that had no story to tell beyond the one on the wall. From the wobbly infant taking her first steps into the world to the Halloween witch with melted makeup, they were the only posters of real life.

You don't win this, you know,

he said.

There is no version in which you win this.

Elizabeth looked past him, at one more photo of Layla. She was bundled up in a hat and fur-lined hood, drinking hot chocolate from a flask cup, with a sweeping valley behind her.

She looked back at Norman.

You took so much of my life.

I won't let you take a second more of hers.

She imagined Layla and Robyn running free across the park and her heart raced to join them.

Elizabeth took a step down.

Norman's arm blocked her.

You're not leaving,

he whispered.

Elizabeth closed her eyes and saw Layla counting trees.

Yes, I am.

Then she barged into the burning building.

For her daughter, for herself.

She walked through his arm, forcing her way past him, but lost her footing on the spiralled step.

Norman caught her, and for a second she was saved.

Then he let her go,

and her life unravelled down the clean carpet.

ROBYN.

They traipsed up the stairs in silence. Robyn was two flights ahead of Layla, and paused to watch her through the diagonal bannister bars.

Come on,

she called, then continued upwards.

The flat was warm. The sun streamed in as a truth-teller. It picked up the crumbs that were strewn across the countertop like rubble and it exposed a vortex of dust that hovered in mid-air. Layla sat down on the sofa and more dust plumed up to disturb the silent display. They didn't interact until early evening, when Robyn poured a second bowl of cereal and thrust it into Layla's hands.

Shall I get ready for bed?

she asked after finishing her dinner.

Ok.

Layla emerged from the bathroom in leggings and a pyjama top, with a lump of toothpaste on her upper lip.

Night, night, Robyn.

Robyn nodded.

Can I leave my door open?

Ok.

When will Mummy come home?

I don't know.

Layla submerged into the shadows of the bedroom. Robyn changed from her work polo to her cleanest vest top, and lay on the sofa. She had no way of knowing what minutes ticked by, only that the sun no longer lit the flat's secrets or the gridded square of sky, and Elizabeth was still not home.

She cartwheeled her legs off the sofa.

Get your shoes on,

she called from the bedroom doorway.

Layla jolted awake, then stared at Robyn with one eye closed.

And bring the biscuit tin.

The hallway lights blinked on in confusion.

Robyn banged the heel of her closed fist against the door until she heard sounds of a chair scraping and multiple latches undoing.

Robyn! Chill chill chill. Grandma's sleeping,

Vinny looked like he'd also been sleeping.

We're going out.

If Elizabeth comes back, tell her to wait here.

Robyn had not said her name aloud before. It had so many syllables.

Vinny looked at Layla, who was stood a metre back dressed in Robyn's hoodie, that missed her wrists by a mile and fell like a dress around her shins.

Ok, sure thing, ladies. You want me to stand guard?

No, just, listen out.

Robyn had already turned to leave and Vinny softly shut his door, saying, *better make a coffee then.*

Layla did up her own seatbelt in the taxi, and held onto the round tin on her lap. They sat next to each other, but faced away, watching different sides of London roll past. Their eyes ran over lit shopfronts and fluorescent signs and glowing streetlamps, anything that stood out against the sleeping backdrop.

Layla had recited her home address to the driver through the plastic partition, but Robyn found herself scanning the pavements, miles from their destination, looking for some navy vision. They stopped at a red light and the constant chug of the car became more obvious. It vibrated under their feet and tickled their arms.

A supermarket's mini-me was on Layla's side. The automatic doors, open all hours, swooshed open for a customer.

An Emergency Department & Urgent Treatment Centre Entrance was on Robyn's. The automatic doors, open all hours, swooshed open for a patient.

We're getting out here.

But you're only halfway!

The driver hadn't turned his mic on, and sounded further away than just beyond the plastic wall.

Give him the money,

she said as she disembarked, and Layla paid the man's fare, with a four-hundred percent tip.

Robyn couldn't be certain what had drawn her in, only that this seemed like an Emergency and this seemed Urgent. She'd never been invested enough in her own life, let alone been embroiled in anyone else's, to make a trip to a hospital, and wasn't quite sure of the circumstances that warranted it.

She approached an open hatch that was signposted Reception. Layla stood behind her like a pocket grim reaper (with a biscuit tin for a scythe).

Hiya,

was all the lady at the desk said.

Robyn waited for a question.

What's wrong?

she finally clapped her hands together, impatiently.

Is her mum here?

Who's mum?

Robyn nudged the cloaked child forward.

The lady crossed her arms and studied the pair of them.

Who's your mum?

Elizabeth Sear,

Layla's impeccable diction melted something in the hospital gatekeeper.

Is she poorly?

Layla looked to Robyn.

No.

Then why would she be here?

her impatience snapped back.

We haven't seen her all day and night.

Ok sweetie,

she picked up her desk phone.

This isn't missing persons, you should go through the police you know,

she fired at Robyn just before –

Hi, Sue.

Robyn looked around the waiting room. Connected chairs grew on blue metal vines, and nearly every one bore the fruit of a person. A young boy fired a pair of crutches as fake machine guns, someone else had a hand wrapped in a tea-towel, but the rest of them seemed only to be afflicted by sullenness.

The receptionist put the phone down and disappeared, appearing moments later in the waiting room with them.

Can I take your names?

Layla.

Robyn.

And surnames?

Have you found her?

Have you got any ID?

Is Mummy ok?

The receptionist called off her search for order, sighing into the depths of another nightshift. Her intrinsic need to help people had not been completely worked out of her. She led them down a white rectangular tunnel, with speckled flooring that squeaked beneath their shoes.

Robyn held a mug of tea. She didn't drink it, because she'd never drunk tea, but she kept her hands tightly wrapped around the ceramic as it burnt against her palms and finger pads, and she watched a man in green scrubs crouched at Layla's level.

Layla was sat in a grown-ups' chair. The blue felt seat swamped around her base.

Her feet were miles from the ground.

It was not a conversation, because only the man in green spoke.

Robyn pressed harder against the hot mug, hoping the burn would deepen and she wouldn't be able to escape this moment, but each time she looked at Layla, the sensation waned and her mind placed herself in the chair instead.

Robyn couldn't remember who had been her man in the scrubs or what they had said. She could only imagine how she had sat there, as passively as Layla, as she had been robbed of her entire world. Had she cried or screamed or kept quiet because there was nothing to say? Had she understood the words they had used? Had she understood them at all? How could someone be asked to envision the night, when they'd only experienced the day?

Robyn knew nothing of the child who had sat in that chair. She'd never thought of her before, never considered the nights she may have lain awake in the dark awaiting a return or the way her delicate hands might have reached out for another or how her heart may have ached so hard that she became a woman, sat in this chair, without one at all. But as she sat there now, watching Layla, she learned one thing about that child.

That it had not been her fault.

For many years, she may have disappointed people or not been what they expected or not been enough, but now she knew, at least, that this original sin had not been hers. Because if Layla could be the one in that chair, so undeserving of such hurt, then perhaps Robyn hadn't been, either.

Robyn refocused on Layla's face. Her eyes, who'd no longer be reflected anywhere but a mirror, were warped with confusion. They barely looked like Layla's at all. This is how it starts, Robyn thought. The transformation.

We're going now,

Robyn stood up.

She would plug the process before it begun. This time, she would accept the help.

Even before the security light came on, she recognised the feel of the paving stones beneath her trainers. The driveway was unchanged. She was sure the moss grew between the concrete rectangles in the exact same pattern. But the house looked smaller.

Robyn had not grown, physically, since she'd last been here, but she'd grown accustomed to buildings that served the masses, to sleep, to fuel, to fight, and this toy house, set apart from its neighbours, seemed more absurd than it had done back then. The striped house number had weathered well this far from the sea.

Robyn rang the doorbell, which was new. It did not ding or buzz, but played a synthetic song. From outside, in the early hours of the morning, the chirpy tune sounded decidedly sinister. She pressed it again and again before even the first melody had subsided. At the emergence of light from within, she took a step back.

A tall man answered the door. His floppy blonde hair was nearly combed by the top of the doorframe.

Robyn hadn't accounted for this.

Can I help you?

His voice had forced depth. He was wearing a stained t-shirt and checked pyjama bottoms, but he didn't look like he'd been asleep. Robyn subconsciously reached for Layla's shoulder, without looking.

Do you need help or ?

He glanced at Robyn's chest, exposed beneath the x-ray security light.

She pressed her soles down hard, trying to reconnect with the familiar flooring. The bungalow seemed to shy away from her, coyly hiding in the shadows, like an old friend pretending not to recognise her.

Ok well, goodbye then,

he started to close the door.

What's going on, Ror?

The voice was soaked in sleep, but unmistakable. Robyn looked past the young man, into the hallway, and saw the gallery of pieces that still decorated the walls.

Sarah appeared at her son's side. She too was unchanged.

Robyn?

She blinked behind her rimless glasses.

Her wheelchair looked younger.

What's going on? Are you ok?

She flicked her eyes towards Layla only briefly, not wanting to look away from Robyn for too long. The young man stood guard, protective of his mother.

I need you to look after her,

Robyn still had her hand on Layla.

Ok,

Sarah said slowly. She was in a floral-printed dressing gown.

Is this, your –

No.

Ok. Is everything ok, Robyn?

And Robyn was back in that armchair, being probed and prodded. Being assessed by those glass eyes that had already determined that nothing was ok. It was if her own memories had not been stored within her at all, but somewhere outside herself, and with this single question, this single look, they were gently handed back to her. She could smell the fake lavender and recite titles of textbooks she hadn't thought about in years. She could feel the urge to answer, and the weight of conscience that suppressed it.

Her mum,
Robyn wanted to press on with the matter at hand.
She,
but for once the truth seemed harder. As the child shivered beneath her fingers, she couldn't say it aloud.
Layla needs a place to live.

Rory looked at his mum. Layla looked at Robyn.

Why don't you come in and sit down? Get warm and we – we can have a chat.

No.
The memory of lavender was enough. And with each minute that passed, on a floodlit driveway in Robyn's possession, Layla's scars were forming.

Sarah wrapped her dressing gown tighter around her chest.

Rory, love, it's ok, you go back to bed.

He hesitated, as the man of the house,

I'll be in the kitchen,

he asserted, then edged away taking a final glimpse at the late-night intruders.

Sarah moved her chair into the freed-up space of the doorway, half in the warm glow of the hallway, and half in the stark interrogation light. Her limp hair was too fair to show any greys, but it hinted at a brief and bold dabble with bangs.

What's your name?

she adjusted her glasses.

Layla,

her voice was smaller than ever.

That's a really lovely na –

Can she come in.

Sarah had always been anxious of saying the wrong thing, of pushing the wrong button, for the sake of what it might do to the other person. But in that moment, never a truer picture of a rabbit in headlights, Robyn felt Sarah was anxious for what it might do to her.

Of course, ok,

she started to back up.

Robyn pushed Layla forward, but she kept her fingertips on Layla's back for as long as possible, keeping connected until her arm was

fully outstretched and she broke away. Her pink sandals inched up the slope. They were all Robyn could see of the child, the rest was buried beneath her own black hoodie. Sarah moved further back, opening up the hallway, and Robyn could see right inside. Layla held onto the doorframe, to step over the threshold,
Wait.

Layla spun around.

The white light immortalised her fear.

Robyn crouched on the slanted doorstep.
You are really great.

You are a really good person.

And you can keep – you should keep doing that.
Robyn pulled Layla into her. She was so small that Robyn's hands came back to touch her own arms.

Robyn had never held anyone just to hold them. *I think we can underestimate how much people are our purpose.*

The detached driver in Robyn, the one who could override her will to give in, pulled away from the child.

She stood up.

Are you staying with me?

No,
Robyn didn't look at her.

Would you like a hot chocolate, Layla?
Sarah asked.

Ok,

Layla accepted out of politeness.

She stepped on the threshold, and looked back for Robyn.
Robyn nodded, an instruction, and the child stepped inside.

Sarah called out to her hidden son and he led the child away for a sweet drink.

What's going on, Robyn? You can talk to me, you know. Are you – are you sure you don't want to come in? Whatever it is, we can figure it out.
She strained her neck forward.

Robyn nudged a puff of moss with her shoe.

I will – I will look after Layla, of course, but I think I need to know what's happened here.

Her voice had a trace more of determination. The assertion of a mother. Robyn still stared at her feet, unsure why they weren't leaving.

> *I'm glad to see you, after all these years. You look – you look great. So grown up. And that you remembered where we live, after all this time, that's – that's very impressive. I'm so glad you felt like you could reach out to me for –*

Why didn't you adopt me?

The cold question froze the night air.

The residential street held its breath. No wind dared whisper through the trees that lined the pavements, and the sleeping policemen did not stir. A curve of moon played host to a sky full of stars. Some shone more brightly than others, but they all looked down upon this moment. Spectacles turned spectators.

Sarah edged her wheels out onto the slope.

> *I didn't – I didn't know that was what you wanted. You were nearly sixteen when we – and you seemed happy, to be getting happier until – I had no idea. I really did care about you, Robyn. And I've thought of you nearly every day since you left. I'm sorry if I – I was doing my job, but I really did care for you. If I'd known…*

Robyn watched the moss moving beneath her feet. She felt the once-familiar driveway become pavement, and her world darken as she strode away from the bright light. She dipped into an alleyway, the friendly kind, that connected neighbours, and stopped. An overgrown clematis peaked over the fence and shook its head. The stars, way above her, lost interest and returned to their own splendour, and she was left all alone,

save for her greatest ally.

The rage started in the pit of her stomach.

It rumbled like thunder, thick and momentous, and gathered in volume, becoming both too loud and too massive for her to escape. It was a sandstorm that she couldn't see through, couldn't capture or outrun. All she could do was hold her breath and be carried along at its mercy. Her feet began to pound the pavement. A route she had run once before.

Her legs and lungs started to burn from sprinting, but their heat disappeared like lit matches in a forest fire. Her autopilot navigated the streets, whilst she concentrated solely on her plan. To foresee the way in which her anger was going to be unleashed was the only way to stop it from consuming her completely right now.

She flew down the stairs and threw open the door.

Her panting echoed in the concrete dungeon.

The lights above the ring weren't on. No lights were, except a couple of half-working fluorescent strips at the far end, next to the wooden wall she'd once been slammed into, and a dim lamp from Darrell's cupboard. Gloves and pads were littered across the gym floor, as if they'd been dropped and abandoned in an instant. The silhouettes of canvas bags and rubber bodies stood still.

Robyn didn't wait to catch her breath. She strode towards the office cupboard that beckoned like a last-resort lighthouse on the ridge of a blackened coast. Darrell jumped when he saw her, just a heaving figure, darkening his doorway. It was only after his truthful shock, that he said,

Jesus fucking christ.

His tracksuit knees were squashed against the filing cabinet.

What the fuck is the matter with you?

A pad of lined paper was open on top of the desk (filing cabinet). The lamp was poised over lines of pencil handwriting.

Give me a fucking heart attack, you fucking prick.

Robyn felt the sweat cooling on her back.

Where's Winston?

He went home, 'cause it's,

he tilted the large gold face to the light,

nearly three in the fucking morning.

Why are you here?

He flipped the pad of paper closed.

Why are you here?

She looked back into the desolate gym. The black hole which had swallowed hours and more of her life. Had it been a kiln which had made something of her crude clay, or simply a furnace.

I need your gun.

Darrell's knees smacked against the metal cabinet.

He jolted his chair back, but it didn't budge. He flustered, trying to wiggle free from where he was wedged.

What?

he snapped, once he'd fumbled to his feet.

The one in the second drawer,

she pointed.

What the fuck are you talking about, Robyn?

She lurched forward to show him, but he stepped in the way.

I mean, why the fuck do you want it?

He whispered, although no one else was there.

Her breath had now simmered but her heart raged on, hammering at her chest as if it were trying to use up a lifetime of power, trying to run down the clock as fast as possible.

Just do.

She saw the plan in her head.

Jesus fucking christ,

he said, gently.

Go home, Robyn.

She looked once more into the disused car park, devoid of life. Just as it was on a packed Friday night, when empty souls clambered for a sensation. When they shouted and stomped and threw their fists, living so loudly because inside they were so deathly quiet. As quiet as her flat would be now. As devoid of life.

I don't know what the fuck's going on with you,

said the man who had chiselled her into a weapon,

who had profited from her pain,

who had taught her the only way to win,

and who could no longer contain the monster he had manufactured.

I just need it.

She punched Darrell in the face.

It had more power than anticipated, assisted by adrenaline, and blood gushed from his nose. She threw another one, transferring the weight, following through, his own lessons ingrained in her muscle memory.

Darrell's head was solid and her knuckles suffered the consequences. He splattered blood as he staggered out of the cupboard towards her. It was disappointing for Robyn, to learn that this man whose words she'd taken for gospel, who'd given tireless lectures on offence and defence, couldn't block or counter a single punch. It was also disorientating, to see the aged coach stumbling about in his own kingdom. It mellowed her a touch and reigned her attack into just the necessary.

Which was one more, a left hook that he didn't see coming. He was still on his feet, but she skipped into the office and dodged back out before he could touch her. She sprinted across the gym, the sound of his tracksuit chaffing struggling to keep up, and she bounded up the twelve flights, out of the fire exit and onto street level before she stopped to notice the weight of what she held in her hand.

The electric gates were as tall as Robyn. They were white plastic, grooved to look like wooden slats and up-lights alluded to the brick posts on either side of them. She stood at the precipice of her destination.

The street was marked with large houses. Some hugged together, in runs of two or three, and others stood alone, such as this one. They were all of the same imposing stature, with neat sash windows and front doors that were aggrandised by steps and columns. They separated themselves from the pavement with pointed iron fences, either backed by privet bushes or bay trees or pampas grasses. But on this house the iron spikes protruded from a low brick wall. The road was dotted with antique-looking lanterns, unsure whether it was safer to light up or not light up their precious homes. The only movement Robyn had seen was a lofty fox, padding along the centre of the road. She held onto two metal prods and climbed over the property's boundary.

She moved so lightly, so stealthily, that even the security light did not turn on until she was inches from the stained-glass door. Old sweat and new sweat were layering on top of her skin, from the miles she had run this evening, in body and mind, and yet she had not exhausted herself of feeling. Her purpose still pulsed through her skin. The colours on the glass shone with clarity.

She knocked on the door.

She needn't have been concerned about waking the slumbering street for their big lives could not be disturbed by her measly tapping. The door opened before she was ready. It was not preluded by lights or sounds, it was open.

And he was there.

Norman was wearing a shirt and trousers, just as he had when they'd met. But this shirt was white, with the sleeves rolled up and the collar open and marred with stains. And he was wearing a velcro boot. His eyes looked as if they'd been hollowed out and replaced with ones that didn't fit right. They sat deeper and darker and bruised around the edges   and they stared at her.

Perhaps his whole being had been scooped out and left empty, because he didn't do anything. There wasn't a hint of recognition. Not of who she was, or that he'd opened the door to anyone at all. The detachment on his face suggested he was neither asleep nor awake.

Even when Robyn pulled the gun from her waistband and pointed the barrel at his chest,

it took him a second to register.

Suddenly, synapses sparked to attention and he took a step back into his dark hallway.

Robyn wrapped both hands around the grip and followed him inside.

What's what's what's going on,

he wheezed.

He held both hands up and his eyes were on stalks now. Robyn was glad they were only lit by the echo of light from the front steps outside. She didn't want to see the empty house. She didn't want to be winded by smiling family portraits. She looked only at him. But then the security light timed out and it was pitch black. Instinctively, she kicked her leg back outside and the dimness resumed. Norman had not moved in the blackout.

The floorboards creaked beneath her as she took a step closer to him.

What do you want? If it's money, you can have whatever you want.
Please don't hurt me.

His face twisted with emotion.

He didn't look anything like Layla. He had pinched eyes and an invasive nose that could never belong on her delicate face. He backed up until he hit a glass-topped sideboard, adorned with candles and decorative bowls, and he convulsed at how he'd trapped himself.

Robyn felt her lungs inflating, trying to make room for her pounding heart, and each smooth extended exhale as she channelled everything into this moment. She gathered every breath she had ever taken, every thought, every feeling, every lesson, every snapped and healed fibre, every single second of it all

and brought it here.

To unfold along the predetermined pathway of her anger's choosing.

Wait – are you – Oh my god.

Norman suddenly saw beneath the bandage, beneath the swollen skin of the petrol station worker who had ruined it all.

I didn't kill her, I didn't, I didn't. If you're here for – I promise – she fell.

His look was only infinitesimal. But he looked.

And Robyn saw, in the lowest of lights, that the carpet was no longer immaculate. That the floorboards at bottom of the sweeping staircase were darkened in wide brush strokes. And when she looked back at Norman, she saw only the brown patches between his buttons,

and then it went dark again.

She fumbled backwards, searching for the open door that had drifted out of reach. Metal clattered against glass and a hard-soled boot thumped on the floorboards. She waved frantically searching for the threshold. The heavy limping moved further away. The security light snapped on, and Norman was gone from the hallway.

Robyn scanned the space, eyes jumping over the stained floor. She squeezed the gun's textured grip with her palms, her forefinger still poised in position. She tried to let the noise of his uneven footsteps echo in her mind's ear, to retrace where they had run to. She walked further into the house,   slowly.

Each step, her trainer only kissed the floor but still the wood rang out.

There were the doors to Layla's playroom and the office but she'd not heard anything open. Instead, she headed for a doorless passageway, the one Amelia had taken to the kitchen on that first night. When she reached it, she was glad the floor changed to tiles underfoot, that would not snitch on her whereabouts. Robyn took one hand off the weapon to feel her way as she ventured further from the front door, deeper into darkness. The walls were cool. Her fingers traced the tiny bumps of the painted plaster. She crept at a steady pace, losing perception of how far she'd travelled into this tunnel. The deeper she got, the quieter she became inside. Until she herself was not living at all, only looking for life.

Wall fell away from her fingertips, and she paused.

She pointed the gun into the kitchen that she could not see.

The thick nothingness didn't evaporate the more she stared. It blurred and waved and grew denser.

Then it struck her from the left.

She was shoved sideways, thrown against barstools. Her hands spread out, reflexes catching her on the lip of a breakfast bar. But only at the sound of metal on ceramic did she realise that that meant she'd dropped the gun. And then hands were on her again. Large, hot hands that could wrap around her humerus in a single grip. She flailed against them. With no sense of a target in the black, she kicked everywhere, twisted wildly and got a knee in her intestines. Still, she shoved against the darkness. The hands groped her, their span the size of her chest. They passed over her ribs and shoulders, such fragile bones that they couldn't make sense of, and came together on her neck. His fingers and thumbs encircled her throat with precision. They didn't need light to feel her cartilage squirming for an escape, to know that her jugular veins were pulsing with panic. Norman strangled her, shoving her backwards until she was pushed up against a wall.

She punched out, but his long arms could keep his body just out of reach.

She kicked out, but as soon as her foot made contact, he retaliated.

His skull butted against her face with full force. He'd missed the centre, in the darkness, but still caught the base of her nose and the top of her lip. She tried to get a grip on the pain, to make sense of it, use it, but it was too disorientating, being choked by the darkness, and his hands. Robyn was gasping for air. The tar in which she was drowning was seeping down her closing throat, spreading across her chest, slowing down her brain. Silky blood trailed from her nostrils. It dripped into her open mouth. She clawed at his wrists and pulled down on his forearms, but they were as solid as stone. They were immovable. Her hands dropped. She no longer knew if her eyes were open or closed. The tar was filling her lungs, dripping from her nose. It filled her mouth, but she couldn't taste it.

Her hands fumbled along the wall, desperate to be swallowed by it, to be nothing but darkness itself,

but instead she was blinded by light.

She'd stumbled across a light switch and the room became a brilliant white. Brighter than she'd ever known. Her vision was too blurred to make out his face, it was a blend of pink and white and red and black looming over her, as if she were beneath a body of water. But over his shoulder was a mirage of navy.

An elegant woman, waiting for a train.

She looked certain and hopeful. Like she was on her way to meet someone.

Robyn gripped Norman's wrists, and rammed her trainer into his torso. It was accurate, blasting through his stained buttons and kicking the wind out of him. He faltered, but his chokehold remained. So she kicked again. She was trained to work with no breath, she was trained to work with no strength. She had fought all her life on nothing but resilience. The third kick knocked him back.

Her free throat gulped and gasped.

He started towards her and she ducked out of the way. She tried to blink back her vision, to make sense of her surroundings, but tripped on the foot of a barstool and she was on the floor, knees and palms slapping against a pale ceramic tile the size of her bed. She was lapping up air, desperate for fuel, when she saw it.

The black right angle.

The weapon, just out of reach.

She crawled towards it, then her chin smacked the hard floor and she was pulled backwards. She frantically tried to shake his grip from around her ankle. Her heel clipped his nose and she was free. She scrambled forward and picked up the gun.

Then got to her feet.

Everything stopped. Robyn's shoulders rose and fell. She kept both hands on the grip and did not wipe the blood that poured across her mouth and chin. Slowly, she came back into her body. She felt her feet inside her shoes that were planted wide. Breath squeezed its way through her blocked nose and bruised throat. And the bright room began to make sense around her. There were white walls and marble countertops, a double sink and a gas stove with half a dozen rings.

Norman was knelt on the floor, his heart hidden behind her gun.

Please,
he drooled.
Please, please, I'm sorry.

Robyn breathed in then out.

Please, please.

I have a daughter.

She lifted her aim to his forehead.
It meant nothing to have someone.
Where's her favourite place in the world?

He panted, spittle sticking in his throat.

His eyes panicked either side of her barrel.
I – I – I don't know.

Robyn's forefinger twitched.

THE LAKE.

The sun was still drying the droplets from afternoon bathers when the festivities began. Half a dozen women lay about on towels on the bank, letting the lake evaporate from their skin, and taking with it the tasks of the day, as they waltzed across the border from journey to destination, from preparation to party, with the simple suggestion of, *Cider?*

Freddie fetched her homemade brew, and slowly, those who still toiled away sloped towards the bank for sundowners. Only Betty and Delilah were amiss, as they topped dishes with seasoning and added the final flourishes to place settings. Only them, and Robyn and Layla.

Shall I go get them?

Maria whispered to Anna, as they took their seats at the kitchen table (which eight of them had laboriously lugged to the lakeside).

Layla and Robyn,

she needlessly added. The two empty places were glaringly obvious.

Ermm,

Anna toyed with what the least intrusive, most inclusive course of action was, when calls of

Speech! *Speeeeech!*

Speech, Anna! *Yes, speech!*

interrupted her thoughts.

Yes, yes, go see them,

she said, hushed and hasty, before standing for her audience. Maria slipped from the table.

Well, ladies, what a glorious feast this is! The best one yet. I know, I know, I say it every year, but it just keeps getting better and bigger and more, scrumptious looking!

She couldn't help but watch Maria marching towards the bell tent in her periphery.

Honestly, you all amaze me. But, erm, truly a huge thank you for not only your hard work today to bring together such a,

Maria dipped from view, inside the tent.

An exquisite looking meal, but also for, for the whole season, for all your hard work, for, for everything you do every day and continue you to do, for all of us here and I know we're not done, the coming months will be,

she scratched the nape of neck, turning to see the tent full on. The doors of its entrance sat still.

Will be, erm, but it, it – Oh god, sorry this is awful. Fred, how strong was that cider?

She laughed, they laughed, her body relaxed.
She held a glass up, half-full of cloudy liquor.

To my wonder women,

I thank you, I respect you, I admire you, I adore you.

Clinking and whooping and clapping and cheering broke out. Anna took a sip to hide her flushing cheeks. As she brought her glass back down, she saw Maria trotting towards the table,

with Robyn and Layla in tow.

Dishes moved around the table like dodgems. They weaved between, and passed under, over, across as each diner piled on spoonfuls of herby bulgar wheat and basilly tomatoes and grated apple slaw and chargrilled asparagus and potato salad. Layla sat on two cushions just to be eye level with the mound of food on her plate.

The sun had drifted off duty by the time they all lay their forks down. Delilah lit the candles she'd pre-emptively dotted on and around the table, to illuminate the dinner conversations that were far from finished.

I think it's time,

Violet stood up.

Her announcement simmered the chatter at once. She possessed an unquestionable knack for being authoritative, not bossy, commanding, not demanding. In truth, they all had the ability, but had been fooled to think otherwise. She lifted a melting candle high above the crown of her silver head. More cheers escaped, and they all began to untuck themselves from the benches.

The bonfire did not ignite as dramatically as the waiting audience might have hoped for. Violet singed the ends of dry branches, and they all watched as the orange live wires began to work their magic. Eventually, yellow flames quivered high into the night sky. Flashes broke away and drifted upwards, as if being pulled home to their sister stars that shone way above. They stood and absorbed the heat, listening to the conversation of crackles.

But soon they began to dance and sing, and the fire became a mere spotlight to the true spectacle.

Rhythmic claps and unrestrained laughter followed the breakaway sparks into the open sky. The strength of joy could have made the lake ripple, as it echoed throughout their private valley. Even Anna and Maria took respite from their obsession with the new guests (who were not dancing, but remained with them, which felt like contribution enough) to be immersed in the celebrations. These women had nowhere else to be, in mind or in body. They had busted the shackles of conformity and danced in their freedom.

A while later, the union of the celebration had petered out and some sat by the fire, some stood, some drank, some meditated alone on the perfection of this moment. Anna and Maria paddled at the edge of the lake.

Though only a short distance from the bonfire, in the deepened darkness, they could see the moon's full light across the water. With no clouds to bar its glow, it shone as bright as a floodlight: security over their precious home. It also grew quiet quickly. The sounds from the revellers blurred into the background, and they could hear the gentle tinkle of water around their ankles.

Beautiful,

Maria said softly, little more than an exhale.

Then she turned her back on the moon's reflection and looked up towards the bonfire. Layla was sat between Cynthia's knees, who teased her hair with a comb. Layla sat patiently as her hair was tugged. If it was not comfortable, there was at least comfort in the familiarity. Cynthia slathered an oil through the curls as she worked, talking animatedly. Layla gave a giggle here and there. Anna watched Maria watching Layla.

She's a precious one.

Yeah.

Maria knew Anna was looking, so she did not wipe the tear that rolled slowly down her cheek. Perhaps it wasn't visible in the dark. Perhaps it would continue to roll and drop silently into the water below.

But Anna reached out and squeezed Maria's hand.

You are a mother, you know. To every one of us.

Maria could only nod.

Anna indulged in another glass. She felt the fermented apple juice warm her insides, a nostalgic sensation. It made her feel childish and alive. It made her sit down next to Robyn, and stare at the fire with her.

Robyn, I want you to know, whatever you're running from, if it's any danger, whatever it is, you can stay here as long as you like. Take as long as you need. I don't know what your exact circumstances are, and I know our lifestyle might not be viable for Layla for a long period of time – she's so young, I'm sure she needs other children in her life – but please, we can figure all of that out. There's space for you both and you're safe here.

The flames rippled shadows across Robyn's face. Sparks crackled in her dark eyes.

Thank you.

Anna's legs buzzed under the cider's influence, as if they were a pair she was only borrowing.

What were you running from then? When you came here.

Robyn asked, and really looked at Anna the first time.

The fire began to dance in slow motion as Anna drifted away, somewhere both deep inside and far outside herself. She could see her years lived as clear as a jet stream across a summer sky, as she stood here, at the farthest point of her existence. It felt peaceful to pause.

To do nothing but exist, and allow her world to zoom into perspective.

I don't think I ever was,

her own voice surprised her.

Not running away. I was running to.

To find my place in the world, to my purpose, to my people.

She returned to the bank,

to the women who lounged, who stood, who danced,

to Maria at the lake's edge,
to the lake itself,
to the stars above
and the dewy grass beneath her feet,
I was running to here. To be exactly here.

For a moment, Robyn held her gaze, a token of understanding, then she turned back to the fire.
Why do you think we're running away then?

Anna snuffed out a laugh.
Once more, her existence was thrown into perspective, but this time the bird's eye view was even higher, high enough to observe her own egotism.

True.

With no forewarning against her own action, she placed a hand on Robyn's shoulder,
and there was a hint of stillness,
before Robyn inched away.

Well,

Anna felt that swell of surety that can rise in the face of rejection.

You let me know if you need anything.

She held her own knees, ready to stand, hesitating only a fraction with the desperation to be interrupted.

But Robyn let her go.
Anna stood and felt the fire almost stinging her cheeks. Then stepped over the bench.

Actually,

there's one thing.

ROBYN.

I – I – I don't know.

Robyn's forefinger twitched.

I don't know, but I love her, so much.
The last of his words were swallowed by tears.
And suddenly,
all her feeling evaporated.

She was drained of all anger. A thousand plugs were pulled and it dispersed in an instant. She was as light as the room, a brightness she wanted to bask in forever.

I don't know much about it, but I think if you love someone, you don't hurt them, you don't scare them.

You want to hold them and make them feel safe.

She pulled on the trigger again and again until it became loose under her touch.
Seventeen holes in the bumpy wall.

Then she threw the gun at his sobbing knees.

THE LAKE.

When Anna awoke, most of the beds were empty. One person, maybe Betty, possibly Jan, was still sleeping in a single bed, on the far side of the tent. Anna smiled to herself, basking in the rebellion of a lie-in. Then she heard voices outside and couldn't resist joining.

Pyjama-clad women sat around the alfresco dining table. They clutched teas and juices, with messy hairdos and bleary eyes. Cynthia sat with her knees up, Maria lay flat on the bench, whilst Violet stroked her hair, Freddie sat at the head. They lounged like a pride of sleepy lionesses, an enjoyable contrast to the formality with which they'd sat behind place settings the night before.

Good morning! *Anna, my love.*

Morning. *Morning!*

She was greeted. Maria began to sit up to make space.

No, no, stay. I'm going to get a cuppa. Anyone want anything?

Anna could not control her grin as she marched towards the main building. Happiness pulsed through her so intensely, she could not stop it from shining out of her face. She walked quickly, despite there being no rush. She practically skipped across the grass, towards the woods, past the bell tent and, she paused. Robyn and Layla were a part of the family now. They should not miss out on hot tea and a debrief breakfast. Anna walked back to the bell tent entrance. She did not dilly dally with knocking protocol this time, but opened it straight away.

The bed was empty.

An attempt had been made to make it. Everything else looked untouched. They'd arrived with no real possessions, so it was difficult to tell, on a logical level, whether they had packed up.

But on an instinctual level, Anna knew they were gone.

LAYLA.

The grass cushioned beneath her feet.
Layla held the worn sandals in her hands and trod her own path, just next to the rocky trail, enjoying the kiss of each delicate blade beneath her healing soles. She watched the green roll under her as she walked on

and on

and on.

Sometimes her toes would touch the soil bedded beneath the grass and it felt damp, as if it had already rained. Perhaps the earth knew what was around the corner. She pushed hard off each foot, conquering the incline as her legs dropped into a constant cycle, as rhythmic as her breathing pattern, that was louder than normal, but not strained. It just reminded her it was there.

She moved at such a speed that she created her own breeze, which grew cooler as she climbed up and up. The ground continued to blend underfoot. All the individual strands of green merged into one moving picture. It was not dissimilar to how her mind felt. How very few blades of memory stood out against the week that had passed in a blur:

The printer that had juddered back and forth spitting out pages of directions on the night that Robyn had come back for her.

The roar of motorway traffic that had pretended they weren't there.

How their bones had bruised one another when Robyn had carried her for hours at a time.

The sunrise that had glowed so fiercely the sky had looked like it was on fire.

How her tongue had forgotten how to speak.

The road turning that had appeared out of nowhere, decorated in friendly trees and dawn light and how it had looked so pretty they'd had to take it.

But that was it.

Her feet powered onwards as these shards of memories jolted around like a broken picture.

Come on.

Nearly there.

Layla paused. She squinted into the sun, to Robyn up ahead. Then she glanced back down the hillside. She could barely see where her path had begun. She forged on, just a few more feet. Robyn disappeared over a ridge and Layla jogged to join her.

On the other side, the land stretched out forever.

They walked across the flat in silence, and Layla slapped her hand down upon the small brick tower.

They had made it, she was here.

Unicorn Hill.

The quilt of greens swept up and down in gentle waves, just as she remembered. Dark lines surrounded lush puzzle pieces that slotted into place perfectly. Shadows shape-shifted across the landscape as fluffy clouds were just passing through. The edge of the image was so far away that she could hardly trace it with her eyes.

She could see the whole world,

and it was all wrong.

Layla's legs buckled and she collapsed to the ground.

She cried so hard that her whole body shook. Her wails pierced the sky. The tears soaked her face and she gasped for air, she pleaded for respite. But still she cried until the sobs were so strong that they threatened to break her and she believed she would drown.

She didn't notice Robyn sit down next to her, until she pulled her into her chest. Layla heaved, drenching Robyn with her eyes and nose and mouth, but she stayed there and, slowly, the cries began to ease.

Her breath rattled in the aftermath and still Robyn held her.

I found out why birds sing,

Robyn said, finally.

Layla's head was rocked up and down by Robyn's chest.

When she was ready, she sat up.

She wiped under her nose and looked at Robyn, who waited patiently.

Anna said it's because they're communicating.

They are telling other birds about food or trying to find a friend, or telling others to leave them alone.

She said there's lot of reasons.

But also they sing because they're alive, *and they're happy about that.*

ACKNOWLEDGEMENTS

To Callum, Jess, Georgia, Fred and Georgie for reading Robyn when it was in its infancy, and providing enough kind words to sew the seed for this book.
To Emily for being so generous with your time and experience, and providing invaluable insight and thoughtful feedback.
To Marcus and Lynne for your sensitive edits and treasured encouragement.
To the countless coffee shops where I overstayed my welcome and the temp jobs where I tapped away when I should have been working.

And thank you to the Skwad, for the endless love and support. I love you all more than you could know.